PRAISE F...
THE MASTERE...

"With *Unwound*, James once again proves she's the master of erotic romance. Filled with unforgettable characters, fiery passions, and an all-encompassing love story, it's a must read for anyone craving more kink in their romance."
—Tara Sue Me, *New York Times* bestselling author of *The Enticement*

"[A] fascinating read that explores the emotions of a woman swept up in a dark world of bondage."
—*Romantic Times*

"...
... Banks

"Sweet, seductive, and romantic . . . an emotional ride filled with joy, angst, laughs, and a wonderful happily-ever-after. Lorelei James knows how to write one hot, sexy cowboy."
—*New York Times* bestselling author Jaci Burton

"The down-and-dirty, rough-and-tumble Blacktop Cowboys kept me up long past my bedtime. Scorchingly hot, wickedly naughty."
—Lacey Alexander

"Known for erotic interludes, [James] never forgets to bolster the story with plenty of emotional power."
—*Publishers Weekly*

continued . . .

"Hang on to your cowboy hats, because this book is scorching hot!"
—Romance Junkies

"Lorelei James excels at creating new and evocative fantasies."
—TwoLips Reviews

"Incredibly hot." —The Romance Studio

"Beware: Before you read this hot erotic from Lorelei James, get a glass of ice. You are going to need it." —Fallen Angel Reviews

"Think it's impossible to combine extremely erotic and sweet? Not if James is writing." —*Romantic Times*

"Plenty of steamy love scenes that will have you reaching for your own hottie!" —Just Erotic Romance Reviews

"Smokin'-hot cowboys [and] lots of Western charm." —Fiction Vixen

"I honestly do not know how . . . Lorelei James keeps doing it, but every new book is a masterpiece, blending an incredible story line, sexy alpha cowboys, and strong women, plus luvin' so smokin' hot, you'll be stocking up on batteries!" —Guilty Pleasures Book Reviews

LORELEI JAMES

CAGED

The Mastered Series

 New American Library

New American Library
Published by the Penguin Group
Penguin Group (USA) LLC, 375 Hudson Street,
New York, New York 10014

USA | Canada | UK | Ireland | Australia | New Zealand | India | South Africa | China
penguin.com
A Penguin Random House Company

First published by New American Library,
a division of Penguin Group (USA) LLC

First Printing, July 2015

 REGISTERED TRADEMARK—MARCA REGISTRADA

LIBRARY OF CONGRESS CATALOGING-IN-PUBLICATION DATA:
James, Lorelei.
Caged/Lorelei James.
p. cm.—(The mastered series)
ISBN 978-0-451-47364-6
I. Title.
PS3610.A4475C34 2015
813'.6—dc23 2015001730

Printed in the United States of America
1 3 5 7 9 10 8 6 4 2

Set in Bembo
Designed by Spring Hoteling

CAGED

CHAPTER ONE

"YOU'RE taking me to a strip club? Seriously?" Molly stared at her friend/coworker/frequent rabble-rouser, Presley, hoping she was joking.

Presley slipped her arm through Molly's. "Good golly, Miss Molly, this'll be fun. I promise. See, Bloody Mary used to work here."

The blond bruiser from Presley's roller derby team known as Bloody Mary walked in front of them. "Why'd she quit stripping?"

"Last year she scored a job as a personal trainer. I guess the bosses at the skin boutique weren't happy she'd put on so much muscle. They prefer their strippers to be tanned bags of bones with fake jugs." Presley shrugged. "I don't get that. If I were a dude paying to see tits and ass, I'd want a variety of tits and ass—know what I mean?"

"To be honest, Presley, I have absolutely no idea what you mean, or why you think I'd want to see *any* tits and ass. Hell, I don't even want to look at my own boobs and butt."

Then they were standing below a neon sign that boasted HOT EXOTIC DANCERS—READY TO DANCE FOR YOU!

"Hot and ready . . . Sounds like a pizza joint," she muttered. When Presley didn't respond, she cast a quick glance around the line of guys ahead of them, waiting to get in. The closer they got to the entrance, the more she was tempted to make a break for it.

"Don't you even think about ditching me, Calloway," Presley warned in her ear. "You *will* walk in and have at least one drink. If it sucks, we'll go."

The bouncer, a big African-American guy, threw open his arms when he saw Bloody Mary. "Marisol! Gimme some sugar."

"Marisol was her stripper name," Presley whispered.

"I gathered that."

"Black Bart, baby," Bloody Mary cooed. "You're looking as badass as ever."

"No need to flatter me. You know I'm waving the cover charge for y'all. Tell me who you're bringing to class up the joint," Black Bart asked.

"You remember Elvis from my Denver Divas roller derby team?"

It took a second for Molly to remember that Presley's team nickname was—duh—Elvis.

Then Bloody Mary snagged Molly's hand and tugged her forward. "We're popping Miss Molly's strip-club cherry tonight."

Black Bart gave Molly a slow once-over. "You don't say."

She fought the urge to fidget. This man was used to seeing women with perfect bodies, naked women, letting it all hang out—literally. *Please ignore me.* That'd be easier than seeing a sneering expression that proved he found her seriously lacking.

But he offered her a hot-eyed stare and a very wolfish grin. "You need anything, pretty eyes—and I mean *anything*—you come find Black Bart and I'll take care of you. Mmm-mmm, sweet thang. Would I *love* to take care of you."

She blushed like a virgin. "Ah, thanks?"

Bloody Mary kept a firm grip on Molly's forearm as she led the way inside. They paused in the doorway. "So, Cherry, behold Jiggles, the classiest strip joint in Denver. Which ain't saying much. But trust me—this is ten steps above the other clubs in town."

Cherry? Awesome, she'd gotten a nickname.

"Let's sit there," Presley said, pointing to a table in the back. "I don't need to see a cooter up close."

"Then why are we at a freakin' strip club?" Molly demanded.

"We drink for free. See, dudes in here ain't ever gonna get with a stripper, no matter how many lap dances they buy. So when they start looking around and see a table of available women . . ." She shrugged. "It's win-win. We flirt, they buy us drinks, and sometimes we end up with a hot hookup."

Molly noticed all the chairs at the table faced the stage, so she couldn't look at, oh, the wall. "You've hooked up with a guy you met in a strip club?"

"In some ways it's better than meeting a guy in a bar." Presley plopped down next to her. "Just steer clear of the ones you can see masturbating under the table."

Her mouth fell open. "You can *see* that?"

"It's obvious by how fast their arm is moving," Bloody Mary said. "I always felt sorry for the cleanup crew. They have to stock some special, industrial-strength jizz remover."

The stripper strutted onstage wearing a spangly fringed top, slinky black pants, and a black cowboy hat. Molly recognized the song as "Wild West." The stripper was gorgeous, with auburn hair that fell past her shoulders, long legs, and—holy crap—she just ripped off her shirt to reveal enormous boobs. After a few twirls around the stripper's pole, another rip and her pants were gone. The woman had no hips to speak of, and her legs bordered on scrawny. Her sparkly G-string was the only item of clothing remaining, besides the five-inch acrylic stilettos.

She gyrated her hips, shook her nonexistent ass, spun around the pole, dropping into a squat and rolling up slowly. On the last spin she performed a backbend, keeping one hand on the pole until she did a walkover and landed in the splits. Then the stripper whipped off her G-string and played pussy peekaboo with her cowboy hat. Her final bow—with her head between her legs— gave everyone a full view.

The DJ warned the patrons to stick around because Madora the Sexplorer would be taking the stage in ten minutes.

Molly tried to play it cool, but she gawked at the women strolling around in ankle-breaking heels and itty-bitty scraps of silk. Even if she had a super-hot body, she doubted she'd ever have the guts to parade around half naked. She wondered if the dancers ever got cold.

Of course they do; look at their nipples.

Then again, with as vigorously as they rubbed a guy's crotch during a lap dance, friction had to at least keep their butt cheeks warm.

The cocktail waitress took their orders. Bloody Mary ordered Jäger bombs. Jägermeister always reminded Molly of *him*.

Deacon McConnell.

Even his name dripped sex.

When Molly had signed up for a kickboxing class at Black Arts dojo, she hadn't known Deacon "Con Man" McConnell was the instructor. He'd strolled into class and scared the crap out of her. It wasn't his killer physique that turned her knees to jelly, although six feet two inches of a massively muscled, heavily tattooed, shaven-headed MMA fighter with icy blue eyes would kick-start any woman's hormones. She'd never been attracted to a man with a don't-fuck-with-me badass attitude, so the pull she'd felt toward him both fascinated and frightened her.

Not that Deacon had noticed. The only time he paid attention to her was to chastise her in class. But even when the man barked orders at her like a drill sergeant, she wondered what it'd be like to hear that sexy southern drawl whispering honey-sweet words against her fevered skin in the dark.

Since Molly's boss, Amery Hardwick Black, was married to Ronin Black, Deacon's boss, they occasionally ended up in social situations outside their class time. One night a group of them had gone out to a bar and Molly had sensed Deacon watching her. Liquid courage in the form of three margaritas had allowed her to meet his gaze. Those crystalline eyes showed no guilt at getting caught staring at her, yet she hadn't seen a glimmer of attraction either, so she'd brushed it aside.

The man sent her mixed signals. He let her know he was pissed off that she'd signed up for private boxing lessons from Fisher Durant—another Black Arts MMA instructor—instead of him. Deacon didn't mention his displeasure again for almost a year . . . until she'd missed three of his kickboxing classes. Then he'd shown up at her apartment—three Sunday afternoons in a row—for makeup lessons.

The following week he'd cornered her at the dojo and asked her out on a real date. She'd been so excited and nervous, it hadn't occurred to her that he might've been messing with her. So she'd felt like a total chump, sitting in the restaurant for two hours waiting on him, only to get a *Sorry, bad timing—C U around* text that wasn't an apology or an explanation.

Then, to make matters even more confusing, Deacon had passed off his kickboxing classes to Shihan Beck, the new second-in-command at Black Arts. So Molly hadn't seen Deacon for two months.

That didn't mean she hadn't thought about him. She had, way more than was healthy, actually—which was sort of pathetic, even when half of her scenarios had a violent comeuppance, where she leveled one perfect punch to Con Man's smug mug, which knocked him out cold. In front of everyone in the dojo.

Yeah? What about the other scenario? Where you lick his bulging, tattooed biceps and stroke his shaved head until he purrs? Tease him into a sexual frenzy so he regrets that he stood you up?

The cocktail waitress dropped off the shots and whispered in Bloody Mary's ear.

Bloody Mary stood and said, "One of my old regulars is here in the VIP section. I'm going to surprise him."

What constituted a regular customer? Was there a VIP punch card? Buy four lap dances and get the fifth one free? And what kind of hard-up loser was a frequent strip-club patron anyway?

"Molly, you all right?" Presley asked. "You're quiet."

She gave Presley a fake smile. "I'm awesome. Cheers." She held up her shot for a toast and knocked it back. "Whoo-ee! That'll put hair on your chest."

"I'd much rather have a hot guy's hairy chest rubbing on mine," Presley grumbled.

"Look around, Pres. You're not gonna find that guy in here tonight." Molly leaned closer. "My cherry is officially popped. I saw a stripper and had my one drink. Let's ditch this place and go somewhere we can dance, okay?"

"Fine. I'll go tell Bloody Mary we're leaving."

Molly stood. "I'll do it. I have to use the restroom anyway."

She wandered to the VIP section, which wasn't cordoned off with velvet ropes, just a small sign that warned membership cards were required. The area was more smoke and mirrors than posh. The chairs were wider—likely for all of those free lap dances. A private bar lined the back wall.

A table of businessmen watched as a guy in the corner got a lap dance.

Single men sat at smaller tables among the groups of guys.

Molly's gaze moved to the man, who had both his hands full of Bloody Mary's ass as she straddled his lap, her boobs in his face.

Then Bloody Mary threw herself into a backbend, which gave Molly an unimpeded view of the "regular's" face.

A familiar face, smiling at Bloody Mary with those icy blue eyes.

Deacon.

His sexy grin dried up when his gaze connected with Molly's.

Her heart plummeted. *Now I know why you stood me up, you bastard.* Face burning, she retreated and kept a leisurely pace as she cut through the tables, her gut urging her to run outside, snag a cab, and go home.

Once inside the restroom, she braced her hands on the sink and dropped her head down, forcing deep, even breaths into her lungs. It didn't help. Mortification had morphed into anger. Mad as hell, she let fly, "You motherfucking, cocksucking sonuvawhore, ass-licking fuckwad!"

The bathroom door opened.

"Whoa. What's wrong?" Presley asked. "You ran in here like you saw your minister in the VIP section."

"No. But guess who I did see?" She paused and met Presley's eyes in the mirror. "Deacon."

"As in our former kickboxing teacher, Deacon?"

"Apparently he's Bloody Mary's regular customer."

When Presley didn't say anything but became very interested in checking her makeup, Molly's eyes narrowed.

"You've seen Deacon in here before."

"Just once, okay? It was around the time Knox and Shiori got married, so I figured it might be a bachelor-party thing."

"Why didn't you tell me?"

"Because I didn't know it'd matter to you." Presley's gaze met hers in the mirror. "*Why* does it matter to you?"

"It doesn't."

"Oh yeah? Then why are you so upset?"

"I'm not upset!" Okay. She sounded upset. Molly slumped against the wall. "Seeing him here clears up the mystery about why he pulled a no-show for our date. I'm not his type."

Presley got right in her face. "Fuck that. And fuck him. You don't want a man who drools over tits and ass, unless it's *your* tits and ass. I'll bet a lap dance is the only action he gets since he's so big, mean, and scary-looking."

Molly had watched ring bunnies hanging all over Deacon because being big, mean, and scary-looking was what made him so compelling. And she was smart enough to admit that was part of the reason he appealed to her too.

Appealed. Past tense. *Let it go.* "I need a drink."

"Come on. I'll buy."

Molly followed Presley out of the bathroom.

Presley stopped in the middle of the hallway so abruptly that Molly ran into her.

When she glanced up to see what'd caught Presley's attention, she froze.

Deacon leaned against the wall, his muscled arms crossed over his chest, one knee bent with his cowboy boot pressed behind him. The pose seemed casual, but she wasn't fooled.

"Beat it," he said to Presley. "I need to talk to Molly."

Her stomach swooped.

"You have shitty manners," Presley said.

Deacon ignored Presley and continued to level his brooding stare at her.

Talk about unnerving.

Talk about hot.

Shut up, hormones.

Then Presley moved and blocked Molly from his view. "Tell me what to do."

"Go. I'll give him five minutes."

"Don't take his crap."

"I won't."

Presley's gaze darted between Molly and Deacon as she backed away. "I'll be right over there if you need anything."

"She won't."

"I wasn't talking to you, asshole."

"I know. Keep walking."

When they were alone, Molly kept the entire width of the hallway between them. "You were rude to her."

"So?"

"So you save your decent behavior for the strippers working the VIP section?"

His eyes flashed. "Sometimes. What are you doin' here?"

"Drinking with my friends and soaking in the naked entertainment."

"Doesn't seem like your scene."

"I hardly think *you* can chastise *me* for being here when it appears you're a frequent patron of this strip club, Mr. VIP."

In the blink of an eye, Deacon had caged her against the wall, his mouth next to her ear.

She shivered when his hot breath tickled her neck.

"Goddamn flowers," he muttered. "You always smell sweet. Even after sweating in class for an hour, you didn't reek like everyone else."

"There's a compliment." Molly put her hands on his chest and pushed him. "Now move it."

A soft growl vibrated against her cheek. "You drive me crazy, woman."

"Hey!" a loud male voice shouted behind them. "Let her go." The bouncer stopped a foot from Molly and set his hand on her shoulder. "Hey, pretty eyes. Is this fucker harassing you?"

"No, I'm not harassing her, but I'll break your hand if you don't take it off of her."

"Deacon!" she gasped. "What is wrong with you?"

"Got a case of *mine*, I'm thinking," Black Bart said. "You know this joker, sweet thang?"

What perfect payback to proclaim she'd never seen him before. But that'd set him off. And Deacon "Con Man" McConnell in a rage was dangerous for everyone. "Yes, I know him. He is— *was*—my kickboxing instructor."

Black Bart grinned. "No kidding. You one of them *ka-rah-tay* chicks?"

"No. I've discovered I like beating the crap out of something a couple of times a week."

"I hear ya there." Despite Deacon's warning growl, Black Bart stepped between them. "Say the word and I toss him out on his tattooed ass. I don't cotton with any women being threatened in my club."

"Our conversation got a little intense, but we're done now."

Deacon's dark look said, *The hell we are,* but he kept his mouth shut.

"Okay. You need anything, come find me."

"I don't like the way he looks at you," Deacon said softly, the menace in his tone unmistakable.

"Like you'd know how he was looking at me," she said hotly. "You haven't stopped glaring at me since the moment you trapped me back here."

"Staring at you and glaring at you aren't the same thing, dar- lin', and you damn well know the difference. Especially with me."

"My mistake. But you're always glaring at someone. Is that MMA badass behavior? Daring someone to screw with you so you can beat the snot out of them?"

"Beat the snot out of them?" A smile curled his lips. "Babe. If I hit a guy in the nose, it ain't snot running out."

"Eww. Thanks for the visual."

Deacon inched closer. "No one here knows I'm a fighter. I keep it my personal business."

"I don't imagine there's much talking going on during a lap dance anyway."

"Not usually, no."

"Whatever. I'm leaving."

He shook his head. "Not done talking to you."

"We have nothing to talk about. I ran into you at a strip club. Big deal. You're a single guy. It's your *personal business* if you pay some chick with fake boobs to grind her bony ass on your crotch." She paused. "Does that about cover it?"

"No. That doesn't begin to cover it." Deacon crowded her against the wall. "You still seeing Jake, that pussy banker friend of Amery?"

How did Deacon know that? Moreover, why did he care?

"What about the douche bag caught your eye? The snappy suit? The nine-to-five work hours? The freakishly perfect groomed hair?"

"Maybe it's that he didn't stand me up for our first date," she retorted. She gave Deacon's shiny head a blatant once-over. "Sounds like you're jealous of his hair, baldy."

His eyes hardened. "Shaving my head is a choice."

"How do I know you're not sporting a chrome dome because otherwise you'd have a bad comb-over?"

Omigod. I cannot believe I said that. To Deacon.

Molly braced herself for his reaction.

But nothing could've prepared her for his mouth coming down on hers in an explosion of heat, need, and possession.

His kiss inflamed her. Head spinning, Molly fought the temptation to hold on to him for dear life—because holy buckets, his kiss packed as hard a punch as his fist. She melted into him, and that changed the tenor of the kiss from passion to sweetness.

The twining of tongues slowed, and he teased her lips with tiny nibbles and tender smooches. Then Deacon buried his face in the crook of her neck and his big body trembled. "Fuck. I knew it."

"Knew what?" she managed.

Deacon stepped back. He didn't act shocked or even contrite. He rubbed his hand over his mouth, and grim determination darkened his eyes. "I didn't mean to do that. Not here, not like this. But I'm considering it a sign."

"Of what?" *My stupidity?*

"That we're gonna happen."

The music had kicked on, so she must've misheard him. "What?"

"We're gonna happen. I've wanted you for too damn long. I see you—I fucking *smell* you—and I can't get you out of my head. I've tried staying away from you—for your good and mine. But now that I've tasted that sweet mouth? No more denying this."

"Are you always this cocky?" she demanded.

His eyebrow winged up. "You kissed me back."

Molly blushed. Dammit. He had her there.

Admit that the man could have you anywhere. Anytime. Anyplace.

"Don't tell me you don't want this."

"I don't even know what 'this' is, so you and I are *never* gonna happen, Deacon."

That dangerous look settled in his eyes again. "Because a guy like me—a tattooed fighter without a college degree—ain't good enough for you?"

"Oh, quit acting hurt. You lost that right when you pulled a no-show for our date. The only reason you want me is because you haven't had me. Or maybe I'm more appealing to you now that I'm telling you no." *I'm not your type, Mr. VIP. Don't make me say that out loud. This is mortifying enough.*

"You sure got a mouth on you these days." He locked his hooded gaze to hers, stalking her until her back met the concrete wall again.

"I'm glad my transformation from mousy to mouthy amuses you."

Then his hands were on the wall beside her head. "I'm not

amused. I'm proud. You should be too. You've come a long way, learning to stand up for yourself—verbally and physically."

There was the mother lode of compliments. But it was too late.

"Happy as I am to have your professional approval of my progress, this is me standing up for myself. Goodbye, Deacon."

Molly ducked under his arm and walked away without looking back.

CHAPTER TWO

THE punishing rhythm Deacon had set on the treadmill finally started to wear him down.

His body had become too slippery for the heart-rate monitor to stick. Even the armband holding his MP3 player had slid down and he'd had to take it off. So he'd run to the sounds of his thudding footfalls and measured breaths.

Black Arts was quiet as a tomb on Sunday—the way Deacon preferred it. After Sensei Ronin Black's sojourn to Japan last year, he'd hired additional jujitsu instructors, which meant Deacon spent less time teaching and more time focused on MMA. Despite Deacon's protests, Shihan Beck had taken over his kickboxing classes.

Not that any of his classes had been overrun with eager students. He had high expectations, and only the hardiest of souls lasted in his classes. So what if his students were afraid of him? If he didn't push them beyond their expectations, they'd show up for class uninspired and unconditioned. Fear was a great motivator.

It'd definitely worked for Molly.

Just the thought of that woman sent fire through his veins. She'd gone from trying to melt into the wall whenever he came near her to telling him he was a sadistic bastard right before she released a flurry of punches at the heavy bag.

That'd been one of his proudest teaching moments.

Her fierceness in class had spilled over into her interpersonal dealings. He'd heard that her managerial skills had lessened his boss's wife's workload. He'd seen her increased confidence when their group went out. Yet, with all the changes, she'd retained genuine niceness, sweetness, and thoughtfulness. He wanted her in a way he'd never experienced. Yeah, he wanted to fuck her and watch those brown eyes heat with lust, but he also wanted . . . more. And since that was a new feeling, he had no fucking clue what to do about it or how to act on it.

As he kept up the brutal cardio, his thoughts drifted to the first time he'd considered taking action with her outside of class.

Last year the Black Arts crew had converged at Fresh, a fetish club, for Ivan Stanislovsky's birthday party. While their friends had been doing shots or sneaking off to see club demos of spankings, floggings, and fire play, he and Molly had gotten into a heated argument.

"Why didn't you tell me you were taking private boxing lessons?" he'd demanded when they had a moment alone at the table.

She rolled her pretty brown eyes. "Because I knew you'd act like it's a personal affront to you."

To keep their friends from eavesdropping, he'd moved in close enough to count the freckles on her nose. "Whose kickboxing class are you in?"

"Yours." She studied him. "You're telling me you're a more dedicated teacher than Fisher?"

"Do I *look* like I give a damn if my students excel in a fitness class? Huh-uh. I try to break them."

"Why?"

"Survival of the fittest, babe."

"Sorry, but that attitude *does* make you a shitty teacher, Deacon."

"Fish-dick is a shitty teacher. I break my students down to build them back up stronger than they were before." He had a hard time keeping his eyes off that lush fucking mouth of hers, which needed his mouth on it pronto. "So did you hire Fisher because you wanted private one-on-one time with him?"

"Yes, that's it," she cooed with sarcasm. "Instead of showing me how to increase my impact and speed, Fisher ties me to the heavy bag and fucks me in front of the whole dojo. I'm surprised you haven't heard about it."

He forced himself to focus on the challenge dancing in her eyes rather than hooking an arm around Fisher's neck and choking him out right there in the booth. Every time he inhaled, Molly's flowery scent floated to him.

"But if you're so desperate to prove your dick is bigger than his, I'll bring a ruler next time."

He laughed. "Better bring a yardstick for me, babe, not a puny ruler."

"I'm surprised you can get pants on over that monster-sized . . . ego."

Speaking of monster-sized. Jesus. All night he'd tried to keep his gaze off her truly spectacular tits. Something had prompted her to ditch the modest clothes she usually favored. And it made him fucking crazy to think she'd dressed differently because Fisher was here.

Needing to push her a little, Deacon lifted his hand to twine a long, shiny brown curl around his index finger. As his finger wound the spiral higher, the backs of his knuckles brushed the creamy swell of her full breast.

Molly's refusal to slap his hand away intrigued him. As did the way her pulse hammered in her throat as he touched her.

"Tell me why you need to take more classes to increase your hitting power?"

"Are you asking if I'm still afraid of my own shadow?"

"From where I'm sitting, you've made great strides in confidence and the ability to defend yourself."

She didn't look like she believed him.

"What?"

"Do you know what I did today? I helped teach a self-defense class. I stood in front of fifty girls and told them about being attacked. How I'd felt like an idiot for being oblivious to my dangerous surroundings. How I'd felt lucky that at least I hadn't been raped. Then I confessed I couldn't go outside by myself after dark for more than a month after it happened. Even if I'd forgotten something in my car, I couldn't make myself leave the safety of my apartment. A big, strong, tough guy like you doesn't have any idea how it feels to be frightened out of your fucking mind. So getting to tell those girls today that I took control of the fear by enrolling in self-defense classes made me feel ten feet tall."

Shit, he knew what was coming.

"But according to you, I'm still traumatized from that attack. I shouldn't speak out publicly about what happened to me. I shouldn't share the precautions other girls can take so they don't end up in that situation." She glared at him. "You think I'm weak. That's why I didn't ask you to teach me. Fisher has never seen me as a victim."

When she attempted to pull her head away, Deacon held tightly to the piece of hair wrapped around his finger. His gaze encompassed every inch of her face. From the fire flashing in her big brown eyes, to the wrinkle in her brow, to the heat and alcohol turning her cheeks rosy, to the pursed set of her lips.

"Let me go."

"You've had your say; now I'll have mine. I told your friends not to assume you'd want to help with the class. The reason I said that? Because you've never spoken to me or anyone else at the dojo about the attack. So I assumed it still had a hold on you. That mistake is on me and I'm sorry. But I've never *ever* thought you were weak—especially since you faced down your fears and have been kicking them in the teeth. Do I tell you to toughen up in my class? Yep. But I tell everyone to push harder.

"The real reason you didn't ask me to teach you? Darlin', you're afraid of this pull between us." His focus momentarily slipped to her cleavage. "The thought of being alone with me, with my hands all over you, my body in tight behind yours, my voice in your ear . . . sent you running. But here's a warning, babe: Don't think I won't chase you." Another round of shots had arrived, breaking the moment.

Molly didn't speak to him the rest of the night.

And he hadn't found the balls to ask her out for another year. A *year.* Talk about fucking pathetic. He might be fierce in the ring and in his classes, but he was a chickenshit when it came to man/woman personal stuff. So when Molly had skipped his kickboxing class three times, he'd seized the chance to turn their teacher-student relationship into something more. He'd loaded his portable fast bag and other training equipment and shown up at her apartment.

The look on her face when she opened the door to him? Priceless.

But then she'd tried to bar him from entering. Rather than laughing and shoving her aside, he'd asked if she really wanted to drop his class. Because the only way he'd allow her to return was to make up the hours she'd missed.

Molly had reluctantly let him in.

Deacon was pretty sure she'd imagined his face on the boxing dummy as she'd pummeled it. After the workout, he'd ordered Chinese. They'd eaten side by side on her couch and watched three episodes of *Bar Rescue.*

So he'd warned her he'd be back the following Sunday for another makeup lesson. After a grueling session, she'd shocked him by cooking a pork roast with all the trimmings. Those few hours with her had been burned into his memory banks forever.

But the third lesson—he hardly remembered that one. Due to an unseasonably warm afternoon, she'd worn spandex workout pants and an eye-popping sports bra. They'd done mostly floor work because watching her gorgeous tits jiggle every time her fist connected with the dummy . . . A man had only so much willpower. He'd given her a lame excuse and left right after the workout.

Then all that crap had gone down.

And she hadn't given him a chance to explain.

Not that he'd know what the fuck to say to her anyway. Because even to his own ears it sounded like a lousy fucking excuse.

"Get off that thing. Now."

Christ. His trainer's booming voice could compete with thunder.

When Deacon didn't immediately comply, Maddox leaned over and stabbed buttons on the console until the machine shut off.

Unprepared for the sudden loss of movement, Deacon smacked into the handles. Then, bracing his feet on either side of the belt, he pulled the towel from around his neck and mopped his face and head.

"What is wrong with you?" Maddox demanded. "Three hours on the goddamn treadmill means you won't be worth a damn for other cardio training tomorrow."

Deacon slowly raised his head, his chest heaving from exertion. He respected the hell out of his trainer. Not only was Maddox Byerly the force driving him to finally get somewhere in his MMA career, but he'd become a good friend. Spending six days a week together, though, meant they had to maintain a line between friendship and training at the dojo.

"Don't pull that silent-treatment crap on me, Deacon. How fucking hard is it to just tell me the problem?"

"Hard as hell, to be honest."

"Tough. Park it. I ain't going anywhere until you start talking."

In the rare instances in the past that he'd needed advice, Deacon had relied on Ronin or Knox. They never pushed; they waited until he came to them. But Maddox was a fucking bulldog—he demanded full disclosure about Deacon's life outside the ring because he claimed it'd affect Deacon's performance inside the ring. So in the last six months, the motherfucker had tried to force—*tried* being the operative word—Deacon into talking about every-fucking-thing. Hadn't worked so far, so he attempted to hedge. "I don't know what your problem is. I thought you'd be happy I got my cardio in."

"Nice try. Take your time working up to the real issue. I've got nowhere else to be today."

"You plan to load me up on chocolate and tampons after I share my feelings with you?" he retorted. Hadn't these new guys gotten the memo that he—Deacon "Con Man" McConnell—did *not* do let's-talk-it-out friendship crap?

Maddox scrubbed his hands over his cheeks. "A bottle of Midol would help you immensely, dickhead."

Deacon wanted to laugh. Maddox didn't take his shit, which was why they got along so well. He grabbed his water bottle and drained half of it.

"What happened to make you punish yourself like you're training for a marathon?"

As much as he wanted to say, *None of your fucking business*, he knew if he didn't lay it all out now, he'd get steamrolled. "An incident at a strip club."

Maddox's head snapped up. "Please tell me you didn't get into a fight."

"Not with guys hanging out in the club, a bouncer, or the owner."

"Jesus, Deacon. You got into it with a *stripper*?"

Deacon dropped into the chair next to Maddox. "No."

"Start from the beginning."

Looking at his ratty-ass running shoes was easier than staring Maddox in the eye. "I couldn't shake off my restlessness after practice yesterday. Sitting at home flipping through channels would just piss me off because I end up watching cage fights. So I went to my strip club." He felt Maddox staring at him, so he looked up. "What?"

"Why do you have such a hard-on for strip clubs?"

"What's not to like, watching hot chicks dancing around naked?" He took another sip of water. "Not all strip-club regulars are pervs who can't get dates."

Maddox continued to look skeptical.

"Some people attend plays, ballet, and opera for entertainment," he said defensively. "To me, it's entertaining to see beautiful women with killer bodies dancing around naked."

"I never thought of it that way."

"It's cheaper than a Saturday-night date to the movies with popcorn. Even after tipping out for a lap dance."

"Nice justification."

He snorted. "I've never fallen prey to the delusions that the hot brunette grinding on me will want to see me outside of the club."

"So you've never dated a stripper?"

"Explain what you mean by *date*."

"Pick her up, take her to dinner, then end up banging the headboard."

Deacon shook his head. "I ain't the dating kind. I've fucked a few strippers."

"I don't get it." Maddox held up his hands. "No judgment on

your choice of amusement. But when I look at the dancers, all I see is their age. It doesn't make me feel pervy watching them. It makes me sad. Admitting that probably makes me sound like a prude."

"That makes you a decent guy because you wanna save them."

Maddox leaned back and crossed his arms over his chest. "Back to the story. So you went to the strip club. You're sipping a drink, minding your own business, when . . ."

"One of my favorite former dancers visited me in the VIP section." Deacon scowled. "She plopped herself on my lap, stuck her tits in my face, and when I glanced up, I saw Molly."

"Molly. As in Molly—"

"My former student who I've wanted to bang like a fucking drum since the moment I saw her? The woman you forced me to stay away from while I was training for the last fight? Yeah, *that* Molly."

Maddox whistled. "So she what? Used some of Fisher's boxing moves on you?"

"A punch in the nuts would've been easier to take than the way she looked at me." He let his head fall forward. "You have any idea how much I hated standing her up two months ago?"

"I've a good idea. I'm sorry for it now, but you won the fight. That's what I needed from you. And what you needed for yourself. You can't deny that you'd never been more focused."

Only because he'd cut himself off from everyone. He trained, ate, slept, and trained some more.

"Being with Molly then would've been a distraction."

"She'll be a distraction now." The best kind of distraction— not that he'd admit that to Maddox. "But now I have a better handle on what you expect of me for fight prep. And you know that I won't hand grenade my career because of some random chick."

"Molly wasn't a random chick for you, Deacon," Maddox pointed out. "That's why we had to intervene."

He shoved aside his resentment for the Maddox-led, Ronin-executed intervention—for the good of his career. "So when I saw her at the strip club, those brown eyes snapping fire at me, all I could think about was how much I wanted her and I'd been patient with her and the situation long enough."

"You didn't tell her that?"

Deacon looked at Maddox sharply. "Of course I did."

"What exactly did you say to her?"

"That her and me were gonna happen."

Maddox groaned. "Then you grabbed her by the hair, threw her over your shoulder, and stomped out?"

"The bouncer was watching me or I would have."

"Been a while since you've been in a relationship, huh?"

"Yeah."

"How long?"

Fuck if he wanted to tell him, but he admitted, "Since I was fifteen."

Maddox shook his head. "I'd laugh and call bullshit, but I don't think you're kidding, D."

"I'm not. After my last . . ." *Hold on. Should you share the ugly part of your past with the guy who's helping you build a future?*

No.

Deacon shrugged. "I've stuck to sex without entanglements. I don't even understand why it feels different with Molly. I sure as fuck don't know what to do about it now that I've royally screwed up again."

"Tell her that."

"Show up on her doorstep and blurt out what an idiot I am?" he said, a little horrified by that thought.

"You really are clueless."

"That's helpful, fuckhead."

"Maybe something will come to you while you're groveling. But make no mistake—that's what it'll take."

"I figured."

"What if she won't forgive you?" Maddox asked.

Deacon shot Maddox a dark look. "I'm blaming you. Then I'll grovel and promise her that it'll be the last time my trainer interferes with my love life."

"Love life, eh?" Maddox nudged Deacon's shoulder. "Speaking of . . . Now that you've poured your heart out to me"—Deacon snorted—"it's time for you to return the favor."

"I'll definitely need to be punching shit while you're jawing on about it."

Maddox smiled. "That I can help with."

CHAPTER THREE

MONDAYS were always busy at Hardwick Designs. But Molly thrived on it. She remembered the lean times—which hadn't been that long ago.

Since she'd taken over as office manager, she'd freed up her boss, Amery, to work more on the creative side of the graphic-arts business. And Molly had streamlined their operations so Amery could spend more time with her husband, Ronin.

Part of the streamlining process had been hiring Presley Quinn—aka PQ, or Elvis—a kick-ass artist and one of the most out-of-the-box thinkers Molly had ever met. But Presley, for all her tats, piercings, funky clothes, and offbeat lifestyle, had no problem with taking direction and was very much a team player. After interviewing a dozen potential employees, Molly knew how rare that trait was in creative types. The irony was they'd met in Deacon's kickboxing class at Black Arts, so they'd become friends first before Molly had approached Amery on the subject of hiring Presley. So far everything had worked out better than either she or Amery had imagined.

In addition to hiring Presley, Molly had convinced their friend, and Amery's former coworker, Chaz Graylind, to work for Hardwick Designs. Chaz had some professional highs, followed by lows, and having a steady paycheck appealed to him. Plus, he'd proven in the last year that he had Amery's back, after a personal issue caused her to question their friendship and his loyalty. The bonus was since they were all adrift from their families in some form, they'd formed their own family.

So after spending most of the day on the phone, Molly was happy when things wound down around four o'clock. Presley had a roller derby bout, so she left early. At five, Chaz breezed by, kissing her cheek, expressing regrets she couldn't come along to happy hour. But she couldn't wait to finish out her day in blessed quiet.

Lost in spreadsheets, she glanced up from her computer screen an hour later, when the front door chimed. Chaz must've forgotten to lock it.

She wheeled her chair around and headed to the reception area. Whoever had stumbled in could just deal with her bare feet, because those killer pumps were not going back on.

"Sorry. We're closed—" was all she managed when she saw Deacon standing in the center of the room, shrinking the space with his presence.

Her intent to order him out of the building vanished when his smoldering gaze rolled over her and he said, "Looking good, babe," in that sexy southern drawl.

"What do you want?"

"To talk."

"I said everything I needed to say Saturday night."

"Fine. Then you'll listen." His long strides erased the distance between them. He grabbed her hand and towed her around the corner. Then he backed her against the brick wall.

And she let him, which annoyed her.

"Don't know if I oughta be worried or excited by the way you're looking at me."

Her face heated. "Go with worried and go away, Deacon."

He didn't laugh. Point for him.

Even being mad at him didn't lessen her attraction to him, which also annoyed her.

"I was a dickhead to you Saturday night. I'm sorry."

She said, "That's it?" with cool detachment.

Deacon shook his head. He opened his mouth. Closed it.

When a few moments passed and he didn't tack on anything else, she said, "Can you get on with it?"

"Can you give me a goddamn minute? I can't think when you're glaring at me. Jesus, woman. You're intimidating as fuck."

Her jaw dropped. "What? Me?"

"Yes, you. You are smart and clever and you can just say what you mean the first time. I had this whole speech prepared, and then I get here and I see you and it's just . . . gone." The tension in his body and the fact he couldn't meet her eyes indicated his distress.

Cut him some slack.

Molly couldn't believe she was about to do this. "The best way to remember your speech is to recall the high points."

His gaze snapped back to hers. "The what?"

"High points. The most important thing you wanted to say."

"I already did that when I said I was sorry."

"And . . . ?"

"And I was a dickhead."

"And . . . ?" she prompted more firmly.

"And I want to start over with you."

"You had the chance to start over and you blew it when you stood me up."

"You never let me explain."

"You never *tried*," she retorted. "You showed up at my house three times when I missed kickboxing class. But after you stood me up, all I rated was a lousy text message?"

"Technically, I didn't stand you up."

"Yes, you did. And it's too late for excuses." She ducked under his arm and pointed to the front door. "Go."

"Not an excuse but an explanation. See . . . I was there that day, the day of our date, sitting in the parking lot, watching you." He described her outfit in detail, along with her facial expressions. "I was a fucking coward, staying in the car instead of coming in and telling you the truth."

"Oh, that you suddenly remembered you weren't attracted to me because I'm not a hot-bodied stripper?"

"Not. Even. Fucking. Close." Deacon took a step forward with each terse word. "Maddox overheard our entire conversation in the dojo when I asked you out."

Molly put her hands on his chest, stopping his advancement.

"He reminded me I needed to focus on my fight. When I told him my life off the mat wasn't his fucking business, he *made* it his business." The muscle in his jaw flexed. "He went to Ronin. They pulled me from teaching to concentrate fully on MMA training. I was pissed as hell." He paused to inhale a deep breath. "Mostly because they were right."

"And?"

His blue eyes shimmered with regret. "And after the fight was over, I figured I'd grovel, but you'd already moved on. I worried I'd lost out on you to that pussy banker."

Molly stared at him. This wasn't the overly confident Deacon she knew. This man had vulnerability in his eyes as if he expected rejection. "It's your career, Deacon. I could've handled you need-ing to focus on training. I would've been disappointed, but not angry and hurt."

"Would you've gone out with Jake?"

Why did that bother him? "Would you have expected me to wait around until you were through with your fight?"

"Probably not." He curled his hand around her face. "I can't change the past, babe. I can apologize for it. Which I've done. I can ask you to forgive me for hurting you, which I'm doin' now. And I can admit I want us to happen." He offered a wry smile. "I did a shit job trying to get that across to you Saturday night."

With Deacon close enough she could feel his body vibrating from nerves, she had a spark of hope this could be the beginning, not the end.

You're such a sickening optimist.

No. You're just a fool.

A fool about to take a big chance.

"Say something," he urged.

"I only went on three dates with Jake and I didn't sleep with him," she blurted out.

Deacon eased back to look at her. "It kills me to ask this, but why not?"

"Because Jake didn't do it for me. Like Fisher doesn't do it for me. It'd be easier if . . ."

"If what?"

If other men did it for me, but they don't. Not by half.

She'd tried, dammit. Telling herself over and over that other men besides Deacon were hot. Other men sported amazing bodies. Other men were inked with cool tats. Other men broadcast that don't-fuck-with-me vibe. Other men spoke with a sexy voice that hit the mark between rough as gravel and smooth as whiskey.

But when all of those attributes belonged to one man and that man owned them without apology?

Goodbye, other men.

"Molly. Tell me."

She swallowed hard at the intensity in his eyes. "You do it for me in a bad way, Deacon McConnell. You always have. Even when you scared the crap out of me."

Then he slanted his lips over hers and kissed her with tenderness. And he seemed as surprised by that as she was. "Give me another chance," he said as he feathered kisses up her jawline. "I can figure out how to do this relationship shit."

"That's what you want? A relationship with me?"

"Yeah."

In that moment, when their gazes collided, the heat in his eyes imparted a few things.

Sex with him would be raw. Borderline rough. Rarely tender.

There wouldn't be candlelit dinners beforehand.

There wouldn't be cuddling or spooning afterward.

Being naked with him would likely ruin her for sex with mere mortal men.

Those thoughts must've been easy to read on her face, because Deacon treated her to the most wicked grin she'd ever witnessed. "I see a whole lot of interest in those pretty brown eyes, and no fear."

"Oh, there's fear."

"Of?"

Right now she had too many to name, so she picked the most obvious one. "That you seeing me naked won't be nearly as thrilling as me getting the full monty from you."

"Not a chance in hell, babe." Deacon's hands landed beside her head. He leaned in, letting his smooth jaw rub against hers. His breaths teased her cheek, then moved lower.

The combination of the soft drag of his lips and the scrape of his teeth turned her skin into a mass of goose bumps.

"You wanna test that theory right now?"

"How would you do that?" she asked breathlessly.

"Unbutton your blouse," he murmured against her throat.

She obeyed him without question—and she didn't stop to ask herself *why* she had zero hesitation. She untucked her shirt from her skirt and started at the bottom, working her fingers up. When she reached the button between her breasts, the back of her hand brushed his chest. After unhooking the last button, she let her shirt hang open.

Deacon didn't waste time. He planted sucking kisses from the hollow of her throat to the V of her cleavage. Then he traced the edge of her bra with his tongue, up the swell of her left breast, back down, then up the right side. He didn't speak; he just tormented her with hot kisses, leisurely licks, and tiny nips. He muttered, "Fuck," then sank his teeth into her flesh and sucked hard.

Molly gasped, more in surprise than in pain.

Keeping his mouth in place, he snagged her left hand and pressed it against the fly of his jeans.

Her palm met a rock-hard bulge.

He broke the suction of his mouth on her skin. "You're *half* undressed and I'm fully hard. So yeah, I'm thrilled by the idea of seeing you naked, babe." He brushed a soft kiss over the mark on her breast.

She glanced down; he'd left a big red hickey on her boob.

Then Deacon nudged her chin back up, forcing her to meet his hungry, sexual gaze. "You look at that mark over the next couple of days and make sure you understand what it means to be involved with a man like me."

"Is that supposed to scare me?" Thankfully, her voice didn't shake when she tossed out, "It doesn't. Know why?"

He waited, those blue eyes still blazing at her.

"Because it's really hot that you used your teeth on me just because you wanted to, so I guess I passed your little test to see if I'd get prudish." Feeling reckless, Molly tilted her head, baring her neck. "I liked it. So mark me here."

He didn't hesitate. He opened his mouth over the spot. When he started to suck, her knees wobbled. But Deacon held her up, pushing his leg between hers. Palming her breasts. Squeezing the flesh with his strong fingers in time with the pulse beating in her throat.

She reached for him, wanting to feel the muscles in his back rippling as he positioned himself over her. Wanting to feel the muscles in his ass flexing as he powered into her. Wanting to feel the muscles in his chest abrading her nipples as he moved against her.

Cool air met the wet spot he'd created as he trailed kisses up her neck to her jawline.

"Deacon."

"That's what I want. My name on your lips." He fit his mouth over hers and delicately licked the inside of her bottom lip until she opened for him fully.

No explosion of need, just pure sensual torture.

He ended the kiss but didn't release his hold on her.

Breathing hard, they stared at each other.

Then Deacon leveled that devilish smile on her. "No more denying there's nothing between us. From here on out, we *are* together."

Not a question; a statement. "So it appears."

"So what are we doin' tonight?"

We. Lord, the man was a bulldozer. "Presley has a roller derby bout in Centennial. I need to change before we go." *We* again.

"Need help?" His gaze swept over her from her unbuttoned shirt to her bare toes.

She pushed past her normal response to hide her body and listened to the voice that dared her to tease him. As she headed for the bathroom, she let her blouse flutter to the floor. She paused just outside the door and unzipped her skirt; then it too hit the carpet. Looking over her shoulder at him, she said, "Maybe next time."

His eyes were firmly on her ass. She might've heard a growl before she shut the door in his face.

As she pulled on her jeans, her gaze caught on the red spot on her breast. Her fingers traced the mark. She'd never had a love bite before—just another rite of passage she'd missed.

When she leaned closer to the mirror to check her makeup, she noticed kissing Deacon had made her lips full and pink. No need for lipstick. She adjusted the drawstring on the hoodie and saw the other love bite. Holy crap. It was huge. She smoothed her hands down her hair, pulling the sections forward to frame her face and mask the mark. After slipping on her pink and black canvas sport clogs, she shouldered her backpack and exited the bathroom.

Deacon leaned against the wall, her blouse and skirt dangling from one finger.

"Thanks for picking those up."

"I figured there might be questions in the morning if you left a trail of clothes."

Molly rolled to her toes to peck him on the mouth.

Instantly Deacon's arm circled her lower back, holding her in place as he kissed her with surprising sweetness. Then he released her and said gruffly, "Let's go."

She shoved her clothes in her backpack, shut off the lights, armed the alarm, and locked the front door.

On the sidewalk, she blocked the late-afternoon sun, noticing that Deacon already had his shades in place. "Do you wanna follow me?"

"Nope. I'll drive us."

"But then you'll have to come all the way back here."

"I don't mind." Then he relieved her of her backpack, slipped the strap up his left arm, and draped his right arm over her shoulder.

He brushed a soft kiss over her temple. "Love the shoes, babe."

"Yeah? Why?"

"They're unexpected. Can't wait to find out what other surprises you've got in store for me."

CHAPTER FOUR

"DO you go to a lot of roller derby bouts?" Deacon asked.

"It's not like I attend them all like some rabid fangirl."

Deacon peered over the top of his sunglasses and looked at her Denver Divas hoodie.

"Hey, I bought this at their fund-raiser." She resisted sticking her tongue out at him. "I support my friend's activities. Presley would do the same for me if I suddenly took up racquetball or golf. Not that it'll ever happen, since me and athletics don't go hand in hand."

"You showed great improvement in kickboxing."

"Improvement doesn't count as much as natural ability."

"Natural ability can only take you so far. Continual improvement is all that matters."

"Are you improving with Maddox training you?"

"Be a sad state if I wasn't with as much time as I spend with him," Deacon drawled. "Did you attend my last fight?"

Molly shook her head.

"Because I stood you up?"

"Yes. You weren't my favorite person. I might've rooted for your opponent that night."

"Harsh." The edges of his mouth turned up, half grimace, half smile. "There's no in between with you?"

"If there weren't, Deacon, I wouldn't be here."

That answer didn't make him happy.

Too bad.

Molly looked out the window. As they drove along the outskirts of Denver with the rolling hills and animals grazing in the fields, she realized it'd been a while since she'd ventured out of the city. In the spring she'd always made a point of hiking several of the wildflower trails in the foothills, but she hadn't this year. The summer wildflowers weren't as vibrant as the spring varieties, and she knew if she didn't make time to do it, it'd be another source of enjoyment abandoned. Maybe she could convince Presley to go with her. God knew Chaz would likely complain about bugs, sun, and dirt. Amery spent weekends with Ronin. Her next-door neighbor, Nina, might be game.

"Why the frown?" Deacon said. "What'd I do now?"

That sounded a little paranoid. "Nothing. I'm just thinking."

"About?"

She faced him. "Are you really interested, or just making polite conversation?"

"Babe. I'm not so much with polite conversation. You *know* this about me."

"True. So I was thinking about taking a wildflower hike in the foothills."

"Lemme know when and I'll make sure my gun is cleaned before we go."

We again? Really? Before she did a total dork move and *squee'd*, the gun comment registered. "Why would you bring a gun?" And why hadn't he shot out a derisive remark about her stopping to smell the wild roses?

Because this Deacon—with the hot eyes and even hotter kisses—isn't the brooding Deacon you know.

"Bears," he said without sarcasm. "Those motherfuckers cover a lot of ground in the summer. Better to be safe than bear meat."

"You like to hike?"

"I've never been. I've never been to a roller derby bout either." A half smile flirted on his lips. "You're getting me to try all sorts of new things."

"I'm sure there are all sorts of new things you'll get me to try too," she returned with a provocative look.

After tossing his sunglasses on the dash, he placed a soft kiss on the inside of her wrist. "I stick to the basics when it comes to sex."

"The basics?" she managed to get out. The heat in his eyes burned away the moisture in her mouth, making it hard to form words.

"Hot, wet, and as often as possible." He sank his teeth into the fleshy part of her thumb.

She bit her lip, but a moan escaped.

"You don't get to do that."

"What?"

"Try to keep quiet when you like the way I touch you."

Molly felt her face and neck flush, but she didn't look away.

"Sexy thing," he murmured. "You tell me when it gets too intense."

"Is that even possible?"

His eyes darkened. "Jesus, Molly."

"I'm not being flip. I've only ever experienced intensity in small, singular doses."

"And yet you say this doesn't scare you?"

"How can I fear what I've never had?"

"Killing me here, babe."

That gruff, sexy tone sent a shiver up her spine.

Deacon continued to stroke her cheek. "One hour."

"What?"

"One hour since I apologized. One hour since you agreed to give me a chance. One hour since I kissed you. I oughta be happy we've come this far in one hour." His thumb returned to her mouth, and he outlined her top and bottom lips. "But it ain't far enough. If I had my way? We'd spend the next hour, the hour after that, and the hour after that in my bed."

Her sex pulsed. If he could rev her up this fast with words, what kind of heat and power could he generate with his mouth, his hands, and his body?

Atomic-level heat.

"You know . . ." she offered, "roller derby *is* overrated."

"Don't even fucking kid about that," he growled. Then he kissed her hard. "Get outta the car."

"But—"

"Leave this for now. We'll revisit it when we've both got clearer heads."

Molly freed her inner temptress—who preferred instant gratification and thought revisiting this later was a bad idea—and unzipped her hoodie.

One tine at a time.

Deacon's avid gaze followed that movement.

She stopped below her cleavage. Then she pulled the tank top aside. "Which mark screams *clearer head* to you? The one you gave me? Or the one I asked for?"

He bent his head over her chest.

She expected a quick nip, not a featherlight kiss.

Locking his gaze to hers, he righted her clothing. "Let's go."

Deacon draped his arm over her shoulder as they walked toward the school. "How long does this last?"

"It depends. I'd say . . . two hours. Why?"

"We're eating after."

They reached the ticket table by the door. She said, "Two, please."

Deacon paid before Molly fished her wallet out. "When we're together, I pay. Always."

"That's archaic."

"Get used to it."

With the large crowd in the gymnasium, Molly was relieved to see seating and not standing-room only. She pointed to the top of the bleachers. "That's the best place to watch."

After they settled in, Deacon threaded his fingers through hers. "Explain how this is played, because it doesn't look like what I've seen in the movies or on TV."

"This is a flat track. It's used more commonly than the elevated track. Presley told me that when the team first started, they didn't have a dedicated training place, so they had to practice in a parking lot."

Deacon winced. "Sounds painful. I did my time training under less-than-ideal conditions."

"I guess sweeping the area off with industrial brooms cut down on road rash. Everyone who started with the team has scars."

"What'd they do in the winter?"

"They only played in a summer league."

A commotion broke out on the floor, and Bloody Mary shoved an opposing team member.

Deacon stiffened beside her.

"She looks a lot different as Bloody Mary, doesn't she?"

"Jesus. Marisol is a roller derby queen now?"

"I don't know about being the queen. She's the jammer. I'm surprised you recognized her with her clothes on."

A heavy pause. Then, "Look at me."

Dammit. She felt his pull and turned her head.

"I thought we were done with the strip-club fallout."

"We are."

"Then you don't get to throw shit like that in my face." Deacon lifted his hand and cupped her cheek. "One hour."

"Deacon—"

"We became this one hour ago. I had a life before that. So did you. What—and who—came before doesn't matter."

"Ignoring things that happened in the past only means they'll be harder to discuss down the road."

"I'm not a big discusser, babe."

"Well, I guess that's about to change—isn't it, *babe*?"

Deacon's eyes narrowed.

Molly offered him a sunny smile. "We *will* have a detailed discussion about our expectations—both social and sexual." She patted his thigh. "Chin up, buddy. It'll give you something to look forward to during dinner."

He stared at her.

She didn't crack—but, lord, perky and determined was hard to maintain when faced with those calculating blue eyes.

Then Deacon smiled. A smile she hadn't seen before. A smile that shot straight to the heart of her.

"Killing me, babe." He kissed her decisively. "Now explain roller derby to me."

The bout started, and the noise level in the gymnasium increased dramatically. Molly did her best to explain what a jam was, what rules a player violated to get a penalty, the difference between a jammer and a blocker. She admitted the scoring never made much sense to her.

When Presley went sailing across the floor and ended up dog piled by the opposing team, Molly stood and booed along with the rest of the Divas fans. Then she booed louder when Presley, who had a bloody nose and a gash on the outside of her calf, was penalized for tripping.

"You suck, ref! Pull your head out!" Molly shouted.

Deacon looked at her strangely when she plopped back down next to him.

"What?"

"You're a vocal fan."

"Embarrassed you, did I?"

"Surprised me is all." He ran his knuckles down the side of her face. "You'll yell and scream at my opponent when you come to watch me fight?"

She couldn't tell him the thought of seeing him bloodied turned her stomach. "Would that make you happy?"

"It'd make me very happy to see you sitting in my corner, babe. Never had my woman cheering me on."

My woman. The growly way he said that just . . . got to her.

Another loud cry arose from the crowd.

Molly looked down on the floor. The players were in a massive fight. Punching, pushing, elbows flying, and more pushing. Even the secondary players skated into the fray.

"What just happened?" Deacon asked.

"I have no idea. I've never seen this before. Usually it's a lot more sedate."

Deacon hissed in a breath. "The chick from the other team just clocked Marisol."

Blood Mary roared. She grabbed her attacker and knocked her down. Before Bloody Mary lived up to her name, whistles blew.

That garnered attention. The coaches separated the players and sent them back to their respective benches.

The ref skated over to the penalty box to confer with someone.

"Is there medical personnel at these bouts?" Deacon asked.

"Not officially. But the Divas' coach's wife is a nurse." She paused. "Speaking of medical personnel, what do you think of Riggins?" Riggins was one of the new jujitsu instructors, who also served as medical adviser for the athletes in the MMA program and took care of injuries in the dojo. Big Rig was intimidating— partially because of his massive size, but also because he was majorly hot. Molly suspected some of the female students faked injuries just to have Riggins put his big hands on them.

"He knows his shit."

"That's not really an answer."

He shrugged. "It's what you asked. But if you meant what do I think of Riggins's role at Black Arts? Whether he'll stay through the building of the MMA program, or if he'll just train with Sensei for belt advancement? Don't think Riggins knows the answer to that."

The referee moved to the center of the floor, brandishing a microphone. "According to regulations set forth by the national organization, in light of actions by both teams, I'm ending this bout as a double forfeit."

A chorus of *boos* rang out.

"That's a weird end to this." Molly nudged Deacon's shoulder. "Means you'll get to eat sooner. But I have to see if Presley's okay first."

Deacon insisted on holding her hand, so she let him lead the way. When they reached the floor, Molly noticed the coaches were in a heated discussion with the referee. The players had spread out to remove their skates.

Presley was perched on the edge of a wooden bleacher seat, holding an ice pack to her face. A smile broke out when she spied Molly. But then she dropped her gaze to Molly and Deacon's joined hands. "I left you three hours ago. In that time you managed to forget every damn thing we talked about?"

"Deacon showed up at the office and apologized. We realize we have a lot to talk about"—Deacon snorted—"but I'd promised I'd come tonight, so here we are."

"I don't know whether to smack you or hug you."

"I wouldn't recommend smacking her," Deacon drawled. "Molly consistently outpunched you in class."

"She outpunched everyone because *someone* gave her special treatment."

"Nope. She's just that good."

"What happened tonight?" Molly asked, trying to change the subject, but secretly she basked in Deacon's compliment.

"Double forfeit. They started the fight knowing we wouldn't back down. Now the forfeit puts our losses even with theirs. So they did it to move up in the standings."

Molly didn't point out the Divas could've avoided the loss by not taking the bait and avoiding the fight. "When's your next bout?"

"I'd have to look at the schedule. But I know we're holding tryouts next month." Presley said the last two words in a singsongy manner. "The Cisco Kid is moving back to Oregon, so there's an opening on the team."

Bloody Mary strolled by and did a double take at seeing Deacon. "Hey, hot stuff. Couldn't get enough of me, eh?"

He lifted one eyebrow.

That's when Bloody Mary noticed Molly and Deacon were holding hands. "You and Cherry? Never would've called that one."

Rather than let it go, Molly said, "Why is that?"

"You lost your shit seeing me fully clothed on his lap. Imagine how you'd react seeing me doing this"—she gyrated her hips and lewdly thrust out her ass—"wearing only a G-string and a grin."

"I'm imagining it, all right. Not sure whether a spinning back kick or an uppercut would be most efficient to knock you off his lap."

"Jesus," Deacon said under his breath.

Bloody Mary looked her over. Then she smiled. "Gotta respect a bitch who don't back down when it comes to defending her gals or her guy." Then she smirked at Deacon. "Watch your balls, 'cause sweet Cherry here is gonna own them."

"And . . . we're done," Deacon said, dragging her away.

Shoot. She didn't even get a fist bump from Presley for her excellent defense of her man.

He's your man? After only a few hours?

Sure felt like it. Especially when Deacon pressed her against the building as soon as they were outside and devoured her mouth. The hot, wet kiss sent her pulse tripping. She became so light-headed she had to clutch him to keep herself upright.

He slid the heel of his hand above her heart. "Babe. Gotta remember to breathe when I kiss you."

She sucked in a lungful of air on a huge gasp.

"Better?"

She nodded.

Deacon eased back and locked his gaze to hers. "Two things. One, there's no fucking way I'll ever let you strap on a pair of skates and run with those crazy-ass bitches. Two, made me fuckin' hard hearing you threaten to take on Marisol for me."

The possessive glint in his eyes? Hot. The decree of what he'd allow her to do? Not hot. At all.

Molly fisted her hand in his shirt, pulling him closer. "Two things. One, I'll try out for the Divas if I want to. Two, now that we're together? No more strip clubs."

They stared at each other.

Surprisingly, Deacon broke eye contact first. He said, "Fine," and kissed her.

But it was hard to maintain the kiss when she couldn't stop smiling.

DEACON took her to a hole-in-the-wall Mexican joint.

He scooted into the booth so she could sit next to him. Then he stretched his arm behind her and played with her hair.

After they ordered, she said, "The staff seems to know you."

"I eat here once a week. It's the only place in Denver that serves Tex-Mex."

"Mexican food is different in Texas?"

"Yep."

"Do you miss the Lone Star State?"

"Sometimes."

"Do you miss your family?"

"Nope."

"How often do you go home?"

"Rarely."

"Don't get along with them?"

"Nope."

Molly decided to stop asking questions that could be answered with one word. She jokingly said, "So I guess that means you won't be taking me home to Texas to meet the family."

He scowled. "I don't do family shit, so no."

She slid out of the booth and moved across from him, folding her arms on the table. "If you keep scowling like that, your face will freeze that way."

Deacon finally smiled. "Good one."

"First-date rule. Tell me something about yourself that you've never told another woman."

A momentary look of panic crossed his face. Then the mask settled in place again. "I don't like to answer a bunch of questions."

"Ha! I'll bet that's standard answer with you. Not new, so try again."

"I hate this shit."

"I know. But that also doesn't count as an answer. Tell me a secret."

"I like to watch skating on TV."

"Men's or women's or pairs?"

"Hockey."

Molly leaned forward. "Hockey is not figure skating, Deacon."

"I didn't say *figure* skating. I said *skating*. Hockey players are the shit on the ice. So hockey counts as skating. Just a rougher version. Your turn." He lifted his beer to hide his smirk.

You asked for this, smart-ass. "Sometimes I fantasize about a rougher version of sex."

Deacon choked on his beer. "What the hell, Molly? Why would you . . . ?" His eyes narrowed. "You're fucking with me."

"Not yet," she said sweetly. "And no more than you were when you said you liked to watch *skating* on TV."

"I was telling the truth." He sighed. "I changed it to hockey at the last second because I thought it might make me sound like a pussy, all right?"

She didn't believe him. "So you really like figure skating?"

"To the point I fucking DVR'd the world championships and the Olympics." He pointed at her with his beer bottle. "And if you tell anyone that, I'll lie."

"I believe you. Anything you tell me, I'd never tell anyone else."

"Good. Back to your answer. Do you really like it rough?"

"I don't know. I've never had it that way, which is why I said I fantasize about it."

"Jesus, woman."

"What? Men don't look at me and imagine pushing me up against a wall and fucking me, pulling my hair as I'm being fucked, or just taking me fast and hard in the heat of the moment." When Molly looked up at him, her stomach cartwheeled at seeing the hunger in his eyes.

"You toss that out there? Expect I'll pick it up and run with it. Because, babe, I can do rough."

"Good. That's what I want."

"Then that's what you'll get," he said softly. "But sometimes you're gonna get it sweet from me too."

Chills skittered down Molly's arms from his first declaration, and her heart went mushy at his second. "I can deal with that."

The waitress dropped off their food.

Molly eyed the two grilled chicken breasts topped with sliced avocado, the cup of whole black beans, and the pile of plain rice on his plate.

Deacon caught her looking at his meal. "What?"

"That's Tex-Mex?"

"A healthier version of Tex-Mex." He shoveled a scoop of rice and beans into his mouth.

"Do you always eat like this?"

He held up his hand while he chewed and swallowed. "Five days a week. Two weeks before a fight, the warden switches me to bread and water."

"Seriously?"

"No. But I get damn sick of protein shakes."

She drizzled a mix of salsa and ranch dressing over her salad greens.

"Do you always eat like that?" Deacon asked.

"I do now. Once upon a time I would've ordered two chimi-changas covered in cheese, sour cream, and guacamole. I would've knocked back two alcoholic drinks, and I'd have finished the meal with a sopapilla sundae." She sipped her water. "I make better choices now."

Deacon gestured to his plate with his fork. "I hear ya. Maddox had me drop ten pounds. It's tough to cut weight."

"I used to fluctuate ten pounds in a week. You look amazing at any weight."

He scowled.

Note to self: not so much with the compliments.

They ate in silence for a while.

Then she said, "Since Maddox discouraged you from pursuing me before, will you tell him about us being together now?"

"He already knows." Deacon scooped rice into his mouth.

"What do you mean he already knows? Did you text him from the bathroom or something?"

"No. I talked to him on Sunday."

Molly set down her fork. "*Before* you talked to me?"

"Yep."

"You were so sure that I'd throw myself into your arms and let bygones be bygones that you told your trainer we were— *happening*?"

Then it hit her. *Isn't that what you did? Deacon blows in, acting sweet, sexy, and sorry, and immediately you're on board with starting a relationship with him?*

She needed to get out of here and look for her brain and her backbone. "Excuse me."

Before she blinked, Deacon was on her side of the booth, blocking her in. "You don't get to run off when you're pissed at me. You'll stay and fight."

"Even if I want to scream in your face?"

"Even then. So let fly, babe. I promise I can take it."

"You are so cocky! Did it ever occur to you that I might've accepted your apology, then shut the door in your face so I could move on from whatever fucked-up thing this has been in the past or what it might become?"

He shook his head.

She wanted to smack him for his presumption. She wanted to cry because he'd been dead-on in making that assumption about her. Was she that easy to read? Was she that . . . desperate-looking?

Deacon gripped her jaw, forcing her to look at him.

"Let go."

"Am I hurting you?"

"I can't move with the choke hold you've got me in."

"That's the point."

Her gaze moved all around the table as she avoided his eyes.

"Molly," he said sharply. "Am. I. Hurting. You?"

"No."

"Listen to me. Look at me." He leaned closer. "Even if you would've slammed the door in my face tonight, I would've come back tomorrow. And every day after that until you let me in. I didn't give Maddox a date when we'd be together. I just knew I'd do whatever it took to make sure it happened. Whatever. It. Took. Understand?"

That soothed the sting a bit. "Yes."

"Good." He pressed his lips to hers and dropped his hand. "I'm relentless in getting what I want. And I want you. I've wanted you for a long damn time." His eyes gleamed. "And you're wrong about something else."

"What's that?"

"That men don't have fantasies about you. You never noticed how hard my dick was in class whenever you reached up to adjust the chains on the heavy bag?"

"Ah, no." She paused. "Why?"

"I imagined chaining your wrists above your head and keeping your back against the heavy bag as a cushion for how hard I wanted to pound into you."

Molly clenched her thighs together.

Deacon placed a soft kiss on the corner of her jaw. "My woman likes dirty talk."

"Uh. Yeah." She traced the thick vein on the inside of his arm. "Thank you. I get the *you're so sweet* a lot."

"When I look at you, *sweet* ain't the first word that comes to mind."

"What word comes to mind?" *Please don't say* full-figured *or* curvy—*both euphemisms for fat.*

His low-pitched snarl startled her. "Whatever popped into your head just now, get it out. I never wanna see that look on your beautiful face again—understand?"

Deacon really thought she was beautiful?

"Did you hear me?"

She managed a half shrug. "Easier said than done when it's been ingrained in me for years."

"By who?" he demanded.

"By my cousins. Which means I won't be taking you to Nebraska to meet my family either."

The waitress dropped off the check.

Deacon stopped and spoke to the owners as he paid.

Another tidbit she learned; he spoke Spanish fluently. Maybe it made her perverted, but she'd love to hear him whispering in Spanish in her ear as he moved inside her.

When Deacon's eyes met hers, she swore he'd read her mind.

She didn't find it odd that he didn't strike up a conversation on the drive back downtown.

At the parking lot where she'd left her vehicle, he helped her out of the passenger side before walking her to the driver's side of her car. "You still hungry, babe?"

"No. Why?"

"You've been eyeing me like a juicy steak all the way back here."

"I can't help it that you're one thick, delicious-looking slab of hot man meat." When his piercing blue eyes pinned her down, Molly imagined him pressing her against the car, or on the ground, or to the tree behind them—any vertical surface would suffice.

He cupped her face in his hands, then sifted his fingers through her hair. The tenderness in the move surprised her, until his fingers tightened, allowing him to maneuver her head wherever he wanted. "Should I kiss you right here"—he licked the curve of her neck— "where I marked you? Where the touch of my mouth to your skin makes you squirm?"

"Deacon."

"Put your hands on me," he ordered hoarsely. "I need proof this is really happening."

With that admission, she untucked his T-shirt and inched her fingers up his warm skin. The hardness of his body and the way his stomach muscles quivered beneath her stroking fingers spurred her on. Then she formed her hand around his rib cage and shifted her thumb to tease his nipple.

He hissed.

Well, if he liked that, he oughta really like this. Molly slid her right hand down to his groin and cupped him.

Deacon jumped back. "Jesus H. Christ, woman, stop."

Startled, she looked up. Lord, the man had the sexiest, fiercest expression on his face.

"You are making it hard—shit, I mean difficult—to rein it in."

"And if I don't want you to rein it in?"

"This is our first date."

"So? You think I don't put out on the first date?" she teased.

He stayed silent a beat too long. Then a smile ghosted around his lips. "Maybe *I* don't put out on the first date."

They stared at each other.

Then Deacon kissed her. "Thanks for giving me another chance. I swear you won't regret it."

CHAPTER FIVE

DEACON showed up on Knox's doorstep an hour before he headed for training. He hadn't called ahead. It'd give his friend too much time to come up with a hundred ways to say *I told you so.*

Knox answered the door with baby Nuri propped on his hip. "Deacon? What's going on?"

"You got a minute"—fuck, it killed him to ask—"to talk?"

"Sure. Come in."

In the living room, Deacon dropped into the lone chair not littered with baby paraphernalia.

Knox pushed aside a stack of baby clothes on the couch and settled in, bouncing his daughter on his knee.

Deacon knew nothing about babies, but he supposed Nuri was cute. She had a ton of light brown hair and the same topaz-colored eyes as her mother. She had dimples in both her pudgy cheeks, and she stared at him solemnly as she gnawed on a hard plastic ring.

"You give kids dog's chew toys?" Deacon asked.

"It's a teething ring, smart-ass. Better she chomps on this than on me." Knox kissed the top of Nuri's head. "Isn't that right, sweetheart?"

Nuri kicked her legs and threw up her arms, smacking Knox in the face with her chew toy.

Knox winced. "I didn't get hit in the face this much at the dojo."

"You wouldn't say that if you trained with Maddox."

"Is that why you're here? To bitch about training problems?"

Deacon shook his head. "It's . . . personal."

"Like a personal problem?"

"Yeah."

"Like with a woman?"

"Yeah."

Dickhead that he was, Knox laughed. "This day has been a long time coming. I'm *so* gonna rub it in that you swore this would never happen to you. Think I'll need to grab a box of tissues and a pint of ice cream before you start sharing your feelings?"

He could admit he deserved this rash of shit. Still, he flipped Knox off.

Nuri started to fuss. Knox snagged a bottle off the coffee table and popped it in the baby's mouth, cuddling her close.

Deacon had seen Knox with his daughter only a handful of times, but the big man had taken to fatherhood like he did everything else—with absolute dedication.

"What's going on, and who's it going on with?"

"Me'n Molly started seeing each other."

"About damn time. When?"

"Last night."

Knox raised both eyebrows. "So you're having problems . . . less than a day into it?"

Deacon rested his elbows on his knees and shook his head. Fucking sucked ass to ask this.

"Yeah. I know, so just spit it out."

Christ. When had his internal thoughts started spilling out of his mouth?

"All kidding aside, Deacon, no judgment, okay?"

He blew out a breath. "I've stuck with one-night stands all my life. Get in, get off, and go home. The expectations are stated up front. I've had a repeat hookup twice."

Knox whistled.

"So last night I couldn't sleep. Kept thinking about how I have no freakin' clue how this relationship stuff works. We didn't have sex on the first date. Is there sex on the second date? Are there rules about that kinda shit? And who the fuck gets to make them?"

When Knox ducked his head, Deacon knew the man was trying not to laugh.

Then he looked up again. "Honest, D. I don't know if there are rules. Keep in mind I belonged to a sex club. There's the same type of expectations as one-nighters. I hadn't gone out on a real date in a long time before I started messing around with Shiori. And our relationship isn't definable by normal standards."

Deacon's gaze dropped to the bracelet Knox wore—an ownership tag of sorts. "Has having a baby changed those things between you two?"

"Some. Nuri's needs come first for both of us." He smiled at his daughter. "It's not a hardship when this little sprout has brought us so much joy. When the bedroom door closes, Shiori is still my Mistress. That part of her will never change—even if we have five more kids—because that's who she is. That's who I need her to be for me."

Deacon couldn't wrap his head around that, but Knox and Shiori were sickeningly happy together, and who was he to judge?

"I don't suppose you've talked to Molly about any of this?" Knox asked.

"Fuck no. What would I say?"

"The truth?"

"She'll be real understanding when I tell her my last relationship was in high school."

Knox's eyebrows went up again. "That was what? Fifteen years ago?"

"Roughly." Right. Like he didn't know the exact fucking day his only relationship had ended. And that was just another issue with being in a relationship as opposed to one-night stands. He'd have to tell her about his epically fucked-up past.

"So what's your plan?"

"No clue." He hated being in the dark about this romance crap. "So I've gotta bring her flowers, give her back rubs, and take her to dinner if I wanna get laid?"

"Is that all Molly is to you? A hole to shove it in?" Knox asked sharply.

"No. Not even close." Deacon slumped back in the chair. "That's why I have to do this right from the start."

Knox lifted his sleeping daughter onto his shoulder and gently patted her back. "I'm not being a smart-ass when I tell you it's not a bad idea to start this out like you were in high school. When She-Cat and I started seeing each other outside of the dojo, we had an entirely different view of each other. My best advice is to listen to her. Women are sneaky. They'll leave hints about what they want. They're rarely direct."

Deacon folded his hands on top of his head. "Even Shiori? I thought she told you exactly what she wants you to do."

"As far as sex? Yes. She tells me exactly what her sexual needs are, but I'd be a poor sub if I hadn't learned to anticipate those needs. The woman ain't complaining about what she gets from me." He gave Deacon a cocky grin. "It's when we're not in the bedroom and are out of those Dominant/submissive roles that she drops hints about stuff instead of telling me directly."

"Explain that."

"Two months ago, she started talking about how much she missed the onsen in Japan. Then she asked if I'd ever soaked in a hot mineral bath after skiing." Knox cocked his head. "Decipher that for me."

"I wasn't expecting a pop quiz." Deacon racked his brain forever—probably fifteen seconds. "That was Shi-Shi's way of hinting she wanted a hot tub." As soon as Deacon said that, he knew he'd nailed it.

"Nice try, grasshopper. But that answer is too obvious."

"What? That was the perfect answer."

Knox chuckled. "I'll break it down for you. She asked if I'd been skiing in a place that had hot springs. So I put together that she wanted a weekend away with me in Steamboat Springs."

"You figured that out from just those few hints?"

"Yep. She acted like I was the most intuitive guy in the world for reading her mind."

"I am so fucked."

"Not if you listen. That's the whole point. If Molly says something like she gets cold at night and wishes she had a quilt like her grandma made, check the area events for a quilt show, because that's what she's hinting at."

Deacon stared at Knox like he'd never seen him before.

"What?"

"Dude," he said in awe. "You are like the woman whisperer."

"Nice shot, dickhead. Just trying to be helpful."

"I'm serious. That is a hard-core skill. Teach me."

"First one is free, my friend. Then you're on your own." Knox gave him a contemplating look. "But I could impart more advice if you agree help me out Friday night."

"Help you do what?" Deacon asked suspiciously.

"Hang shelves in Nuri's room. The kid's toy collection is out of hand."

"Sure. I can do that."

"Cool. As long as you're here, what's this I heard that Terrel and Ito got into it in the training room?"

Deacon bit back a smart-ass remark about Knox turning into a gossipy housewife—sometimes he forgot the big dude with the higher belt rank could whip his ass. "Ito's daughter, Simone, has been fucking Terrel on the sly. And Daddy ain't happy about the color of skin that's been all over his baby girl."

Knox looked shocked. "How can that be? Ito is Japanese. He's pissed off that his mixed-race daughter is sleeping with a mixed-race guy?"

Deacon could see where Knox would take issue with that since his wife—and now his daughter—were both of mixed race. "I know, man. It's fucked-up. But Ito cornered Terrel and knocked him out before Maddox could intervene. Blue wasn't happy when Sensei only put Ito on probation."

"Why isn't Shihan Beck handling it? That's his job."

"He tried to handle it. I don't gotta tell you, Ito can be a condescending prick."

"I don't remember there being this much drama when I was Shihan," Knox said.

"There wasn't. We were too understaffed to bitch at each other because we couldn't afford to piss off one of the teachers and take a chance they'd quit. Now, between the dojo and the MMA program, there are a dozen new people."

Knox kept lightly rubbing on the baby's back, but the kid didn't stir. "Do you miss teaching?"

"Kickboxing, yeah. Jujitsu?" He shrugged. "Some days. But it's a relief to focus on just one thing."

"Will getting involved with Molly screw with your focus when you're both in the dojo? You had problems with that when she was working with Fisher in the training room."

"I have to prove to Maddox she's not a distraction. Besides, it's not like she'll be working with Fish-dick anymore. And I won't be fucking her in the dojo either."

Knox didn't say a word. But his smirk said everything.

"It never bothered you when I caught you and Shi-Shi sneaking out of the damn supply closet? Ronin and Amery weren't any better, slipping into the Crow's Nest for a quickie. They couldn't keep their clothes on until they got to the penthouse?" He shook his head. "You all are the reason it won't happen there for us."

"Guess we'll see how that plays out, huh?"

Deacon looked at the clock and stood. "I gotta get. Uh, thanks for . . ."

"Being a friend?" Knox supplied. Then the jackass started singing the theme song from *Friends* and woke up his baby.

Served him right.

CHAPTER SIX

MOLLY had a dozen things on her mind when she walked into Hardwick Designs Tuesday morning.

Presley jumped her first thing. "What the ever-lovin' fuck, Molly? You and Deacon? Seriously? Everything you ranted about Saturday night just vanished when he showed up yesterday looking hot and horny?"

"What? No."

"So you just tripped and fell onto his mouth when you were chewing his ass?" Her gaze zoomed to Molly's neck. "You suck at hiding hickeys."

"Because I haven't any practice at it." Molly sent a quick glance to Amery's closed office door. "We'll talk about it later."

Presley leaned forward, giving Molly a close-up of her bruised and scabbed face, which was almost as interesting as her retro Betty Boop T-shirt. "I don't think I can wait until lunch."

"Me either," Chaz said from behind Presley, propping his chin on her shoulder. "I'm starved. I'm thinking about doing Five Guys for lunch."

Molly rolled her eyes. "Only you, Chaz, could make eating a burger sound dirty."

He smiled. "What can I say, doll? It's a gift."

"While we'd love to watch you do five guys," Presley said dryly, "aren't you lunching with Amery today?"

"That's right. I am so glad you're keeping track of my schedule, honey. Thank you." He sauntered over to Amery's door and knocked. Only after the door closed behind him did Presley speak again.

"I'll wait, but you'd better make it as juicy as the burgers I'm missing out on."

DOWNTOWN Denver was chock-full of restaurants with outdoor seating. Even basking in the summer sun for only an hour rejuvenated Molly after staring at a computer screen all morning.

Presley hadn't chimed in about the situation with Deacon beyond saying she was happy he appeared to be making an effort. "Do you have plans with him tonight?"

They gathered their stuff and started walking back to the office. "Deacon knows I have kickboxing class. I wish he were still teaching. Shihan Beck is all right, but he doesn't have Deacon's mean streak, which made me mad but also made me work harder."

"Will you continue taking private boxing lessons with Fisher now that you and Deacon are happening?"

"I don't know. Why?"

"If Deacon hated you spending time with Fisher before you two got together, he'll really hate it now. I just worry he'll dictate stuff like that to you."

"He can try. But I'm not the pushover I used to be." And it was a moot point since Fisher had been too busy to work with her one on one in the last month.

"Good." Presley looped her arm through Molly's. "Speaking of dicks . . . Any idea what size he's packing?"

Molly groaned. "That's your segue way into discussing his penis? From *dictate* to *dick*?"

"Hey, I'm an artist, not a wordsmith. As a woman who's been around that fine fucking specimen of manhood, I'm curious, Mol. And maybe a little jealous."

She stopped walking and faced Presley.

"What? Now that you've got Deacon in the bag, I can admit he's the one guy at Black Arts that I'd consider bagging."

"And you're telling me this . . . why?"

"Full disclosure. Deacon is a five-alarm-fire kind of man. The body, the tats, the chiseled face, the shaved head, the facial scruff, those blue eyes, the pissy attitude. You think it's escaped anyone's notice that he could be Daniel Craig's younger, better-built brother? No. As far as looks and physique, he's the total package. But he's always been kind of a dick, so that lowers his stock value."

She snorted at the phrase *stock value.*

"But in class he had eyes only for you. It never made sense why he stood you up after he finally asked you out. So after the shit went down in the strip club, I assumed he'd walk away when you didn't just drop your panties for him. But he came after you. That he apologized? Hot. The way he looked at you in the gym last night? Hotter yet. I don't have to tell you Deacon defines intense, and that's scary." Presley reached for Molly's hand. "I have to ask if you can handle that about him."

Presley had been her friend for long enough that relaying the issues from her past probably wouldn't earn her pity. "The truth?"

"Between us? Always, Mol. You know that."

"I grew up believing no one wanted me. After my mother died, my grandma did her duty and took me in. As I grew up, I was shy, overweight, bookish. I never rocked the boat, never shared my opinions. That made me a ready target for my bitchy cousins and everyone else. I survived. In college I became . . . me. The me I'd always wanted to be. My life is better than I'd ever imagined. But the one thing I've never had?" Molly met Presley's concerned face. "I've never had a man look at me the way Deacon McConnell does.

So no. It doesn't scare me; it thrills me. Can I handle it? You bet your ass I can."

"If I haven't said it enough, I'll say it now. You amaze me." Then she yanked Molly against her in a fierce hug.

Molly squeezed her back. "I doubt this thing with Deacon will be long-term. And guess what? I don't care. I will be well versed in covering up hickeys all over my body by the time this ride ends."

"Good attitude." Presley hooked her arm through Molly's again as they started down the sidewalk. "And not to make this about me, but you being with him is a bonus for me."

"How?"

"Because you'll be so distracted by thoughts of going all 'hi-ho, Silver,' riding Deacon's naked bod all the time, that I'll sneak in some funky design concepts, rope in new clients, and become Amery's new favorite."

"Don't bet on it."

AN hour of kickboxing coated her entire body with sweat.

Despite the heat burning her face, the pulse pounding in her throat, in her head, and in her hands, she stayed focused.

Somehow Molly had ended up sparring with Shihan Beck at the end of class. It surprised him when she didn't fall for his abrupt switcheroos and could adapt on the fly. She gave herself a mental high five.

"All right. That's it. Wrap it up and return to the mat."

They gathered around Shihan.

"Starting next week we'll rotate instructors. I'll be gone from teaching this class for a month."

Grumbles sounded. Mostly from Liv, who had a massive hard-on for Beck. And Molly suspected it was an actual hard-on. Although Liv dressed like a woman, her body was ripped like a man's, and no woman had an Adam's apple that prominent.

Molly wiped her face with a towel and started for the door. It might make her a masochist, but she loved the rubbery legs and tingling arms she got from working out, followed by the gradual cooling of her skin.

Shihan fell into step with her. "Impressive as always, Molly."

"Thanks."

"I won't give up on getting you into our jujitsu program."

In the hallway, Molly saw Deacon propped against the wall, waiting for her, giving her a hell of an eye fuck.

"It's all about showing up for class," Shihan said, oblivious to Deacon advancing on them. "Consistency assures you won't develop bad training habits. You could be an instructor in no time, if you put in the time. Isn't that—"

Deacon grabbed the ends of the towel draped around her neck, pulled her against his body, and laid a possessive kiss on her. After he staked his claim, he murmured, "Sweet and salty. My favorite combination, babe." Deacon tucked her against his side and looked at Beck. "Shihan."

"Yondan."

"Just so you know? My woman is skilled enough to move up the jujitsu belt ranks at a rapid pace, but she's never gonna slip on a gi."

Molly gaped at him when he planted another kiss on her lips to forestall her argument.

Beck folded his arms over his chest. "I think the lady has something to say about that."

Had the tension always been this thick between the new Shihan and the former Shihan's best friend?

"Over the last year Molly has lightened Amery's load at Hardwick Designs, which allows Amery to spend more time with Ronin. I'd guess if anyone has objections to Molly enrolling in extra classes to become a jujitsu instructor, it'd be Sensei. I doubt he'd be happy if his wife had to start working those crazy hours again." Deacon shrugged. "But it's your neck."

"Point taken."

"Sucks when your plans are foiled, huh?" Deacon drawled.

"You don't know the half of it." Shihan Beck's gaze winged between Deacon and Molly. "Guess you're not coming out for a beer with us?"

"Sorry. Got a better offer."

"I'll say, you lucky bastard." Beck sent Molly a quick smile. "See ya." He walked off, leaving them alone.

Without a word, Deacon towed her down the hallway into the conference room. He didn't bother to turn on the lights. He just wrapped his arms around her and buried his face in her neck.

Okay. This was . . . unexpected. And sort of weird, because Deacon had trapped her arms so she couldn't hug him back.

He held her like that for several long moments. "How do you smell like goddamn flowers after you've been sweating your ass off for an hour?"

"I am sticky and sweaty. I reek." She sniffed his breath. "You don't smell like you've been drinking."

Keeping their gazes connected, he brushed his mouth across hers once. Twice. Three times. "You always gonna babble before I kiss you for real?"

"For real? So the kiss in the hallway was what? Fake?"

He slowly shook his head, movement dragging his lips across hers again. "That was a preview."

"That was a show of machismo."

"Needed to happen. Put your hands on me."

Molly curled one hand around the back of his neck and pressed her palm over his heart.

Deacon's tongue parted her lips and he took ownership of her mouth.

Talk about a breath-stealing kiss. She had no choice but to hold on tightly.

Once he'd finally relinquished her, she murmured, "Sorry for the nail gouges."

He scraped his teeth over the hickey on her neck. "I'll wear your marks with pride, babe, same as you wear mine."

Could this man be any sexier? "I didn't expect to see you tonight."

"I hadn't planned on bein' here, but tomorrow Maddox is driving to Cheyenne to watch a guy he's interested in signing. I told him I'd go along. We're staying over, so I won't be back until Thursday."

"That sucks. Presley and I are headed to Boulder on Thursday for a photo shoot. The Divas have a bout there, so it'll be late when we get back." She paused. "What about Friday night?"

"Knox asked me to help him put up shelves in the baby's room as a surprise for Shiori. Don't know how long that'll take."

"Are you training Saturday?"

"Only until noon." He hesitated, and she swore she felt the man blush in the dark. "Then we're going hiking."

"Really?"

"Yep. Pick a trail or two you wanna try."

Thrilled that Deacon had actually listened to her, she peppered his face with kisses. "Thank you! Thank you! Thank you!"

"Babe," he growled. "You missed my mouth."

"Oh yeah?" Molly teased him like he'd teased her. A whisper-soft lash of her tongue across the seam of his mouth. Sinking her teeth into his plump lower lip. She wanted him as desperate for her kiss as she'd been for his. By the time they finally took a breath, her lips were kiss-swollen.

"Damn. It's gonna be a long four days."

"We could text."

"Nope."

"Why not?"

"I text slowly and I suck at spelling."

"That's a shame. I've always wanted to try sexting."

His deep voice rumbled in her ear. "No words can describe

how fucking hot it'll be when I have the wet kiss of your pussy around my cock. Or how hard your heart will pound against mine when our bodies are slamming together."

"You're pretty good with words."

"I'm even better with the real thing." He stepped back, keeping his hands curled around her upper arms. "You hungry?"

"I'm never hungry after class. But I could sit with you while you're eating."

"I ate. So I was offering to sit with you."

Molly laughed. "Walk me to my car before we get into trouble."

"I think it's way too late for that."

CHAPTER SEVEN

THE sun glinted off Molly's shiny brown hair as she waited in front of her apartment complex, looking as perky and fresh as a sunflower.

You are gone for her, man, and you haven't even fucked her.

Yet.

She climbed in before he could jump out to help her. "Hey, I didn't recognize—"

Deacon's need to take the kiss he'd been craving for four long days overruled any warring thoughts about acting cool.

After sating himself on her taste, he rested his forehead to hers. "New rule. You gimme this mouth first thing."

"Even before we say hello?"

"Yeah." He pressed a kiss to the corner of her lips and murmured, "Hello."

"You are high-handed. I can't believe I like that about you . . . sometimes." She buckled her seat belt. "Where's your Mercedes?"

"In the parking garage."

"So you have two vehicles?"

"Define vehicles."

Molly held up her phone, and he watched her flick past screens.

"Whatcha doin'?"

"Opening my dictionary app."

"I didn't mean to literally define it."

"Live and learn that I'm always literal." Her thumbs moved fast. "Aha. Here it is. Vehicle: a means or machine used to carry or transport people or goods from one place to another." She gave him a haughty look.

"Sometimes I fucking hate smartphones."

"Answer the question."

One corner of his mouth kicked up. "No, I don't have two vehicles."

"You have more than two vehicles."

"Yep."

"How many total vehicles do you own, and what kinds?"

Deacon swept her hair over her shoulder. "We playing twenty questions?"

"With your one-word answers, it'd take two hundred questions," she grumbled. "So just tell me what you've got, since I prefer to be direct."

So much for Knox's assumption that women played coy. "I have a Mercedes, this SUV, a Jap bike, a Harley, a four-wheeler, and a dirt bike."

"You drive all of them regularly?"

"My bikes are for warm weather. This and the Mercedes get the most drive time." He squinted at her. "Why? You secretly a car chick?"

"I don't have the money to be a car chick. But you don't seem like a car guy."

"I'm not. I drove this because I wasn't sure how far back into the mountains we'd have to drive. Hit me with the address for the GPS."

"There's no street address, city slicker. I'm your copilot. I'll give you directions, and you'll follow them."

He stared at her.

"What?"

"I hate getting lost."

"We won't get lost! Get on C-470 south. I'll tell you when we get close to the exit."

"I ain't the only bossy one, babe."

"Aw. You say the sweetest things." She pecked him on the mouth.

He checked his mirrors before pulling into traffic.

"If we need to pick up water, there's a convenience store about a mile up."

Inside the convenience store, Deacon grabbed a twelve-pack of water bottles. It would've taken him a minute to get in and out. But Molly had wandered to the snack aisle.

Deacon pressed the front of his body to the back of hers and rested his chin on her shoulder. He noticed the packages in her hands. "Trail mix? Seriously?"

"There's a reason it's called trail mix, Deacon."

"Is there a rule we have to take it on the trail?"

"Smarty." She grabbed four packages. "Just for that comment, I'm not sharing with you. You can eat squirrel poop, gnaw on tree bark, and forage for nuts, for all I care."

"I'd rather you foraged for my nuts, darlin'."

A beat passed. Then she laughed.

Why was it so damn easy to tease her and flirt with her? He'd never been so comfortable with a woman. A sense of happiness had Deacon impulsively spinning her around and kissing her thoroughly.

"Fine," she said a little breathlessly. "I'll share."

Back in the car, Molly pulled a paperback out of her purse and flipped to the page marked with an owl-shaped sticky note. "The Hayden/Green Mountain Trail is closest to Denver. It's where the

Front Range meets the plains. It's a three-mile loop. The difficulty level for the hike ranges from easy to moderate."

"Show me that map."

"It's not a map. It's a trail guide."

Three miles after Deacon turned onto 470, he said, "What exit?"

"It's a ways up yet."

"Is 'a ways' an actual measurement of distance?"

"It's between 'as the crow flies' and 'down the road a piece,'" she said sweetly.

"Funny, farm girl."

"Take the Morrison Road exit, cowboy."

He shot her a look. "Not all Texans are cowboys."

"Not all Nebraskans are farmers either," she retorted.

"But weren't you raised on a farm?"

"Yes. And don't you have at least one pair of cowboy boots, a hat, and Wranglers?"

Deacon laughed. "I give."

After they'd parked, Molly rummaged in her bag. "Did you put on sunscreen?"

"Nope."

"You're in luck, because I brought some."

"I don't need any."

She looked at him—studied him really. "Deacon, you don't have any hair. You'll fry your head."

"That's why I'm wearing a hat."

"But it won't shade your neck."

"I'll be fine."

"Men who kick ass for a living are too tough to get skin cancer?"

"You're a real laugh riot, babe."

"Suit yourself." Molly squeezed the plastic and a white splotch landed on the upper curve of her breast. On the next squeeze, a dozen white dots spattered on her chest.

Did she know what those white spots and that milky trail looked like?

She caught him staring and said, "What?"

Offhandedly, he said, "Reminds me that I'd planned on giving you a pearl necklace, but not so early in our relationship."

Molly's face went bright red. Then she said, "You can finish coating me outside. It'll give you a better angle to squirt all over my back."

He groaned. "How am I supposed to hike with a hard-on?"

"You started it."

He'd worn camo cargo shorts—handy for holding water bottles and snacks. Molly had slipped on a wide-brimmed straw hat, which would've looked ridiculous on other women, but she looked so damn cute in it he wanted to just eat her up.

After she tucked her cell phone in her pocket, she grinned at him, fairly bouncing in the toes of her hiking shoes. "You ready?"

Just to fuck with her, he squinted at the trail ahead. "Not enough trees to hide bears, but rattlesnakes are thick out here. Glad I'm armed."

"You're seriously carrying a gun right now?"

"I'm always packing. Wanna see?" He grinned. "I have to keep it hidden out of sight in my pants because it scares most women . . . and some men."

She whapped him on the arm with the trail guide.

As they ascended the first hill and dropped into a section of the trail shaded by rock formations, he was thankful for the mild temperatures.

They didn't talk much. Every time Molly wandered off the trail, Deacon went with her. She paid little attention to her surroundings besides searching for flowers, so he scoured the dense brush for snakes. He'd seen a few of these scraggly ground bushes around Texas.

He'd expected they'd take breaks—not that they were exerting themselves—but they stopped only upon reaching the summit.

A cool breeze blew up from the valley below. Molly took off her hat.

With the wind blowing through her hair, the late-afternoon rays shining on her, and the happiness on her face, Deacon couldn't take his eyes off her.

"Gorgeous," he managed.

"It is pretty here." She angled her head toward him. "But I'll admit some disappointment."

"What?" Deacon moved in behind her and set his hands on her hips.

"I thought there'd be meadows full of wildflowers. Like in the guidebook."

"Did you wanna run through a field of wildflowers? Or did you see us rolling around naked in a meadow?"

Tilting her chin, she gazed at him coolly. "So what if I did?"

Deacon nibbled on the side of her neck. "I'd ask if you brought a condom." He caught the scent of her skin beneath the sunscreen, and his dick started to stir.

"What if I told you I have one in my pocket right now?"

"Since there's no field of wildflowers, I'd take you down to that rock outcropping." He pointed to the area about four hundred yards downhill. "Once we were in the shadows, I'd yank your pants to your ankles and eat your pussy until you came against my mouth." He paused to nuzzle the hollow below her ear. "Would you come quietly? Or would you scream loud enough to be heard across the valley?"

"I've never had a man make me come hard enough to scream."

"That's about to change."

Molly wheeled around and kissed him with near brutality. Clawing at his chest. Rocking her pelvis into his.

Voices on the trail brought a fast dose of reality. As much as Deacon hated the interruption, he needed it—they both did.

But he wouldn't let her break away from him. He kept his arm around her shoulder and whispered, "Soon," into her hair.

SOON.

What did that even mean?

It hadn't meant Deacon ravaging her in his SUV after they finished hiking. He said he needed to satisfy his appetite for food first. So did that mean he'd satisfy his other appetite as soon as they left the restaurant?

"Babe."

She looked up at him. "I'm sorry. What did you say?"

"You okay?"

"Just tired. The trailhead sign should've said six miles, not a three-mile loop. Not that it's a big deal to you, since you run a billion miles a week—"

"Running ain't hiking. I'll feel it tomorrow."

"Such a sweet lie."

The waitress returned and flirted with Deacon.

"I brought the dessert menu." She slid it in front of Molly. "I don't eat dessert myself since modeling is so competitive I can't afford to put on a single pound." She turned her simpering smile on Molly. "But I've heard the chocolate gold-rush dessert is delicious."

"I'll pass."

"There's also an apple streusel cake with caramel sauce."

Molly wanted to ask if it was restaurant policy to push desserts on women who weren't skeletal clothes racks. But she just shook her head.

Deacon said, "The check. Now."

She scrawled something inside and then slid the black vinyl ticket holder in front of Deacon. "I'll be your cashier, whenever you're ready."

Molly stirred the remnants of her rum and Diet Coke as Deacon got out his wallet.

"Let's go," Deacon said tersely.

"Don't you have to wait for her to run your credit card?"

"I paid cash."

"Did Miss I'm-a-Model leave her phone number?"

Deacon's eyes went flat.

"She did!" Molly snatched the ticket holder and cracked it open. Sure enough. Arisol—seriously, her mom had named her after a spray can? And misspelled it—had written her number below her name, complete with a little heart.

"Forget it."

"Nope." Molly circled the digits with the girl's hot-pink pen and added her own message. She slid out of the booth and headed toward the exit.

When they passed the hostess stand where Spray Can stood, Deacon whispered, "*He's my dessert—eat your heart out*. Nice one, babe."

"I couldn't let her bitchiness slide."

"I expected to see something like, *I took a dump bigger than you last week*."

"Eww. I'd never say anything like that!"

"I know you wouldn't. You're too fucking nice."

And so are you, because you didn't do anything to discourage her.

Okay. That wasn't fair. Deacon was hot. Women didn't care if he had a girlfriend. It'd be different if he'd somehow encouraged Spray Can, but he'd ignored her.

Before Deacon opened the passenger door, he pulled her body against his. "You inviting me up when we get to your place?"

"Well, you *are* my dessert."

A low growl emerged, and he kissed her.

The ride to her apartment felt like the calm before the storm.

As many times as she'd fantasized about getting naked and wild with Deacon, now that it was happening, her nerves kicked in. Then she remembered—with some embarrassment—Deacon's horrified expression the first time he'd seen her apartment.

She'd been so pissed off that he'd shown up to give her a freakin' makeup lesson, she'd snapped, "What?"

"Looks like a lace factory blew up in here and someone threw flowers and shit everywhere to cover up the evidence."

Molly loved the romantic, cozy cottage look she'd created. "Leave if it offends you."

"It's too cute and girly to ever be offensive." He'd smirked at her. "Kinda like you."

Shaking off the memory, she fled to the kitchen in the guise of being a good hostess and offering him a nightcap.

But Deacon caught her and kissed her for a good long while— long enough she wondered if the light-headedness was from him or from the last drink she'd had.

Definitely him. Booze had never made her feel this way.

"You hum," he said after releasing her mouth.

"What?"

"Sometimes you make a humming noise when I kiss you."

"Sorry."

"Don't apologize. I like it."

"Oh." Something about the darkness urged her to say what was on her mind. "I like being with you. Am I breaking second-date relationship rules by admitting that?"

"Babe. Do I *seem* like a guy who'd know that shit?"

"No, you seem like a guy who'd glory in breaking the rules."

"I'd rather glory in you," he murmured against her throat. "Take me to your bedroom."

Molly's belly flipped. Gooseflesh broke out. Her heart beat

madly when she took his hand and led him down the short hall-way.

Moonlight shone across the carpet in her dark bedroom. Before she could turn on the lamp on the nightstand, Deacon spun her around.

The man was gorgeous in any light, but he was a deity with silvery moonbeams highlighting his face. She knew the muscled body beneath the clothing was unparalleled.

"Relax." He tipped her head back to gaze into her eyes. "I'm not gonna throw you on your bed and fuck you. But I do want to play with you."

"Play with me," she repeated.

Deacon stroked her bottom lip with his thumb. "We start this, I'll ask you to do things for me. Things I need. If you can't give me those things, let me know now."

"Can you be specific about these 'needs' of yours?" Her gaze searched his. "Or will you surprise me with ropes like Ronin did to Amery?"

His lips curled up in a half smile. "Did Amery tell you about Ronin's rope mastery?"

No, but you just did. "Or maybe you'll take me to Twisted?"

"Where'd you hear about Twisted?"

"From you and Knox." She paused, waiting for a reaction from him. Getting none, she continued. "What is it?"

"A private club that caters to like-minded individuals."

"Are you a member?"

"Not my scene." He smirked. "Literally."

"What is your scene?"

Warm lips brushed her ear. "My scene is you, babe." The hand on her lower back glided down to her ass. "Ask me what I want tonight."

His deep, rough voice sent an electric zap straight to her core. "What do you want from me tonight, Deacon?"

"To watch you."

"Watch me what?" she managed.

"Watch you get yourself off."

Molly's entire body flushed with heat.

"If you don't wanna do this, tell me no."

But she knew if she told him no . . . he'd leave and never come back. This would be over with him before it even started.

That thought caused her more distress than the idea of masturbating for him. She blurted out, "I've never done that particular act of self-love in mixed company."

A rumble of approval vibrated against her neck. "Good. Then it'll belong only to me."

"Tell me what you want—exactly how you want it."

"What I want," he whispered, "is to watch you come."

"Where will you be?"

"In the chair, waiting for the show to start." Deacon disappeared into the shadows.

Ask if he plans on joining you in your bed after you get off. Ask if he'll be jerking off while he watches you. Ask why this turns him on.

Duh. It turns him on because he's a voyeur. The guy has a VIP pass to the hottest strip club in town.

When she didn't move, he said, "Go out and come back in."

In the kitchen, Molly poured three fingers of Rumple Minze into a juice glass and downed it.

Immediately the liquor warmed her. Not that she needed it; her body was already hot. But she welcomed the buzz.

You can do this and make it the sexiest thing he's ever seen.

After grabbing her e-reader and her phone, she wandered to her bedroom, putting an extra sway in her hips.

She clicked on the fringed lamp on the nightstand. Torn between rummaging through her drawer for a nightgown, or bucking up and baring all . . . she chose the latter. It'd be easier if Deacon saw how she looked naked when she couldn't read his expression.

Even though she'd transformed her body, she still had a hard time not hiding it.

Molly unbuttoned her blouse, facing the chair in the corner, although she didn't look that direction. No reason for a peekaboo tease when she removed her bra. When she cupped her breasts, her fingers caressing the swells and then the hardened tips of her nipples, she swore she heard a sharp intake of breath.

She ditched her capris and her underwear. Now what?

Deacon wants you. He said he's wanted you for a long time. Make him want you more. Be the siren, vixen, temptress you've always dreamed of being.

Naked, she lifted her arms above her head, swaying from side to side in a delicious stretch. She tilted her neck so her hair spilled down her back and brushed her skin, letting herself enjoy the sensation.

Then, buoyed by the laser-hot stare she felt coming from the corner, she perched on the edge of the mattress, resting her heels on the bed frame. That allowed her to spread her knees wide, giving Deacon a peek at her pussy.

A low rumble drifted to her from the corner.

Molly grabbed the bottle of lotion from the nightstand and squirted a thick dollop into her hand. She thoroughly coated her arms in long, sensuous sweeps. Finished with that, she rubbed lotion on her breasts, making sure she got some on the sides and the under swell, by squeezing the mounds together, and releasing, squeezing and releasing. Again she let her head fall back. She loved breast play. She couldn't wait until Deacon put those big mitts of his on these. With the way he constantly stared at her tits, she knew he liked what he saw.

Pretending it was just another Saturday night alone with BOB—her battery-operated boyfriend—Molly stretched out on the side of the bed that gave Deacon the best view. She powered on her e-reader and scrolled to her favorite erotic book, which always got her hot and wet enough to get off.

Once she'd become engrossed in the words, she forced herself to go slow and tease him. Touching herself like she wanted Deacon to touch her. Trailing her fingers between her hip bones. Pinching her nipples. Biting her lip as she arched into her own caresses.

Almost too soon her sex became hot and slick. The need for friction had her rubbing her thighs together. But that wasn't enough. She spread her legs and glided her middle finger up and down her slit, separating her flesh, priming herself.

When she reached the part in the book where the hero went down on the heroine for the first time, Molly quickly moved her finger over her clit. It made her so hot that after the heroine's first explosive orgasm, the hero kept sucking on her pussy, driving her to orgasm again and again, showing her how an alpha male took care of his woman. Somehow she knew Deacon would be just like that. And that made her hotter yet.

That tightening sensation began behind her pubic bone. As the heroine thrashed on the bed, begging her lover to enter her, Molly had the same sense of frustration. Then the hero finally plowed inside, fucking the heroine with the force of a battering ram.

Molly pushed a finger into her pussy and slid the base of her thumb back and forth over her clit, grinding down until she came, gasping. But it ended too soon. If the hero could give his woman two back-to-back orgasms, she'd use her hand and BOB to get that for herself.

Tossing her digital reader aside, she reached into her nightstand and pulled out her personal massager. She cranked it to high, outlining her pussy lips with the pointed tip.

Images flashed behind her closed eyelids. Deacon ordering her to spread her legs wider, his fingertips digging into the tops of her thighs with enough force to leave tiny bruises. Deacon belly crawling up the mattress, shoving his tongue into her pussy. Then those compelling blue eyes of his locked to hers as he feasted on her and fucked her with his mouth.

Molly clutched the vibrator and began to move the head around, delaying that first moment of pleasure even as she craved the instantaneous explosion of it. Whimpers stuck in her throat as she tried to keep them from becoming needy moans.

So close, so close, so close.

Her body couldn't hold off any longer. She arched when the first pulse hit with enough power to make her cry out. She found herself holding her breath until that last hard throb. Then she gasped, air filling her lungs, her head buzzing as loudly as her vibrator.

Once her heart stopped racing and her breathing leveled out, she blindly reached out to set her vibrator aside. Her hand connected with something solid and warm on the side of the bed.

Deacon.

Soft lips brushed her forehead, her temples, the corners of her lips. "Fucking hot, babe."

Still floating in the fuzzy aftermath of her orgasm, she reached for his hand and peered at him from beneath her lashes. "Show me how you touch yourself."

Deacon's eyes were molten as he lowered the zipper, and his camo shorts whooshed to the floor. "Lick it," he said gruffly, holding his palm closer to her mouth.

Licking and nibbling on his rough and warm skin, she relished his taste: salt and musk.

He dragged the rough fingertips of his other hand across her breasts. When she sucked his pinkie into her mouth, he said, "Enough."

Then Deacon wrapped the damp palm around his cock, showing her how he primed himself, with long, slow pulls, from root to tip. Then he started to stroke without pause.

The sound of his hand slapping his own flesh was one of the sexiest things she'd ever heard. Watching him was one of the hottest things she'd ever seen. The way his eyes glittered. The sheen of sweat on his shaved head. The dichotomy of the hard set of his jaw and the soft set of his lips. All a visual feast.

A groaned, "Fuck yeah," accompanied the first warm splat on her breast. He jerked his shaft faster, aiming at her nipples. He made a satisfied grunt when a milky rivulet of his come disappeared into her cleavage. The last spurts landed on her belly.

A satisfied gleam settled on his face as he looked at the marks he'd left on her body.

He said, "Close your eyes."

Before Molly's eyes drifted shut, she saw him yank his shirt over his head. Then she felt gentle swipes of cotton as he cleaned her.

Deacon placed a featherlight kiss on her lips. "I'll lock up and call you later."

Molly's last conscious thought was, *How sweet.*

HER phone buzzed on the nightstand.

She blindly reached for it and rolled to her back. Never good news at midnight. Never good news when Uncle Bob's name showed on the caller ID. "Hello?"

"Molly. It's Bob. Your uncle."

She didn't snicker at her usual *Bob's your uncle* joke. "What happened to Grams?"

"She was having some problems, so I took her to the hospital. They were keeping her overnight for observation." He paused. "It's a good thing because she had a heart attack."

All the air left her lungs.

"Her heart is in bad shape. That's all the doctor will say."

"Which hospital is she in?"

"The one in Norfolk."

"They didn't transfer her to the cardiac unit in Omaha or Lincoln?" Molly said sharply.

"She refused to go. Said she'd have Doc Danvers treat her and not some stranger."

That sounded like her stubborn grandma.

"Molly, you need to come home," he said gently. "As soon as possible if you wanna say goodbye."

She closed her eyes. But it didn't stop the tears. "Is she conscious?"

"In and out. Jennifer and Brandi were here talking with her earlier . . . Now she's not responding."

Molly had to hold her tongue. Why hadn't they called her? *Beside the point now.*

"I'll leave Denver within the hour." Driving straight through would be faster than waiting for a flight to Omaha from DIA and then renting a car to get to her small hometown outside of Norfolk.

"I'll tell her you're coming. I know she'll hold on until then."

She swallowed the lump in her throat. "See you soon."

After she hung up, she sent out a silent plea. *Please, Grams, hang on until I can see you one last time.*

One last time.

Sobs racked her whole body. Tears streamed down her face. She rocked, trying to calm herself, holding her pillow to her chest to try to keep her heart from hurting.

Get a handle on your sorrow, girl, and get a move on. There'll be plenty of time for crying later.

Hearing Grams's voice gave her the push she needed. She dragged herself into the bathroom. Splashing cold water on her face helped the blotchiness but did little to reduce the swelling in her eyes. She swept her toiletries into a travel bag. As she stared at her closet, she couldn't decide what to bring. Annoyed with her indecision, she pulled random clothes off hangers and dropped them into the suitcase at her feet.

Packed, she rolled her suitcase into the living room. She snagged the cords for her various electronics and shoved them into the outside pocket of the suitcase.

Now what?

Let people know she'd be gone. She'd text Amery and Presley in the morning. No reason to freak them out now. Her finger hovered over Deacon's name. Should she call him? He hadn't left here long ago. He'd probably still be up.

And what will you say to him? When you don't even know what's going on?

Good point. Besides, he'd warned her that he didn't do family shit. And her family shit was about to get real shitty, real fast.

Car loaded, gas tank full, a six-pack of Red Bull on the passenger's seat, Molly pulled onto I-80 going east. She'd be in her Nebraska hometown in roughly eight hours.

During the long-ass hours in the car, she wondered if this was the last time she'd ever make this drive. With her grams gone, she'd have no reason to go back.

CHAPTER EIGHT

THE last thirty hours seemed like a bad dream.

The only bright spot was her grandma had come to for a few minutes.

"You're here, sweet girl."

"Don't I always turn up when you least expect it?"

"Yes." A long pause. "I've missed you."

"I've missed you too." Molly *rubbed her thumb across her grandmother's hand, the paper-thin skin a bluish white, not the chafed red she knew so well. "I love you, Grams."*

"You're a good girl, Molly."

That was their last conversation.

She'd felt her grandma fading further away. She and Uncle Bob stayed by her side in silence, until she slipped her earthly bonds, freed from pain.

Molly shook herself and fished out her house key as she started up the sidewalk to the farmhouse she'd grown up in. Flowers bloomed in pots on the porch. The rug from the kitchen hung over the railing. The place had the aura of waiting for the owner to return.

The front door stuck, forcing her to throw her shoulder into it.

After it opened, she decided to leave it open, and entered the house. Immediately, a lifetime of familiar scents engulfed her. The persistent mustiness. The faint aroma of coffee. The pungent scent of Spic and Span cleaner.

She didn't venture very far into the house. Just to the window that overlooked the garden. She must've been lost in thought, because she didn't hear them come in.

"We were surprised you could tear yourself away from the all-you-can-eat buffets in Denver to come back here," Jennifer sneered.

Molly schooled her features before she faced her cousins. "I should be grateful you held your tongues while we were at the hospital. I'm guessing your stab at civility is over?"

Jennifer and Brandi exchanged confused looks.

They weren't the sharpest pencils in the drawer. "Is Uncle Bob with you?"

"No. He's meeting with the funeral director."

"Alone? Why didn't you go with him?"

"Because he told us to look after you."

Great.

"You had one of those stomach-shrinking surgeries, didn't you?" Jennifer said.

"That's what you want to talk about?"

"She's not denying it," Brandi pointed out.

Molly closed her eyes and counted to five. "Can you please, for once, act like adults?"

"Excellent suggestion."

They were all surprised by Reverend Somers's sudden appearance.

"As a neutral party, I'll ask you all to refrain from bickering. Keep your past petty grievances private. Hold it together for your grandmother's memory."

Jennifer placed her hand on the reverend's arm. "Of course we will. We loved Grams. We'd never disrespect her. It's just easy to fall into those old habits. Isn't it, Molly?"

Easier for some of us—namely you. "Reverend, why are you here?"

He sent Molly an apologetic look. "With all you've been through . . . I'm sorry to say that you'll have to stay elsewhere. Torch Robbins, your grandmother's attorney, has documentation requiring the house be locked up until the will is read."

Now she had to shell out money to stay at a motel? Fantastic. Molly looked at the notebook the reverend held. "I assume you have the official documentation?"

"Molly! What is wrong with you?" Brandi pushed into Molly's personal space. "We have no reason to question what the reverend tells us."

"You've been living in the big city too long," Jennifer retorted. "We trust our friends and neighbors around here."

"Which is good and well, but we all know break-ins occur as soon as word gets around there's been a death and a house sits empty." Not to mention she wouldn't put it past her cousins to keep her out of the way so they could go through the house, picking the items of value.

Reverend Somers smiled at her. "Of course you're entitled to see the paperwork." He opened his notebook and handed her the first loose sheet of paper. "Erma had this drawn up last year."

Molly scrutinized the text. For once Grams had made a sound decision, although she hated that Grams was planning ahead for her own death. "It appears to be in order. Thank you."

"We're not a bunch of rubes, Molly," Brandi said snottily.

"Neither am I." She looked to the reverend. "You've been entrusted to lock up?"

"Yes."

When her cousins asked a question, Molly fled outside.

It hardly seemed fair the day was so beautiful when she was so filled with sadness. It should be gloomy, cold, and rainy. Rather than wait for more attacks from her cousins, Molly wandered to the end of the lane—Grams's term for the dirt track that connected to the main road.

Early summer in Nebraska meant the scents of dirt and diesel. The air hung heavy with humidity. Bugs buzzed around her feet and head. Birds chirping and the occasional croak of a frog drifted up from the ditches. When she reached the tractor-shaped mailbox, she tipped her head back, letting the watery sunlight heat her face.

A sharp pang jabbed her heart.

Erma Calloway had come to this farm a blushing bride of nineteen. After Grandpa Pete died, Grams had sold off what land she could and rented out the rest. As a widow with no skills outside of being a farmwife, she'd needed the income. Now they had to pack up sixty years' worth of stuff accumulated over a happy, well-lived life.

Mostly happy. One child had given her joy; the other, trouble. Molly's mother, Pauline, had skipped town with the carnival the day after she graduated from high school. Almost twenty years passed before Pauline had returned, unmarried, with a two-year-old and addiction problems. Molly's memories of her mom were of stale cigarette smoke and the sour scent of booze. Within a month of being back on the farm, her mother had bought the farm—she was killed by a train at an unmarked railroad crossing in the middle of the night. During her teen years, Molly suspected her mom had parked her car on that railroad track on purpose. But Molly's grandmother insisted it was an accident—not suicide.

But the truth was, as she grew up, Molly understood why her mother might've done it. Life on the farm wasn't Norman Rockwell idyllic. Neither was living in small-town Nebraska, where everyone knew everyone, their dirty laundry, family secrets, and shame. Where your relatives judged you, shunned you, hated you, and made your life hell.

Growing up, her cousins Jennifer and Brandi had been the bane of her existence. Being the quiet, shy type, she'd suffered their insults and attacks in silence. The one time she'd complained about their excessive meanness, her grandmother had snapped that they were her family—the only family she'd ever have—and she'd better be grateful that she wasn't living in foster care. Then she'd told Molly to find a way to deal with it. So she had. She'd become invisible.

In high school her outstanding grades had earned her a full-ride scholarship to University of Nebraska at Lincoln. She'd chosen business accounting—a smart, safe, employable major.

Following college graduation, Molly had returned home for a temporary visit while waiting to see where she'd been accepted to grad school. It had shocked and dismayed her when she'd overheard Grams asking Uncle Bob to find a position for her in his insurance business. One, because nothing could ever make her stay in her hometown permanently. Two, because both Jennifer and Brandi worked there—if sleeping off hangovers in the conference room was considered working. The rest of her life played out before her as a nightmare.

Then the acceptance letter for the graduate program at University of Denver arrived and saved her from that life. And she hadn't looked back.

"Molly," Jennifer yelled. "Pull your head out and get back here."

Lovely. She wandered back to the house.

A bicycle chain had been strung across the front door, locks on both ends.

"The back door is locked too," Brandi informed her.

Molly walked the reverend to his car. Before her cousins could waylay her, she took off.

As she hit the edge of town, she debated on driving another thirty miles to Norfolk for a hotel room. But it'd be convenient to have a place to escape when everything overwhelmed her over the next few days.

The exterior of the Motor Inn Motel had been remodeled. She parked beneath the carport and entered the reception area. The space smelled like new paint.

A young woman slid behind the counter. "Welcome to Motor Inn."

"I need a room for at least three nights. Possibly more."

"Would you like a single room? Or I have a room with a kitchenette available."

"The kitchenette would be great." Molly handed over her credit card.

"Are you just passing through?"

"I'm here for a funeral. Then there's all the legal stuff to deal with, which is why I won't know how long I'll need to stay."

"I'm sorry for your loss."

"Thanks." She looked around while she waited for the paperwork. "The place looks a lot different."

The young clerk beamed at her. "My husband and I took it over last year. Lots of sweat equity, but it's coming along. Room by room." She slid the paper and a pen across the counter. "Sign in the boxes and fill in your vehicle information."

Molly scrawled her name and palmed the key fob.

After parking in front of her room, she unloaded her suitcases. The space was better than she'd expected. An apartment-scaled couch and chair were positioned in front of a flat-screen TV. The compact kitchenette had new countertops, appliances, and cabinetry. A modern bathroom and a bedroom with a king-sized bed rounded out the place.

She secured the chain on the door and breathed a sigh of relief. She desperately needed a nap after driving all night and then spending the last twenty-four hours in the hospital. Her cell phone was dead, so she plugged it in before she face-planted on the puffy bed.

Molly woke up completely disoriented. She squinted at the alarm clock. Crap. Had she really slept six hours? She needed a shower and food.

She checked her phone. The first message was from Amery. The second from Presley. The third from her friends Fee and Katie, who both worked at Black Arts. The fourth message was from Chaz. All basically the same, her friends expressing their condolences.

But calls five, six, seven, eight, and nine were from Deacon. He'd left the first message nine hours after she'd left Denver. "It's early. Where are you? Call me."

She moved to message six. "You always have your damn phone on you. Call me. Not kidding, babe."

Charming. Phone manners weren't his forte.

Call seven from last night: "I'm at your apartment. You're not. Call me."

Call eight, two hours later. "Not cool, not hearing from you at all in twenty-four goddamn hours . . . Jesus, Molly. Call me."

The last message had been left at nine o'clock this morning. A pause, followed by a sigh. "Sucks about your grandma. But, babe, you don't have to go it alone. You need me, I'm there. Period. You know that." A muffled noise, then, "Fuck it."

She hadn't purposely kept him in the dark. She'd just been so focused on the inevitable that she'd shut down. And Deacon was wrong. She did have to go it alone. She was used to it.

Her stomach rumbled. She shouldered her purse, slipped on her flip-flops, and set out on foot since most places were within walking distance.

Few streetlamps lit Main Street. The buildings weren't connected, making it easy for someone to lurk in the shadows and grab an unsuspecting, defenseless person.

Stop. You're not defenseless. Besides, this is Nebraska. The worst thing that'll happen to you is you'll run into someone you know and they'll bore you with talk of pesticides and projected corn yields.

When Molly reached the Silver Dollar Tavern, she pushed open the heavy door and walked in, hating the immediate silence that her entrance caused, a stranger among the locals. She chose a seat at the bar and smiled at the bartender, who looked familiar.

"What can I get you?" he asked.

"A rum and Diet Coke. And a menu, please."

"Sure thing."

The menu consisted of bar food. By the time he'd brought her drink back, she'd decided. "I'll have a hamburger."

"Fries with that?"

"No."

He ripped the top sheet off the green ticket pad and walked to the pass-through window to the kitchen. "Order."

Molly had barely taken a drink when a guy plopped down at the barstool next to hers.

"My buddy over there thinks he knows you."

Lame pickup line. "What's your buddy's name?"

"Alan Rossdale."

She pretended she was trying to place him. "I think he gradu-ated a couple years ahead of me."

The guy scrutinized her. "You're from around here?"

"Yes. What's your name?" she asked, even though she knew it.

"Marcus Olney."

"Ah. The football player. You were in Alan's class."

He grinned. "How we survived high school is a miracle. So, pretty lady, what's *your* name?"

"Molly Calloway." And she waited for the jaw to drop.

There it was.

"But you're . . . Well, shit. You don't look nothin' like you used to."

"We all change." *Some of us for the worse.* Marcus, the good-looking, well-built quarterback had morphed into a pudgy average Joe with thinning hair.

"Why are you back here?"

"For my grandma's funeral."

"Right. I'd heard about that. Sorry."

She'd fantasized about this scenario when Marcus was the senior-class stud and she a lowly freshman—him taking notice of her. But now he didn't interest her at all. She didn't want conversation. She wanted to drink alone and wallow.

"How long you staying?"

"Depends."

Marcus rambled about this person or that person, not noticing Molly hadn't chimed in at all. His rude behavior, half facing her/half facing the room, rankled.

When the bartender strolled by, she asked for a glass of water since she'd drained her drink.

Thankfully, her hamburger arrived, and Marcus mumbled about letting her eat and left.

She'd finished half her burger when the barstool creaked again.

"Hey, cuz. I heard you were trolling in here."

Brandi. She'd definitely end up with indigestion now. "Word gets around town almost as fast as you."

"You've got a bitchy attitude these days, doncha?"

The hamburger turned to dust in her mouth. Still she managed to chew and swallow. "I'm just trying to get through this an hour at a time."

Brandi rested an elbow on the bar. Her whiskey-laden breath stirred the air. "You like playing the grieving granddaughter? Think it'll get you attention from guys like Marcus and Alan? Dream on. No matter what you look like now, they'll picture you like everyone else in town does: a sad, fat, unwanted girl."

Molly spun her chair and faced her cousin. "And they see you as you've always been? A skanky bitch with a mean mouth?"

"Watch yourself."

"Or what? I'm beyond being bullied by you. In fact, I feel sorry for you. Talk about stunted growth. You haven't changed since third grade. You can't even come up with new insults."

Her booze-dulled eyes narrowed. "So your backbone *was* hidden under all those rolls of fat."

Molly laughed.

Marcus cleared his throat. Then he made the time-out sign. "Ladies, let's set aside the family shit for one night."

Where had he come from? And who the hell was he to butt his busted nose into their business?

Brandi put her hand on his chest. "You're right, Marcus. Where's Alan?"

"Right here." He parked himself on Brandi's other side. "Hey, Molly," Alan said, ignoring Brandi completely. "Do you remember me?"

"Of course she remembers you. *Everyone* knew who you were," Brandi assured him.

Alan tried to send Molly a smoldering look. "We'll have to catch up."

Right. You never deigned to speak to me before, and I'm not so hard up that I'll swoon at your feet now. "I'm only here for a short while, and I'll be busy."

"I'll make time for you."

"Are you seriously trying to pick me up on the day my grandma died?"

Alan blinked in confusion.

Brandi snorted. "I'm thinking she'd be more into you if you had tits and a pussy."

Silence. Then Alan sneered. "You're gay?"

Unreal.

Molly handed the bartender cash and said, "Keep the change."

"See? She's not denying it," Brandi said.

"I'm not gay, but it wouldn't be your business if I were. And for your information, I have a boyfriend."

"A boyfriend. Uh-huh. Why haven't I heard anything about this"—she made air quotes—"boyfriend before now?"

"Because I haven't talked to you in a year. Oh, and because I can't fucking stand you."

A nasty look crossed Brandi's face. "What a faker you are. Acting innocent when you have the mouth of a truck driver. I'm sure Grams would be ashamed of how you've treated me on the day she died. You're not the only one grieving for her." She affected a sad look. "Even the reverend had to get after Molly today for acting out."

How many times had she dealt with Brandi or Jennifer lying to cover their own bad behavior? Too many to count. Molly felt herself reverting into that old role, keeping her mouth shut and letting it go.

You're not reverting. Not calling your cousins out on their lies and walking away isn't cowardly; it's the smartest option, because you know no matter what you say, you can't win.

Molly bit off a civil, "See you in the morning," to Brandi and escaped from the bar. On the walk back to the motel, she stayed alert just in case one of those drunken bozos followed her.

After she'd made it inside the safety of her room, the day's events overwhelmed her and she couldn't stop the tears. She clapped her hand over her mouth to muffle the gasping sobs.

"Your tears fuckin' wreck me, woman."

She screamed. Luckily she'd already covered her mouth, but still she froze. She lowered her hand and whispered, "Deacon?" into the darkness.

"You expecting someone else?"

"No. But I wasn't expecting you."

"You should have." He moved into her line of sight, fury and frustration burning in his eyes. "I shouldn't be the last to know this important shit. I oughta be the first one you call."

"You're mad."

"Damn straight I am."

"That's not fair. You don't know what I've been through."

"Tell me."

"I stayed by Grams's side until she . . ." She closed her eyes against the sharp sense of loss that sliced through her. "I hadn't slept in more than twenty-four hours, so after I checked in, I crashed."

"But you had time to text Amery and let her know what was goin' on," he pointed out.

"I would've texted you, but you're Mr. I Don't Like to Text, remember? I planned to call you tonight. But it sounds like Amery already filled you in."

"Wasn't like I gave her a choice." Deacon reached out and curled his hand around the side of her neck. "Goin' crazy knowing how bad you were hurting. Knowing you shut me out."

"What was I supposed to do? You've already told me you don't do family shit. This is big family shit, Deacon."

He stroked his thumb across her jawline. "I said I didn't do *my* family shit. I didn't say a damn thing about yours."

"Oh."

"We decided to do this relationship thing, babe. That means you don't decide to take off without a word to me. It makes me do crazy stuff."

"Like hopping on a plane to Bumfuck, Nebraska?"

"Yeah. Would've been faster to drive. I had to get a damn rental car anyway."

"I could've told you that."

He made an annoyed noise. "I wouldn't have *had* to fly if you'd told me what was goin' on. Then I would've driven with you."

"I can't believe you're here." Molly turned her head and kissed the inside of his wrist. Then she looked at him. "Hey. Wait a second. How did you get into my room?"

"Told the chick at the front desk you're my girlfriend. I said you were so upset, you left Denver damn near in the middle of the night and forgot to tell me where you were staying."

Who said small towns weren't dangerous? "What was she thinking? Giving a big, mean-looking, tattooed badass access to my room?"

His full lips formed a smile. "Her husband checked me out. I assured them I wasn't here to hurt you and you'd be happy to see me." Deacon bent down, forcing her to meet his gaze. "Don't make a liar outta me, babe. You *are* happy to see me, right?"

She said yes without hesitation.

Then Deacon's mouth was on hers. He kissed her slowly, steadily, and sweetly. She teared up, grateful for his tender concern.

Tender concern? The man probably dropped two grand getting here on such short notice.

Molly broke the kiss and tried to get away from him.

But his arms just clamped around her more tightly. "Don't."

"Deacon—"

"Lemme hold you and say what I need to."

She stopped struggling.

"Know what I thought when I couldn't get in touch with you? That we were done. You were freaked-out and disgusted by what happened in your bedroom Saturday night."

Since Deacon always acted so cool and confident, she'd never considered he might need reassurance that his sexual quirks hadn't sent her running from him. "Saturday night was hot. I wanted that from you. No regrets on my side, Deacon."

"But?"

"But we've had two dates. I wouldn't ask you to drop everything and come to Nebraska with me, a woman you're not even sleeping with."

He stretched his fingers beneath her jaw, lifting her head so his gaze bored into hers. "We're involved."

"I know."

"Then you also know that I want to fuck you until you can't move."

Need spread in a rush of heat from her core outward, warming her body from the inside out.

His thumb grazed the underside of her jaw in an erotic arc. "But that ain't the only reason I'm with you or that I'm here. So fair warning. I won't take advantage of you when you're in a sad place any more than I would if you were drunk."

"You're chivalrous."

"Ain't no other way for a real man to be, where I come from."

Keeping her eyes on his, she sucked his lower lip between her teeth and lightly bit down.

A low warning rumbled up his throat.

"While I appreciate your consideration and restraint, Deacon, it's not only your decision when we become intimate."

"That's what I'm trying to tell you. We're already intimate, regardless of whether we've fucked. Which is why I was pissed off you didn't come to me first when this family stuff went down."

"I am sorry."

"I know. And it won't happen again."

A statement. Needing space from his intensity, she retreated. "It's been an exhausting day."

"No kidding. I'm beat." Deacon fisted his hand in his T-shirt, yanking it over his head.

When his fingers unhooked the button of his camo shorts, Molly said, "What are you doing?"

"Getting ready for bed."

"Oh. I'll get out of your . . . space. I'll grab the extra blanket from the bedroom for the couch."

Deacon stared at her. "Contorting my body on that tiny couch ain't happening when there's a king-sized bed in the next room."

"But . . ." Her mouth dried when he lowered the zipper and his clothing hit the floor.

Her *don't look, don't look* mantra was overruled by the greedy sexual bitch inside her that screamed, *Fuck yeah I'm gonna look! It was dark the last time and I didn't see much!*

Molly's eyes followed the line bisecting his upper torso, down his pecs, over his sternum, past his belly button, her gaze straying to the rigid pillows of flesh that created his six-pack, and then, whoa, there was his cock, growing right before her very eyes.

Then he gritted out, "Molly."

"What?"

"Get ready for bed."

She took longer than usual in the bathroom. It seemed the mirror exposed every one of her flaws in brightly lit detail. *Screw it. He's seen me naked before.* She slipped on her frilly baby-doll nightgown and marched into the bedroom.

Deacon was propped against the headboard, watching TV. Immediately, his gaze roved over her, from the tiny pink bow between her breasts to the sheer ruffles hitting her midthigh.

"What?"

His tone was even, but his eyes were filled with male appreciation. He pointed at her with the remote. "It's a damn good thing I'm bein' chivalrous; otherwise I'd be . . ." He closed his eyes and groaned. "Fuck it. Never mind."

Molly inched forward. "Tell me."

"Otherwise I'd be ripping that sexy nightie off you with my teeth."

Lust and regret landed a one-two punch in her gut and she huffed out, "Oh."

He pulled back the covers to reveal he'd slipped on a pair of boxers. "Get in here and cover yourself up, woman."

"You're acting awful bossy for a man who's a guest in my bed," she retorted.

"Babe. I'm bossy in *any* bed."

Molly clicked off the lamp on the nightstand before she crawled in. She curled onto her side, her back to Deacon, giving him almost all of the bed.

"You mind if I watch TV?"

"That's fine. I'm so tired I'll sleep through it."

Shadows flickered from the TV images even after she closed her eyes. Exhaustion overtook her.

The last thing she remembered was Deacon kissing her cheek and murmuring, "Sweet dreams, sweetheart. You could use them tonight."

CHAPTER NINE

MOLLY woke up and squinted at the clock.

Dammit. She'd overslept. She had to be at the church in twenty minutes.

She got ready in record time. When she came out of the bathroom, Deacon was up. Still in bed with the covers up to his chest but looking at her curiously.

"Hey." She shoved her feet into her sandals. "I'm meeting my family at the church."

"You want me to tag along?"

"No. Thanks, though. After I'm done I'll head to the store. Anything in particular you want me to pick up?"

Those crystalline eyes narrowed. "We'll go to the store together."

"Fine. I'll see you later."

Molly stopped at the convenience store for a giant coffee before she pulled into the church parking lot.

Reverend Somers sat outside on the stone steps. He smiled at her warmly. "Good morning, Molly."

"Morning."

The sun shone between the clouds, sending shards of light

skipping across the lush green grass. Growing up, she'd attended this church every Sunday. As she'd gotten older and had the freedom to make her own choices, she'd understood that her grandmother had a heavier hand than god in forming her.

"Erma was proud of you," the reverend said softly.

Molly faced him. "I know. But as she'd raised me not to brag, I have a hard time believing she'd boast to you, Reverend."

"You're right. She wasn't one to boast. Especially not in mixed company. But whenever she invited me for supper, we talked for hours. That's when she spoke of you. I will miss her."

Tears sparked in her eyes. "I'll miss her too."

Uncle Bob pulled up in his boat of a Cadillac. Jennifer exited on the passenger side and Brandi from the back.

Reverend Somers stood and unlocked the church door. They filed inside after him, falling into silence.

In the parish office, Molly settled in the lone chair off to the side of the reverend's desk. As much as it dismayed her to imagine Grams discussing particulars of her funeral with her pastor, it made planning the service easier. It also indicated that her death wasn't as unexpected as Molly had believed. Had she been so wrapped up in her own life she hadn't recognized the signs of her grandmother's failing health?

Guilt rolled over her.

Molly was preoccupied when they left the reverend's office an hour later.

But when Jennifer grabbed the back of her arm above her elbow—a move she'd been doing since they were kids—and squeezed with enough force to leave a bruise, Molly reacted. She twisted her arm free, grabbing Jennifer's wrist, stepping sideways, and jerking Jennifer's arm behind her back.

"Fuck. Ow. Jesus. Let go," Jennifer complained.

"Don't. Ever. Touch. Me. Again. Understand?"

"Fine. Whatever, you stupid cow."

Molly dropped her arm.

Jennifer rubbed her wrist. "You have turned into a real head case."

"You'd know all about that," Molly said sweetly.

Jennifer leaned in and whispered, "I hate you. I've always hated how you were Grandma's spoiled, fat, favorite grandkid."

"Jennifer Marie, stop badgering Molly and get moving," Uncle Bob warned.

Jennifer muttered something to Brandi and stormed down the hallway, Brandi on her heels.

Molly exited the church and allowed herself a moment to breathe in the fresh air.

Jennifer and Brandi lounged against the hand railing, ensuring Molly had to pass by them.

"You should've seen her last night, Jen. Throwing herself at both Marcus and Alan. As if she'd ever have a shot at either of them. It was embarrassing for her."

"Didn't you accuse me of being a lesbian last night?" Molly said. "Then why would I care about the guys you're so desperate to impress?"

"You think you're so smart," Brandi sneered.

Doesn't take a whole lot to be smarter than you, dumb-ass.

Molly had reached the bottom step when she glanced up and saw Deacon leaning against her car.

It took every bit of resolve not to break into a run.

When she reached him, he pulled her into his arms and softly kissed her lips. "Hey."

"Hey. How'd you know where I was?"

"Only so many churches in this town, babe." His gaze searched hers. "You okay?"

"Not really. This sucks. But I'm better now that you're here."

"You ready to hit the grocery store?"

"I'm ready to hit something," she muttered.

Footsteps sounded behind them, and Deacon's gaze moved over her shoulder.

"Who's your friend, Molly?"

Molly turned, and Deacon stood beside her, keeping his left hand on the small of her back. "This is my boyfriend, Deacon McConnell. Deacon, this is my uncle, Bob Calloway."

Deacon offered his hand and Bob shook it.

Jennifer slunk forward. "Molly didn't tell us she had a boyfriend." She held out her hand. "Jennifer Calloway. Molly's cousin."

He lifted his chin and ignored her outstretched hand.

Then Brandi horned her way between her father and sister. "Molly did mention a boyfriend, but I didn't take her seriously."

Deacon cocked an eyebrow at Brandi. "Why not?"

"Because she was flirting her ass off at the bar last night." Brandi sent her a triumphant look.

"I let you outta my sight one day and other guys are already sniffing around you. Will I have to bust some heads?"

"You know you have nothing to worry about. Save your head busting for the ring."

Her uncle had been watching the exchange. "Ring? What do you do for a living, Deacon?"

"I compete as a mixed martial artist."

"You don't say. Karate and such?"

From the corner of her eye, Molly saw her cousins exchange a look and then give Deacon a slow perusal.

Eat your hearts out, bitches. He's mine.

"Not karate. I'm a jujitsu instructor at Black Arts in Denver." He pulled Molly more firmly to his side. "We met in my kickboxing class."

"So that's where Molly has tried to lose some of her weight," Brandi said.

"I'd watch the insults or you might be tasting blood," Deacon warned.

Brandi's mouth dropped open. "Are you threatening me?"

"Not me. Molly. The woman's got a mean right hook. And I oughta know, since she learned how to throw a punch from me."

Molly sent Deacon a look of adoration. "Of course, I'd never hit someone out of anger." Then she looked at Brandi. "Besides, if I used my fists on you every time you insulted me, you'd be black-and-blue from head to toe."

Without another word, Deacon opened the passenger door for her.

Then he skirted the front end and climbed in the driver's seat. "Keys."

She dropped them in his hand. "Thank you."

"For?"

"Showing up."

He pressed his lips to her forehead.

When she buckled her seat belt, she noticed Brandi glaring at them before she got into her father's car.

"What is up with those bitch cousins of yours? Jesus. I've always had a 'no hitting women' policy, but they're tempting me to break it."

"They've been that way to me my whole life."

"And your grandma let them get away with it?"

She ignored his probing gaze and stared straight ahead. "Everyone let them get away with it, claiming they'd outgrow it. They never have."

"That's bullshit."

"As a kid, I had no power. As an adult, I moved away. I'd always been so malleable . . . until I wasn't. I've had minimal interactions with Jennifer and Brandi since I went to college. After all this is over, I'm done with them."

"Good. No one needs bad people in their lives that make them question who they are."

Sounded like he was speaking from experience, but she knew better than to ask.

The trip to the grocery store was uneventful—weird as it was shopping with Deacon.

At the checkout she said, "Am I missing anything?"

Deacon peered at the meat, veggies, bread, canned goods, and fruit in the cart. "Where's the ice cream?"

"I didn't buy any."

His eyes turned shrewd. "You aren't lactose intolerant or something?"

"No. I'm intolerant of fat on my belly, hips, and ass after I've worked so hard to keep it off," she said dryly.

"We'll share. What's your favorite kind?"

"Coffee or vanilla," she lied. Both those flavors would be safe from her.

He strolled to the frozen-foods section while she unloaded the cart.

The last item that rolled off the conveyor belt was a carton of rocky road.

Deacon put his mouth on her ear. "You're a shitty liar, babe." Then he deftly shunted her aside and handed the clerk his credit card. His death glare meant she'd be wise not to protest.

At least not here.

He pushed the cart outside. As soon as he'd opened the hatchback, she got in his face.

His mouth was on hers before she'd uttered a word. The kiss wasn't sweet and gentle. It was decisive. When she eased back to speak her mind, he murmured, "Let it go."

And so she did.

Back at the motel, Deacon carried in the groceries while she put everything away. She fixed her favorite comfort food for lunch—canned chicken noodle soup and deviled ham sandwiches. Halfway through the meal, the reality of why she needed comfort food hit her. The first couple of tears fell in silence. But then they came too hard and fast to maintain decorum.

When the first sob broke free, Deacon picked her up and carried her to the couch.

THE sobbing woman in his arms was killing him.

Killing. Him.

Fuck.

He rarely felt helpless, but he sure as hell did now. Molly's keening wails might just do him in.

Deacon pressed his lips into her hair. Her tears dampened his shirt. How was he supposed to comfort her?

First off, don't be a dickhead.

Amery's warning had given him pause after he'd stormed into Hardwick Designs Monday morning, demanding to know where Molly had gone. Hearing that Molly's grandmother had died was bad enough. But when Amery shared her concern about Molly being back in her hometown and dealing with her family members, who had had made her life hell, he'd booked the next flight to Nebraska.

Molly's sobs had morphed into hiccups. Then she wiggled to free herself from his embrace.

"Where are you goin'?"

"To get a tissue."

He released her.

She pushed off his lap and shut herself in the bathroom.

Deacon got up and waited for her.

When Molly finally emerged, she jumped at seeing him leaning against the doorjamb to the bedroom. "I'm sorry I'm such a blubbering mess."

"Come here."

"But I'm better now," she continued as if she hadn't heard him, "so I'll just go clean up the kitchen—"

"I said come here."

"Deacon—"

"Now."

"Fine." She marched over to him. "What?"

Deacon curled his hands around her shoulders. "You need to crawl into bed."

"I'm not tired."

"Bull." He turned her and gave her a gentle push toward the bed. "In."

She stopped at the edge of the bed and stared at the neatly folded-back covers. "Did you do this?"

"Yeah."

"Did you fluff my pillows too?"

He dropped his hands to her hips. "Babe. I draw the line at that."

Molly snorted and crawled between the sheets fully clothed.

He pulled the covers over her and smoothed his hand over her hair.

She closed her eyes and sighed. "If I ask nicely, will you stay here with me? Just until I fall asleep?"

Say no. You're not a fucking monk. If you lie next to her, you'll be hard as a brick. You want a repeat of last night? Thinking of Iceland as you're in her warm bed, feeling her curves pressed against you, with her scent tempting you as you listened to her soft sleep noises? Say no. Say hell no.

But Deacon found himself crawling onto the mattress and curling in behind her. The comforter wasn't much of a barrier between their bodies, but it was enough.

For now.

His lack of sleep caught up with him, and he drifted off.

The dream always started the same. Surrounded by fog as thick and sticky as a spider's web. But he was safe inside. Then ghostly fingers crept in through the air vents, covering his mouth and eyes.

So wet and cold. He couldn't breathe. He couldn't see. He couldn't hear. Where were they? He opened his mouth to call out, but their names bounced back as if he'd shouted against a wall.

In the next instant the fog dissipated and an image appeared in the distance. A ridged gray and black object. Getting closer and closer.

A tree.

He stared wide-eyed as the massive oak morphed into a talking tree from *The Wizard of Oz*. The knothole became a mouth open in a silent scream at the moment of impact.

Then the screams became real.

Not his screams, he thought as darkness overcame him.

Breathe, man. Come on!

Then he was floating, watching the scene above his own body, lying lifeless on the gurney along the side of the road.

The EMT yelled at him to breathe, to fight.

Not to die.

He felt his soul being sucked away, vanishing into nothingness like the fog, forever gone. Like he never was.

Until excruciating pain had him gasping for breath.

"That's it," a disembodied voice said. "You're a fighter. Stay with me."

Deacon shot upright in bed. His heart hammering, his body bathed in sweat, his hands clenched into fists so tight he couldn't get them unclenched.

It's not real. It's not real. It's not real.

Except . . . it was.

In a panic he glanced over at Molly, afraid his thrashing around had awoken her. Or worse, his scream.

Thankfully, she remained curled into herself, still asleep.

Deacon carefully eased off the bed. He never wanted her to see him like this. Shaken. Haunted.

Broken.

By the time he reached the living room, he no longer felt like he might throw up.

By the time he raced out of the room and reached the playground in front of the motel, he'd stopped shaking.

He'd been shaking so hard he hadn't realized his cell phone had been vibrating in his back pocket.

The phone had kicked the caller over to voice mail.

Good. He needed a distraction. He waited to return the call until his voice wouldn't betray him.

Deacon hit RETURN CALL, and the other line rang twice.

"Please tell me you're on a plane back to Denver," Maddox said instead of hello.

"Not yet."

"Any idea when that will be?"

"Nope. There's still a lot of stuff up in the air."

"Is she glad you're there?"

Deacon had asked Ronin if he should go. He said yes. So had Knox, and even Beck had told him to take off. The lone dissenter had been Maddox. "So far."

"Are *you* glad you're there?"

He grunted. "What do you think?"

"I think this is a bad time for you to take off from training and become your girlfriend's counselor."

"That's why you called? Jesus, Mad, I'm not a fucking idiot. It's not like I'll be gone a month. I'll do what I can with cardio and strength training."

"You also need to spar every day, Deacon." He paused. "Speaking of sparring . . . guess who walked into the dojo today?"

"Dana White."

Maddox snorted. "Micah Courey."

Deacon froze. "No shit?"

"No shit."

"What did he want?"

"To train here. Specifically, to train with me."

Fuck. "What did you say?"

"I told him to come back in a few days after I brought it up with Ronin since he has final approval on adding new fighters to the program."

Pacing in the gravel parking lot kicked up puffs of dust. "Is this your way of cutting me loose?"

"No."

"Then why are you even considering taking on a champion in my weight division?"

"Nothing has been decided, and nothing will be until you get back here. But you can understand why I'd want that to be sooner rather than later."

"I've been gone one fucking day, Maddox."

"Deacon. These next six weeks are crucial. You win the next fight against Needham and one of the big fight organizations will sign you. This is what you've been working toward."

"You think I don't know that?" he shot back. "Fuck. I know Micah Courey is a better bet than me. He's already signed with Smackdown. He's already proven himself."

"Some say he's already hit his peak. There are arguments for and against bringing him on board."

Deacon didn't have a vote since the Black Arts MMA program had become a separate entity from the dojo. As a jujitsu instructor, he had a say in the new hires. As a fighter . . . he kept his mouth shut and did what his trainer told him to do. "So you called to freak me out because I don't have enough shit on my plate right now?"

"No. I called because I hadn't heard from you and I was worried."

"I'm eating my veggies, washing behind my ears, changing my underwear every day, and working out," he snapped.

"Such a smart-ass. Which means you're not okay. So for a second, you *will* suck it up as I step outside my role as your trainer and speak as your friend."

Everything in Deacon seized up against advice he didn't want and likely wouldn't take. "Huh-uh, Maddox. You had your say one time where Molly was concerned, and it fucked everything. I'm here because her grandma is dead, her relatives are assholes, and she's alone. I've been there, man. I know how much it sucks. I could have a title fight on the line tomorrow and I still wouldn't walk away from her. I won't ever walk away from her. She needs me, and I sure as fuck need her."

A soft gasp sounded behind him.

He whirled around. A white-faced Molly stood five feet away.

A pause. Then Maddox sighed. "I get it. I wish I didn't, but I do. Take care. I need you back here no later than four days from now."

"Understood." Deacon hung up and pocketed his phone before he reached for Molly. "Hey. I tried not to wake you."

"Did you mean what you said? About not walking away from me?"

"Wouldn't have said it if I didn't mean it."

"But . . ."

"What?"

"But I don't want to distract you from your career, Deacon. Maddox already—"

"Maddox can suck it," he said hotly. "I set you aside once before, and I ain't gonna do it again. Period. Understand?"

"It's so soon in our relationship! I didn't think you—this—was serious."

"I don't do half-assed, babe. If we're in this . . . we're *in* this." He stared into her eyes, trying to mask the worry in his own that his feelings were more one-sided than he liked. "So are you in or what?"

"I'm in. I'm *so* in."

"Good." He wrapped her in his arms and breathed a silent sigh of relief when she rested her cheek against his heart.

After a bit, she said, "I heard some of what you said. Sounded like you're no stranger to grief."

Her statement didn't demand his response, so he said nothing. They'd talk about his demons another time, when her sorrow wasn't so fresh and raw.

"Is that why you don't talk about your family?"

"Probably."

"You have relatives worse than Jennifer and Brandi?"

"My cousin Clive makes them look like angels."

"Are you close in age to him?"

"He's a year younger than me." He wanted to drop it, but he forced himself to share something with her. "Tag, my only other cousin on that side of the family, is three years older. He's not so bad. I can stand him. Even when he's always been too fucking cocky for his own good."

He felt her smile against his chest. "No wonder you got along with him."

Deacon swatted her ass.

She laughed softly.

It lightened his load to hear her laugh.

"Is Maddox upset you're not in Denver training?"

"He'll be fine as long as I'm back in four days." He tilted her head to look into her eyes. "When's your grandmother's funeral?"

"Tomorrow."

"So soon?" That forced him to revise his plans for dragging her back to bed for the rest of the day and all night.

"Surprised me too. But we have a small family and we're all here, so there's no reason to put it off. I guess she had it all planned out. Her death wasn't as unexpected as I'd thought."

"Babe. I'm sorry."

Molly's hands slid up his chest. "I was kinda hoping you'd still be next to me when I woke up. We could pick up where we left off Saturday night."

As much as Deacon wanted her, and fuck did he *ever* want her, he needed her to come to him with a clear head, not with a heavy heart. He clamped his hands on to her hips, holding her body away from his. After pressing a kiss to the hollow beneath her ear, he murmured, "Gonna be wild exploring this heat between us. But it's not happening tonight."

A beat passed. "I thought you might say that."

When she tried to retreat, he trapped her face in his hands. "Don't think for a second it's because I don't want to fuck you until you can't move this sexy body without thinking of me on you and in you. Because that's what will happen the next time we're naked together. You really wanna be limping, sore, and covered in my marks on the day you bury your grandma?"

She blinked at him, then shook her head.

"Understand this. Tonight is the only night I'll say no to you."

That seemed to satisfy her. She gave him a quick peck on the lips. "I hope you have ideas on how we can keep ourselves occupied."

"Funny you should mention that. Get your workout clothes on. We're going for a run."

"Funny." When he didn't crack a smile, she said, "You're serious."

"Yep. Not the way I envisioned getting sweaty with you, but I need cardio."

"So go without me."

He shook his head.

"You're not my teacher anymore. You can't make me."

Deacon laughed. "You really wanna test that theory?"

"You're mean. Maybe I'll lag behind and yell insults at you."

"You cursing at me will be the highlight of the run, babe."

CHAPTER TEN

DEACON had been her rock, holding her up when she'd been weighted down with sorrow. She'd needed him to take charge. Forcing her to run, to eat, to sleep.

Amery had correctly assumed that in Molly's rush to leave Denver, she hadn't packed funeral attire. She'd found three outfits in storage at her loft and had sent them with Deacon.

At first Molly refused to try the clothes on. But after Deacon threatened to strip her and dress her in them himself, she'd locked herself in the bathroom. No surprise neither of the first two outfits fit. The third option, a long-sleeved black knit dress with a modest neckline, was snug, but it worked. Not that anyone would be looking at her. They'd all be too busy gawking at Deacon.

His suit was obviously custom-tailored, since the black pinstripes managed to both camouflage his big body and accentuate his amazing build. The high-necked white shirt covered his tattoos. The pale blue patterned silk tie matched his eyes. The man looked just as good dressed up as he did completely naked.

Deacon caught her staring. "What?"

"I've never seen you in a suit before."

"So?"

"So you look spectacular."

He brushed aside her compliment and jiggled the keys. "Let's go."

Uncle Bob, Jennifer, and Brandi were already in the family room when she and Deacon arrived at the church.

No one broke the somber mood with idle chatter. Then the funeral director escorted them into the front pews of the church and the organist began to play. Grams would've been happy to see all the people who'd come to pay their respects.

Deacon held her hand and supplied her with fresh tissues during the service. The reverend's words were fitting, but Molly doubted she'd remember specifics. Deacon stood beside her during the internment.

Afterward, during the repast in the church basement, he never ventured more than four feet from her side, supporting her as people she'd known her whole life offered condolences. Although her cousins were on their best behavior, Deacon kept an eye on them too.

Finally, the day had ended.

Molly barely remembered getting into Deacon's rental car and driving to the motel. Inside the room, he slipped off her shoes, forced her to drink three shots of scotch, and tucked her into bed.

At first when she'd awoken, she'd hoped it'd all been a bad dream. But Deacon's scent on the pillow next to her and the taste of booze on her tongue reminded her that the day's events were all too real.

After using the bathroom and brushing her teeth, she sought him out.

He'd settled on the sofa. His eyes were closed. His head was back. Light and shadows from the television flickered over his angular face. He'd removed his suit coat and loosened his tie. His black dress shoes were off, and he'd propped his bare feet on the coffee table. His arm hung over the edge of the couch, a tumbler dangling from his fingers.

He sensed her and lifted his head. "You get some sleep?"

"Of course I did—after you dosed me with scotch."

"You needed it." Deacon shifted, setting his feet on the floor and moving the glass to the table.

"Did I catch the unflappable Deacon McConnell napping?"

His lips twitched. "Just resting my eyes."

"You tired?"

"Not at all."

Molly meandered toward him with deliberate intent.

He didn't say anything as she stood in front of him; he just studied her with that calculating stare.

She hiked up her dress and straddled his lap. Then she put her hands on him. The knot in his tie gave way when she tugged. She tossed the silky material aside.

Deacon's breaths became labored as she slowly undid the buttons on his shirt. When she reached the waistband of his pants, she stopped.

"Darlin', you lookin' for permission to keep goin'?"

She loved how his accent deepened when he got turned on. "Yesterday you said you wouldn't tell me no today."

"You think I've changed my mind?" he growled. "No fucking way."

"Good. I've been in a holding pattern with everything since I've been here. I don't want to be in a holding pattern with you anymore." She traced the portion of the scroll tattoo beneath his collarbone. "Take me to bed, Deacon. Keep your promise that you'll fuck me so many times I can't walk."

Deacon muttered, "Fucking hell, woman."

The next thing she knew, he stood, keeping his hands clamped on her ass as he set her on her feet and towed her into the bedroom.

He crowded her against the edge of the mattress and loomed over her. "Be very, very sure this is what you want."

"It is. Not because I need a distraction from family stuff. Or that I need to feel alive after dealing with death for days on end. But because I want you. I've wanted you for a long time. You know that. You've wanted me equally long. I know that too." She rubbed her fingers over the slight stubble on his jaw. "So I'm very, very sure."

"Once we start this? Once I've been inside you? Things will change. I'll want to be all up inside you every chance I can get, in every dirty way I've imagined."

That was the hottest thing any man had ever said to her.

"Let's get it started, then." She pulled his mouth to hers. The kiss hit the ignition point from the first touch of his tongue to hers. Wet and hungry. But after a few glorious moments, he toned it down. Seducing her rather than ravaging her.

Impatient, she reached between them and cupped the bulge behind his zipper.

But Deacon's hand circled her wrist, stopping her. "Finish the top half first, then work your way down."

"Bossy." Molly dragged her mouth across his pecs once she'd gotten him bare chested.

He bunched up the fabric of her dress until she felt her ass exposed. "Lift your arms."

Her arms went up and her dress was gone.

Deacon affixed his gaze to her breasts and lowered his head. His soft lips started at the upper swell of her right breast and followed the edge of her bra down to her cleavage. "Fuck. I need my mouth on you. Bra. Off," he growled against her skin.

"Nope." She trailed her fingers over his erection. "Your pants off first." As she slid the button on his dress slacks through the hole and slowly worked the zipper down, she fastened her mouth to the flat disk of his nipple.

His head fell back, and he groaned when she started to suck.

Feeling powerful, she switched sides and focused on the tiny tip pebbling beneath her flickering tongue. One quick yank and his pants hit the carpet. Molly followed the delineated line between his pecs with her mouth, kissing a straight line down his belly until she had to lower to her knees. She'd just mouthed the outline of his cock, when she was hauled to her feet again.

"My pants are off, babe. I want those tits." His rough-skinned hands glided up her spine and she shivered from the sensation. Deft fingers pulled the hooks on her bra. Deacon paused. "Eyes on mine."

That command made her breath catch.

He leaned back only far enough to slide the straps down her arms, letting the bra cups fall away and reveal her bare breasts. That's when she understood why he'd demanded she watch him, so she could see the hunger in his eyes that was all for her.

The first hot touch of his mouth to her nipple made her knees buckle.

"Hold on to me." He placed her hands around the back of his neck.

Deacon focused his attention on her breasts. Vigorously sucking her nipples. Dragging kisses across the upper and lower swells. Burying his face in her cleavage. Squeezing, pinching, nipping, licking, turning her inside out with his single-minded dedication to her chest.

"Deacon."

"Not yet. Fuck me, you have the most perfect tits."

The pulse in her sex mimicked the hard pulls of his mouth on her nipples. Another rush of wetness coated the insides of her thighs. "Stop teasing and give me your cock."

That got his attention.

Keeping their eyes locked, he ditched his boxer briefs and kicked them away. Then he curled one of her hands around his shaft. He hissed when she squeezed and jacked him twice.

Her thumb swept beneath the head and over the wet tip. "You're big."

"Fuck. Don't do that."

"What? Tell you you're big? Or this?" She traced the flared rim of his cock.

"That. Put your hands to better use and take off your panties."

"Help me."

Deacon yanked down one side while she did the other.

The heat of his skin where his thighs brushed hers sent a tremor through her.

He palmed her breast and spoke directly into her ear. "Spread your legs for me."

His touch, his voice, the hard press of his body nearly had her coming before he traced her slit with his middle finger.

He pushed the thick digit into her pussy. "You're wet."

"Because I'm ready for you to fuck me," she panted.

"Not yet." Deacon pumped one finger in and out and added another. "Tell me where you want my first mark."

Molly let her head fall to the side, exposing her neck. "Wherever you want."

His approval reverberated across her skin as he latched on to the spot that made her mindless.

"Deacon."

"Come around my fingers."

"Harder."

"Where?"

She swallowed, wetting her dry mouth. "On my neck. Suck harder."

As the suction increased and he plunged his fingers deeper into her pussy, her brain started chanting, *almost, almost, almost.* Then Deacon pinched her nipple and she was done.

She didn't utter a peep as the orgasm crashed through her. Her pussy throbbed; her nipple stung. Her brain tried to slow time so she could feel every single pulse in her body. She'd reached number fourteen when everything went hazy.

"Babe. Gotta remember to breathe."

Molly sucked in a lungful of air.

"Better?"

"Uh-huh."

He gently pulled his fingers out of her. "Don't. Move."

"Where are you going?"

"To get a condom." He took a box out of his suitcase and tossed it on the nightstand.

Molly squinted at the box. Had it been opened? Was that a jumbo-sized pack? When she looked back at him, she wondered why he was pulling a condom out of his wallet.

Deacon maintained eye contact when he said, "One time ain't gonna be enough. I don't want to have to go far before I have you again."

She'd never felt more wanted. Need pulsed through her body.

He ripped the packet open with his teeth and rolled the condom down his length. Then his mouth was on hers, his kiss electrifying her until her lungs were saturated with his scent and her mouth was steeped in the potent taste of him. He continued nuzzling her after he broke the kiss. "Get on the bed."

Molly scooted to the middle, and Deacon was immediately on her, his hips against hers as he positioned himself above her.

He balanced on one hand and reached between their bodies to align his cock. He didn't kiss her as he pushed inside. His focus remained on her face.

Once he was fully seated, he stopped.

Feeling ornery, she drawled, "Darlin', you lookin' for permission to keep goin'?"

A devilish glint entered his eyes as he withdrew completely.

He waited, poised in a push-up position, his breath close enough to tease her lips but his mouth not close enough to kiss.

The blunt head of his cock rested at her entrance. "Deacon."

"Tell me what you want."

"Fuck me."

He tormented her, giving her his cock a little at a time. Leisurely pulling out. Holding back the hard, deep thrusts.

Molly squeezed his ass. "You proved your point."

"Which was what?"

"You're a sadist."

Deacon lightly bit her earlobe. "Babe. A sadist would stop right now."

"No. Please, don't." The slow and steady pace was making her squirmy. Making her pant. Making her beg.

"Then it's a good thing I'm not a true sadist." He slammed into her with enough force she slid up the mattress.

"Yes."

On the next dozen strokes she arched up and bore down with her pussy muscles.

Then she shifted her hips side to side to get some connection on her clit.

"Stop trying to get off."

"Stop trying to keep me from getting off," she retorted.

Deacon reverted to a slow and steady rhythm. But this time he gave her toe-curling kisses as he tortured her.

Molly's hands skated across his shoulders. His powerful muscles bunched and flexed as he moved. Seeing the sheen of sweat on his forehead, she realized she'd never touched the shiny, hard skin on his head. And she wanted to. Bad.

He stopped moving. "What?"

"Can I put my hands on your head?"

"Yeah. But you don't have to ask."

"Well, I wasn't sure if you liked it."

Deacon put his mouth next to her ear. "I fucking love it. And you'll love how it feels between your thighs when I fuck you with my mouth."

Imagining his mouth licking, and sucking, and, god, *biting* the tender flesh there sent a delicious shiver through her, and she moaned.

"Molly."

She refocused on him—sort of hard not to with him being right in her face and all. "What?"

"Are you trying to make me stop fucking you?"

"No! Why would you ask that?"

"Because of that sexy noise you made when you thought about me goin' down on you. Jesus. I'm tempted to stop fucking you and start eating your pussy."

Her face heated. Dammit. The man was naked on top of her, his dick stuffed inside her, and she still blushed when he said something dirty. Annoyed with herself, and him, she slapped his ass. "No pussy eating yet. Get moving."

"Christ. This is not how I imagined the first time we fucked."

"Disappointed?"

"Just that we waited this long. You feel so damn good."

"So do you." Molly slid her hands up the back of his neck, letting her fingers follow the contours of his skull before she stroked her palms over the smooth skin.

Deacon groaned and turned in to her touch, wanting more.

Speaking of sexy noises, she could get used to hearing Deacon's grunts and moans as she learned what he liked.

Time seemed to stand still as they moved together. Kissing. Tasting. Touching. Until their bodies were slick with sweat.

"Deacon," she murmured against his throat. "I need—"

"I gotcha, babe." He lifted up to push her legs farther apart with the heels of his hands and moved back over her without missing a single stroke.

Every upstroke put direct friction on her clit.

She clung to him, holding herself rigid as she waited for the hot tingle that unleashed her pleasure.

"Relax," he panted in her ear. "Don't force it."

"But I've always been responsible for my own orgasms."

"Not anymore. Now they're mine."

Deacon's soft, teasing kisses were in opposition to the hard-driving snaps of his hips.

When he changed the rhythm, she arched up, hanging on to him as her orgasm blasted through her. Her brain fragmented. She floated on a cloud of bliss until she realized the low rumble in her ear was his voice and he was trying to rouse her.

"Fuck, woman. You are the sexiest thing I've ever seen."

She peeked at him from beneath slumberous lashes. "How long was I out after you fucked me into a coma?"

"No more than a minute." The pride in his voice was unmistakable.

She shifted her body and realized his cock was still hard inside her. "Tell me what will get you there."

"This." He braced his hands beside her head and drove into her with short strokes, his eyes dark with primal lust as he watched her tits bounce. His head fell back and he came in silence, except for the shallow exhalations as if he'd gone a few rounds in the training room.

Molly stroked his scalp, loving the way he twisted his neck and angled his head so she touched him everywhere.

After Deacon caught his breath, he rested his forehead to hers. "You're beautiful and you just rocked my fucking world. I never want to move from right here. But I've gotta be squishing you." He watched her face as he pulled out. "You okay?"

"Mmm-hmm." She stretched her arms above her head.

The bed jiggled as he scooted to the end.

She rolled onto her side, her eyes glued to the round globes of his ass as he went to ditch the condom. For the shitty way the day started, it sure ended with a bang.

It's a slap in the face to your grandmother that a few hours after you bury her, you're lost in lust. It's disgusting how quickly you've forgotten your grief and sorrow as you pursue your own pleasure.

Molly curled onto her other side, squeezing her eyes shut at the ugly reminder of what this day had been.

The bed dipped. Deacon slipped his hand around her waist and pulled her body against his. "Don't."

"Don't what?" she snapped.

"Don't do this guilt trip." His warm breath tickled the fine hair on the back of her neck. "Now, if you'd skipped your grandma's funeral to bang me all afternoon, that'd be entirely different."

When had Deacon become so intuitive?

He's not. He's trying to justify getting his rocks off.

"So this wasn't a 'take her mind off her troubles' mercy fuck?"

Deacon had flipped her onto her back and straddled her hips, pinning her arms above her head before she could blink. "Don't try to piss me off so I'll leave you alone to wallow in guilt. Not happening, babe."

"Don't use jujitsu on me, Yondan."

They stared at each other. Winning a stare down with him was impossible.

Molly caved. "Fine. But I doubt I'll be good company."

"I'm not looking to be entertained." He touched the side of her face. "I'm taking care of you. That includes me bein' a dick and calling you out on your misplaced guilt."

"Get off me."

He backed off.

But as soon as her feet hit the floor, he said, "Where are you goin'?"

"To make something to eat." Without a robe nearby, she snatched Deacon's dress shirt and put it on.

His eyes flared with heat. "If that's supposed to keep my hands off you, you oughta know it ain't gonna work."

"I'm not trying to be provocative. I'm just borrowing it."

"Don't matter. I still have the right to demand it back at any time."

DEACON didn't let her cook. He didn't ask her what she wanted to eat. He settled her at the table with a glass of scotch and a lingering kiss.

He'd slipped on a pair of athletic shorts, but his upper torso remained bare. She shamelessly studied the ripple of the muscles in his arms as he chopped cabbage, carrots, green onions, celery, broccoli, and peppers. It struck her in a fresh wave of lust that this man was simply breathtaking. A head as perfectly shaped as his shouldn't have hair. His face was a beautifully masculine study in angles. High cheekbones, a square jaw, a broad forehead. The full lips beneath his narrow—and slightly bent—nose provided the only hint of softness in his face. His dark brown eyebrows were furrowed in concentration. His jaw was set. The tendons in his neck were rigid.

Molly's gaze moved down. The front side of his body wasn't as heavily tattooed as his back. The tats were swirls of color instead of black and shades of gray, but the scrolls and images melded together to look seamless.

She gulped a mouthful of scotch, hoping the alcohol would dampen her sudden need to trace every curve and line of his ink with her fingers and her mouth. She imagined being behind him, using her teeth across the slope of his shoulder while running her hands over the smooth pate of his shaved head. Then she'd nibble on the backs of his ears, sucking on his earlobe before she followed the outer rim with her tongue. She'd whisper dirty, raunchy things as she touched and teased him.

"Stop making that noise," he half growled, not looking up from the chicken he sautéed in sesame oil, soy sauce, and garlic.

"What noise?"

"The noise you make when I'm sucking on your neck right before you come."

"I can't stop it. I can't help it. You're just so . . ."

Deacon's gaze snapped to hers. "So . . . what?"

"Hot."

"Fuck." A pause. "Gimme two minutes."

Ask him what happens in two minutes.

But she knew.

It might be the longest two minutes of her life.

She closed her eyes and let her anticipation build. What would Deacon do to her first? She wanted burn marks on her neck from his razor stubble. She wanted purple love bites on her breasts, on her belly, on her ass. She wanted her lips swollen and chapped from kissing him. She wanted her pussy sore and all the muscles in her body aching from his total possession.

"Molly, look at me."

She opened her eyes.

Deacon stood by the sink, drying his hands with a tiny tea towel. "Get up on the table, hands behind you."

But the time he crossed the small space, his cock was tenting his shorts.

She licked her lips.

He reached down to the seat next to hers and came back up with the entire box of condoms.

Did he take that box with him everywhere? "Been planning this?" she asked breathlessly.

"Only since before I had you the first time." After he'd suited up, he undid the buttons on his shirt she was wearing. "You ready for me?"

"You mean wet?" She pushed up far enough to nip his stubbled jaw. "Yes. Seeing you half naked does things to me."

Deacon moved his hands up the center of her torso, stopping to palm and squeeze her breasts before he tugged the shirt off her shoulders and down her arms.

When Molly tried to take it completely off, he said, "Leave it like that."

"But I can't move my arms."

He smiled against her throat. "I know." Then his hands were on her hips, pulling her forward. "Hard and fast, babe."

Like she'd say no to that.

He guided his cock to her opening, his gaze engrossed on watching his length disappear into her.

Molly felt every inch of him since her tissues were still swollen. It didn't hurt, but she knew she'd understand the phrase "well fucked" before the night was over.

As soon as Deacon anchored his hands to her hips, she braced herself.

Two smooth glides in and out and then he hammered into her.

The powerful thrusts shook her entire body, making her thighs and her breasts bounce. For a brief moment she was thankful Deacon's eyes were on her bouncing boobs and not her jiggling thighs. But being on the receiving end of Deacon's passion sent all thoughts like that into the background as she lost herself in the heart-pounding, sweat-dripping, body-clenching rush of his sexual magnetism.

There was something so primitive and male about the way he fucked her. His fascination with how her body moved as his body powered into hers. She'd never felt so . . . taken. She closed her eyes and let his need drive hers.

Then his mouth was on her throat. Teeth scraping, followed by tiny bites. Soft flicks of his tongue. Heated breath. "Arch into me," he rasped in her ear. "I want this hot pussy milking me as we both come."

Deacon changed the angle of his hips, pressing into the low rise of her mound on every upthrust.

"Oh. I like that." She put her heels on the edge of the table and rocked into him. "Harder."

A soft snarl burned across her skin as he bottomed out inside her faster and faster.

Molly didn't chase her orgasm. She just let the sensations build, one grinding hard thrust at a time until she couldn't stop herself from sliding side to side and then gasping, "Shallow thrusts. I'm right there."

"I fucking love when you tell me what you need."

When she started to come, Deacon latched on to her nipple and sucked with the pulsing rhythm of her blood. She felt the orgasm in every muscle and pulse point in her body. All she could do was let the storm crash over her again and again, spinning her around and around until she didn't know which end was up and the waves of pleasure receded.

After she'd reached her peak, Deacon didn't return to the skin-slapping thrusts, but he continued the slow, steady movements. When he buried his face in her neck, his harsh breathing and the stiffening of his body above her were the only indications that he'd found his own release.

They remained like that, their chests plastered together by sweat, trying to catch their collective breaths. With his hands still squeezing her hips, Deacon planted kisses down her neck, across her collarbones, dragging his mouth down to her left nipple. He teased that hardened tip until she started to squirm beneath him.

"Deacon."

"What?" he said in an annoyed whisper, as if he didn't want her to interrupt his worship of her breast.

"You wrecked me."

He lifted his head. His lips were full and wet from suckling her. Something dark skittered through his eyes.

Molly nuzzled his cheek. "In a good way. In the best way ever."

Deacon's hands glided up to cup her face. He smoothed her

hair away from her damp forehead. The tenderness in him delighted her, how effortlessly he soul kissed her. Intently, not just intensely.

He tugged her upright so she could wreathe her arms around his waist.

After the kiss shifted into soft smooches, he rested his forehead to hers. "You wrecked me too. I didn't know . . ."

His body language—the way he clung to her—said everything his mouth didn't.

They'd been intimate on a level before they'd had sex. They'd both felt the urgency about taking that next step to become lovers. But being this . . . Neither one of them had been prepared for it.

She twisted out of his hold and flattened her palms on his forearms, taking in every inch of muscle, every ripple of sinew. "As much as I'd love to continue to worship at the altar of Deacon the sex god, we could both use a break."

He lifted an eyebrow. "Deacon the sex god? Seriously, babe?"

"Mmm-hmm. New nickname for you. In fact, Deacon 'Sex God' McConnell has a much nicer ring than Deacon 'Con Man' McConnell, don't you think?"

"I think you're delirious from lack of food." He kissed her decisively. "Off the table before I'm tempted to eat you for supper."

CHAPTER ELEVEN

THEY'D both overslept the next morning, allowing no time for Deacon to fuck Molly in the shower like he'd planned.

There wasn't any time to stop at the C-Mart for a quick cup of joe, either. But on the way to the lawyer's office, Deacon did bring up one thing that'd been weighing on him. "Torch Robbins is your family lawyer?"

"If by 'family' you mean Grams's and Uncle Bob's lawyer . . . then yes."

He picked up her hand to stop her from fiddling with the crease in her pants. "You're nervous."

"I've never been to the reading of a will before."

"It's pretty boring. It's the shit that happens afterward you oughta be worried about." He parked in front of the lawyer's office and faced her. "Babe, I gotta be honest. I'm not sure this guy"—he pointed to the fancy lettering on the glass window—"has *your* best interests in mind."

"I've thought about that. But what are my options? I'm leaving tomorrow. Torch Robbins is the only game in town."

He curled his hand around her neck and turned her face toward him. "My cousin Tag is a lawyer. Lemme ask him if he's got colleagues in Omaha or Lincoln. We'll go from there."

Her brown eyes softened. "That'd be a huge relief to me. And make sure your cousin knows I'll pay him for his time."

"No worries. Tag owes me. Just don't sign anything until I talk to him, okay?"

"I won't. You're too good to be true. You know that, right?"

"Wrong. I'm a bad bet." He stroked the edge of her jaw. "Don't say I didn't warn you."

"So noted. But I still think you're sweet. Showing up here, knowing what I need before I do—"

Deacon brushed his mouth over hers to stop the stream of praise he felt he hadn't earned. "I'll wait out here."

He called Tag's home phone and left a message. Pussy move, not calling Tag's office at JFW or his cell phone, but Deacon wanted legal advice, not family guilt.

It'd gotten stuffy inside the car, so he'd found a shady spot in front of a barbershop. While he waited, he checked sports scores and mined through MMA sites for news on his phone.

Less than an hour later, Molly exited the lawyer's office.

"How'd it go?"

Molly shot a look over her shoulder. "I don't want to talk about it here. I need some damn caffeine."

He drove to the C-Mart.

After she'd taken a few sips from her jumbo cup of coffee, she blurted out, "That was bizarre. Everyone acted so civilized until Torch read the will. Then Jennifer and Brandi started yelling at me and Uncle Bob asked if the will could be contested."

"What the fuck happened?"

"Grams bequeathed some of her belongings to the church. We're meeting Reverend Somers at the house in an hour— evidently she already had that stuff sorted. Once the place is empty, the house and the land will be put up for sale. The money is to be split equally between Uncle Bob and me. Anything left over in the house will be auctioned off. That's Brandi and Jennifer's inheritance."

While that seemed fair, since Molly was the sole heir of her grandmother's other child, Deacon knew her cousins wouldn't see it that way. "Tag left me a message. He's tracking down an estate lawyer. He'll follow up with you soon."

"Did he say something else? Because you seem distracted."

No surprise she'd picked up on that. "Just wondering how long it'll take to empty the house. I have to be back in the training room by the day after tomorrow."

"Deacon, if you have to go, I'll understand. Everything you've done for me has been above and beyond."

"I'm not leaving you to deal with angry family members. Let's help them get the stuff in the house sorted. But, babe, you're only doin' that as a courtesy since they own everything inside now. There shouldn't be any reason we can't leave tomorrow morning."

"You're right. I'm just used to doing everything."

"Time to let that go."

"Time to let a lot of things go," she said softly.

He knew how that felt, but as usual, he said nothing.

BY the time they arrived at the house, the locks had been removed. Reverend Somers and two parishioners were carting out boxes of books and craft supplies.

Neither Molly's uncle nor her cousins were there yet. He suspected Brandi and Jennifer planned to show up late—after Molly had done most of the work.

Before they started tearing up the house, Molly gave Deacon a tour. She held it together until they reached the living room.

As she ran her hand over her grandmother's worn easy chair, she took a moment to firm her wobbling chin. "Growing up I wasn't allowed to eat in the front room. Seeing this"—she gestured to the dishes on the plastic-coated TV tray—"makes me sad. I wonder when she broke that rule. After I left for college? Is that when she realized she'd be eating alone regardless if she sat in front of the TV or at the dining room table?"

Deacon moved in behind her and wrapped his arms around her.

"This is supposed to be the easy part, right? These . . . things are just things. Sellable and replaceable. I shouldn't have any attachment to that chair. No matter how many years she sat in it. Because I know she'll never sit in it again. I don't need that around as a reminder."

He kissed the top of her head, strangely moved by her unsentimental view.

She disentangled herself. "This stuff won't sort itself."

And there was his shove-the-emotional-stuff-aside Molly. They were strangely alike that way. "What's the plan?"

"Personal things in one pile. Auction items in another. Throw away the stuff that doesn't fit in either category." Molly faced him. "If you bring in the four big trash cans from out back, I'll get the garbage bags."

"I'm yours to command, babe." He'd do Molly's bidding today, because once this task was done, he could get her naked beneath him again and he'd be the one calling the shots.

As he carried in the garbage cans, he thought about how things had changed between Molly and him. Being lovers was a big part of it, but she'd given herself over to his care in other ways. It'd been a long damn time since he'd felt needed, and it didn't scare the fuck out of him as much as he'd feared it would.

In the living room, Molly was hitting her fists into the window frame, which appeared to be painted shut.

"Trying to break your hand?"

"Ha. I'm trying to open the windows. It's so stuffy in here I can't breathe." She grunted and banged into the wood even harder.

"Move."

"There's a trick to this; I just can't remember what it is."

He crowded her, intending to elbow her aside, but she whirled around and slapped her palms on his chest. "Whoa there, big guy. It's not a big deal if I hurt my hand, but yours are a different story."

"Babe. I ain't gonna hurt myself opening a fucking window."

"That's right. Because your job is to stand there looking all hot, scowly, menacing badass while I do it."

"Christ. I remember when we first met you couldn't even look me in the eye. Now you're bossing me around and insulting me."

"Turns you on, doesn't it?" she said with a sexy purr before she faced the window again and smacked her palms along the top of the sill.

Deacon circled her wrists with his fingers, pulling her arms above her head and pressing his groin into her ass. "Know what really turns me on? Imagining how hot it'll be when I take you like this."

She melted against him. "Deacon."

"Fuck, woman. What you do to me." He let his lips follow the curve of her cheek to the corner of her mouth. "And the things I want to do to you."

The front door slammed against the wall.

When Molly jumped back, he moved into her space and pounded his fists into the wood casing until the window opened.

"Show-off."

Jennifer stormed in, dragging a trash can to the dining room table. "For years I've been looking forward to throwing away all this crap. Who keeps magazines, knitting patterns and old Christmas cards?"

"Don't throw out any pictures, ledgers, or records. Put anything you're not sure of, like the crocheted afghans, in the kitchen, and we'll go through it later."

Jennifer got right in Molly's face. "You may own half of this house now, but what's inside belongs to us. Not you. You're not in charge. I am. I want this shit done. The auction house will be by later today. Sort the stuff upstairs first."

Deacon was disappointed when Molly said, "Aye-aye," but didn't salute.

In Molly's old room, Deacon noticed the twin bed had been stripped. A cheap pressboard desk and an old metal chair were shoved against the wall. A battered chest of drawers anchored the opposite end of the room. No posters or plaques adorned the walls. "Did your room always look like this?"

"Jennifer and Brandi wrecked anything nice, so after a while I didn't bother making it personal."

"It sucks that not even this was a private space for you growing up."

"Makes me appreciate the freedom to decorate however I want—even with flowers and lace and shit."

"Hilarious."

She checked the closet and every dresser drawer. "This room is done. Guest bedroom is next."

Deacon hauled in the garbage can, but the room was already sparse. A double bed, a dresser, and a bentwood rocker. He leaned against the doorjamb, watching Molly rifle through the contents of the drawers and dump everything into the trash.

The two plastic tubs she'd designated for keepsakes were both empty.

"What can I do? I'm just standing around."

"Take down the curtains?"

That killed four minutes.

"Now what?"

"A big, strong man like you could probably lift that bed frame with one hand."

Deacon did just that.

Laughing, she yanked out the oval rug beneath the metal feet. "Be still my heart."

He snagged her around the waist and pulled her close.

"What?"

"Gimme that mouth." Her lips parted on a soft sigh, which he caught as he kissed her. Normally he wasn't a kissing guy, but being mouth-to-mouth with her punched all his buttons.

The stairs creaked and she broke the kiss. "Stop tempting me away from work."

He smirked. "Not sorry."

"I know. Make yourself useful." She pointed to the garbage. "Take that out and dump it."

Deacon was in the kitchen when he heard the front door open. A male voice called out, "Molly?"

Fast footsteps sounded above his head. "Omigod, Tim? Is that really you?"

"In the flesh, baby."

Molly let out a happy shriek.

What the hell? Deacon moved to the open doorway and watched as Molly flew down the steps and launched herself at another man.

"I can't believe you're here!"

"I came as soon as I heard. Sorry I missed the funeral." Then he planted his mouth on hers in a really fucking far-from-friendly kiss.

Then Mr. Soon-to-Be-Bleeding framed Molly's face in his hands and spoke softly to her.

Jennifer sidled up next to him. "Why the angry look, Deacon? Surely since you and Molly are *involved*, you know all about Tim."

"Who is he?"

"Her best friend from high school. They were constantly together. She mooned over him like a lovesick calf. I think he dated her out of pity. But now that she's not such a porker . . . maybe you'd better watch your back."

"Maybe you'd better watch your mouth, because you don't know a fucking thing about her."

"Doesn't seem like *you* know as much as you think you do either," she retorted.

The slam of the back door broke Molly and Mr. About-to-Be-Punched-in-the-Kisser apart.

Molly glanced over at him with a measure of guilt.

Deacon's eyes narrowed.

Mr. Gonna-Be-Handed-His-Ass looked at Molly and then Deacon.

Clasping Tim's hand with a challenging look, she towed him over to Deacon. "I'd like you to meet my good friend. Tim Bakke, this is Deacon McConnell."

With his build and coloring, this Tim guy was a dead ringer for Sandan Zach from Black Arts—a guy Molly had once dated.

Now it's on, motherfucker.

Tim offered his hand first. "Nice to meet you, Deacon."

Shaking the proffered hand, Deacon muttered "ass-licker," knowing it'd pass as likewise. *Good one, bro.* Dante laughed in his head, as he always had when they'd pulled that old gag. *Never not funny.*

Deacon refocused on Molly. Why hadn't she clarified who he was? Or when she'd said *good friend*—maybe she hadn't been referring to Tim.

Fuck that.

Tim grabbed Molly's hands. "I'm here; put me to work while we catch up. God. You look amazing. I'll bet you have to beat the guys away with a stick."

E-fucking-nough.

Deacon stood behind Molly, gliding his fingers down her arms in a deliberately sensual caress. He pulled her hands free from Tim's and tugged her back against his body. "I don't need a stick to beat down the guys dumb enough to touch her. I just use my hands."

Silence.

Tim raised his eyebrows at Molly. "He's your boyfriend?"

Deacon almost snapped that he was a fucking *man*, not a god-damn boy.

"Yes. We're together."

"Huh."

"Who'd you think I was?" Deacon demanded.

"A moving guy here to help with . . . stuff." Tim didn't budge at Deacon's nonverbal expression of displeasure.

Molly squeezed Deacon's wrist as a warning. "Be nice."

Keeping his gaze on Tim, he said, "This *is* nice for me, babe."

"We're working upstairs. Come on."

Deacon had no choice but to let her go.

"This should go fast. Then we'll head down to the cellar."

"I hate the cellar," Tim said.

"Well, at least Grams cleaned out the majority of crap down there two years ago, or we'd be stuck down there for a month," Molly said as she started up the stairs.

Tim followed her, but he paused to look at Deacon.

That's right. I'm watching you. And you'd better keep your beady eyes off her butt.

He grabbed the garbage can and headed up the stairs. He'd make sure that motherfucker kept his hands off her too.

FOR the next two hours Molly and Tim reminisced.

It went like this:

Cue Tim's braying laughter after they journeyed into the dank cellar: *Hey, Mol, remember when we were fourteen and stole a bottle of homemade dandelion wine from down here?*

Cue Molly's tittering laugh. Yes, the woman fucking *tittered* at Tim: *All I remember about that night was puking outside, next to the grain bin.*

And so it went. On and on.

Deacon pretended to tune them out. But that meant his

thoughts drifted to his own memories. He hated getting sucked back into that time of his life, before life as he knew it ended.

That was how he defined his life. Before. And after.

What will happen when Molly asks about your childhood?

He'd do the same thing he did when anyone pried into his life before; he'd hedge. Or flat-out lie if he had to. With her, he could fuck her until she ceased to think at all.

Brandi and Jennifer clomped down the stairs.

The one good thing about Tim showing up was the cousins had steered clear of them.

Molly tossed an empty bottle in the garbage. "We're almost done."

"Good. The auction guy will be here soon."

Jennifer stepped forward. "We need to talk to you alone."

"About family business that's none of theirs," Brandi said, gesturing to Tim and Deacon.

"Nice try," Deacon drawled. "Any family business will be handled by Molly's attorney from here on out."

"You've just completely taken over her life, haven't you?" Jennifer said.

"Nope. Molly can take care of herself. I just ride shotgun and don't let anyone run roughshod over her."

Tim snickered.

"Whatever. We'll be in the barn taking inventory."

"I guess we're done here." Molly stood and slapped the dust off her hands. "I need to wash up before I leave."

The mood was more subdued as Molly walked through the house one last time. Deacon would've left her alone, but he didn't trust her cousins not to ruin this moment for her too.

Finally she reached for his hand and said, "Let's go."

Tim was waiting for them in the driveway. His focus was entirely on Molly. "You okay?"

"It's surreal to think this is the last time I'll be here." She shook off her melancholy. "Would you like to have supper with us since we're leaving in the morning?"

Tim's gaze winged between Molly and Deacon. "Actually, my folks made plans."

"I've hardly seen you. Can you come to the motel when you get a moment so we can say goodbye?"

Deacon set his hands on her shoulders and pulled her firmly against his chest. "You'd better call first. We probably won't hear you banging on the door when we're in the bedroom."

"Omigod, Deacon! What is wrong with you?"

Tim frowned. "Molly, you sure you'll be all right?"

"She's fucking fine. I take care of what's mine."

Molly looked up at him.

Deacon pressed his lips to hers. As much as he'd love to kiss her until the passion consumed them, if he didn't back off, he'd be fucking her right here in front of her good *friend* Tim. When he rested his hand on her throat and stroked her jaw, her brown eyes were black with lust.

For him. Not for that fucker who stood ten feet away, trying to encroach on his territory.

"Uh, yeah. I'll be heading out now," Tim said. "And I'll definitely give you a call before I swing by tonight."

Deacon said, "You do that," without looking away from Molly.

Only when he heard Tim's car door slam and his engine start did he release her.

Neither spoke on the drive to the motel.

He parked in front of their room.

Molly scrambled out of the car.

Deacon followed her. He moved in behind her, watching her struggle with the room key. "Don't run from me, babe. You've got nowhere to go."

She shoved the key in the lock.

"Here's what'll happen once we're alone," he murmured in her ear. "I'll be on you. In you. My mouth. My fingers. My cock. I'll remind you who I am to you." Deacon grabbed a fistful of her hair and pulled it aside to get at her neck. He opened his mouth and sucked a love bruise on the tender skin.

Her knees buckled. "Deacon."

"Open the goddamn door."

As soon as they were inside, he crushed her mouth beneath his.

This was what he needed—to gorge himself on the taste of her. To revel in her response as she kissed him back with equal voraciousness.

Between kisses he demanded, "Lift," and yanked her shirt over her head. He twisted the front clasp of her bra until her tits tumbled into his hands. After tossing the bra aside, he undid the button on her pants and lowered the zipper. "Off. Everything."

Molly kicked off her shoes. She wiggled her hips and her pants hit the floor.

Planting his lips on hers, he backed her into the alcove. After he curled her fingers around the half wall, he said, "Brace yourself," and dropped to his knees. He opened his mouth over her sex, sinking his teeth into the top of her mound as his tongue stroked her slit.

When her legs bobbled, he gripped the back of her knee, lifting her leg up and draping it on his shoulder.

"Oh god. What are you doing?"

The first taste of her sweet pussy on his tongue turned him into a wild man. He moved his head back far enough only to spread her wide-open with his thumbs, fully exposing her hot, wet flesh. Burying his tongue deep in her tight channel. Coating his face with her essence.

Now that I've had this, you're mine.

Deacon wanted to tell her how fucking addictive her taste was. How hard he was going to make her come. But he couldn't tear his mouth away from this fragrant flesh to even speak. He mapped her folds with his lips. He curled his tongue into the opening to her body to lap up the sticky sweetness.

Above him, Molly whimpered and moaned, but she held herself upright . . . until the moment Deacon's mouth connected with her swollen clit.

Four hard sucks, a few flicks of his tongue, and she detonated.

More sweet juice coated his chin as he ate at her. He felt each hard pulse of her sex against his lips. When they tapered off, he released her, lowering her foot to the floor as he nuzzled the soft skin between her hips.

He looked up to see her beautiful face flushed with pleasure.

I did that. No other man gets to see you like this.

Deacon rolled to his feet. He latched on to her right nipple and suckled softly, in spite of the need riding him.

Her head lolled forward. "I don't think my legs will keep me up much longer."

"Good thing they'll be wrapped around my waist as I fuck you into the wall."

She opened her eyes.

Deacon dug the condom out of his pocket before he ditched his jeans and boxers. His mouth sought the warm skin below her ear as he ripped the condom package open and rolled it on.

He lifted her left leg, pressing the soft inside of her thigh against his hip bone. The head of his cock gravitated toward her wet center like a heat-seeking missile.

One hard snap of his pelvis and he buried his cock in those snug pussy walls.

She gasped.

Deacon paused for a moment and realized Molly was still shaking. "You okay?"

"You overwhelm me."

"Babe." His eyes searched hers, his body vibrating with the

need to get them back to the place where words weren't necessary. "I'm not scaring you?"

She shook her head.

"Then why is your whole body trembling?"

"Because of that."

"What?"

"That look in your eye." Molly touched his chest. "You're all this. I'm just me. Nothing special. But when you look at me like that, you make me feel . . ."

"What?"

"Precious. Like I'm worth having."

"You are. And you're mine." Possession roared through him. "Hold on to me."

Molly clutched the back of his neck.

He plowed into her, hips pumping at full force. The all-encompassing need to imprint himself on her was stronger than he'd imagined.

Her mouth was on him, treating him to tender kisses. On his lips. On his neck. On his jaw. This reverence destroyed him.

Deacon pushed her knee out. Every time he drove in, he canted his pelvis, putting friction directly on her clit.

"Yes. God. Don't stop."

One. Two. Three thrusts and Molly unraveled.

Fuck. He fought the deep rhythmic pulling of her cunt muscles, milking his cock. Not yet. He had to see this. Her total abandonment to the moment. To him. He had to hear the sexy moans drifting from her kiss-ravaged lips.

That's fucking mine too.

He murmured, "Beautiful," against her throat.

She clamped her hands on his head. With her breath in his ear and her pussy tight around his cock . . . he felt the beginning of that spiral into the ultimate bliss. He clenched his ass cheeks, holding his breath through every hard spurt.

White spots danced behind his lids.

Molly whispered, "Babe. Gotta remember to breathe when you're fucking me."

The noise he made was half laugh/half gasp.

Deacon panted against her neck. Seemed to take forever to find his balance.

"You okay?"

"Fuck. I came so hard my balls hurt."

"It's only fair if I'm chafed you should be too."

"I don't care."

"There's a lover's concern," she said dryly.

He raised his head and gazed into her eyes. "I warned you it'd be like this."

"I know." She paused and whispered, "One day."

"One day what?"

"One day we've been lovers and you're already fucking me into acceptance of your caveman ways."

"You're not complaining," he said, lightly sinking his teeth into her chin.

"No, I'm not. But can you let me go so I can clean myself up?" Almost on cue, her stomach growled. "We forgot to eat today."

Deacon's lips followed the arc of her throat up to her chin. "I forgot to work out today too."

"You carted stuff and moved stuff around for hours!"

"Fetching and carrying doesn't count as cardio." He swept his lips across hers, unwilling to break their connection. "I can't go without it. Not this close to a fight."

Guilt darkened her eyes, and she looked away.

"Molly. Don't. There are enough hours left in the day to get my workout in. I didn't tell you that to make you feel guilty, dammit."

"But I do feel guilty. You'd be sparring and doing all the training stuff if you weren't here."

"There's no place I'd rather be. I'm in the best shape of my life. That will sustain my body when I have a light training day."

Her fingertips drifted up and down his arms. "Speaking of . . . are there no-sex-before-a-fight rules too?"

"Not at Black Arts."

"I'm serious."

"If I was in a title fight? Maybe. But for a regional fight?" He kissed her again. "Don't worry about goin' without, babe."

Molly put her hands on his chest and nudged him back. "Gotta dismount, cowboy."

He grinned against her throat as he withdrew from her body. "I sure like plowing into you, farm girl."

She slapped his ass. "I'll hit the shower. Then I'll cook."

ACCORDING to his distance calculator, he'd run seven miles. In an hour.

He stayed outside until his breathing returned to normal. He'd forgotten how much farther he could run when the elevation was three thousand feet lower than the Mile High City.

Deacon sat on the low rock wall separating the children's play area from the parking lot. Cornfields stretched as far as he could see. Everything was so damn green. He'd grown up in west Texas, where the dirt, the trees, and even the sky were a dull brown.

His stomach gurgled. He'd waited an hour after eating before hitting the pavement. An hour where he'd stretched out on the puffy bed and watched Molly sleep.

After she'd showered, she'd strolled into the kitchen in her bathrobe. Being the horny bastard he was, he slid the robe off her shoulders to play with the amazing tits he couldn't get enough of. Under the fluorescent lights, Deacon got a full look at the marks he'd left on her chest.

And on her neck.

And on her belly.

And on her hips.

And on the insides of her thighs.

And on the outsides of her knees.

He must've looked appalled, because she twined her body around him.

"Know the places I don't have marks?" She nuzzled his pecs. "Along the backs of my shoulders, the nape of my neck, and on my ass. Seems you've been lax in your promise to mark me everywhere, Deacon. So you'd better remedy that by bending me over and putting that mouth of yours to good use."

"Now?"

"Right now."

"I thought you were chafed?"

"And I thought you didn't care."

Deacon was done for. He herded her into the bedroom and fell to his knees behind her to gift her with suck marks on each of her ass cheeks. Before she'd stopped wiggling that ass for more, he'd slapped it hard—and again she'd made those sexy fucking needy moans. He positioned her on all fours on the bed, caging her body beneath his, biting on the back of her neck until her pussy was thoroughly soaked. Then he'd impaled her. Fucking her nice and slow, bringing her to the edge three times before sending her soaring. Twice.

The crunch of tires on the gravel yanked him out of the memory. He glanced over to see a car pulling in and parking.

Tim exited from the driver's side. "I tried to call, but no one answered."

"We were . . . busy."

"Before I come closer I should ask if you still plan on beating the fuck out of me."

"Not unless you plan on putting your hands on her."

"Nope." Tim held out a beer. "Peace offering?"

"Sure."

Tim plopped down beside him with a beer of his own, acting like he wanted to talk.

What the fuck? Deacon wasn't a talking kind of guy. Maybe he should've just beaten on him.

"So you threaten every guy who looks at Molly?"

"Pretty much."

"Women eat that stuff up, don't they?"

Deacon looked at him with complete confusion. "Not Molly. She said it'd serve me right to choke on my own machismo."

Tim laughed. "Sounds like her. Look, Molly and I go way back. It's obvious that you care about her. I care about her too."

He nearly crushed the beer bottle in his fist.

"But I don't care about her in the same way you do." Tim swigged his beer. "I'm not a threat to your relationship with her, Deacon."

"You hugging her, kissing her, fucking *touching* her . . . I should ignore that shit?" He shook his head. "Not gonna fly with me, dude. I'll always see that as a threat."

"While I'm happy that my affection for her came across to you that way, I need to clarify why that was my intent."

Fucking guy talked in circles. Why couldn't he just say what he meant?

"I'm gay."

Okay. No circles there. Deacon looked at him. "Pardon?"

"I'm gay. Molly has known that since seventh grade, when I figured it out. No one else knows. At least not in this ass-backward town."

"Your parents don't know?"

Tim shook his head. "My folks are good people who live by the good book. They're happy. Coming out to them would serve no purpose. It's not because I'm ashamed. It's not like I lie to them. We simply don't talk about it, because we don't talk about anything real. From the time I realized girl parts didn't interest me like boy parts did, I knew I'd leave here and never come back."

While Deacon should've been relieved, he wasn't. He was pissed. Maybe more so than before. "So you're just another person in her life who uses her? Who doesn't give a damn about her beyond what she can do for you? That's bullshit."

"You're right. It is."

"You're just like her cousins."

Tim scowled. "No, I'm not. I came here because I assumed no one would have Molly's back and she'd be dealing with those nasty bitches alone." He sent Deacon a sideways glance. "I'm happy to be wrong about that."

"That's the only reason you're here?"

"No." He shoved a hand through his hair. "I'm a selfish prick, okay? This was also an excuse to come home and not to have to stay longer than two days."

"That is fucked-up." Deacon sipped his beer. "And I oughta know because I've done the same thing with my family."

Tim laughed. "So I came by tonight to make sure she was all right with you."

"I'll knock your face in the dirt if you think I'd *ever* raise a fucking hand to her," he snarled.

"Whoa. Not what I meant."

"Explain it, then."

"It'll make a big, macho guy like you blush, especially coming from a gay dude."

Deacon snorted. "Unlikely."

"Brother, you ooze sex. From your muscle-bound body, to the raspy southern drawl, to the tats, to your shaved head. The way you looked at Molly earlier . . . Fuck, man. That's what she's always wanted. I hated I couldn't be the one to give it to her." He paused. "See. Molly and I were each other's firsts."

Deacon's head whipped around. "Are you *trying* to get me to beat the fuck out of you by telling me shit like that?"

"Hell no. You need to understand the context because it'll help you understand her. So few have. We were both virgins our senior year. She wanted to know what the fuss was about. I wanted to know if having sex with a girl would make me think less about having sex with guys."

"You were a fucking dog," Deacon scoffed. "You just wanted to nail her."

"No. We both wanted to be with someone we trusted. We did the deed. What stuck in my mind afterward was hearing Molly question whether passion was real."

That broke his fucking heart.

"Like I said, I couldn't give her that. I blamed her unrealistic expectations on the romance novels she devoured. She argued that *Pride and Prejudice,* and *Outlander,* and *The Thorn Birds* gave her hope for an epic love story of her own someday."

As much as Deacon wanted to be the guy who could give that to her . . . what if he couldn't?

Footfalls falling fast on gravel echoed to them.

Tim stood and stepped over the wall. "You don't need to run interference, Molly. We're fine."

Deacon rolled to his feet. "You get some rest?"

"Barely." Molly stepped into Tim's arms and hugged him. "I wish we could've spent more time together."

Even when Deacon knew there wasn't anything but history and friendship between them, he couldn't watch their casual affection. He stepped over the wall and headed back to the room.

As soon as Molly returned, Deacon pressed her against the door, pinning her arms above her head.

"Again?" she murmured.

"Can't get enough of you, babe." He lowered his mouth, teasing her lips with little bites and nibbles. Slowly sweeping his tongue across the fleshy inside of her bottom lip.

She heaved an impatient sigh, which he swallowed in a deep, wet kiss. He wouldn't speed up even when she made a soft whimper.

When he'd had a thorough taste of her, he sighed. "We have to go back tomorrow."

"I know."

"Things have changed between us."

"I know that too." She wiggled, forcing him to release her arms. "What's going on?"

"I need to know that you can handle it," he said softly.

"Handle what?"

"Me being completely obsessive when it comes to you." Since he'd never felt this way, he knew he was about to tell it to her all wrong, but he couldn't keep his mouth shut and just let it ride. "Maddox told me I have two speeds. Full throttle and dead stop. Which do you think applies to you now that we're fucking?"

"Hearing the word *obsessive* is an automatic freak-out for me."

Deacon wasn't sure if anger or fear flared in her eyes.

"By obsessive do you mean you'll need to know where I am at all times?" she continued. "You'll get irrationally pissed off if I don't answer my cell phone within a few minutes of you calling? You'll expect me to spend every second of my free time with you? You won't let me make a decision about anything without your input? Will you dictate my clothing styles? If we're out at a bar, you'll blame *me* if guys hit on me? You'll keep me away from my friends?"

"Not that kind of obsessive, Molly." He stepped away from her, hating how bad he sucked at this stuff. "Fuck. Never mind." Then he turned around.

Wrapping her arms around his waist, she pulled him to a stop. Then she ducked under his arms and got right in his face. "Remember when you told me I had to stay and fight with you? I'm telling you, mister"—she drilled her index finger into his chest— "the same rule applies. You've pushed me not to hide my body from you. You don't get to hide your emotions."

"This isn't about my fucking emotions." He crowded her until her back hit the wall again. Then he flattened his palm at the hollow of her throat and curled his hand around her neck, not surprised to feel how fast her pulse leapt. "This is about the beast you bring out in me."

That startled her. "Wait. We're talking about sex?"

"Yes, we're talking about sex, goddammit. I've already had you three times today. And all I can think about is shoving you to the floor and fucking you until you scream my name. As soon as I finish, I want to bury myself inside you again. I'm that obsessed with fucking you."

"Deacon. Honey—"

"Don't try to placate me. You saw how crazy I got when I thought Tim wanted what was mine. Turned me into a beast."

She rolled her eyes.

His big goddamn confession and she rolled her motherfucking eyes at him.

"You're a fighter. Of course you're a beast."

"That's not what I—"

"Let. Me. Finish. You're a beast in the ring. Did you really think I expected you to be any different in bed? You are powerful, skilled, and focused in every single aspect of your life. A force unlike anything I've experienced. I like that about you, Deacon. Why wouldn't you think I'd be just as sexually obsessed with you as you are with me? Have I said no when you've touched me?"

"Not yet."

"Oh. So you think I'll get tired of having the hottest man I've ever met touching me and getting to touch him back whenever I want? I'll get bored with multiple orgasms?"

"Smart-ass."

"Only because you, Deacon McConnell, are a dumb-ass." She scraped her fingers over the scruff on his cheek. "If it gets to be too much, I'll tell you. I don't want you to keep that beast side of you leashed. I'm not breakable."

The challenge in her eyes made his dick stir. "Good." Deacon slid his hand down from her neck. "Remember you said that."

CHAPTER TWELVE

"YOU sure you don't wanna drive by the house?"

"No."

"I don't need to ask if you wanna say goodbye to your cousins and your uncle. But should we stop and get food?"

Molly shook her head. "Not here. I just want to go. Put this behind me."

Deacon gathered her in his arms and kissed her temple. "I understand. But, babe, I want you to be sure. Regrets suck."

She sagged into him. She never would've attributed intuitive and sweet to Deacon, but the more time she spent with him, the more she realized he kept so much of his true self hidden from the world. And little by little, he was letting her in to the part of him that no one else got to see.

So how long do you think you can keep this relationship just sexual?

"No regrets. Let's hit the road." She handed him the car keys without him having to ask.

Deacon slipped on his sexy, mysterious shades and took the wheel.

She'd managed to nap for the first hour, lulled to sleep by the perfect temperature in the car and Deacon's gentle stroking on her bare leg.

After a quick stop for fast food and a bathroom break, they were back on the road. Deacon was the perfect road-trip partner. He didn't listen to the radio. He didn't blather on endlessly. He didn't snack on sunflower seeds. He remained still and alert as they cruised across Nebraska.

Molly kicked her shoes off and grabbed her e-reader from the backseat. Within a few minutes, she became engrossed in the story. The next time she glanced at the clock, she realized almost two hours had passed.

Deacon looked at her. "Good book?"

"Yeah. Sorry I'm not great company. I tend to get lost when I read."

He picked up her hand and rubbed his callused thumb across her knuckles. "I'm not much of a reader."

"You play video games?"

"Some."

"What do you like to do in your off-hours? Now that you're no longer hitting strip clubs."

"Hilarious, babe. It seems I don't have many off-hours."

Molly turned in her seat. "Do you do that on purpose?"

"What?"

"Pack your free time with MMA or martial arts stuff so you don't have to figure out a hobby?"

"I ain't exactly the hobby type."

"Because you turned your hobby into your job?"

It took him a few moments to answer. "Yeah, I guess. Now I'm getting paid to fight."

Ask me my hobbies, Deacon. This is what people in a relationship do.

"What kind of books do you read?"

"Promise not to laugh?"

"Nope."

She laughed. "I read romance."

His lips twitched. "I knew that."

"How?" Had he noticed the books in her living room?

"Tim told me. Pissed me off that he knew your favorite books. But I saw you finger yourself while reading a dirty one, so I win." He gave her a full-out bad boy grin.

Her cheeks heated. "I read more than just erotic romance. I like historical, paranormal, and suspense."

"What makes a book erotic?"

"More sex scenes. Erotic novels also have some kink, which is, ah . . . fun to read about."

He snagged his water bottle from the cup holder. "What kind of kink?"

"Spanking. Multiple partners. Bondage." Molly sent him a sideways glance. "I've wanted to ask Amery about the rope stuff she and Ronin do, but I always chicken out."

Deacon choked on his drink. "Jesus, Molly. Warn a guy first."

"So what do you know about that?"

"It's not my place to say. So if you wanna know more, ask Amery."

"Fine." She swiped her finger across the screen and the text reappeared.

She'd finished maybe a page when Deacon spoke again.

"Why do you like erotic books?"

"The level of intensity between the hero and heroine always seems . . . higher. They express themselves to each other through sex."

"What else?"

Pushy much? "Never mind."

"Oh, no, darlin'. You don't get to admit you like them kinda books and then act pissy because I wanna know *why* you like them."

"Because they make me hot, okay? The only place I'll ever get

to experience that kinkier stuff is through the pages of a book."
Embarrassed by that admission, she directed her attention out the
window.

Deacon's hand landed on the back of her head. "Look at me."

She shook her head.

"Please."

"No. Keep your damn eyes on the road, Deacon."

He slowed down and pulled onto the shoulder. After putting
the car in park, he curled his hand below her jaw and turned her
head, forcing her to meet his gaze.

He'd shoved his sunglasses on top of his head, and those icy
eyes were scary as hell.

"Understand this. I'm not making fun of you for what you're
reading."

"You're not?"

"No." He gave her a look she couldn't decipher.

"Then what?"

"Read it to me."

When her jaw fell open in shock, he took advantage and kissed
her. A sweet, coaxing kiss, with teasing flicks of his tongue and the
hot and sexy glide of his wet lips across hers.

Against her mouth, he murmured, "I wanna hear what gets
you hot."

That caused her belly to swoop. "You're serious. You want me
to read to you."

"Yeah, babe, I do." Another soft brush of his lips across hers.
"And not just the dirty parts. But you could mark the kinky spots
and we could try them out later."

Molly laughed.

He settled himself in his seat again and put the car in motion.

Since Molly was halfway through her current book, she picked
an erotic contemporary she hadn't started yet. "You ready?"

"Yeah. What's the title?"

"*Teacher's Pet* by Cherry Starr." She flipped her e-reader around. "The cool thing? Hardwick Designs did the exclusive book cover."

Deacon squinted at it. "Whoa. Is that chick wearing a . . . collar?"

"Yes. It was fun watching Amery direct this couple as she maneuvered them around."

"Now I really wanna hear you read this."

Molly jumped right in. She didn't attempt to lower her voice to portray the male character or force an accent for the foreign characters. This was one of the first times she appreciated the slow buildup to the first sex scene.

Every once in a while she'd glance over at Deacon at a funny part and it gave her a feeling of relief to see his lips curled into a smile.

When she reached the scene where the heroine sees the hero naked for the first time, she started to skim it to gauge the level of heat.

Deacon's hand squeezed her knee. "No fair reading ahead."

"I'm not. I just . . ." *Don't know how I'll get through this, and it's not even a full-blown sex scene.*

"You're blushing, which means it's gotta be good. Read," he commanded.

Molly sipped her water and cleared her throat.

> *I shouldn't have walked into his bedroom without knocking. I know that now. But in my own defense, I was thinking of ten other things. I had my hand on the door handle and stepped into the room before the words* knock-knock *occurred to me.*
>
> *Colin had his broad back to me. His muscles stretched and rippled with every movement of his arm. I saw droplets of water glistening across his shoulders and, oh, how I thirsted.*
>
> *I clenched my hands into fists and let my eyes wander down*

his spine. The golden hue of his skin ended abruptly at his waistline, making his pale buttocks stand out even more. I bit back a moan at seeing the firm, round globes. I'd had my hands in the pockets of his jeans, so I'd felt the masculine curve and hardness once before. My fingers clenched and released, as if they had a mind of their own—a mind to grab a handful of that tight white ass and hold on.

I gave his legs a cursory glance, then let my gaze travel back up his body, savoring every inch. But my visual appreciation didn't get any farther than his lower half because I realized his right arm was still moving in front of his body, his well-defined triceps straining and bunching with the movement.

Then Colin's head fell back. Those dark curls covered the nape of his neck as he expelled a loud, "Fuck."

I gasped because I figured out what he was doing.

He confirmed my suspicions when he spun to face me and I saw his fist wrapped around his cock. "Caitlin? Why the bloody hell are you in my room?"

"I don't know." My feet carried me forward even when I knew I should've stayed put. "I'm sorry I barged in and interrupted—"

"Me jerkin' the gherkin?" he said in that deep, menacing tone.

"It's not a gherkin, from where I'm standing," I replied without thinking.

Then his entire countenance changed. "Like what ya see, do you, lass?"

I couldn't respond. The lust I'd felt had somehow seized my vocal cords and I could only nod.

"Jesus, Mary, and Joseph. Can ya get your eyes off my junk?"

I continued to move forward.

Colin breathed heavily, although he'd stopped sliding his hand up and down his rigid shaft.

Once I was close enough to fill my lungs with his scent and feel the heat from his naked body, I stopped. My hands definitely had a mind of their own and landed on Colin's thickly furred chest.

With his free hand, he tipped my head back and got nose to nose with me. "Do ya mean to make me mad with wanting you?"

"I'm not the one who said no, Colin."

"Because I'm trying to protect you!"

"From what? From you?" My eyes couldn't stay in one place long. I drank in every feature of his face. The stormy gray eyes were brimming with lust. His lips had lost the pinched look and were parted from his rapid breaths. Color rode high on his cheekbones. His dark hair, nearly black, was slicked back and wet from his shower.

"Aye, from me, dammit." Then his mouth crashed down on mine and he finished the kiss he'd backed away from earlier. A growing hunger consumed him, as it did me when he gave in to it.

Colin kissed me with the finesse of a man who understood kissing was an art, a journey of itself, not just a prelude to full-body contact and sliding part A into slot B.

That kiss destroyed me piece by piece even as it built me up brick by brick. I became stronger the longer his mouth remained on mine. I knew this was right between us. Damn the age difference. Damn the supposed impropriety between teacher and student. Damn everything but this passion that was the only truth between us.

Colin's lips—soft and warm and damp—glided across my cheek to my ear. He tried to hide his labored breathing from me, and for that reason it burrowed into the very heart of me.

"Do you know how bloody hard it was to push you away, Caitlin?" He nuzzled the hollow beneath my ear. "When I

*really wanted to push you onto the bed and do every dirty thing
I've been fantasizing about for weeks?"*

"I'm not busy right now," I breathed.

*A small chuckle broke free and vibrated against my skin.
"So why do I feel dirtier that you caught me rubbing one out
than I did when thinking about your hand on my cock?"*

*"You think too much," I murmured back. "You can have
the reality instead of a fantasy." I arched as he placed sucking
kisses from beneath my earlobe down the column of my neck.
"You know you want to push me to my knees. So do it."*

*I waited, expecting he'd say no and act as if he knew what
I needed rather than what I wanted. So I braced myself for his
rejection.*

*I should've braced myself for his strong grip on my shoulders
as he forced me to kneel.*

Molly's cheeks were warm. Her eyes burned hot. Her voice
had turned scratchy, and she paused to take a drink. Then she felt
Deacon's eyes on her. "What?"

"Keep goin'. That's fucking hot."

She swigged her water again before she read on.

*A sense of power rolled through me as my lips met the wet
tip of his cock. I barely had time to ready myself before his big
hands cradled my head and he guided his cock into my mouth,
which was already wet with anticipation.*

*The musky taste of him was as potent as the man himself.
I flattened my palms on his upper thighs and squeezed the muscles as I pulled him deeper into my mouth. I'd make this blow
job the best he'd ever had or choke trying. His girth stretched my
lips, and the weight of his thick shaft rested heavily on my
tongue. My throat felt overly stuffed and my gag reflex kicked
in, but I pushed past that and began to work him.*

Colin spewed a bunch of curses and Gaelic words, but I had drifted into that state where seeing to his pleasure increased mine.

I slid my hands around to grip his ass. To encourage him to plunge into my mouth without holding back. Needing him to see me differently—not as his graduate assistant, but as his sexual equal. Wanting him to understand that as his lover, I'd deny him nothing. Silently promising him that fulfilling his kinkiest, dirtiest desires, anytime, anyplace was my ultimate fantasy.

And I sensed when that shift occurred. His hands were rougher, as were the sounds working out from deep inside him. I knew he wouldn't hold back. There'd be no warning when he started to come in my mouth. He'd take his pleasure in the manner I'd offered—with no restrictions.

That's when I drifted into the sexual high I'd experienced only once before.

Colin rammed into my mouth and stopped.

I started to swallow immediately after that first spurt slid down the back of my throat. The muscles contracted around the head of his cock, and he groaned and twitched until I'd milked every drop.

He threw his hand against the wall to keep himself upright, his lungs heaving and his body damp with sweat.

There was the dirty, sexy man I wanted—not the staid professor.

That was as good a place to end as any.

Deacon didn't say a word. With his sunglasses on, she couldn't read his eyes.

She refused to look at his crotch to see if the scene had affected him.

Without taking his eyes off the road, Deacon asked, "Did that scene get you hot?"

"A little. Did it do anything for you?"

"I'm hard as a fucking barbell."

Then Molly did sneak a peek at his groin. She clearly saw the outline of his cock off to the left side of his camo shorts.

"When you read stuff like that, do you put yourself in the story?"

"Like I was Caitlin, on my knees, gobbling up Colin's cock?"

Deacon groaned. "Gobbling? Jesus, babe."

She laughed—a trifle nervously. "Do you think it was easy for me to read that to you?"

"Answer the question."

Molly tried to find the right phrasing. "It wasn't me in the story. It's more like I'm a voyeur—which is a kink you're very familiar with."

He snorted.

"Your turn. While you were listening, did you—"

"Imagine it was your hands touching me, your lips on mine, my cock plunging into your mouth? You're goddamn right it was you and me."

"Why?"

"Because it was like that for us in the beginning. I wanted you like fucking crazy but had convinced myself I couldn't have you and I had to stay away from you."

Molly set her hand on his forearm and followed the dips and grooves of his muscles with the tips of her fingers. She feathered her thumb over the crease in his elbow and continued her exploration of his upper arm, stopping to map the deep cuts of his biceps and trace the ripped edges of his triceps. "You have me now, Deacon. So what are you gonna do with me?"

He turned and looked at her over the tops of his sunglasses. Twin blue flames of pure desire shone in his eyes. "Show you that real passion"—he pointed to her e-reader—"is way better than what's written on the pages of a book."

Holy crap.

"Any fantasy you got? I'll make a reality."

Holy, *holy* crap.

"You down with that, babe?"

Internally, she'd busted into the *Yay me!* happy dance. Outwardly, she blushed from the roots of her hair to her toenails. Rather than sit there in shock like a goof, she unbuckled her seat belt and leaned closer. She kissed a path up his jawline to his ear, loving the rough feel of his stubble on her lips. "Very down with that. In fact, I could be very *down* with a lot of things right now."

"Buckle up," Deacon warned. "The first time your mouth is gobbling down my cock won't be in a moving car."

Not even his use of *gobbling* softened the sting.

After she'd buckled up, Deacon said, "While we're on the subject—"

"Is this where you tell me you don't like blow jobs?" she retorted.

He snatched her hand and pressed it on the bulge straining against his zipper. "Does that *feel* like I'd hate the idea of my dick buried in your mouth?"

"No." Molly removed her hand and blew out a frustrated breath. "Sorry. It's the first time a man has offered to fulfill all my sexual fantasies. I got excited and wanted to reciprocate."

"Killing me here, woman."

"What can I say? I've always been a giver."

That earned her a smile.

"As soon as we're outta this car, I'm gonna be on you. Now, get back to the book."

She murmured, "Yes, sir."

CHAPTER THIRTEEN

DEACON unloaded everything—including his own luggage since he planned on spending the night with her—from Molly's car onto the sidewalk in front of her apartment building. Then he curled his hand around the back of her neck and brought them face-to-face.

"Don't even think about hauling all this shit upstairs by yourself, understand?"

Molly briefly berated herself for liking his bossy behavior before she let it go. She flattened her palm on his chest. "Will you punish me if I disobey you?"

Those pale blue eyes flared with heat.

Intrigued by his response, she closed the distance between their mouths. Keeping their eyes locked, she brushed her lips across his. "Will you spank me? Or tie me up? Like Colin did to Caitlin?"

"Maybe I'll not touch you at all."

She couldn't help but laugh.

Deacon's lips twitched. "Yeah, pretty much an idle threat, because you know I can't keep my hands off you, babe." He kissed her hard and slapped her ass. "But I'm not kiddin' about you taking that stuff up without my help."

"Gotcha."

Immediately after Deacon turned the corner toward the parking area, the front door to the apartment complex opened and Molly's friend Nina walked out.

Nina seemed startled to see her. "Hey." She eyed the pile of luggage. "Going somewhere fun, I hope?"

"No. Just getting back from my grandma's funeral."

She crossed over and hugged Molly. "Damn. I'm sorry."

"It wasn't . . . unexpected, I guess."

"Still. It's gotta be hard."

Molly didn't know what to say to that. She'd better have a stock answer ready, since Nina likely wouldn't be the only one to express concern for her mental well-being.

"Anyway. It's good to see you."

"You're on your way to work?" Nina wore bright blue scrubs with images of grumpy cats.

"Yeah, but I can take a minute and help you carry this stuff up to your apartment."

"Thanks, but my boyfriend is parking the car. He'll help me."

Nina smiled. "Boyfriend, huh? Is that why I haven't seen much of you?"

"Partially. It's also been crazy at work."

"I feel you there. But I miss hanging out with you. We always managed to find trouble somewhere."

"That we did. So what about you? How's the hospital?"

"The ER is always busy. I've been working tons of OT since we're short staffed."

"Any new guys in Nina's love life?"

Nina shook her head. "All the men I've run into lately are douche nozzles. Even a fast fuck hasn't been worth the hassle." She sucked in a quick breath. "But I'd make an exception for the badass dude strolling up the sidewalk."

"Nina—"

"Don't be scared, but there is an extremely dangerous-looking hottie moving toward us."

Before Molly could respond, Deacon's hands landed on her hips and he planted a hot kiss on the side of her neck. "Hey, babe."

Deacon's show of possession thrilled her to her toes.

"Nina, this is my boyfriend, Deacon. Deacon, this is my next-door neighbor, Nina."

"It's great to meet you," Nina said with a grin. "You have excellent taste in girlfriends."

"That I do."

Nina's gaze kept zooming between them. "Well, I hope we can catch up soon, Molly."

"We will. I promise."

As they watched her walk away, Deacon put his mouth on Molly's ear. "I hope her bedroom wall isn't on the other side of yours."

"Plan on banging my headboard loud enough that it'll scare the neighbors?"

"Oh yeah." His breath teased her ear, sending chills down the right side of her body. He released her and loaded himself up like a pack mule, leaving Molly with just her roller bag.

"Show-off."

Molly was surprised Mr. Cardio didn't insist they hoof it up the three flights of stairs but allowed them to take the elevator. Her apartment complex tended to be quiet since the majority of the residents were students. But tonight the silence felt stifling, as if the floor were deserted. And it didn't help that Deacon was breathing down her neck as she cranked her keys into the door locks. "Stop crowding me."

"I haven't begun to crowd you." Deacon used his teeth on the section of skin where her shoulder flowed into her neck. "I've had a hard-on since you started reading that book. Imagining all the ways I wanna do you." He flicked his tongue over the cord straining in her neck. "Fuck, woman. Hurry up."

Click. The last lock tumbled.

After she'd opened the door, she reached back for the handle of her roller bag. Her hand connected with the hardness between Deacon's legs, and he hissed.

Molly spun around. "Sorry."

"Inside."

She snagged the handle and had made it into the living room when she heard the door slam, followed by a series of thumps.

Then Deacon was on her. His mouth hungry. His hands greedy as he pulled her tank top over her head.

Molly yanked on his skintight shirt, equally eager to strip him. After he ditched his shirt, his mouth was back on hers, his fingers tugging to unhook her bra as he backed her down the hallway toward her bedroom.

Her heart beat like mad. Her thoughts went fuzzy, the word *more* repeated in her head—even her blood began to thrum with a tribal cadence. Her near nakedness only increased the burning need to feel his skin gliding against hers.

The instant he freed her breasts, his hands were squeezing and caressing. Deacon's fingers followed the curve of her belly, slipping beneath the elastic waistband of her capris, tugging the material—and her underwear—down her hips.

Panting, Molly stopped to kick her bottoms away and flattened her palms on Deacon's bare chest, pushing him against the wall.

"Gimme that mouth."

Deacon's fevered kiss fueled her raging need. She fumbled with the button on his camo shorts and attacked his zipper. One quick tug and his shorts hit the floor. When she realized he'd gone commando, she ripped her mouth free and dropped to her knees. She had her lips around the wet tip of his cock and was sucking his shaft into her mouth before he knew what hit him.

"Jesus!"

She got only two bobs of her head in before Deacon hauled her back to her feet.

He wrapped one hand beneath her jaw to keep her from talking. "I'm too far gone to handle a blow job. I need to fuck you first." Then his mouth was on hers again, his voracious kiss laced with sweet desperation.

Molly moved Deacon's other hand from where he'd clamped it on her ass and pushed it between her thighs.

He groaned in her mouth.

Her smile ended the kiss.

"Bed. Now." He bent down and snagged a condom out of his back pocket. Then, amid soft kisses on her neck and collarbone, he propelled her backward into her bedroom.

The sheets and pillows were still rumpled from the night she'd left for Nebraska. The night Deacon had been here watching her. It seemed like ages ago.

Deacon flung the covers aside and rolled on the condom.

The man wasn't messing around.

Molly stretched out on the mattress, her fingertips grazing the headboard, every muscle and tendon vibrating with anticipation.

Crawling between her legs, he leveled his body on hers. He didn't ask if she was ready. He guided himself inside her with a slow glide. "You're wet for me, babe."

She twined her arms around his neck. "You're hard for me, babe."

He laughed. Then he started to move, his eyes intent on hers. "Every time is different with you. But every time is good."

"This is my favorite." Molly ran her fingers down his spine. "Your weight on me. And I can touch you and taste you."

Deacon slanted his lips over her and started with the drugging kisses that matched the slow and steady rhythm of his thrusts.

This was perfect.

He was perfect.

No one else saw him this way. She'd never expected he could be so loving—and still be so . . . Deacon. While they'd fucked half a dozen times in the motel room, this was different.

"Wrap your legs around me," he urged against her mouth.

As soon as she'd locked her ankles over his thighs, Deacon shifted his weight, allowing his mouth to reach her breasts. The angle change put almost constant pressure on her clit. By the sixth grinding thrust, she felt that warning tingle.

"I'm not gonna last if you keep doing that, Deacon."

He lifted his head from her chest to say, "Why do you think I'm doin' it?"

"You're already close?"

"Been thinking about doin' you for hours, so yeah." He pressed a kiss in her cleavage. "Come for me. I wanna watch."

Before she could ask him to ramp it up, he did. She slipped her hands down his back, reveling in his shudder when she dug her nails into his tight butt cheeks. "Like that. Don't stop." When his cock connected with her G-spot, she flattened her palms and held him there while he continued to pump his hips.

The tiny warning throb became a full-blown orgasm; her pussy tightened, her clit spasmed, and her nipples went diamond hard against Deacon's chest.

Toward the end, when she bowed upward to prolong the mind-blowing sensations, Deacon opened his mouth over her throat and sank his teeth in before he sucked softly on her skin.

That set her off again.

By the time her sanity returned, Deacon had rested his full weight on her as he buried his face in her hair.

They stayed like that, catching their breath, Molly's hands running over his head, neck, and back. Finally, she murmured, "Deacon, you have to move so I can get my pajamas on."

"No."

"No?"

"You'll sleep naked with me."

She bristled. "You're a little bossy in my bed, aren't you?"

"Warned ya, babe. I'm bossy in *any* bed."

"But I don't like to sleep in the nude."

"If you get cold, I'll warm you up."

More like he'd get her so hot the mattress might combust.

He did move to ditch the condom. When he returned, his face immediately went to her chest. He nuzzled the swell of her left breast and tenderly caressed the same spot on her right breast. "You don't wanna wake up to me doin' this to you?" He followed the curve of her flesh to her nipple, softly brushing his warm lips over the puckered tip.

She sighed and arched into him.

The reverence in his attention thrilled her. She'd never had a boyfriend who constantly had to have his hands on her the way Deacon did.

Had it been like this for all the women he'd been with?

"Ask me."

That startled her. "What?"

"Something's on your mind. Ask me."

Molly let her palm drift over the top of his perfect head. "I like how you're always touching me."

"But?"

"No buts." She lazily swept her knuckles down the stubble on his jaw. "I just wondered if you've been touchy-feely with your other girlfriends."

Deacon froze.

So did she, afraid he'd be angered by the question and revert to his *what—and who—came before doesn't matter* answer.

"I'll answer that if you tell me how many boyfriends you've had, including Tim, who was all too fucking happy to share that he'd popped your cherry."

Tim, you jackass. "I didn't date Tim. In fact, I had zero dates in high school. I dated a few guys in college. I didn't have sex with all of them. None were ever serious. I hit a boyfriend dry spell after I moved to Denver. So fewer than six boyfriends total." She paused. "Wait—am I supposed to include one-night hookups in that?"

"Jesus. No." He propped himself up on one elbow and toyed with a section of her hair. "Two things. First, I wanted to ask you out for a long damn time before I actually did."

"What stopped you?"

Deacon's eyes searched hers. "At first? You."

"Me? Yeah, sure. I was so freakin' intimidating in all my timid, doughy, out-of-shape glory."

"Molly, you started taking self-defense classes because you'd been attacked," he said gently. "You'd cringe whenever one of the instructors you didn't know got close to you. Including me."

Embarrassment heated her face. "I don't remember doing that." Without downplaying the assault, she knew the random mugging had given her the wake-up call she'd needed to change all aspects of her life. But it made sense now when she'd dated Sandan Zach that he'd insisted on taking the physical side at a snail's pace.

"The day I walked into my kickboxing classes and saw you in the back row? You might've been scared shitless, but you were there. After a few weeks, I'd stand outside the room before class and listen to you. Christ, woman. You had this genuine happy laugh that just . . . got to me. As the weeks went on, your determination told me a lot about the kind of person you are."

"The jerky way you acted to me in class should've told you that I didn't like the kind of person you are."

Deacon grinned. "I know. Makes me a pervert, but when you started sassing back? That's when I knew—"

"That you and me were gonna happen?" she teased.

"Smart-ass."

"You knew what?"

"That you weren't scared of me." He continued to play with a long curl of hair. "A lot of women are."

Oh, you sweet, tough man. She had to ignore his show of vulnerability and keep things light or he'd close right back up. "And yet you didn't ask me out."

"That's the second thing." Those blue eyes shone in the dark. "I didn't know how to ask. And before you laugh or get sarcastic, you should know that I don't date."

"Ever?"

"Ever. I haven't asked a girl—woman—out since I was fifteen." Deacon watched his finger twirling that section of hair. "I haven't had a girlfriend since high school, Molly. I've been with women, but never for more than sex, and never for more than one night."

Molly could've asked him why, but she suspected he'd hedge. She slanted her mouth over his for a smacking kiss. "So I'm special? Awesome. I am so glad you figured out a way to *tell* me we were going out. Because, babe, you didn't *ask*." She smooched him again. "Even if it did take you for-freakin'-ever."

His sheepish smile . . . just got to her.

"So the long answer to your 'sleep naked' question is yes. I'll crash in the raw if you'll tone down your seductive mojo and let us both actually get some sleep."

"I'll try, but no guarantees." He planted kisses in random spots across her chest. "So the long answer to your 'girlfriend touching' question is no. You're the first and only. Fair warning, babe. If you're nearby, I'm gonna be touching you."

"I can deal with that."

He tucked her body in to his so they touched head to toe.

Normally Molly did a starfish imitation on her mattress, but she much preferred being skin to skin with a hard-bodied man.

She'd drifted into that floaty pre-sleep place when Deacon murmured, "You sure you're tired?"

"You're not?"

"I'm wide-awake."

"Do you want to watch TV or something?"

She felt him grin against the top of her head. "I was thinking you could read me a bedtime story."

That yanked her out of her sleepy state. Self-professed non-reader Deacon wanted her to read to him because he was interested in the story? Not just because he'd been bored during the drive?

How freakin' awesome. She'd always envied couples who read together. As far as she was concerned, reading to him counted.

"Well, we did leave Colin and Caitlin hanging." She threw back the covers. "I'll grab my e-reader."

CHAPTER FOURTEEN

DEACON walked into the training room on Saturday morning ready to do battle.

Maddox went back to working with Ivan after pointing to the jump ropes.

So that's how it's gonna be.

He warmed up first with a few stretches, push-ups, pull-ups, frogs, and gator rolls. Then he snagged a jump rope and hit it.

Most of the time when Deacon was training he could block out everything and focus on form. But today his thoughts kept straying to Micah Courey. If he'd been training here all week. If Ronin had made a decision on adding him to the roster. If any of this training mattered. If he'd ever get past being a contender to being a champion.

The years he'd spent in the underground fighting scene, the unrecognized championships hadn't made him complacent. He'd always wanted more. Ronin had recognized that from the first time they'd met.

That'd been an eye-opener. Deacon had been undefeated for two years. He'd craved a challenge to the point he'd started to travel to other cities to fight. He hadn't found a worthy opponent in Albuquerque, Santa Fe, Tulsa, or Oklahoma City. But when he showed up in Pueblo, Colorado, that's where he'd learned the difference—the hard way—of fighting a true master.

Of course, at the time—five years ago—he hadn't known Ronin Black held a seventh-degree black belt in jujitsu—a black belt designation was the only requirement to fight. As Deacon had climbed into the ring, he'd been less than impressed by this Ronin guy. Although they were in the same weight class, Ronin wasn't bulked up—his physique ran more toward lean. That right there should've set off Deacon's warning bells. But he'd dismissed it.

Mistake.

Big mistake.

Ronin had toyed with him the first two rounds. Testing him. He'd even let Deacon get in a couple of body shots with both his kicks and his fists.

But when the third round started, Ronin brutalized him for an eternity—he'd later learned it'd been only two minutes—before he knocked him out.

When Deacon had come to, his fury had overtaken his embarrassment. And that fury hadn't lessened when Ronin had stuck around to talk to him after the match. Ronin's Zen-like attitude and watchful eyes seemed to bore into Deacon's soul. That put him on edge and pissed him the fuck off. He'd been a total dick to Ronin. Why the man had stuck around still boggled Deacon's mind.

Now Deacon was grateful that the great man had seen something in him that he hadn't seen in himself.

Ronin had shown up in the hotel bar. After a couple glasses of whiskey, they'd both loosened up. Deacon had finally found a kindred spirit in Ronin—a man who understood the addictive side of fighting. No judgment, no excuses, just the need for violence. And the sometimes shameful feelings that accompanied that near-obsessive need to prove yourself with blood, bruises, and pain.

And so Deacon had found himself opening up to Ronin, telling him some of the ugly details of his life that'd prompted him to leave everything behind and start over. In turn, Ronin had shared his struggles with his family, the dojo, and how his disillusionment had sent him back into the world of underground fighting.

Everyone always talked about life-changing events, but Deacon hadn't put any stock in those types of claims . . . until he'd met Ronin Black. Within a month of that meeting, Deacon had relocated to Denver. If he passed the six-month probation time, he'd become a jujitsu instructor at Black Arts while keeping up his MMA training. In Ronin keeping Deacon's secrets about his past, Ronin had entrusted Deacon to keep his secrets too.

"McConnell!"

Deacon let the jump rope fall to the floor. He reached for the towel on the bench to mop his face before he turned around and said, "What?" to Maddox.

"You warmed up enough to spar?"

"With you? Bring it."

Maddox shook his head.

That's when Deacon noticed the Black Arts MMA fighters—Ivan and Sergei—as well as Black Arts instructors Fisher, Blue, Ronin, and Knox had gathered around. He was about to toss off a snarky comment about not needing a formal welcome back, when he saw a guy in a hoodie, arms crossed, waiting beside the ring.

Micah Courey.

"Is he my new sparring partner?" he asked Maddox. "Or am I his?"

Deacon glanced at Knox—who looked very pissed off. Knox opened his mouth, but Ronin's headshake had him snapping his mouth shut.

What the hell?

"Come on. I'll introduce you," Maddox said.

Knox left Ronin's side and stood in front of Deacon. His six-foot-four-inch frame blocked everyone from view. "I had nothing to do with this. And I'm pissed the fuck off about it."

"I can handle myself, Knox."

"I know that. All's I'm saying is you shouldn't have to." Then he walked off.

Maddox got into Deacon's personal space. "Problem?"

"You tell me."

"We'll talk later about the bug that crawled up the former Shihan's ass. Right now come meet Courey."

Rather than follow Maddox, Deacon cut in front of him and reached the hooded figure first and thrust out his hand. "Deacon McConnell."

The guy clasped his hand hard enough to fucking break it. "I know who you are; you know who I am. So let's cut the shit and get to it."

"Deacon, you're up first with the mitts," Maddox said.

Deacon forced himself not to react. He rarely held the mitts; his sparring partner did. After he returned with them, Maddox frowned at him. "What?"

"Headgear too."

"I never wear headgear."

"You've never needed to before now."

Tell him to fuck off.

No. Do what he says and knock that smug motherfucker out when you're throwing punches.

The cooler, revenge-seeking part of his brain prevailed. "Fine. It's buried in my locker." Deacon headed to the corner where the lockers were.

After Maddox had taken over the MMA program, he'd installed private lockers so none of the fighters had to rub elbows with the jujitsu students or instructors in the dojo's locker room unless they wanted to shower. He dug through the bottom of his locker until he found the modified helmet. His extra mouth guard

had gotten caught in the strap, so he took it to the drinking foun-
tain and washed it out before returning to the ring.

Maddox and Courey ended their conversation as soon as they
saw him.

"Work punching only. No lower-body work," Maddox said.

Courey said, "What's the level of practice?"

"Prefight. Don't pull back, but no blows to the head."

"Even if I see a chance for a clean hit?" Courey asked.

Good luck with that, asswipe.

"Deacon? What level are you prepared for?" Maddox asked.

"Any level you think is best, Coach."

Maddox's jaw tightened, and he addressed Micah. "Bump it to
fight level, then."

"No," Ronin interjected from the sidelines. "The last thing
Deacon needs is to pull out of the fight because of a training injury.
Stick with prefight level. If you two get bored, then we'll bump
it up."

Thanks for the vote of confidence, Sensei.

Since he wasn't in gloves, he didn't take off his shoes or his
shirt.

The first thing he noticed about Courey was he didn't bow
when he entered the training ring—a blatant show of disrespect, in
Deacon's opinion, since they were in a martial arts dojo. The second thing he noticed was the man thought he had something to
prove. Courey didn't warm up; he immediately started throwing
speed-punching combinations.

And as the time passed by in a series of jarring thumps, Deacon
saw the benefit in being the former champion's sparring partner.
Within the first fifteen minutes, Deacon had zeroed in on a couple
of weaknesses. He didn't get too cocky about it. The weak spots
might be apparent only because Courey wasn't able to switch it up
with kicks.

For the first time in a long time, Deacon remembered what it was like to be the one with his back to the cage. To be the defender, not the aggressor.

Just when he thought he had Courey's tells figured out, Deacon dropped the mitt to block what he assumed was a rib shot, and Courey landed a right hook to the jaw. A punch hard enough to snap Deacon's head, which sent him careening backward, ass hitting the mat.

His hearing went wonky, but he couldn't be sure if it was from the blow or the headgear blocking normal noise.

Surprisingly, Fisher was the first guy to reach him. Deacon removed the mitts and his headgear and said softly, "He doesn't hit as hard as you, so why am I on my ass?"

Fisher didn't crack a smile. "Because your equilibrium is off due to the head protection. You don't wear it in the ring, so it's stupid for you to train with it." He leaned closer. "And don't get me started on why the fuck you're wearing mitts and being his bitch. Should be the other way around."

One thing Deacon respected about Fisher—the man was loyal to the Black Arts fighters. Even their dustup about Molly taking private lessons from him hadn't damaged their professional working relationship.

Deacon moved his head side to side, trying to work the tension out of his neck. He saw Maddox advising Courey. He saw Ivan and Sergei on the bench. He saw Ronin off to the side, keeping an eye on everyone. Blue had disappeared.

Then Maddox wandered over and crouched next to him. "If you've caught your balance, get back to it. Courey's turn with the mitts."

He wasn't feeling real cooperative, but he forced a cool tone. "Another day."

"Why? You've taken hits harder than that."

"No shit. But I wasn't expecting to get knocked on my ass first thing this morning after being gone from training for six days. I've still got Saturday drills to do. Ito's coming to work throws with me, right?" He paused. "Unless you were planning on having Ito working with Courey. In that case I'll do footwork with Fisher, Sergei, and Ivan."

If the sour look on Maddox's face was any indication, he knew he was fucked. Deacon had covered all his training possibilities for the day—none would be with Courey. "I get that you're pissed off he's here, Deacon, but you're supposed to be learning from him."

"Maybe he'd better learn what Sensei means by *prefight* power level." From the corner of his eye, he saw Ronin walk away.

"I'll give you a pass today, but Courey will be training here off and on over the next few weeks, so get used to the idea you'll be partners."

Fuck that. Maddox could force him to do a lot of things, but being a punching bag for Micah Courey wasn't on the list.

Before Maddox could force the issue, Ivan and Sergei climbed into the ring and stepped between Deacon and their trainer. Maddox took off. Ivan held out his big hand to help Deacon to his feet.

"Thanks, man."

"No problem. You ready to play footsie?"

Deacon snorted. Footsie. Ivan poked at Sergei for his expertise in savate, French foot fighting. Sergei, whose English was minimal, trash-talked Ivan's specialty in sambo, the Russian martial art that was a weird combination of wrestling and judo.

One thing Maddox could be given props for—all of the fighters he'd brought on board had different specialties. "Yeah, I'll see what punch-kick or kick-punch combos Sergei has been working on to trip me up."

"Trip you up. Funny." Ivan translated for Sergei, and he barked out a laugh.

"Hey, where's Blaze?"

"Pulled his calf muscle. Same day you left. Riggins told him to rest it for a week minimum," Fisher said. "He'll be hobbling around for Beck's thing tonight."

"Beck's thing?" Deacon asked.

Ivan shot a quick look over his shoulder. "Birthday thing. Not everyone is invited."

"Aw, but I am?"

Fisher clapped him on the shoulder. "At a strip club. Right up your alley, huh?"

Fuck. It would be, if he hadn't promised Molly he'd steer clear of them.

Sergei frowned and spoke to Ivan. The big Russian shook his head. Deacon made out three words—Dave & Buster's.

While Ivan and Sergei went back and forth, Deacon watched Maddox and Courey confer with Ito, who'd just walked into the training room.

Ivan pinned Fisher with a hard look. "We're going to that game-playing place first, right?"

"Yeah. Why?"

"Sergei's girlfriend forbids him to go to strip clubs."

"And he lets her dictate that to him?" Fisher said. "Lame."

Two weeks ago Deacon would've been railing against that too. But now . . . he wouldn't break his promise to Molly even to save face with the guys.

"Like Sergei said, he'd rather not piss off his girlfriend and get cut off from pussy just to look at some random stripper's tits."

That gave him an out. "That'll work for me too. I'll hang at Dave and Buster's, but then I've got plans with Molly."

Fisher sighed. "Didn't you just spend an entire week with her?"

"Because her grandma died. A funeral ain't exactly fun."

"Guess it's up to me'n Blaze to get Beck his birthday lap dance," Fisher said.

"If you guys go to Jiggles, I'll give you my VIP pass," Deacon offered.

His eyes lit up. "No shit? You da man, bro." He held his fist out for a bump.

Ivan thrust his fist at Fisher and Deacon for a bump. "No woman tells Ivan what to do. I'm in."

Sergei snickered and said something in Russian that caused Ivan to gut punch him.

"If you ladies are done swapping spit," Maddox yelled, "how about you get those lazy asses in gear and get to fucking training."

Deacon picked up his gear. Then he said quietly, "Why isn't Mad invited? He and Beck are always doin' stuff together."

"Knox said Beck and Maddox had words this week and Sensei had to step in," Fisher said.

"Words about what?"

"You, evidently."

"Fucking awesome. Seeing that Courey is still here, I know who won that pissing contest."

Ivan loomed over Deacon. "It's not what you think. Maddox trains you. But Beck has your back. He proved it." Then Ivan walked off.

Weird.

But Deacon didn't have time to dissect what that meant because he spent the next four hours sweating his ass off and working his muscles to the point of exhaustion.

ABOUT an hour after he'd returned home, his phone rang.

Deacon debated ignoring it—but he pushed ANSWER. "Hey, Dad. What's up?"

"Nothing earth-shattering," he drawled in his thick Texas accent. "Just hadn't heard from you in a while and I thought I'd see what's new. How's training?"

He slumped back into his recliner. He could handle this conversation. It was the other one his dad regularly brought up that set him on edge. "It's going good. Sometimes Maddox drives me so hard I wish he were my sparring partner so I could knock him the motherfuck out. Then, after training ends, we have a rational discussion about my progress or setbacks."

His dad chuckled. "Coaches like that are rare, son."

"I know."

"When's your next fight?"

"Next month. Here in Denver."

"Let me know when the date is set. I'll fly in for it."

His dad was supportive of his MMA career—as much as he could be given that he'd set his sights on Deacon taking his place in the family business.

"Your mother sends her love."

Deacon snorted. That was a fucking lie.

For the next five minutes his dad filled him in on the stuff going on at JFW, the family company. After that they talked sports, his dad's golf game in particular.

"Anything new with Ronin?" his dad asked.

"Since Black Arts has been under the House of Kenji, he's had to step up his responsibilities."

"Responsibilities to what?"

"The American Jujitsu Association. The politics of jujitsu ain't his favorite thing by any stretch. But there are only five other instructors in the States that are at his belt level—none even close to his age, so his knowledge is valuable."

"I'd say so."

"He flies to San Francisco a lot. His understanding is he'll be holding seminars with other dojos associated with House of Kenji." Deacon paused. "I'd lay odds at some point during his travels he'll find another punk-ass kid who needs direction like I did." The instant the words were out of his mouth, he regretted opening the can of worms his father had been keeping the lid on.

"He gave you what you needed at the time. I'm grateful to him for that. Maddox is giving you what you need now. But what happens a few years down the road, after you're done fightin'?"

"No idea. It depends on how far I go."

"What're the odds you'll ever get a title shot?"

Fuck. Not this again. "Slim. But that don't mean I won't try. I realize I'm not twenty, but I'm not washed-up at thirty, either."

"I didn't say you were."

"I'm in the best shape of my life," he said defensively. "I finally feel like I'm getting somewhere."

"And getting somewhere will always take you farther away from Texas, won't it?" his dad said softly.

"Don't. You fuckin' *know* why I'm not there, wearing a monkey suit, collecting a big goddamn check, nothin' but a waste of space—"

"You'll never be a waste of space. Jesus, boy. When will you ever get it through that bald head of yours that after Dante—"

"Not goin' there, Dad. Talk about something else or I'll hang up."

"I hate this. I can't even say his name or you lose your shit."

"I lost a fuck load more than my shit when my brother died and you fuckin' know it. So next goddamn question."

A phlegmy cough sounded and faded, as if his dad had put his hand over the phone to hide it.

"Dad? You sick or something?" he said gruffly.

A beat later he answered. "Just old-age stuff."

"Sixty-five ain't old."

"I feel it every damn day. And I'll channel your mother here for a moment and remind you that when I was your age, I'd just gotten married."

Only because a social-climbing, money-grubbing beauty queen hooked you as her lifetime meal ticket.

Nice way to talk about Mom, bro.

Deacon closed his eyes. He used to welcome his brother's voice inside his head, because he'd always been the more reasonable one of the two of them, but today that superior tone annoyed him.

Shut it, Dante.

Would it kill you to give him something? So he knows you're happy outside the ring?

Fuck.

"I'm a long way from that stage, but I am, ah . . . seeing someone."

See? That wasn't so hard, was it?

Fuck off, Dante.

Phantom laughter echoed in his head and then vanished. People would think him certifiable if he admitted it was more than just his dead brother's voice; it felt like part of Dante's conscience hadn't moved on but had remained with Deacon all these years.

"Tag mentioned to me that you'd met someone."

Gossipy damn family.

"So? Tell me about her," his dad prompted.

"She's . . . smart. And strong." *And gorgeous, and sweet, and funny, and sexy, and I'm so crazy about her it scares the shit out of me.*

"What's her name, and how'd you meet?"

"Her name is Molly. We met at Black Arts when she took my kickboxing class. She's the office manager for Hardwick Designs— that's Ronin's wife Amery's business."

"How long have you been dating?"

"A couple weeks. But I've known her for almost two years." Why had he shared that?

"I'd like to meet her."

I'm sure you would. "She'll be at my next fight."

"There's an added incentive to go." His dad chuckled. "I imagine you won't be bringing her home to meet your mother. Does that mean I can't tell her you've met someone?"

"Why ask? You'll do whatever you want. But Molly isn't up for discussion with either of you."

"You sound happy. That's all I care about. But I won't speak for Julianne. Take care, son, and keep me informed on the fight."

"Will do. Later." Deacon hung up.

He ran his palm over his bald pate. His head was wet. Why did talking to his dad make him sweat?

Because you're still convinced he's judging you.

Christ, Dante. He is. You're dead, and I still don't measure up to you.

Bull. Your perception has always been majorly skewed.

Way to remind me I didn't get the math brain.

Quit brooding. I got the brains. You got the heart. Which one of us is still alive? So you tell me which one is more important.

The voice disappeared again, leaving him feeling bereft.

CHAPTER FIFTEEN

AFTER Deacon found the semiprivate room at Dave & Buster's and exchanged the customary hand-jive, half-bro hugs with the Black Arts MMA crew, he focused on the birthday boy—who wore a Burger King crown, for fuck's sake.

Beck grinned. "Like the crown? Ivan's idea. I'd tell you to get on your knees . . . but you'd take it the wrong way, D."

"Ya think?" Deacon looked around. There were monitors in this section that gave a live overview of the different game areas. "Dave and Buster's? What are you? Ten years old?"

"Piss off, Deacon. This place rocks. Besides, it's a tradition. Twenty-fifth year in a row I've spent my birthday in an arcade."

Deacon swiped his light beer off the table. "So you didn't discover video games until you were twenty?"

"Not even on my worst day do I look ten years older than I am, unlike some bald-headed dudes, so fuck off, ass-monkey."

"Can you guys tone down your lovers' quarrel? I'm trying to figure out what to eat here," Blaze complained.

"But their bromance is legendary," Ivan deadpanned.

"Fuck both of you."

Deacon looked around the table. Beck, Ivan, Sergei, Blaze, and

Fisher. Surprisingly, Blue—not Gil—rounded out the group. Then again, if Beck and Maddox had words, Gil wouldn't be invited since he and Mad were so tight.

"You looking for someone in particular?" Beck asked.

"The creepy guy who ties balloon animals at kiddie parties. Thought he could fashion that big dick you've always wanted."

"Bite me." He smirked. "Unless your jaw hurts too much from taking one on the chin from Courey earlier this morning?"

A chorus of *oohs* echoed back to him.

"Ha-fucking-larious, douche bag. No. I just thought . . . Never mind."

Beck swigged his beer. "Yes, I invited Ronin, Knox, and Riggins, but they all had other plans."

"Riggins never comes to nothin'," Blaze pointed out.

"Training at Black Arts is a hobby for him. If he's not being paid for his medical assistance with the fighters, he's not hanging around with us. That's who he is." Beck shrugged.

"Where'd you find him?" Deacon asked.

"I didn't find him. Knox did. So I assume they were military buddies or Riggins works for GSC, the same security place Knox does."

Or Knox and Ronin recruited him from Twisted—not that Deacon could share that suspicion.

"Dinner's on me tonight, so pull that damn menu away from Blaze," Beck said. "The redheaded imp will bankrupt me."

"I hate when you call me imp."

"Dude. You're like five five, and you weigh a buck thirty-five. Imp applies."

"Whatever. Just don't call me rooster. Or red. I'll prove size don't matter when I come out swinging, 'cause them's fighting words."

Food ordered, they all kicked back and decided to hit the games after eating. Talk turned to sports. Being raised in Seattle,

Beck was a diehard Mariners fan. No one else followed baseball as fanatically as he did, so Fisher brought up the Broncos heading to training camp. Which generated Beck's impassioned speech about the Seahawks.

"You lived in Denver for three years and in San Francisco for almost five years and you didn't switch to teams that actually win championships?" Fisher asked snidely.

"Spoken like a native Coloradan who's never lived anywhere else," Beck said. "My allegiance remains with the teams I've followed for years—no matter where I live." He pointed at Deacon. "Tell him, Yondan."

"What?"

"Who's your team?"

"The Cowboys. Ain't only my team; they're America's team."

Arguments followed, and Beck started spouting off stats for all the teams. The man had a head for figures. Reminded him of Dante in a lot of ways.

Deacon noticed Ivan, Sergei, and Blue were talking among themselves. "Care to share with the class, boys?"

"We're talking real football. You Americans wouldn't understand," Ivan said with an air of superiority.

"You mean soccer," Blaze scoffed.

"Football," Blue corrected.

"So why's it called the World Soccer Cup, huh?"

"It's not, dumb-ass. It's called the World Cup."

"Oh."

Sergei slammed his fist on the table. "Hockey!"

"Whoa, there, Sergei. You'll scare the kiddies. Besides, hockey is over for the year. The Rangers won the Stanley Cup."

"*Nyet.*" Then Sergei went into a very animated conversation with Ivan that made Deacon wish he understood Russian.

"What'd he say?" Fisher asked.

"Sixteen, seventeen games for football players is nothing. Hockey players play eighty-two games. That is the true test of athletic ability."

"I'm assuming Sergei used to be a hockey player?" Deacon said dryly.

Ivan shook his head. "His brother, Semyon, is. He's a skate-on for the NHL draft, hoping to get picked up by the Avalanche."

Enough food arrived to feed a hockey team.

"So, Deacon, you're really not going to the strip club with us?" Beck asked.

"Nope."

"He's blowing us off to get blown by Molly."

Deacon leaned across the table so he had Fisher's full attention. "I won't put up with disrespect where she's concerned, so watch your fucking mouth."

"Oh, I see how it is. Last month when I took Jewel out, you said a bunch of lewd things—like showing Jewel the family jewels and asking how well she polishes them with her mouth. Now, when you're with a woman for longer than fifteen minutes, she's off-limits? Total bullshit, Deacon."

"Fisher has a point," Blue said. "You were such a dick about him going to the ballet with Jewel."

"Come on. It was the fucking *ballet*."

Ivan smacked the table. "*I* was in the fucking ballet, remember? Even in a pair of tights, I can crush the life out of you, redneck."

Jesus.

Beck made the time-out sign.

Reaching into his pocket, Deacon pulled out his VIP pass. "Happy fuckin' birthday, motherfucker."

"Hey. You were gonna give that to me," Fisher complained.

Deacon flashed his teeth. "And now I'm not."

"Asswipe."

The food didn't last long. Sergei, Ivan, Blaze, and Fisher took off to play games. Deacon opted for a second beer—which he wouldn't have had if Maddox sat across from him.

Maddox. The man was up to something.

"D? You doing okay?" Beck asked.

"I guess. Weird situation with Maddox bringing Courey in. Don't know what to make of it. Maddox ain't saying shit, which puts me back to square one. Speculating just makes my damn head hurt."

"I'm sure you heard me'n Maddox had words last week."

"Yeah, I heard. Words about what?"

"You."

Deacon glanced at Blue. "You disappeared awful damn fast today. You get into it with Maddox too?"

Blue shook his head. "With Ronin."

"No shit?"

"I'm aware Sensei pays Maddox's salary. But when he brings in outsiders when he has a perfectly viable solution to the sparring and training partner problems, it pisses me off."

"I'm lost."

Beck and Blue exchanged a look. Then Beck folded his arms on the table. "As Shihan, I deal with problems before I bring them to Sensei. That's my job. We've rebuilt the staff since Knox and Shiori are both part-time. You were always part-time. Ito was always part-time. I took over all but three of the black belt classes. That's a lot. So we hired Jaz, moved some of the black belts into teaching the lower-belt classes. More-advanced students teaching less-advanced students. But I didn't have a fuckin' clue that Maddox would pull both you and Ito from the teaching rotation entirely. I had to scramble to fill those instructors spots."

"You ended up taking over kickboxing."

"Which I don't mind. I'm just not as good at it as you are. We've lost some students because of it. And when I bring it up with

Ronin, he reminds me that your hard-assed stance chased off more students than my unimaginative teaching efforts."

Deacon allowed a small grin.

"Black Arts still needs more teachers. At least one full-time higher-level black belt that I don't have to worry is gonna get pulled from the jujitsu roster and moved to the MMA roster. A paid employee." Beck exhaled slowly. "I compiled a list of instructors who'd love to relocate for the chance to work with Sensei Black. I gave it to Ronin with the understanding he'd have to run all the potential instructors through House of Kenji first. It's been three weeks. I worked for Kenji for four years, so I know they put a priority on these types of requests. I called my contact there, and she said they hadn't received any paperwork from Black Arts."

"Fuck. Seriously?"

He nodded. "I asked Sensei about it. He said he'd gotten behind since he'd been helping Maddox scout training partners for the MMA club."

"Which is where I got into it with Ronin," Blue interjected. "I have three guys who are ideal training partners. It'd solve a couple of problems. One, the pay would help them out. Two, they're already trained. Three, they're fighters or teachers and it'd up their skill sets."

It made sense to Deacon, so he didn't understand why Ronin was dragging ass. "Who're the guys?"

"Terrel. He's in your weight class and he no longer has aspirations for an MMA career. But Ito told Maddox if Terrel became your training partner, he'd quit. And evidently Ito is untouchable— since he's allowed to beat the fuck out of my instructor and he isn't disciplined at all."

"Ronin condemned Ito's actions," Beck said, "but he sided with Maddox that Terrel wasn't a good fit for you."

"Bullshit."

"That's what I said. Then I offered to be your partner—"

"Jesus, Blue. You're far too fucking good for me."

"Doesn't matter. Maddox dismissed me out of hand. Which proved my point."

Deacon looked at Beck. "What am I missing?"

"We're not sure. This all came to a head Monday."

"The day I left."

"Yeah. I'll throw out there that I was half joking with Ronin about you returning to teach the Tuesday-night kickboxing class, since you'll be at the dojo glaring at any man who looks at Molly anyway. Maddox blew a fucking fuse and said you were done teaching. And I blew one right back. I said, according to the House of Kenji rules, you were listed as a jujitsu instructor and you were required to teach at least one class a week. Then I got really pissed the next day when I found out that Maddox had nixed both Blue and Gil as your training partners, but he just let that thug Micah Courey wander in off the goddamn street?"

"Dammit. I never wanted any of this to happen."

"Not laying blame," Beck cautioned. "Just filling you in on why Maddox wasn't invited to my birthday party."

Deacon laughed. "Since I choose how to spend my off hours, I'll take over the kickboxing class. Maddox can suck it. We'll have it be a surprise when I show up. As far as sparring partners, I'd love to rotate Blue, Gil, and Terrel in. I'll bring it up with Ronin. He didn't seem too happy that Courey was there today."

"You're right. But Ronin is the type to weigh everything from all angles. I'd guess he'll keep Courey around another week or so to see how you react." Blue drained his beer. "Enough. Let's whip the birthday boy's ass at a racing game. I know he sucks at Grand Theft Auto."

For the next two hours, Deacon challenged each one of his friends to a game. Sergei kicked his butt in pool. That little fucker Blaze whipped up on him at the hoop shoot. Blue destroyed him twice in the virtual NASCAR race. Beck bested him at *Guitar*

Hero. Ivan won the strongman contest. Even Fisher beat him at the shooting game.

He had fun, but the place was too loud, too many people running around, and what the hell was he supposed to do with all the damn tickets the machines spit out? He'd tried to leave them, but a sweet little girl pointed out he'd forgotten them. And he felt like she'd started following him to make sure he didn't forget.

Stalked by a ten-year-old.

Deacon had briefly spoken to Molly as he'd been en route to the arcade. She'd worked a full day to try to catch up. And he hadn't pressed her on her plans for the night.

After being together nearly twenty-four/seven for the last five days, he missed her.

When he returned to the party area to retrieve his jacket, he just happened to look at the monitor. He froze when he saw a woman who looked a helluva lot like Molly from the back.

Wishful thinking, man.

He watched, willing the woman to turn around. When she did and he saw it was Molly, he nearly whooped with joy.

What did it mean that she'd shown up at the exact moment he been thinking about her?

That you are one lucky bastard. And she can't stay away from you any more than you can stay away from her.

Fuck yeah, it was *on.*

Even on the crappy monitor she looked like a million bucks in a summery floral number. She'd worn fuck-me heels the same deep orange as the flowers on her dress. She'd swept her glossy brown hair into a ponytail showcasing the curve of her neck. The cut of the dress did amazing things for her body, specifically her tits.

He curled his fingers into a fist. He needed to get his hands on her. Right now. Before some other guy touched her—guaranteed his hot woman would get hit on in here—and he ended up in jail for protecting what was his.

Deacon tracked her to the gigantic four-player *Ms. Pac-Man* game. He leaned against the wall and watched her as she watched others. She smiled softly at a pigtailed, redheaded girl. Something about that smile tightened his groin.

When she turned and meandered toward the six-player trivia game in the corner, his cock went harder yet, seeing her ass sway in those do-me stilettos.

He expected she'd continue to wander. But she hung back, observing the trivia game. When a spot opened up, she slid into the seat against the wall—a grandmotherly type sat on her right—and took out a plastic power card.

Well, well. The girl knew how to play.

Deacon didn't bother reading the trivia question on the screen; he was too busy watching Miss Competitive be the first player to buzz in. Molly answered all six questions right and buzzed in fastest for bonus points. The ticket machine by her feet started spitting out tickets. She swiped her card and waited for the next round.

Molly won, same as before, and she looked mighty pleased with herself.

The next round she ended up second, and it appeared she planned to take her tickets and bail.

So Deacon moved in behind her, setting his hands on the back of her chair. "I'm a lucky man that my woman is whip smart, into games, *and* sexy as hell." He rubbed his cheek along hers. "I'm happy to see you, babe."

"You're not mad I showed up?"

"Never."

"What if your dojo buddies see me and accuse you of being pussy-whipped?"

"Don't care." He scraped his cheek over hers, and that sweet floral scent tickled his nose. He whispered, "I saw you."

"Where?"

"On the monitors." He dragged his lips across her jaw. "The second I saw you, I got hard."

"Hold that thought. The next game is about to start."

"Yes, it is, because you'n me are playing a game too. First question." He let his breath drift across her ear, holding on to her biceps to absorb her shiver. "How many more times can I make you come today?"

Molly sucked in a soft breath and missed being the first player to buzz in—probably because she was thinking about the last orgasm he'd given her this morning.

"No fair."

The timer went off on the screen, and Molly hadn't even made a guess.

Deacon kissed her temple. "Finish up the trivia game. Then we're outta here."

"Maybe you don't get to decide that. Maybe I had plans for you."

"What kind of plans?"

Her sultry laugh burrowed into his ear, traveling down the center of his body to tighten his balls.

Fuck.

She didn't say another word until the game ended. Then she leaned down and grabbed her tickets from the machine. She noticed the cup of tickets clutched in his hand. "Quite a lot of winnings." She accordioned her tickets and tucked them in his cup. "Now you can think of me when you're spending your load."

He groaned. "Killing me, babe."

"I saw another game I wanted to play." She took his hand, and they wended through the crowd.

He had to give the *eyes off her or I will fuck you up* look to several douche bags with a fucking death wish.

She half turned and said, "Stop growling."

"Better than throwing punches," he muttered.

They ended up in the farthest corner, where the lame games were collecting dust. An old Kiss pinball machine had been shoved against the wall.

Molly swiped her card and "Rock and Roll All Nite" blasted out as the balls loaded.

"You like pinball?" he asked as he moved in behind her.

"Not really. I like that there's no one back here."

Deacon rested his hands on her hips, pulling her ass against his dick. As he pressed his lips to the back of her head, her soft hair caught on the rough stubble on his cheeks. The scent of her was another punch of lust.

"Deacon."

"Yeah."

"Were you serious?"

Ping, ping, ping sounded. "About what?"

Molly turned around and gripped his shirt to keep him from taking a step back. "About fulfilling my fantasies."

He brushed his lips over hers. "Damn straight."

"I have one." She released his shirt and smoothed out the wrinkles. "It's a game called 'get off, get gone.'"

"Sounds dirty. I'm in."

She laughed. "See, we take turns surprising each other. So I'll start tonight." Locking her gaze to his, she rubbed her lips over the stubble on his chin. "If there weren't so many people around, I'd shove you in the corner and blow you."

"Jesus." His cock jerked against his zipper, and she felt it.

"I've had to improvise. So instead of getting head, you're getting a hand job while you're playing pinball. No one will think anything of the way you move your hips and ass as I'm standing in front of you, jerking you off."

"And then what?"

"I go home. Next round is yours. The only rule is payback

can't be immediate. There is a minimum twelve-hour wait between rounds."

"That's not fucking fair. I want to surprise you tonight."

She shook her head. "That's the second part of the fantasy for me, Deacon. I've never done anything like this. You need to let me be the woman who shows up unexpectedly, jacks you off, and leaves."

"Leaves me wanting more," he murmured.

Those beautiful brown eyes lit up. "Exactly."

Deacon kissed her nose. "Hope you brought a paper towel."

She stepped aside and walked backward until she was in the shadows beside a *Dukes of Hazzard* pinball machine. Smirking, she slid her left hand beneath her skirt and . . .

Holy fuckballs, the woman took her panties off. Right there. In the arcade.

He just about shot his load right then.

With her panties bunched in her fist, she sauntered back over and situated herself between him and the pinball machine—her ass against his groin. She looked over her shoulder. "Unzip your jeans and pull your cock out."

In that moment, he saw no sign of timid Molly and he knew he'd do everything under the sun to fulfill her every fantasy. Also in that moment, Deacon fell a little bit in love with her. This good girl who wanted to be bad—and wanted to take him along for the ride.

She set the power card on the glass.

Deacon whipped his cock out and had a brief flash of paranoia. What if someone saw them? What if security busted them for fucking around? What if the dudes manning the security feed knew what they were doing and whacked off while watching them?

Made him a pervert, but the idea of someone else watching them got him harder yet.

Molly stretched her left arm up and dug her nails into the back of his neck. "Come on, pinball wizard. Time to put the balls in play."

He loaded three games. Then he rested his palms on the glass above the flipper controls and tightened the cage he'd created around her with his arms.

Silky material wound around his cock, followed by the firm grip of her hand. She started to stroke him.

"Jesus, Molly. Feels so damn good I wanna close my eyes."

"Watch your balls," she whispered against his neck.

Deacon could barely see the damn pinball machine his blood was pulsing so hard in his neck and head, making his vision waver.

"Thrust your hips into my hand."

Just that small movement kicked the sensation from pleasure in his cock to pleasure coursing throughout his entire body.

"Deacon. You are so sexy. So fierce. Every time I look at you I get butterflies in my stomach. When you kiss me? My heart races. I lose myself in how perfectly your mouth fits to mine. And when you put your hands on me, it feels right and yet it's never enough."

The words, so sweet, hot and earnest, arrowed straight to the heart of him. He couldn't even speak.

She stroked him harder. "Come for me. I want you to blow in record time. I need to know my touch can do to you what yours does to me."

And . . . he was done. He closed his eyes and pressed his lips to her temple as his cock pulsed in her tight fist. He bumped his hips and she pulled on his shaft until not another drop of come remained. The loud whooshing in his head muted the continual sounds of the games.

Molly faced him, kissing his neck as she cleaned up his dick. Then she whispered, "Thank you for playing along, Deacon."

"What goes around comes around. Remember that."

"I'm counting on it." She stuffed her panties in her purse while he zipped and buttoned.

"Before you run off . . . I wanna see you tomorrow."

"I'm not being coy when I ask if I can get back to you, because I might have something else going on."

Deacon didn't like that she'd hedged. But he played it cool. "Yeah, babe. I know you're not messing with me."

"How?"

"You can't lie for shit. Those pretty eyes tell me everything I need to know." He kissed her softly. "Hope to see you soon."

Then he forced himself to grab his cup of tickets and walk away.

CHAPTER SIXTEEN

DEACON trained alone on Sunday, focusing on cardio and strength. He limited himself to dumbbells since he didn't have a spotter in the weight room.

At the end of three hours, when he'd exhausted himself, he hauled out the training dummy and worked on kicks and body blows. This training aspect was his secret weapon. If he could maintain fighting form—Muay Thai or kickboxing—for forty-five minutes, after hours of endurance training, he should be able to stay on his feet for three five-minute rounds.

He was on the mat, stretching his muscles as he cooled down, when the training-room door opened and Maddox strolled in.

Great.

Maddox seemed as surprised to see him. "Hey, D."

"Mad. What are you doing here?"

"I don't always get my workouts in while I'm training fighters during the week, so I catch up on the weekends." He sat on the bench across from the mat. "What'd you work on today?"

"Cardio and endurance. Why?"

"Just wondered if you'd recovered from Courey's hit yesterday."

"Oh, you mean from his cheap shot? Yeah."

"I know you don't like him."

"He's an arrogant prick." Deacon pushed to his feet. "So I can see where you two would get along famously."

Maddox laughed. "There's method to my madness. I swear."

"Tell me."

"Not yet. Yours is not to question; yours is to do."

That shitty Yoda impression always cracked him up. "How much longer will Courey be training here as your guest?"

"Depends."

More of the usual cryptic bullshit from Maddox. He liked the guy, but sometimes he fucking hated him too. "That cleared things up. Thanks."

"You're welcome. Did you hit the strip club last night for Beck's birthday party?"

Deacon shook his head. "Now that I'm with Molly, my strip-club days are over." He narrowed his eyes at Maddox. "And if you tell anyone that, I'll tell everyone you're cruising nursing homes for your new girlfriends."

Maddox whistled. "Low blow, my friend."

"Hey, you're the one who confessed hooking up with your senior-citizen lady friend after I told you about my strip-club fall-out with Molly."

"Because I thought we were male bonding over our woman problems," Maddox shot back and batted his eyelashes.

"Fuck off."

"You're too easy. And FYI: Alicia does *not* qualify for senior-citizen discounts."

"*Yet,*" Deacon stressed. "But her hitting that golden-age mile-stone next year *will* make your date nights cheaper."

"You're an ass. I don't know why I tell you anything."

Deacon grinned. "Now you're getting it, Jedi Master."

"Get outta here."

"I'm goin'. See you tomorrow."

He shouldered his bag and left Black Arts through the back door. Two o'clock. Normally he'd go home, shower, eat, and spend the rest of the day watching fights on the UFC channel or destroying his opponents at WoW.

But that seemed like a waste today.

Deacon wanted to be with Molly. And he hated that she'd acted cagey last night when he'd asked about her plans today.

She's your girlfriend. It's your right to know what she's doing. And aren't couples supposed to be joined at the hip and shit on weekends anyway?

With that justification in mind, he headed to her place.

MOLLY needed a personal spa day.

She waxed and shaved. She soaked in a lavender-infused bath while deep-conditioning her hair. Then she coated her skin with a coconut-oil-based lotion.

As she plucked her eyebrows, saggy, sallow skin stared back at her. Yuck. It was past time for a toning mask treatment. She slathered a thick layer of clay on her face. While that dried, she decided to give herself a pedicure.

She settled on her sofa, surveying her spa-day essentials. Miranda Lambert playing on her iPod. A detoxifying kale, spinach, cucumber, and lemongrass shake for lunch. The latest issue of *InStyle* magazine queued up on her tablet. Her nail buffer and the glittery orange polish for her pedicure.

Time alone to reflect on the recent changes in her life while she pampered herself was the perfect way to spend her afternoon.

She jammed the pink foam spreaders between her toes and slicked on the first coat of nail polish. After she propped her feet on the coffee table, she hummed along with "Gunpowder & Lead" and sipped her shake. It tasted like crap, so it had to be good for her.

Four loud, hammering knocks rattled her apartment door.

Had to be Nina. She'd sent Molly several text messages since she'd run into her Friday night.

Molly tightened the belt on her robe as she carefully walked on her heels, trying not to smudge her toenail polish. She detached the safety chain and unlocked the door, not bothering to check the peephole. She should have.

Because it wasn't Nina standing in the hallway, but Deacon.

A wide-eyed Deacon as his gaze roved over her from her forehead to her toes and back up. Then he said, "Babe. Why did you hit yourself in the face with a cream pie?"

She screamed and slammed the door in his face.

This was not cool. He did *not* just show up unannounced and interrupt her personal time after she'd told him last night that she couldn't see him today!

Two knocks sounded, less forceful than before.

"Molly, let me in."

"Go away."

"I'm worried about you."

She frowned at the door. "Why?"

"Did you hurt your feet or something? I saw those splints between your toes."

For the love of god. Seriously? He thought she was injured? Had he never seen a woman give herself a pedicure before?

Then she remembered his confession she was his first girlfriend in fifteen years—so he'd probably never seen this girly shit, either in real life or on TV. She doubted Deacon McConnell watched anything that didn't have explosions, car chases, gratuitous sex, and violence.

But the pie-in-the-face comment was insulting.

So educate him.

Molly slid the safety chain back on and opened the door as far as it'd allow, but she stayed out of his line of sight. "Deacon, I'm fine. I'm having a home spa day. Painting my toenails, conditioning my hair."

No response. Then, "That gunk is conditioning your face, too?"
Don't beat your head into the door. "It's a mask."

"You're beautiful. Why would you need to wear a mask?"

"Now you're just being"—*sweet, damn you*—"obtuse."

"Whatever that means."

Be nice, Molly. "Why are you here?"

Deacon slid his big hand in the opening, curling his fingers around the door. "I don't like not seeing you every day."

"In other words . . . you missed me."

"Isn't that what I just said?" His fingers tightened on the door. "I'm tired of talking through this damn crack. Let me in." He paused. "Please."

So much for her personal spa day.

"I'll let you in only if you don't make fun of me."

"Tall order, but I'll try my best."

As soon as he moved his hand, she opened the door.

But the second he crossed the threshold, she slapped her hand on his chest. She wrinkled her nose. His shirt was soaked clear through. "Deacon. You reek."

"Well, yeah. I just got done training."

"And you didn't think you should go home and shower before you showed up unannounced at my door?"

"I needed to see you. I didn't think. I just drove." He leaned forward, like he wanted to kiss her, but his eyes were wary, scrutinizing the clay mask.

Molly grinned and smashed her lips to his. And yeah, maybe a little bit of the clay crumbled onto his face as she kissed him.

"You've got a mean streak, babe," he said when they came up for air.

"Mmm-hmm. I'm going to wash my face. Then you'll scrub the stench off in the shower while I put another coat of paint on my toes." Her gaze dropped to his gym bag. "You have clean clothes in there?"

"Yeah."

"Good." She drilled her finger into his chest. "Do not sit your sweaty self on my couch or I will kick your butt."

Deacon wrapped his hand beneath her jaw and held her in place while he ravaged her mouth. Then, after he finished blowing all her circuits, he pressed his forehead to hers, heedless of the mask. "I like this. I like us together. I've gotten used to it and missed it when I didn't have it. So I came over."

"So you're not here just to fuck me senseless?"

"Babe. I've told you it's more than that between us. When are you gonna believe it?" He paused. "Ah, hell. Do I have to keep my hands off you for a couple of days to prove it?"

"God, no. I like us together out of bed too. I just didn't want to overwhelm you by expecting we'll spend weekends together."

"Everything about you overwhelms me, so it's too late for that," he said softly. "And I'm really fucking sick of spending my weekends alone."

"Me too."

"Good. I've got plans for us as soon as you get that dirt off your face and I get cleaned up."

"What kind of plans?"

"There's some flower show, farmers' market thing at the Botanical Gardens. I thought we could stroll around. See what's what, since you like flowers and shit."

Flowers and shit. She fought a grin.

"Oh, and I used all the tickets we won from last night and got this for you." He dug in his bag and handed her a box.

"For me?" Molly grinned so widely more clay crumbled from her face. She tore open the end of the box and tipped the object into her hand. Her heart clenched at seeing the retro, miniature black cat with a curved plastic tail, complete with oversized cat eyes that moved back and forth with every tick of the clock centered in the cat's belly. A larger version of this clock had hung in Grams's dining room for as long as she could remember.

"I saw you looking at the one in your grandma's house when you walked through the last time. I thought about stealing it for you, but I figured your asshole cousins would get pissy and blame you. I saw this last night and . . . figured it'd be the next best thing."

She swallowed hard, completely undone by Deacon's sweetness. No one had ever taken such care and consideration in giving her a gift. "It is perfect. Thank you."

Molly knew right then she could totally fall in love with this man.

THE look on Molly's face when Deacon strolled into kickboxing class on Tuesday night was priceless.

Surprise, babe.

He surveyed his students. Then he grinned. "Miss me?"

A loud chorus of no's rang out.

"Aw, now my little feelings are hurt. And if I hurt, you hurt. Push-ups. We'll start with twenty."

"Start with?" a young guy he'd never seen before repeated.

Liv elbowed him and shook her head.

"You're right, newb. Twenty ain't near enough. Forty."

No one dared complain.

"And, ladies, none of those 'on your knees' girl push-ups. Everyone does everything the same in my class unless I say differently. Drop to plank position." He wandered between the rows, making them hold plank, just for fun. "And . . . go."

By the end of the hour, newb looked ready to puke, Presley was red-faced and breathing hard, Liv was actually lying on the mat groaning, and Molly . . . Well, good thing he was wearing a cup.

Hell yeah, he'd missed teaching.

★   ★   ★

FRIDAY afternoon Molly cut out of work early to make Presley's roller derby match in Colorado Springs. Since they had a photo shoot scheduled for Saturday, she and Presley planned to stay over.

Deacon insisted on attending the match, but he had five-a.m. training Saturday, so he'd drive back to Denver afterward. Which was why they were in separate cars.

Molly hadn't seen the need to caravan to Colorado Springs, but Deacon insisted. Of course, he insisted on being the lead car in his fancy-ass, fast Mercedes. He'd started off nine miles an hour above the speed limit. She'd followed him at that pace for ten minutes, until paranoia about higher insurance rates forced her to return to the speed limit. Within five minutes she'd lost sight of his car completely.

Her phone rang. Hmm. Wonder who that was. She answered, "Yes, Deacon?"

"Where are you?"

"Behind you. Driving slower than you because I can't afford a ticket."

"They're not gonna ticket you for *nine* over, babe."

"I'm a rule follower, *babe*, which means I obey traffic laws. I don't care if that makes me lame."

His sigh indicated he thought it was lame. "I'll slow down. Speed up until you catch me." He hung up.

Tempting to ignore his order. Instead she cranked on the radio and sped up, passing cars until she reached his. She pulled in behind him and waved like an idiot.

Mr. Badass NASCAR didn't wave back—big surprise.

That night the Denver Divas kicked serious ass. The bout was a rout and the ladies were ready to celebrate, so it sort of sucked that all the Divas except for Presley hopped in their team van and returned to Denver.

Molly checked in at the front desk, while Presley and Deacon waited in the lobby. When she returned with the room keys, she winced at seeing her friend's injuries.

The right side of Presley's mouth was swollen. Two spots of blood remained crusted beneath her nose. A bruise had started to form on her cheekbone. Presley managed a wan smile. "Looks worse than it hurts—doesn't it, Con Man?"

"Yep."

Presley snatched a room key. "I need a shower. See you up there."

Deacon threaded his fingers through Molly's and led her out of the hotel.

The summer night air held a sultry hint—an oddity since Colorado had low humidity. Once they reached the parking lot, Deacon directed her to his car with his hand in the small of her back.

She wrapped her arms around his waist. "I hate saying goodbye."

"Me too." Deacon's hands slid up to cradle her head, holding her in place for his kiss.

The kiss didn't veer into blinding passion, but it bubbled below the surface, waiting to erupt. It took more control from him to show her it was there than to just give in to it.

And then he gave in to it completely. "Need you," he rasped against her throat. "In my bed. All weekend."

Molly angled away from his wicked mouth to look into his eyes. "You're inviting me to your place?"

"You're surprised."

"You've been secretive about where you live."

"Not intentionally." He pushed a hank of hair over her shoulder. "It's just a habit."

"Why?" Did he live in a scary neighborhood and worry that'd freak her out?

"I don't take chicks to my place. Ever."

Chicks. Sometimes she wanted to smack him. "Because you're a slob?"

His lips twitched. "No. Just private."

"Wow. I must be special," she joked.

Deacon's eyes softened. "You are." Then he proved it by gifting her with a sweet kiss.

Molly's belly performed a slow roll. Her head told her this was all going way too fast. Her heart agreed. Her body . . . well, it had a mind of its own when it came to Deacon McConnell. As it'd proved every night this week, basking in the worship Deacon focused on every inch of her flesh.

"You make that noise again and I'm fucking you right here against the car," he grumbled against her lips.

"Sorry." She forced herself to release him. "I know you have to go. Drive safe."

"I will. Call me when you get into town tomorrow. Pack a bag and plan on staying until Monday morning, okay?"

"Okay."

CHAPTER SEVENTEEN

DEACON lived in a condo complex in the part of Denver known as the golden triangle, closer to Black Arts than Molly's apartment in the university section.

After meeting her out front, he climbed in and directed her to one of his parking spots in the underground garage. "Must be nice not to have to scrape your windows in the morning."

He shrugged.

They took the elevator to the sixth floor.

Deacon hadn't said much—nothing new for him. But he seemed tense.

As soon as he unlocked the door and shunted her inside, he had her pressed against the wall. He didn't kiss her. He just studied her.

"What?"

"Tell me you're hungry."

"Uh, why?"

"So I don't fuck you right where you stand."

Molly stroked Deacon's freshly shaved head. "Then you'd better feed me after you give me a tour."

He gave her a quick kiss and backed away. Clasping her hand, he pulled her from the foyer around a wall that revealed the living room.

The openness of the space brought to mind Amery's loft. But the kitchen was walled off and had an eat-in bar on one side like a restaurant pass-through. "I like this feature." She ran her hand along the countertop. "It's funky yet functional."

They skirted the wall and entered the kitchen. It wasn't huge, but wasn't as dinky as hers either. Cleaner than hers too. Talk about spotless. He hadn't left as much as a spoon in the ceramic sink.

The space had warmer tones than she'd expected: honey-colored cabinets, rust-colored walls, and small turquoise accents. No ostentatious appliances like a six-burner gas stove, a double oven, or an industrial-sized refrigerator.

Deacon wasn't paying attention to her checking out his kitchen. He rummaged through a stack of take-out menus. "What're you in the mood for?"

Molly stood beside him and rested the side of her face on his biceps. "You choose. Something fairly healthy."

"House of Chicken makes a mean chicken spinach salad."

"I'll have that." She pressed a kiss on the ball of his shoulder. Then another. "Whatever light dressing they have."

He hadn't moved.

"But if that's not what you want—"

Deacon wrapped his hand around her neck, below her jaw. "You don't even have to try, do you? You are just naturally affectionate."

She blushed.

"There. That right there. Jesus. When you blush it's like waving a red flag in front of me." He brushed his lips over hers. Just a back-and-forth glide.

She could melt into a puddle from these pockets of sweetness he showed her.

Then, as quickly as he bowled her over with his physical contact, he let it go. "I'll call the order in."

Molly wandered out of the kitchen while Deacon talked on the phone. Again, she'd imagined Deacon living in an ultra-modern space, not one so welcoming with warmth and comfort. No black leather furniture. No Jumbotron TV. But she wouldn't be afraid to sit on the furnishings in here either.

His arms circled her as she studied the framed art on the walls.

"Where'd you get those? They're amazing." The western paintings were vibrant and detailed, down to the ripped leather of the cowboy's boot.

"Guy I worked with. When he showed me his paintings, I recognized his talent and hated seeing the hands that created such beauty stuck washing dishes."

"Is he still painting?"

"No idea. Lost touch with him when I changed jobs." He shrugged. "Most art is shit. But this? When I looked at it, I could almost smell the puffy tacos at the *mercado* in San Antonio."

"Ah. So it's an image of Texas—the people, the place, and the artist—that speaks to you." She looked at him. "I'm jealous. Unless someone paints pictures of cornfields, I'll never have that kind of connection."

"I still think you should've taken the John Wayne on velvet painting from your grams's house."

"Now you're just being mean."

Deacon laughed. "Busted."

"Just for that I want a tour of your bedroom first."

"Not happening. I get you in there and we ain't leaving."

Molly pointed. "Maybe a trip to the balcony will cool you down."

"Not likely." He opened the sliding-glass door. "Go ahead. I've seen the view before."

She loved being able to see Denver from different angles around the city. She could sit out here for hours. Yet she didn't see a single piece of patio furniture. When she walked across the concrete to peer over the railing, Deacon warned, "Careful."

"Why? Is this rickety or something?" She tried to jiggle the metal to test it, but it seemed solid to her.

"Jesus, Molly. Don't."

She whirled around and saw the pinched set to Deacon's mouth. Now she understood why this space was empty. "You're afraid of heights."

He leveled the deadly stare that used to scare the crap out of her.

Not so much anymore.

"You know what I'm afraid of?" she asked as she walked back to him. "It's stupid. But I've always had nightmares about being invited to an important party and when I get there, I'm wearing something completely inappropriate. Sometimes I'm dressed like a clown or a witch. One time I wore the papal stylings of the pope. Another time I looked like a punk-rock hooker. Everyone is laughing at me and yelling horrible things at me."

"Nightmares aren't the same as phobias, babe. I've suffered from both."

At least she'd gotten him to admit that much. "Is your fear from something that happened when you were a kid?"

He shook his head.

"So, Deacon, if you've got an issue with heights, why did you buy a condo on the sixth floor?"

"I asked for ground floor when they were building this. But something got fucked-up. The real estate developer cut me a deal, and it was too good to pass up."

"Where's your bedroom?"

"Patience, woman. Let's head back to the kitchen."

Molly was out of patience. She needed to see where he rested his shaved head at night—why was he denying her? To distract him so she could make a break for it, she said the first thing that popped into her head. "Look! There's Batman!"

When he turned to look—gullible much?—Molly ducked under his arm and booked it down the short hallway.

She flung open the door and frantically patted the wall until she found the light switch. Then she stopped in the middle of the room, taking it all in.

This was where Deacon slept. This was where he dreamed. Where he hurt. But this wasn't a place he chose to fuck or make love.

Until now. With her.

Large hands landed on her hips. "Batman. Seriously, babe?"

"Hey, *you* looked." She paused. "I have to ask you something. Am I really the first woman you've had here?"

"I wouldn't lie about that."

"I wasn't accusing you," she said softly. "I don't know whether to be nervous or flattered."

"Neither."

"Then what? Why me, Deacon?"

"Jesus. You're here. That's what matters. Why do you have to dissect it?"

"I don't." Molly crossed over to the bed and braced her hands on it. "Wow. This is firm."

"This is firm too." Deacon scooted in behind her, rocking his groin into her ass, performing a sexy bump and grind that seemed almost . . . playful for him.

Probably moves he picked up after spending years at strip clubs.

She willed the cynical voice to pipe down.

"Something wrong?" he asked as he brushed his lips against the hollow behind her ear.

"Yeah, there is."

Deacon froze.

Molly spun in his arms and fisted her hands into his T-shirt. "Let's christen this room."

"I plan to. After we eat."

"You know what they say about the best-laid plans," she murmured. Her greedy hands followed the hard muscles of his chest, past his chiseled abs to that sexy flexor muscle beneath his hips.

She dropped to her knees. He wore athletic shorts. No belt, no zipper—one tug and his clothing hit the floor—no underwear either.

"What the fuck, Molly."

Feeling ornery, she dragged her tongue up his shaft, keeping her eyes on his as she licked the hard, meaty goodness. In the two weeks they'd been together, Deacon had kept his dick away from her mouth . . . and that was stopping right now.

He exhaled loudly. "We—you—can pick this up later. The food will be here shortly."

"Don't care." She teased the head of his cock, flicking her tongue over the sweet spot. Then she parted her lips and slipped the length into her mouth, over her teeth and across her tongue. She sucked experimentally and glanced up to see Deacon's reaction.

He hissed in a breath and his hand cupped the back of her head. He didn't use his grip to drive his cock deeper into her mouth; he gripped her hair tightly, as if he needed to hold on.

The taste of him was . . . so perfectly him, so utterly male. Hot and dark. A little salty. A little musky. Smooth. Hard. Molly closed her eyes and savored him, even as she drove him mad with long, slow sucks. She even attempted to work past her gag reflex, wanting to get the whole of him inside her mouth.

"Fuck." His legs started to tremble.

Imagine that. She could make him weak-kneed. But she wanted more than that. She wanted to hear her name exploding from his mouth as his seed exploded on her tongue.

"Babe," he panted, "stop."

Molly ignored him and just kept on taking what she wanted.

When he realized she wasn't stopping until he came, he became more aggressive. Pulling her hair. Rocking his hips into her face. Muttering dirty things.

She loved it.

"Sweet Christ. Fuck yeah. Feel that. Feel what you're doin' to me."

She felt it; his cock had suddenly gotten harder.

"Gonna come."

The first splash of heat surprised her, as did Deacon's hoarse, "Suck hard."

She swallowed. Again and again, until the jerking pulses stopped. Only after his semihard cock slipped out of her mouth did she feel shy. She rubbed her cheek on the tops of his thighs, loving the rasp of his hair on her skin.

Deacon's hand fell away.

When Molly finally glanced up at him and saw the fire burning in his eyes, her heart slammed into her throat.

His rough-skinned fingers stroked her face—her cheekbone, her jawline. "You have any idea how fucking hot it was watching my dick disappearing between these pretty lips?"

"No, I don't. Tell me."

"Fuck, woman." He laughed. A bit shakily. "I don't know whether to turn you over my knee or get on my knees."

A chime sounded.

Deacon allowed one last caress before he stepped back and yanked up his shorts. "That's the food. Don't move until I get back."

Screw that. She was not eating chicken salad on her knees.

Molly stood and walked into the master bathroom. It wasn't overly done, just basic cream tiles with navy blue accents. A white counter with two inset glass sinks topped the oak vanity. She peeked in the shower. Yeah. It rocked. The space had to be big to fit Deacon's large body. She could see multiple showerheads on three walls, and along the back was a bench seat.

The mirror above the vanity stretched almost wall-to-wall. The mirror in her bathroom was pocket-sized compared to this one.

A tremor rolled through her, remembering when Deacon had bent her over the counter in her bathroom. He'd fucked her slowly, making her watch them fuck, forcing her eyes to stay on his as she came. It'd been hotter than she'd ever imagined.

She knew the man would have her in here at every angle and position imaginable so he could watch.

When Molly glanced up, she jumped at seeing Deacon in the doorway, watching her. "Oh, hey."

"Food's here."

"Great. I'm starving."

He stared at her, his eyes dark with an unmistakable gleam.

"What?"

"I'm gonna fuck you in the shower."

"Now?"

He shook his head. "Soon."

"Okay. Good to know."

"At least twice."

Her stomach pitched at the thought of their wet, slippery bodies sliding together, creating their own steam. "That means we're gonna get really dirty more than once?"

"Count on it."

DEACON wanted to watch a couple of fights after they ate, so Molly curled up next to him on the couch. He trailed his fingers up and down her arm, the touch both soothing and erotic in its repetitiveness.

After dating a couple of sports guys, she expected he'd yell at the TV, trash-talk the guys fighting, but he didn't. He grunted a couple of times when the welterweight challenger landed hard kicks. Besides that, he watched in near silence.

"How many fight tapes do you study before a bout?"

"Every one I can get my hands on. But at my level it's slim pickin's."

"Why?"

"Because of my professional amateur status," he said dryly.

"But you are a professional."

"My win-loss record will back that up. The number of fights I've been in over the years will also back that up. But the officially sanctioned fights by the big fight organizations? I'm still an infant. I've had to beat any guy in my weight division that's up-and-coming or even washed-up. That's why the Needham fight is important."

"Does he watch fight tapes of you?"

"He should. But rumor is he thinks I'm a joke. He's called me 'a street thug with a questionable fight record.'"

Molly turned her head to look at him. "Who'd you hear that from?"

"Needham trains in a public gym. Shit gets said and passed around. And that's a perfect example of why Maddox insists on a closed practice. No one can video our training drills with their phones." His lips curled into a nasty grin. "That fucker Needham has no idea how helpful the bootleg videos of his practices have been to me."

"Where do you find them?"

"YouTube."

"Really?"

"Yeah. All my fights from smokers the last three years are on there. So when I beat Needham, any organization that's interested in signing me will look there first to see my progression." He kissed the top of her head. "Sorry for boring you."

"Nothing about you bores me, Deacon."

"What job did you have in Colorado Springs?"

"A couple of updated exterior shots of businesses. We probably would've turned it down if we hadn't been right there."

"Why?"

"The need for custom photography has dropped off significantly in the three years I've been at Hardwick. Presley and I had fun, though." Until she got that stupid phone call on the way back to Denver.

Deacon tipped her face up. "What happened?"

Man. He'd picked up on that fast. "Jennifer and Brandi decided to include me on a phone conference."

His gaze sharpened. "Does your lawyer know about this?"

"He does now. And it was stupid. I shouldn't have answered."

"I'd tell you to block their numbers from your phone . . . but I know you won't do it."

He was right—she hated that he was right. It made zero sense why she couldn't just end all contact with them. She'd sworn she'd do it. But she hadn't followed through.

"What is the worst thing that could happen to you if you block them?"

"Nothing. My life would be better, wouldn't it?" She sighed. "Maybe I should hand my phone to you and have *you* do it."

"Nothing wrong with cutting people out of your life who treat you like dog shit, babe."

"Speaking from experience?" she asked.

He snorted. "You have no idea."

"Who'd you drop-kick out of your life?"

Deacon didn't answer for so long, she assumed he wouldn't. Shocked the hell out of her when he said, "My mother."

Major reveal about his family. "How long ago since you excised her from your life?"

"Fifteen years."

"So you never see her?"

"Not if I can help it."

Molly nuzzled his chest. "I don't even remember my mother. But I still resent her."

He didn't ask why.

She decided to tell him anyhow. "I'm pretty sure she killed herself. Grams called it an accident, but she was the only one who believed it. I'm not resentful that my mother abandoned me by a selfish act of suicide. I'm mad because she never left behind any indication of who my father was. Grams suspected, given my 'coloring,' as she called it, that my father was Mexican. Sometimes I caught her staring at me like she feared I'd start speaking Spanish."

"Babe."

"When I think about it, which I try not to because it's so screwed up, my mother left home without a word and disappeared for twenty years. Her parents had no idea whether she was alive or dead. Who does something like that?"

Deacon's body went rigid beneath her.

"Then she returned home to Nebraska a few months after her father died. My uncle Bob said that my mother never got along with her father and he was the reason she left."

"Most people don't understand when leaving isn't an option; it's the *only* choice."

Molly had the feeling Deacon knew about that firsthand. "Of course, my nasty-minded, bully cousins had a theory on why my mom took off." The first time they'd shared that theory with her, she'd gotten violently ill. They teased her about that and kept detailing scenarios that were more disgusting than the last. When she became numb to it and didn't react, they moved on to some other verbal torture.

"What did they tell you was the reason?" he said tightly.

"That my grandfather had sexually abused her. They had no proof. Now part of me thinks they said that only because they wanted me to go to Grams to see how she'd react."

"Gimme your goddamn phone, Molly. I'm blocking those bitches from your life forever. Right. Fucking. Now."

When Molly thought of all the years of verbal abuse, all the years she'd cowered in fear of them, all the things they'd taken from her—not just makeup and toys and candy, but her sense of self—not to mention the atrocious lies they'd told . . .

Deacon's hands framed her face, forcing her to look at him. "Tell me why you just gasped like you're in pain," he demanded.

"Because I'm sorry. I didn't mean to talk about any of this."

"Tell me."

That Sunday morning after church became so clear in her mind, she could see the heat shimmers on the blacktop leading out of town. Her cousins had begged her to come along with them because they had a big, secret surprise for her. And they promised they'd be back at the church before the annual meeting that Grams and Uncle Bob had to stay for ended.

So because Jennifer and Brandi had been so nice to her the last two Sundays, she'd gone with them. She'd secretly hoped that Grams was right and they were outgrowing their meanness.

The August day had been a scorcher. The blacktop squished beneath her white dress shoes. The sun beat on her head. Sweat poured down her back, and she wished she'd left her sweater in the car.

They cut through Mr. Stewart's pasture and climbed under the barbed-wire fence that surrounded the junkyard.

Before Molly could point out the NO TRESPASSING signs, or ask about the pit bulls that patrolled the area, Brandi and Jennifer had taken off. And unlike her, they were fast runners.

She'd run up and down every row, looking for her cousins, and had fallen down twice. When she saw the blood welling on her scraped-up hands and knees, she'd panicked, positive the mean junkyard dogs would smell blood and attack her.

She'd stayed very quiet until Brandi jumped out from behind a car. That'd scared her so much she'd screamed and wet her panties a little.

Embarrassed, hot, out of breath, and bleeding, she knew this had been another trick. She turned to hide her tears and to start walking back to the church.

But Jennifer had come up behind her. Pinching the back of the arm to direct her where she wanted, steering Molly to her surprise.

They stopped in front of a twisted heap of metal.

"What is that?"

"That's the car your mom died in."

She'd been too horrified to speak. The car had been mangled so badly it didn't resemble a car.

"We thought it was time you saw it," Jennifer said. "Can you imagine how much it must've hurt to die in that? With a train ripping your body to shreds?"

By that time Molly had been all-out weeping.

"Oh, shut your fat face," Jennifer sneered.

"Yeah. We're not done with the story," Brandi added.

"What story?"

"The truth Grams was too ashamed to tell you. About the night your mom died."

She remembered wanting to ask . . . and not wanting to know. Not that Brandi and Jennifer had given her a choice.

Jennifer had pinched her arm harder and leaned in to whisper in her ear. But she never whispered. She thought it was funnier to yell in Molly's ear at close range.

"Listen," Brandi hissed.

"The night your mom died? She wasn't alone. You were in the car with her."

"I don't remember."

"Of course you don't, stupid. You were, like, two. Anyway, your mom drove to the railroad tracks late at night and left the car there." That's when Jennifer's eyes glittered. "And she left you sleeping in the car. See, she realized after coming back here that she didn't want a fat, ugly kid like you. She knew you'd never fit in and no one would like you. So she was gonna make it look like an accident that you died when the train hit the car."

"But you climbed out of the car window," Brandi inserted. "Your mom tried to catch you, but you hid in the ditch. That's when she knew her plan wouldn't work, so she got back in the car to move it."

"That's when the train hit her and killed her dead. So it's your fault she died."

Molly fell on the ground, spewing out her morning milk and Raisin Bran. Her stomach muscles spasmed even when she had nothing left in her belly.

Brandi dropped onto all fours beside her, making the same retching noises and laughing.

Jennifer crouched on the other side. "They found you wandering along the railroad tracks the next morning. Grams knows your mother didn't want you. She didn't want you either, but she felt so guilty that your own mother tried to kill you, so she took you in."

The images went black, and she struggled not to let that darkness suck her in. As a child she didn't have that ability. It'd taken her months to crawl out of that pit of despair.

"Babe." A pause. "Molly." Another pause. "Darlin', look at me please."

Deacon's insistent voice broke through the sensation of her being underwater. She looked at him, but his face was a blur.

He wiped her tears. "How old were you when that happened?"

"Eight. It sounds far-fetched now, but when I was a lonely eight-year-old girl, it was all too easy to believe. They knew I was too mortified by the possibility it could be true to ever ask Grams. And even if I had found the guts to ask and there were questions about where I'd heard the story, Jennifer and Brandi would both claim they'd never said anything like that and I was lying, making up stories to get attention. A couple months later, my logical brain had picked the story apart completely. There wasn't any way that anyone knew what'd happened that night. And living in a small town that size? If I'd been found wandering on the railroad tracks after the accident, I would've heard about it."

"I hate that you had to go through that."

"I hate that I even told you. You must think I'm the most pathetic woman on the planet."

"No." He got right in her face. "Fuck no. I . . ." He rested his forehead to hers. "I've had ugliness like that in my life too."

"Will you tell me about it?"

"Someday. Not now. Right now I'm taking you into my bed." He placed a possessive kiss on the spot on her neck that he'd claimed as his. "I'll make all that bullshit disappear."

WARM woman. Soft, bare flesh nestled against him. Deacon had his hands on Molly, but he needed his mouth on her. Needed to feel her squirming and moaning beneath him. Needed urgency and a reminder of the passion between them.

Last night had been about comfort. About making her mindless and boneless as he made love to her. Wearing her out so she slept without bad dreams and bad memories.

Thankfully she'd slept like a rock, so she hadn't known his restlessness.

He shifted his weight, moving over her, bracketing her hips

with his knees. He smiled when she turned, seeking his body heat. Yeah, she liked sleeping naked with him, despite her half-assed protests.

Deacon backed down the mattress until his head was directly above the thin strip of hair covering her mound. Keeping his knees pinning her legs together, he closed his eyes and let her scent be his guide in the darkness as he lowered his head.

She smelled of flowers and sex. He parted her slit with his tongue, tasting her warm musk. She moaned. By the fifth long lap, she'd become aware, if not fully awake. Her hand landed on his head and she tried to spread her legs farther apart.

He stopped long only enough to say, "Hands above your head," and then he buried his mouth in her pussy.

Molly's immediate compliance, her unwavering trust in him . . . He'd never had this before—never wanted it. Now that this lush woman was his for the taking, he'd take her as often as possible.

Deacon zeroed in on her clit, alternating between licking and sucking. Plumping the little nub beneath his lips. Hearing her breath change from the slow, deep rhythm of sleep to fast, short pants of passion.

Her thighs went rigid, but her hips didn't shoot up when she started to come. She gasped softly, eliciting his own growl as he tongued her clit past the first wave. He stayed there, consumed by the need to bring her to orgasm again before he sated his body's needs.

"Deacon," she breathed. "Stop."

He shook his head. Within a few short minutes, he proved that stopping would've been a bad idea.

That time she came so hard she released a small scream.

Hard not to feel really fucking cocky about that.

Deacon rubbed his damp mouth between her hip bones, fascinated by how this section of her skin quivered. In the past two weeks he'd spent hours putting his mouth and hands over every inch of her body, memorizing her every reaction.

He was beyond obsessed with her. Last night, after hearing the depth of her suffering at the hands of her family, he'd felt the bonds between them change. No longer a tenuous tie, they'd solidified. He knew she was the one who could anchor him but not weigh him down.

Molly's hand gently stroked his head. She didn't say anything. She just breathed heavily as she touched him with the comfort that made him want to purr and the eroticism that made him want to roar.

Roaring won out.

He pushed onto all fours. Then he pressed his face into her neck and murmured, "Roll over."

"You sure?" Molly arched into him, teasing him, rubbing her chest against his, knowing he was helpless to resist those fantastic tits.

After placing a sucking kiss on the mounded flesh, he said, "I need you hard, babe." Then he turned her onto her belly himself and stretched her arms to the headboard.

Above her, Deacon said, "Lift up, but keep your legs together." He shoved a pillow beneath her hips. Then, balancing on one arm, he gripped his shaft at the base and aimed the head at her wet center.

As her pussy enveloped his cock, he had to grit his teeth against the need to ram into her. Had anything ever felt this damn good?

No.

Once his cock filled her completely, he placed his lips on the nape of her neck, letting his breath and the damp heat of his mouth tease the fine hairs, knowing it drove her wild.

"God, yes. I love how you feel on me. I've never done it this way."

When she said stuff like that, he wanted to beat the hell out of every man who'd failed to be the lover she needed. Then a cocky sense of possession roared through him. He'd give her everything she'd never had and then some.

"Make that growling sound again." She nuzzled his jaw. "Because that means you're about to bring out the beast."

"Fuck, woman. You test me when you say shit like that."

Deacon started to move. Kissing all his favorite spots. Nipping and scraping his teeth on those same sensitive sections. Keeping as much contact between their bodies until the heat and the friction made their skin slick with sweat.

Every time he bottomed out, Molly made a small grunt of satisfaction that echoed his own.

He slid his mouth up and down the slope of her shoulder, feeling her skin break out in gooseflesh beneath his lips.

"Deacon, you said hard."

"Patience, babe," he murmured. "Feels good like this."

"Yes." She moaned when he thrust in harder. "Feels good like that too."

"I wanna take my time with this pussy that's so hot and wet and ready for me," he said into her sweet-smelling hair.

Molly tightened her cunt muscles around his shaft.

"Fuck." He hissed in a quick breath. "Do that again."

She bore down harder.

Deacon picked up the pace. The faster thrusts sent him speeding toward release. He buried his face in the curve of her neck, rocking his hips, his skin sliding across hers, the scents of Molly and sex filling his lungs. Nothing had ever felt so amazing. And then he realized why it felt so amazing.

No condom.

But he'd hit the point of no return. He pulled out, and his shaft slipped up the crack of her ass. The damp skin and tight depth hugging his length had him sliding faster and faster, because that felt fucking fantastic too.

"Deacon? Why'd you—"

"No condom," he panted. "Too fuckin' close to stop."

"Yes, come on me. Mark me."

The circuits in his brain went haywire.

He pressed his hand down over his shaft, keeping it tightly sandwiched between her buttocks, grinding down hard on every thrust. Her wet pussy kissed his balls, and then they drew up tight and his shaft jerked, sending come spurting onto her ass and the small of her back.

Fuck yeah. His orgasm went on and on. Finally he stopped moving, but he couldn't tear his eyes away from the wet spots that glistened on her skin.

He snickered, a little sex drunk this early in the morning.

Molly looked over her shoulder. "It's impolite to stare at someone's ass and snicker, buddy."

"Sorry. My come just looks so fucking hot on you. But, babe, there's a lot of it."

"Guess you'd better get that fancy shower warmed up so you can clean me up."

"Guess I'd better." He kissed the side of her mouth. "Thanks. I love that you're up for anything."

"With you? Always." She pushed up on her elbows to look at him. "We haven't talked about it, but I am on the pill."

He dropped beside her, propping himself up on his forearm. "So no more condoms?"

"Not unless you have a secret love of them."

"Hell no. But my latest health certificate is at the dojo. Had it done before my last fight. I haven't fucked anyone since way before that."

He sensed she wanted to say she trusted him, but he didn't want her blind trust any more than he wanted her blind obedience.

"I think my last doctor's visit was six months ago. I'll set up an appointment to get tested—"

"Have you been with anyone in the last six months?"

Her cheeks heated. "No."

"Then there's no need for a retest."

"You trust me? Just like that?"

"Yeah, I do." Deacon knew she understood what that meant. He kissed her. "So we can be spontaneous now, huh?"

"Like we haven't been before? I think the only place we haven't fucked in my apartment is the hall closet." She smirked. "But then again, you did fuck me against that door."

"So it counts."

Molly laughed.

Deacon brushed her hair out of her face. "Looks like we'll have to fuck in every room here today to even things up."

"You've got a much bigger place than mine. It'll take more than just one day, Mr. Insatiable." Her eyes searched his. "Don't you have to train today?"

"I deserve a day off from the dojo." At least here he wouldn't have to face off against Courey. And Maddox could suck it. Sundays were light training days anyway. "I'll run on the treadmill in the fitness room downstairs."

"Deacon, you're not blowing off training because of me—"

He stopped her from talking with a kiss. The last thing he needed was her nagging him about training like everyone else.

Then Deacon reached down and swirled his finger through the come spots that were cooling on her back. He held it up to her beautifully, sexily kiss-swollen lips. "Open."

Keeping her heavy-lidded gaze connected to his, she sucked the digit into her mouth, then swirled her tongue around and around.

After she released his finger, he kissed her, his tongue darting in for a taste of himself in her mouth. Then he murmured, "I like waking up with you in my bed. Go back to sleep, but stay like this for me—warm, wet, wearing only my marks. After cardio, I'll clean you up as we get dirty in the shower." He tucked the sheet around her.

Deacon watched as she closed her eyes, a self-satisfied smile on her lips.

This would be his fastest cardio workout all year.

CHAPTER EIGHTEEN

MONDAY morning Presley asked, "Why are you dragging ass so bad today?" after the tenth time Molly yawned.

Molly shifted in her office chair, and her sore spots protested. "Because I am a hopeless slut when it comes to Deacon McConnell."

Presley's eyes widened. "Come again?"

"Yes, I come again, and again, and again," she muttered. "That's the problem. And yet . . . it's not a problem. Deacon is—"

"Horny?" Presley supplied.

"You have no idea. And he's insatiable and relentless. I'm not complaining, because it's amazing every freakin' time."

"But?"

"But I'm also wondering if this excessive sex is normal." Her gaze searched Presley's. "Is it?"

"Give me a second to bask in the fact you think I've had a normal life of any kind, let alone a normal sex life."

"Pres, I'm serious."

"I know." She tucked a hank of orange hair behind her ear. "If he rocks your bed frame so often, then why are you questioning it?"

"What if that's all there is between us?"

"You told me you didn't care if this was a temporary fling with Deacon. Have you changed your mind?"

I don't know. Okay, yes, I do. I think it's been more than sex all along.

"This sex-a-thon will run its course," Presley continued, oblivious to Molly's inner turmoil, "and you'll have great sex stories to tell—after you marry a boring guy who isn't hot enough to toast your marshmallows in that way."

When Presley's gaze sharpened, Molly knew her face betrayed how awful that life sounded.

"That's not how you see your life playing out?"

"Maybe at one time I did, but not now."

"Since you started things with Deacon or before?"

"What do you think?"

Presley threw her arms up. "I think you are confusing the fuck outta me. You cannot look at that tough, brooding, snarling man and not see passion, Mol. Passion drives him. You should've expected he'd focus that passion on you."

"You think I don't know that? But I've never been with a man who is as physically demonstrative as he is sexual. It's usually either/or."

"We're still talking about *Deacon*, right? The man who'd grunt his instructions in class if he could? He's touchy-feely in private?"

"Unbelievably." Wait. Did sharing that break a relationship rule?

"Like how?"

"He always has to be touching me. Even when we're just sitting on the couch watching TV, one or both of his hands are on me somewhere."

"What about during meals?"

"I sit on his left side so he can keep his hand on my leg while we're eating. But even that's become an issue since a simple touch leads to wanting more hands on skin, mouth on skin, skin on skin. Then my clothes are flying off, and his clothes are flying off, and I don't give a damn that my bra is in the butter and my panties have become a toaster cozy. We're body to body, it's fantastic and everything else in the world just disappears."

Stunned silence.

Then, "For the love of Loki, Molly. Are you drunk? You never tell me shit like this."

"I never tell you shit like this because being a ho is a new thing for me."

Presley's owl-eyed gaze flicked over Molly's shoulder. "Uh, hey, Amery."

"Morning, Pres. Morning, ho."

Molly put her forehead on her desk. Then she heard the sound of metal scraping across the floor. She looked up to see Amery settling in next to Presley.

"Keep talking. This is way more interesting than itemizing expenses. What did I miss?" Amery prompted Presley.

"Just Molly complaining about being overly tired since she's a sex fiend obsessed with Deacon's magical dick and it's keeping her up at night."

"At least he can keep it up all night for his greedy ho-bag girlfriend, amirite?"

Presley laughed and high-fived Amery.

"You two oughta take your comedy act on the road." She pointed at Amery's office and then at Presley's work space. "Seriously. Get. Out."

"Oh, don't be a bad sport," Amery said. "Keep talking."

"I don't know if I feel comfortable talking about this with you, boss."

"Please. I'm the perfect person to talk to because you see what a ho-bag I am for Ronin." She smirked. "I'm pretty sure you've figured out when he stops by to 'discuss something' with me and my office door is locked that we're usually not talking."

Presley held her hand up for another high five.

"Fine, but you can't share any of this with your husband, because I don't want this getting back to Deacon."

"I won't. Spill."

Molly slumped back in her chair. "Deacon is the most sexual man I've ever been with."

"How often are we talking about with you and Deacon's sexy times?" Presley asked.

"At least once a day. Sometimes twice. Sometimes more."

Presley mouthed, *Holy fuck.*

"You tell him no when you're not in the mood?"

Molly sighed. "There's the *ho* problem—ha-ha. He gives me that look, puts those big mitts on me, and I'm freakin' putty in his hands. I can't say no. I don't *want* to say no. I'm never not in the mood."

"You feel dirty afterward?" Amery asked softly.

Her directness surprised Presley. But their newest coworker didn't know how Amery had struggled with her strict religious upbringing when it came to her sexuality. "No, I don't feel dirty. I feel fantastic. He knows me now." She briefly closed her eyes. "I've never let any guy know me like that because I've never trusted anyone like I do him."

"It's scary, powerful stuff—isn't it?"

Molly's eyes met Amery's. "Very."

"So you're not really complaining."

She shook her head. "I'm just tired."

"Well, you have been spending all of your off-work hours with him," Presley pointed out. "I miss hanging out with you."

"Same. I'll see if Fee and Katie are up for going out this weekend."

Presley said, "Cool. Set it up. I'm in."

"I'm out," Amery said. "We'll be at Knox and Shiori's all day Saturday, spoiling Nuri, and Ronin has plans for us Saturday night."

Molly was too chicken to ask if Ronin's plans included an evening of twisting ropes on her at Twisted. "Too bad. We'll knock back a margarita or two for you."

Amery's eyes bored into Molly's. "You sure you're okay? Nothing else going on with Deacon?"

She knew voicing her concerns about Deacon missing training yesterday, with his next fight coming up so soon, would violate a relationship rule, since she feared Amery would mention that to Ronin. Molly didn't know whether Amery was aware that Ronin had put the kibosh on Deacon starting a relationship a few months ago, and again, she was too chicken to ask. She manufactured a believable smile. "That's it. I've just never been oversexed. I should've come to you—our resident expert on being oversexed."

"No such thing." Amery stood and disappeared into her office.

Presley stood and tapped her palms on the desk. "Good talk."

"You don't have anything to share?"

"Trust me—if I was getting laid as much as you are? I'd be bragging about it all the damn time. You couldn't shut me up about it."

Molly held her next yawn until Presley was gone.

AFTER work she headed to the dojo and managed to catch both Katie Gardiner, who ran the Black and Blue Promotions arm of Black Arts, and Sophia "Fee" Curacao, a Brazilian jujitsu instructor, an MMA fighter, as well as Blue's sister, upstairs in the Black and Blue Promotions office.

Beautiful blond Katie crossed her arms and leaned back in her chair. "My god. You are disgustingly well laid."

Fee smacked Katie on the arm. "Shut it. Jealousy gives you wrinkles."

"Ouch! Don't do that, Fee. You're a like a fourth-degree black belt; I'm a delicate flower and you hit like a man."

"You deserved it. Be happy for our friend."

"I *am* happy, but I'm still going to pout."

"I think your Botox injections prevent that, K." Then Fee waggled her eyebrows at Molly. "Hooking up with Deacon regularly *has* put a satisfied look in your eyes."

"Umm . . . thank you for noticing?" Molly said.

"Hard not to," Katie complained. "I need a man who makes my whole damn body glow like that. It's been ages since I bumped uglies with a dude."

"Maybe because you call sex *bumping uglies*? Anyway, it hasn't been ages, ho-bag." Fee tilted her head at her BFF, Katie. "Didn't you and Ivan break your mattress last month?"

"Shh," Katie hissed. "Ronin and Blue would ream us both if they found out."

"Why? There's not a 'no fraternization' policy at Black Arts, is there?" Molly asked.

Katie shook her head. "Between an instructor and a student like you and Deacon? No. But people might think I'm giving Ivan more press time and coverage if it's discovered *he's* giving me the Russian salami."

"Seriously, Katie, what is wrong with you?" Fee demanded, her voice escalating. "The Russian salami?"

"The what?" Blue asked as he strolled in and grabbed a folder off Katie's desk. "Did you say Russian salami?"

"Yes, we were talking about sandwiches," Katie lied with a straight face.

"If you're making a sandwich run, I'll try a Russian salami." He tossed out, "Make sure it's twelve inches," before he left the room.

Molly laughed so hard she feared she might've wet her pants.

All she had to do was look at Katie clutching her belly and Fee wiping her eyes and they dissolved into laughter again.

"Thanks a lot," Fee grumbled. "Now I'll have my brother asking me if I ever got that twelve-inch Russian salami for him."

"I guarantee Ivan's twelve-inch Russian salami is a lot harder to get in your mouth than out of it."

Molly reached over and stopped Fee from whacking Katie again. But she couldn't help asking, "You're kidding about twelve inches, right?"

"Ivan is a big guy all over. But his Rasputin is closer to ten inches."

"Can we be done talking about cocks now and find out why Molly is here?" Fee asked. "What brings you by?"

"Do either of you have plans Saturday?"

Katie clapped her hands. "Yes, yes, yes, yes, yes! Guess whose birthday it is?"

"Yours?" Molly said dryly.

"Ask Fee what she's got planned," Katie said smugly.

"You bitch! The party was supposed to be a surprise!" Fee's shoulders slumped. "You suck. Now you'll just have to go to Dave and Buster's like everyone else over twenty-five does on their birthday."

Molly choked and tried to pass it off as a cough.

Katie eyed her suspiciously before she refocused on Fee. "You can still have a party for me. You were being stealthy, Fifi, I promise. I just overheard you talking to Jaz."

"*Jaz* knew about this surprise party before I did?" Molly demanded of Fee. Jaz was the new black belt instructor that Sensei Black had hired six months ago. No one knew too much about her. She mostly kept to herself. Apparently Fee had broken the ice with her, which was good. Molly remembered what it felt like to be on the outside looking in.

"I was gonna call you this week, okay? I only decided to do this yesterday. Jaz offered to help." Fee sighed. "I'll need all the help I can get so the princess isn't disappointed."

"I will need to add a few people to your guest list," Katie said, grabbing a pen.

"Fine, but you aren't planning this," Fee warned. "I am."

"While I'll be happy to help you celebrate, Katie, I was really looking forward to girl time."

"It has been a while," Fee said. "But your lack of girl time is self-inflicted. You've been holed up with Deacon."

"She means with Deacon filling your holes," Katie said with a *rowr.*

"Presley mentioned the same thing. Only not so crudely."

Katie tapped her pen on her desk. "We'll do that the weekend after the fight. Shopping, food, drinks, then hitting someplace for kinky fun. I suppose I have to be budget conscious when making the plan?"

"Since it'll be me, Fee, and Presley? Yes. So it's three slim wallets against one fat one, moneybags."

"You have to admit I *am* getting better at the budgeting thing," Katie said to Fee, buffing her perfect manicure on her silk shirt.

Fee snorted. "You spent fifty-eight hundred dollars on a pair of leather pants last month. Your idea of budgeting was *not* buying the twenty-seven-hundred-dollar matching vest."

"Hey! Denial of self-gratification counts as budgeting for me. But luckily for you, I am equally adept at sussing out cheap thrills for us."

"Cool. Text me the details about the princess's partay, Fee. Later."

Molly took the stairs and ran into Deacon.

Immediately he hooked an arm around her waist and his mouth landed on hers. His lips and tongue were cool, but his mouth heated up as the kiss became urgent. As if holding her and kissing her was exactly what he needed.

The post-workout musk of Deacon's body filled her lungs with a giddy sense of possession. Now she knew his scent intimately. His taste was addictive, the hint of salt from his sweat, the underlying sweetness of the protein bars he ate all day, and the dark flavor of the man himself that no mints or gum could mask.

He kissed her harder, pulling her closer. His happiness had shifted into hunger.

Molly found her back against the cement wall and one hundred and eighty-five pounds of turned-on fighter grinding against her. And like always, when faced with his passion, she melted into him.

Deacon shifted until he could fit the upper section of his thigh between hers. He slowed the kiss and moved his mouth to her ear. "I've had a shit day. And I was thinking . . . I can't wait to see my woman." His breath left his mouth in ragged bursts of air. "Can't wait to touch her. Can't wait to slide inside her deep. Can't wait to lose myself in her. Gotta be fate or karma or something. I was thinking of you, babe, and here you are."

She released a little squeak when he nipped her neck.

"Fuck, I love that noise." Then he heaved himself away from her and grabbed her hand. "Come on."

"Where are we going?"

"Someplace more private," he said as he started up the stairs. When they reached the fourth floor, Deacon swiped the ID/key-card he wore on a lanyard around his neck down the lock. The green light flashed and he pushed the door open.

The training area was eerily quiet. Every time she'd been up here, the sounds of striking echoed from corner to corner.

Deacon towed her around a curtain used to divide the spaces and into a small area that resembled a study room in a library. Blue light spilled across the lone table from the emergency light in the corner.

As soon as he shut the door, he was on her. Devouring her mouth, one hand clamped on her ass, the other freeing the buttons on her blouse. His frantic kisses made it impossible for her to catch her breath.

Molly put her hands on either side of his face and pulled him back to break the seal of their mouths. "Deacon," she whispered against his lips.

He buried his face in her neck. "I need you like this."

His desperation inflamed her. Later she'd worry about what in his day had gotten him to this point. "How naked are we getting?"

He tugged his muscle shirt over his head. He kissed her wildly as he unbuttoned her blouse and freed her breasts. Then, after he slid his hands under her skirt to remove her panties, he growled, "This is all I've got patience for." He pushed her backward until her butt connected with the table.

Deacon didn't have to direct her; she knew what he wanted. She shifted one buttock onto the table and then the other. Her skirt rode up and Deacon's hands were shoving the material out of the way, baring her pussy to him.

His fingers teased the insides of her thighs, making her tremble, making her ache for a more complete touch. He used the little things he'd learned about her shamelessly and constantly found new ways to drive her crazy.

After a lip-tingling kiss, he dragged his mouth down the side of her throat. Once his wandering hands reached the juncture of her thighs, he drew his knuckle through her wetness. His low-pitched hum reverberated against the upper swell of her breast as he lowered her down.

When Molly's head fell back, her hair spilled over the edges of the table. The hot fire of his mouth engulfed her nipple as his cock breached her body.

She arched into him. *Yes*. So good. Every time.

Deacon held on to her hips as he started to power up. The long, slow glide gave way to harder thrusts. He moved his mouth back and forth across her nipples, nipping with his teeth and sucking hard, then switching to achingly soft kisses and rubbing the scruff on his cheeks over the mounds of flesh as he pounded into her.

Sometimes he talked when he fucked her, whispering dirty words, sweet words, nonsensical words. She loved that. But his mouth worshipping her breasts needed no words. Although they were alone in the vast space, remaining quiet as they surrendered to the driving need heightened the fervor.

The legs on the table creaked as Deacon's damp, muscled body ground down on hers with every dedicated thrust.

With one hand curled around the nape of his neck, she flung her other arm above her head, her fingers clamping to the edge of the table to keep from sliding off. Her body was a live wire, electrified by the sucking pressure of his mouth. His firm grip on her hips kept her from thrashing, reminding her that he was in control.

More. Please. I need . . .

As if he'd read her mind, his rough-skinned hand moved across her belly and down her slit to where they were joined. Then his thumb, wet with her juices, circled her clit in the same pattern as his tongue on her nipple.

So close. She whimpered and canted her hips.

Deacon didn't miss a stroke as he spread her legs wider, giving her the friction she needed. "You're there. Give it to me."

The orgasm ricocheted through her—a hot detonation that throbbed with such force she swore her eyeballs pulsed. Her body was so revved up she couldn't slump back and bask.

Then Deacon buried his face in her neck, pumping his hips fast. She felt the heat of his release, her spasming walls milking him as he came in a drawn-out groan.

Sometimes Deacon immediately pulled out and brought her tissues to clean herself up. But today she silently begged him to stay put, needing this connection with him as long as possible.

"MOLLY."

"Mmm?"

"Babe. You gotta let go of me."

"But I don't wanna," she murmured. "I like your weight on me." She rubbed her lips over the stubble on his cheek. "I like the stickiness between my legs. I like feeling you soften inside me, knowing if I did this"—she squeezed her pussy muscles around his semihard cock—"you'd get hard and fuck me again."

"Don't tempt me, woman. We're damn lucky we didn't get caught." What the hell had he been thinking, rutting on her in the dojo like a crazed man?

Because you are crazy about her, man. Beyond crazy, heading straight into those three-little-words territory, which is completely new fucking territory for you.

He fit his mouth to hers and kissed her, slowly easing out of her body and then laughing as she tried to hold on to him and keep him on her and in her.

"At least I know you were happy to see me," he murmured.

"Very happy. As always."

He'd been in a lousy mood since first thing this morning when Maddox pushed him to work Courey—meaning he'd been relegated to chump again. Holding the mitts while Courey tried to pummel him.

Luckily—maybe unluckily—Deacon had left his phone on, in the training room, during practice—a strict violation of practice and not intentional on his part—but the phone call from his cousin Tag served as an excuse to leave the dojo. He'd mumbled something about "family shit" and no one had questioned him because they all were aware Deacon never made excuses not to train and he never talked about his family.

By the time he'd finished dealing with Tag, he'd been pissed off for real and wished Courey hadn't bailed for the day because he could've used him to work out his frustrations.

The last thing he needed was Tag showing up in Denver. The fucker had resorted to threats to force the dinner meeting, so Deacon had to ask Beck to sub for him tomorrow night.

Then he'd seen Ronin talking to Shihan. Deacon knew Sensei was questioning whether it'd been a waste of time to add Deacon back into the teaching rotation when he bowed out again within the first two weeks.

Realizing he'd zoned out, he refocused on Molly buttoning her blouse.

"You're staring at my boobs again. Didn't you get enough of them?"

"Never." He reached down to snag her panties. After he handed them over, she used them to wipe between her legs. Then she wadded up the blue silk and stuffed them in her purse.

"What? My panties were soaked anyway. I'd rather go commando than wear wet panties."

Deacon hauled her against him and kissed the hell out of her.

When they broke free, Molly said, "What was that for?"

"For you being the best thing that's happened to me in a long time."

Her brown eyes softened. "Deacon."

He plucked her panties from her purse and shoved them in his pocket.

"Hey! Give those back!"

"Nope."

Molly poked him in the chest. "If I ever see those hanging up in your training locker like some kind of trophy—"

"For my eyes only. I promise." He rested his forehead to hers. "This is ours. No one needs to know how it is between us."

"You are so sweet sometimes. And don't worry. I won't tell anyone that either."

Deacon held her hand as they exited the training room. "What're your plans for tonight?"

"I've been spectacularly fucked, so I can cross that off my 'to do' list."

"Hilarious, babe."

"I actually have some work to catch up on. What about you?"

He had to check over the financial statements from JFW and the investment reports Tag had e-mailed him. "I've got stuff to look over."

"Fight tapes?"

"Yeah." Not a lie since he still hadn't watched Needham's last training tape.

When they exited the stairwell on the second floor, Knox and Shiori were standing outside the office door.

Knox's shrewd gaze zoomed between Deacon and Molly. Then he flashed a shit-eating grin the size of Texas and mouthed, *Busted*, before he elbowed Shiori.

Shi-Shi turned those cool eyes on him and shifted Nuri to her other hip. Knox said something that caused her to smirk.

Asshole.

"Hey, Deacon. Hey, Molly. I thought your kickboxing classes were on this floor."

"They are. Tomorrow night. What are you doin' here?"

"I'm teaching the advanced black belt class tonight," Shiori answered, "since Beck has requested I fill in more often."

Molly ditched him and stopped in front of Shiori. "Gimme the precious."

"Our poor, neglected baby. No one ever wants to hold her." Shiori passed Nuri over, and Molly kissed the baby's head. Then she started walking around with her, pointing out stuff that Nuri was too young to understand.

Her nurturing instinct with Nuri gave Deacon a funny feeling.

"Never gonna do it in the dojo, huh?" Knox teased.

Shiori cocked her head. "His usual snarl does look much less pronounced. So I'm curious. Where did you nail her? I'm betting the locker room. What say you, Knox?"

"Nah. Too many kids running around. I'm betting—"

"It's not up for discussion. *Ever.* So fucking drop it."

"Hell no. What goes around comes around, my friend."

"What did you say to me the time you caught Knox and me sneaking out of the Crow's Nest?" Shiori asked.

"He said you had that high-pro glow," Knox answered. "Who's the dog now?"

Shi-Shi howled and Knox laughed.

Everyone was a fucking comedian. "I was a dick, okay?"

"*Was* a dick? You're still a dick, Yondan. Even when you're smitten and acting all embarrassed about it, we owe you massive amounts of payback."

"Look, I had a shit day and she made it better by just walking in the damn building. The rest between her and me is just a bonus. A private bonus."

"Damn. He does have it bad," Shiori said to Knox.

"Told ya."

"Bring her over for dinner one night next week. Knox will cook. We'll play charades. We'll show you vacation photos from our week in Japan."

"So it'd be like a couples' dinner-party thing?" he said with mock horror.

"Yes."

He grinned. "Cool. Sounds fun."

Shiori tried to get in his face. But at five feet nothing it was a stretch for her. "Knox, get Riggins. I think Deacon sustained a serious blow to the head today."

"Ha-ha, Shi-Shi. This is me bein' all mature and in a relation-ship and shit." He kissed her forehead. "Get used to it."

CHAPTER NINETEEN

MOLLY doubted Deacon liked surprises.

But here she was, dressed to the nines, cursing Tag Westerman and his southern charm, because she was about to horn in on a family dinner.

When Deacon's cousin called to ask if the lawyer he'd recommended in Nebraska was working out, she'd thanked him because the house and land sale had turned into a big mess. Having a lawyer looking out for her interests had saved her sanity.

After some small talk, Tag casually mentioned being in Denver and then he'd invited her to dinner as a surprise for Deacon.

For some bizarre reason, she'd justified saying yes by reminding herself that Deacon had shown up in Nebraska without warning. And he'd handled her relatives just fine. Since she knew Tag was the one cousin Deacon got along with . . . well, how bad could it be?

She approached the hostess stand inside Ocean Prime. "I'm meeting the Westerman party."

The hostess typed on her computer. Then she frowned. "Could it be under another name?"

"Look under Bishop," a deep male voice drawled behind her.

Molly turned.

The tall, slender man offered his hand and a smile. "Molly? I'm Tag Westerman."

Tag had dark blond hair and pale green eyes. He'd dressed casually in a button-down shirt the color of celery, khaki slacks, and a pair of tan cowboy boots. Once her gaze returned to his handsome, almost pretty face, she returned his smile. "Yes, I'm Molly."

"I hope you don't mind me saying so, but, darlin', you're lovely."

"Thank you. I hope you don't mind me saying that I don't think you have a reservation here. Did you maybe make it at Oceanlandia instead? Easy to get the two places mixed up."

"Ah, here it is," the hostess said triumphantly. "Under the name Bishop."

Confused, Molly asked, "Bishop is a family name?"

"No. It's a joke. A bishop outranks a deacon in the religious hierarchy, and since I'm older than him . . ." He grinned. "I'll admit I sometimes use *Cardinal* and *Pope* just to keep my cousin on his toes."

The hostess said, "If you'll follow me."

They headed up a staircase and down a hallway. Then a tuxedoed waiter opened the door to a private room.

Molly was so busy checking out the ambience of the space—glass windows, candlelight, sheer curtains—that she didn't notice the man sitting in the corner at first.

"Punctual as usual, Mr. Bishop," Deacon drawled.

"Thought I'd beat you here, Deacon," Tag returned in an equally thick drawl.

Deacon stood and crossed over to Molly.

"Your cousin called and asked me to come. If it's not okay, I can go."

"Stay." He curled his hands around her face and planted a very possessive kiss on her. "Looks like someone blew off class tonight."

"Says the teacher who isn't barking orders at his students cowering in the dojo right now."

"Luckily, I've got very explicit makeup requirements for you for missing class." Then he pulled out a chair. "This seat has the best view. I planned to let Tag sit there, but he can lord over us from the corner."

"Relegated to the naughty corner within the first two minutes. Usually that's you, Deacon."

Deacon grunted and sat next to Molly.

Before additional conversation started, the cocktail server popped in and pointed out the specialized handcrafted cocktails. Molly chose a blackberry-and-blueberry-infused sparkling wine.

Deacon ordered a light beer, which caused his cousin to snort. "Some things never change."

The menu boasted fabulous food. She settled on the gorgonzola-and-pine-nut-encrusted tenderloin, with a side of lemon-finished asparagus. Deacon didn't deviate from his training diet of lean protein and vegetables.

After the waiter departed, an uncomfortable silence filled the room, and Molly wished they had the noise and conversations from other diners as a distraction.

Deacon reached for her hand underneath the table. "So, Tag, what brings you to Denver?"

"Short answer? I need to talk to you face-to-face. We'll have a breakfast meeting in the morning to discuss the particulars." He smiled. "I wanted to enjoy a leisurely meal with you and your lady tonight."

"You assume a lot."

Tag shook his head. "You've known this was coming for months."

Molly hated cryptic conversations. If they had business to discuss—which was none of her business—Tag shouldn't have invited her. "Deacon hasn't told me much about you, Tag."

"That's where we have a commonality; I was shocked—and delighted, of course—to hear my cousin has a girlfriend. So how about you tell me all about yourself?"

"That will kill two minutes of the evening."

Tag laughed. "Indulge me."

Molly gave him the basics.

"How did you meet Deacon?"

"I started with a self-defense class at Black Arts and moved on to kickboxing, which Yondan teaches. He tortured me endlessly."

"So you're a masochist to his sadist?" Tag mused.

"Something like that."

Deacon squeezed her knee.

"You've seen him fight?"

"Twice. I haven't decided if I can stomach seeing him exchanging blows with his opponent next month."

Deacon looked at her crossly. "Fine time to spring *that* on me, babe."

Molly shrugged. "It's not the same thing to see my instructor fighting as it is to see my boyfriend in a cage with a guy who's determined to cause him maximum physical damage. And it shouldn't be a surprise to you."

"Why's that?"

"Ronin never let Amery see him fight. And Knox had to leave when Shiori fought." She sipped her cocktail. "Dealing with the aftermath of injuries is hard enough without seeing how those injuries were received."

"It ain't a picnic to get hammered on and after the fight is done to realize there's no one in your corner. So you will be there."

That caused a pang of guilt and hurt her heart a little.

"Even if Molly can't be there, your dad will be," Tag said diplomatically.

"I didn't know anyone in your family came to your fights. Have they ever come to the after-party?"

He snorted. "My dad is the only one who comes to anything. But the smokers don't count. Real fights, like the one next month, he'll show up. Look for the white-knuckled man in the back row."

"Maybe I'll sit back there too. We can hold hands."

Deacon leaned over and brushed his lips across her cheek. "I'd like that."

She lowered her eyes, basking in her man's sweetness.

When Molly looked up, she noticed Tag watching them with undisguised interest. "Now it's your turn, Tag. How did you get your name? Was it confusing when you were a kid to hear, *Tag, you're it.*"

Tag let out an amused laugh. "Damn, Deacon. If I lived in Denver, I'd be pulling out all stops to lure this woman away from you."

"Be wise of you not to throw fightin' words at a fighter, cuz."

"My first name is Taggart," he said, ignoring Deacon's snarling response. "It was my mother's maiden name. Only time anyone used it was after I'd gotten in trouble."

"Which he'll now loudly proclaim was rarely," Deacon tossed out.

Their ribbing seemed good-natured and not pure meanness like her cousins' constant barbs.

The salad course arrived and they dug in.

After Deacon finished his beer, he switched to water. "Does Clive know you're here?"

"No. He'd have to show his rat face at the office more than twice a week to know anything."

"It's not goin' any better with him?"

"Worse, actually. It was goddamn blackmail that our fathers agreed to give him a position in the company."

Blackmail sounded harsh.

"They could've said no. Instead they both bent over for Aunt Suzette just like she wanted."

Tag's posture went rigid. "Now we've got a chance to kick his worthless ass to the curb and cut him out, if you'd just—"

"We're not discussing this shit tonight, Tag, so fuckin' drop it. Keep it up and we won't be discussing nothin' tomorrow neither."

Molly tugged her fingers out of Deacon's death grip. As she debated on whether to excuse herself and head to the ladies' room, the door opened and the food arrived.

Every bite lived up to the hype. She moaned when the first bite of tender steak and sharp cheese hit her taste buds.

Tag's phone rang and he excused himself from the room.

The second the door closed, Deacon placed a hot kiss on the side of her neck. "Word of advice."

Crap. Had she mistakenly used the appetizer plate instead of the bread plate? "What?"

"That sexy little fucking moan you made when you were enjoying your food sounds awful damn close to the sexy little fucking moan you make right before you come."

That's when she knew it was possible to blush from head to toe. "It is?"

"Yep. And that noise belongs to me. Just me." His soft lips feathered across her jawline. "So if you keep your nonverbal approval to yourself, you'll save my cousin a bloody lip."

"God, Deacon. You are paranoid. I doubt Tag heard anything besides you thumping your chest every time he looked at me."

"Oh, he heard it, all right. I saw his face. That's why I wanna punch him in the mouth. Fucker is probably in the bathroom right now, rubbing one out."

Ridiculous man.

"And you are gonna make them noises with me later, and it won't be because of food."

"I'll do my best. But no promises if the chocolate crème brûlée with raspberry sauce tastes as orgasmic as it sounds."

Deacon's mouth captured hers in a kiss more seductive than any decadent dessert, and she couldn't help but moan. He murmured, "That's what I'm talking about, babe. That noise is mine."

Tag returned and they finished the rest of the meal in silence.

The plates were cleared and the waiter took dessert orders.

"How long are you here for?" Molly asked Tag.

"I'll leave after the breakfast meeting with Deacon."

"Do you practice law outside of the family business?"

"No. JFW began as an oil company, but we've diversified over the years. Plenty of legal scrabbles to keep me employed and I also handle investments."

"Oil?" She sent Deacon a sidelong glance. "Your family is in the oil business? I didn't know that."

"Because that's their business, not mine. Fighting is what I do."

"I'm a third generation oil man, as is Deacon and our cousin Clive. Granddad started the business in the 1950s."

"Jesus, Tag. Don't bore her to fuckin' death with a family history lesson."

Two sentences wasn't exactly a history lesson. "The only experience I've had with multigenerational business is farming," Molly said, trying to smooth things over. "And not much experience, since my grandmother sold most of the farmland after my grandfather died because she didn't have anyone to pass it down to."

Tag lifted a brow. "You weren't interested?"

"In farming? No. I watched my friends struggle with not wanting to take over the family farm. But most of them ended up doing it anyway."

"That happens in a lot of family businesses—doesn't it, Deacon?" Tag asked. "One person shirking responsibilities."

Deacon stiffened beside her.

So much for smoothing things over. Tag seemed intent on riling Deacon.

"Not everyone is cut out to be cutthroat, Tag."

"Says the man who beats up other men for a living."

Tag and Deacon glared at each other.

This macho family crap drove her crazy. "So it's just you and Clive toiling in Texas?"

"Granddad left the business to his three kids. After he passed, my dad and Deacon's dad had to buy out Aunt Suzette's shares, but she forced them to keep her only kid, Clive, on the payroll. If my dad and Deacon's dad had their way, they'd continue to run the company and work past retirement age, like our granddad did, despite the road bumps JFW Development has hit recently."

Deacon said nothing.

The waiter delivered dessert and coffee, interrupting the awkward silence.

Molly nearly drooled over the luscious caramelized crust and the artful drizzle of raspberry sauce across the plate. A cluster of chocolate-covered raspberries on mint sprigs completed the presentation. "This looks almost too beautiful to eat."

Deacon picked up her spoon and cracked the crust, scooping out a bite of the crème brûlée. "Open," he said huskily.

She parted her lips, and the smooth creaminess flowed across her taste buds. She managed—barely—not to moan with delight.

A devilish light entered Deacon's eyes, and he took a bite, since he'd forgone a dessert of his own. "Almost as sweet as your kisses, darlin'."

Molly popped a chocolate-covered raspberry in her mouth. *Don't moan.* But it definitely deserved a moan.

"Speaking of sweet, D, hand me the sugar, please," Tag said.

"One of these days you'll learn to drink your coffee like a man, without all that froufrou shit."

"If I stirred it with my dick, would that make me more of a manly coffee drinker?"

Deacon held his hands up. "Go for it. It'd be a change for you, having blisters on your dick from something besides excessive use of the palm of your hand."

These two. God. They fought like siblings. "Deacon is the only one not involved in the family business?"

"Yes, but I'd argue that Clive isn't contributing much," Tag said dryly.

"As an only child myself, I find it interesting that all of your parents had only one kid."

"Well, they each have only one kid now."

That pulled her attention away from her dessert. She looked at Tag. "Did one of them have a child die?"

Total silence.

Tag's gaze moved from Deacon to Molly and back to Deacon. Anger flared in his eyes. "She doesn't know?"

Deacon remained statue still.

A bad feeling took root. "What don't I know?"

"Jesus. What the hell is wrong with you?" Tag demanded.

"Shut your fucking mouth, Tag."

"What is going on?" Molly asked Deacon.

He wouldn't even look at her.

Tag said, "Molly—"

"Leave it be." Deacon slammed his fist on the table. "I'm fucking warning you."

Whatever this was, it was bad. She locked her gaze on Tag. "Tell me."

"This should've come from him, not me." Tag paused, giving Deacon a chance to jump in.

But Deacon stayed frozen in place, hands in fists, his jaw clenched, his lips firmly closed.

"Deacon had a brother. Dante. He died when he was fifteen."

The blood drained from her face. Deacon had a brother he'd never mentioned? Why would he keep something that big from her?

"You had no right," Deacon said in a quiet, deadly voice that made the hair on the back of her neck stand up.

"She's your girlfriend—the first one you've had since—"

"Shut up!"

Molly gaped at Deacon.

Tag kept talking. "She should know this about you because it sure as fuck changed you. It changed all of us, but we haven't locked it away like you have."

"It's not locked away. It's with me every goddamn day."

Molly found her voice and addressed her surly, secretive boyfriend. "How old were you when he died?"

"Fifteen."

That jarred her. If Deacon had been fifteen and Dante had been fifteen . . . Her stomach clenched. "My god. You were twins?"

"Identical twins. Now you know, so can we please fucking drop it?" he snapped.

"Drop it? First I find out that your family is in the oil business, which I didn't have a clue about." Something occurred to her. "Is your family like J. R. Ewing—Texas-oil rich?"

Deacon didn't respond.

Floored by these revelations, she addressed Tag. "I'm right, aren't I?"

"Yes, darlin', you are. We've got the Ewing family drama, too, because of it."

"Right. So he's heir to an oil fortune, his twin brother died, which would both explain why he doesn't do family shit . . . What else has he kept from me?"

"Don't answer that," Deacon said tersely.

Then something that'd been niggling in the back of her mind solidified. "Wait. If your fathers are brothers, then why don't you two have the same last name?"

"Bingo." Tag looked back and forth between them. "I'd tell you to ask Deacon why he legally changed his name from Westerman to McConnell, but since he hasn't told you fuck-all about anything else, I doubt he'll come clean about that either."

She faced Deacon and whispered, "Who are you?"

"This"—Deacon stood and jabbed his finger at Tag—"is why I stay the fuck away from you."

"You aren't honestly blaming him—"

"Yes, I am." He whirled around. The panic, horror, and anger in burning in his eyes scared her. "Drop it, right now."

"You're an ass," Tag snapped. "This is all on you."

The second he turned back to rip into Tag, she snatched her purse and raced out, just as the waiter came in, buying her time to get away.

She'd made it down the stairs, out the front door, and almost to the parking garage entrance when she felt a hand on her shoulder.

Molly reacted as she'd been taught. Grabbing the forearm below the elbow, she twisted her body into his, jamming her knee up while trying to inflict damage on his arm.

Deacon easily countered her moves. "What the fuck? Why would you attack me?"

"Instinct from self-defense classes."

"I'm not a fucking threat to you."

"You're right. Because I don't even know you." She tried to level her breathing. "Go back to your cousin."

"I don't give a shit about Tag. He never should've—"

"Told me something that should've come from you?"

His jaw tightened and his eyes went icy. "No. He shouldn't have invited you to dinner without asking me first."

Any sadness and shock she'd initially felt had been replaced with anger. She wanted to scream at him. But she forced herself to start down the sidewalk.

"Don't you fucking walk away from me."

She stopped and spun around. "That's all you have to say to me?"

"I won't be guilted or goddamn browbeat into talking to you about this until I'm ready."

"And when will that be? You could've shared this major life-changing, traumatic event with me when you came to Nebraska and stood by my side every damn hour of the day. I asked you how you knew so much about dealing with grief. I asked you," she repeated, "and you told me nothing. *Nothing.*"

"This is why I don't talk about it. Because now it's about me not opening up to you—not that my brother fucking *died.*"

That remark knocked the breath out of her so fast he might as well have punched her in the gut.

She steeled her resolve and her spine. "I would've accepted not knowing specifics about your past if you would've told me there were things—like your brother's death—that were too difficult to discuss. But this? All of this together—not knowing about your twin brother, finding out you changed your name, hiding your connection to your family business—goes beyond crossing a line of privacy into . . . some fucked-up psychological thing of yours that I can't even begin to understand." She couldn't stop the tears or her voice from cracking. "I trusted you. I thought you trusted me too. But apparently not."

"Molly—"

"I can't . . . I'm not doing this with you. Not anymore."

"So what? You think we're done?"

"Goodbye, Deacon."

She walked away, and this time he didn't chase after her.

MOLLY didn't remember driving home.

She didn't remember getting undressed.

She didn't remember turning off her phone, locking her door, or downing four glasses of Rumple Minze.

That's probably why she didn't remember much.

The alarm went off at six a.m. She climbed in the shower.
How had everything gone to hell so fast?
She'd never been in this situation.
Where her anger outweighed the hurt.
Where she wanted to scream, not cry.
Why hadn't he told her?

Because now it's about me not opening up to you—not that my brother fucking died.

And now . . . it was about her not being able to tell anyone why she and Deacon were over.

AT the office, Presley greeted her with, "Hey, ho-bag. What's up besides your skirt?"

For a brief moment Molly feared she'd burst into tears. But she rallied, like she always did. "Not exactly the most professional way to begin an office conversation."

Presley's eyes widened. "I was joking. I'm sorry. We get along so great that sometimes I forget you're my boss and I say the same stupid stuff to you that I say to the Divas."

"I get it. But sometimes we all need a reminder of our place." Like Deacon did to her last night. Now she had to call in to question everything he'd ever said to her. And she hated—*hated*—that she'd been so damn gullible. She'd opened up to him. She'd told him things she'd never told anyone.

What had he told her?

Nothing.

Fuck. Her chin wobbled.

"Molly, you're not acting like yourself. What is going on?"

Just say it. "Deacon and I broke up last night."

"What?"

"We broke up and I don't want to talk about it."

"But—"

"Seriously, Pres, I'm hanging on by a thread. I almost couldn't get out of bed this morning. So please, don't push me to talk about this. It's over."

"Did that fucker hurt you?"

Molly shook her head.

Presley got right in her face and bit off, "Swear to me that Deacon didn't do anything to you to cause physical harm anywhere on your body."

"I swear it."

"If you change your mind and want to talk . . ."

"Thanks for your concern, but get to work. We have a lot to do today."

CHAPTER TWENTY

DEACON had self-medicated with a bottle of scotch after the shit had gone down with Molly and Tag. He woke up late in no better mood than when he'd passed out last night.

That fucker Tag could just fuck the fuck off. The instant his cousin had walked in with Molly, Deacon had known the night would turn to shit. Maybe it made him a delusional dick, but he blamed Tag. What the hell had he been thinking, contacting his cousin's girlfriend and inviting her to dinner? Especially when Tag had made it clear they'd be discussing family business.

You're really blaming Tag?

Yes.

Tag knew how little Deacon talked about his brother. Tag also knew Deacon and Molly's relationship was new. Tag should've expected that Deacon would share the ugly truth about his past gradually. But by convincing Molly to accompany him to dinner, he'd forced the issue before Deacon had been ready to discuss it.

So fuck yeah, he blamed his goddamn cousin. If Deacon lost Molly over this . . . He clenched his hands on his steering wheel. Fuck. No way. He couldn't think about that right now. Right now he needed to deal with the anger consuming him, not the fear.

So when he'd entered Black Arts training room nearly three hours after he was scheduled to start training, he felt every pair of eyes on him like he was a criminal walking death row.

Maddox waited for him, his arms crossed over his chest. "What the fuck, Deacon. You're late."

"No shit."

"Where you been?"

"Doin' cardio outside. Thought you'd be happy."

"I'd be happy if you didn't disappear whenever the hell you felt like it."

Deacon didn't defend himself or try to explain.

"That's how it's gonna be? Fine, you stoic bastard. Let's knock you down a peg. You're sparring with—"

"Courey," Deacon finished.

Silence.

Courey wandered over from the heavy bags, smirk on his face. "Finally find your balls and ready to face me, Con Man?"

"Depends. You have the balls for full-contact, Crusher?"

"No way," Maddox said, stepping between them. "Mitts and headgear."

"Then I'm not interested in sparring." Deacon walked away, heading to the locker bay.

"Goddammit, Deacon. Get back here."

Deacon stopped and turned around to look at Maddox.

"I'm the trainer. If I tell you to get your mitts and headgear on, you'll goddamn well do it."

"No. Full-contact with Courey or nothing."

Maddox got his mean face on. "Then it's nothing. And by nothing, I mean I'll pull you from the Needham fight, McConnell."

"Do what you have to, Coach."

"I'm not kidding."

"Neither am I. All I've heard for two weeks is you bitching at me for not sparring or grappling with your new pet. Now it's two weeks closer to the bout and I'm ready to up my game, and you're the one saying no. Why?"

"All right, wiseass, I'll tell you why. Because with the piss-poor showing I've seen from you in the training room recently, I'm afraid he'll hurt you and you won't be able to fight."

Deacon laughed. Which startled everyone, because he never cut up during practice. Never. "Whatever. The odds are better that I'll trip over my own feet and twist my knee before Courey can ever hurt me bad enough to keep me from that fight."

Courey puffed up his chest and bumped it into Deacon's. "You've got a big fucking mouth, McConnell. How about I shut it with my fist?"

"You can try, dipfuck."

"Back off. Both of you," Maddox warned.

"You gonna let us spar, right here, right now?" Deacon asked Maddox without breaking eye contact with Courey.

"No."

"Fine. Then we'll go someplace else."

Courey grinned. "One hour. Chico's Gym on South University."

"I'll be there."

"The hell you will!" Maddox roared. "You're my fucking fighter. I say when you fight, where you fight, and who you fight."

"You can't stop me."

"And I don't recommend you try," Ronin said from behind them.

They all watched Sensei move forward in that deceptively lazy gait that meant he was ready to strike at any moment and strike hard.

"What the fuck, Ronin?" Maddox demanded.

"This is what you've been pushing for. So let them spar. Full contact." Ronin gave both Deacon and Courey a cool once-over. "Then we'll know who is ready to move to the next level."

Maddox looked unhappy as his gaze flicked between Courey and Deacon. He rubbed the frown line between his eyes. "You heard Sensei Black. Suit up. Ring check, five minutes."

Deacon grabbed his gear out of his locker and got ready, trying to focus on what he remembered as Courey's weak points.

No one attempted to talk to him. Good thing, or else he might've used them for a warm-up.

Blue checked his gloves. Deacon spared a quick glance at the guys standing around the ring, then at Maddox and Ronin on opposite sides of the netting.

Deacon bowed before he crossed the threshold into the ring.

Courey did not. Once he got inside, he bounced around like he'd loaded springs in his feet. He swung his arms. Moved his head side to side until all the vertebrae in his spine cracked. Then he grinned and popped in his mouth guard.

Terrel served as ref. "Clean fight. Three three-minute rounds. You both know the rules. Blatant disregard of common rules will result in forfeiture. Understand? Now, touch gloves."

After that they returned to their respective "sides" to await the signal to start.

Courey attacked first.

Deacon let him.

Courey tried an outside leg kick, which Deacon blocked.

Then Courey landed a punch to Deacon's jaw, which Deacon didn't even attempt to dodge. That singular hit fueled the rage and he released every bit of pent-up anger. Toward his cousin. Toward the fucked-up situation with Molly. Toward his motherfucking coach, who'd lost faith in him. Toward the sadness at losing his brother and the self-hatred for his part in Dante's death.

But within that firestorm he became a fighting machine. He

remembered why he'd earned the nickname "Con Man." Because neither Courey—nor anyone else—knew what to expect.

By the end of the first round, Deacon had Courey on the run, on the ropes, on the mat. And he'd executed a picture-perfect takedown—a judo hip throw that even skimpy-praise Ito would've applauded.

During the quick break, Deacon grabbed the bottle of water from Terrel and drank deeply, never taking his eyes off his opponent. Strategizing his next round. Not bothering to sit down because he wasn't tired; he was exhilarated.

At the start of the second round, Deacon kept Courey guessing by implementing every fighting style that he'd been perfecting. Faster hands courtesy of Fisher. Faster feet courtesy of Sergei. Faster takedowns courtesy of Blaze.

When Deacon had Courey in a rear naked choke, he freed him before the man could tap out. Tapping out would be too easy. Deacon wanted to make the cocky motherfucker suffer.

So before Courey caught his breath from the near choke out, Deacon rolled him to his back and started a ground and pound until Terrel broke them up.

That signaled the end of the second round. Courey hadn't landed a single kick or hit in those three minutes.

Riggins entered the ring to tend Courey's wounds. Hard not to smile about that.

Again, Deacon didn't sit down during the break. He paced as he remembered Molly's disappointment, the shock and the hurt on her face when she'd learned what he'd kept from her. Then the anger when he refused to explain.

With that one scathing look, she'd had him retreating far faster than any blows any fighter had leveled on him.

She couldn't walk away for good. He wouldn't allow it. He couldn't imagine never seeing that beautifully expressive face

again. Never touching her body as they moved together in pleasure. Never hearing her laugh. Not being a part of something bigger and better than he ever thought he'd have.

He couldn't fathom his life without her. He'd lost too much
already. No fucking way would he lose her. He was a fighter. He
would fight for her. He would win. Because that—not Needham—
would be the most important fight of his life.

That train of thought sent him back into the red zone. He
started to yell, "Can we finish this!" and only Riggins moving in
front of him kept the words from spewing out.

"Let me look at you," Riggins said.

"I'm fine."

"Then it shouldn't be an issue for me to take a look."

"Then why don't you check my balls?" he snarled. "Tell these
guys who thought I'd lost them that they're still intact."

"Jesus." He dropped his voice. "You fucked Courey up. I
oughta call this fight right now."

"But you won't," Deacon said.

Riggins studied him dispassionately. "No. I won't. But I suggest if you wanna go another three minutes, stop reopening his cuts
or Terrel *will* call it."

"Maybe Courey oughta keep his face away from my fists."
Deacon looked across the ring as soon as Courey stood up.

The last round Deacon switched to Muay Thai–style kicks.
Once he got bored with that—because lookee there, the "Crusher"
was on the run—he used a jujitsu takedown.

On that move, Courey scored a reversal and they were back on
their feet. Then he rushed Deacon until they were up against the
side of the cage.

Uh-uh. Wasn't his problem Courey was too fucking tired to
offer much challenge. So while Courey clung to him, Deacon landed
blows to his upper body with both his hands and his knees.

When they stumbled backward, Deacon did the man a favor

and decided to end it by pummeling him in the face with a flurry of fists.

Courey hit the mat like a drunken rag doll.

Finish him. So he can't get up on his own. He'd do the same goddamn thing to you.

Before he could put the final hurt on Courey, Terrel stepped in front of him. "He's done, man. Let it go."

Deacon bypassed Riggins on the way out. He didn't look at Maddox or anyone else. He just picked up his equipment bag and left the training room.

Of course there was no such thing as privacy at Black Arts— not even in the fucking stairwell. He ran into Beck as he cut down the stairs.

"Whoa. Deacon. What the hell." Beck glanced at Deacon's hands, still in gloves and dotted with blood. "What happened?"

"Don't wanna talk about it."

Beck blocked him in. "Tough shit. With the way you're sprinting outta here like the hounds of hell are nipping at your heels, I need to know what's going on."

"Had enough of Courey's big mouth. We went three rounds of full contact."

A pause, then Beck stated, "Courey lost."

"Yep." Deacon sidestepped him.

Beck countered and moved in front of him. "The whole Black Arts crew up there watching?"

"Yep."

"Where you going?"

I don't fucking know. "I've got an appointment."

"Bullshit. You're running from everyone."

He flashed Shihan a nasty smile. "Except Courey. He can barely fucking walk, let alone run."

"Jesus, Deacon." Beck didn't back off. "So you shut up the fuckers who've doubted you. I don't see that's made you happy."

"Ya think?"

"Why aren't you up there rubbing their faces in it?"

"I don't want to talk about it."

"I don't care. You need to talk about it."

"Move."

Beck said, "Make me," knowing Deacon wouldn't take action against his Shihan.

"Why the fuck do you care?"

"Cut the macho bullshit. Yeah, yeah, I got the memo. You prefer to keep to yourself. I don't know if you've noticed, but in the last year, you've become less like an island—at least in the dojo. There are far worse things than having people who care about you, trust me. So suck it up, cream puff, and pour your black heart out, because you know I'm not going anywhere until I either see tears or your gooey marshmallow center."

"You're such a pain in my ass." Deacon rested his shoulder against the concrete wall. "Everything in my life is as fucked-up as it can get. My way of dealing with it is to fight. I could go another ten rounds, I'm that wound. So I'm going somewhere where I'm not tempted to beat the living hell out of my friends." Why did people talk about this shit? It didn't solve anything.

"Will you be back to teach kickboxing this week?"

The thought of facing Molly in a roomful of people, seeing her hurt and scorning him while his students speculated about their private business, twisted his guts into knots. That's when he knew the first fucking place he planned to go when he left here was her office. "I can't. You'll sub for me?"

"This has to do with her, doesn't it?"

"Yeah. And no, I don't want to motherfucking talk about it," he snapped.

"And I don't motherfucking care." Beck ran his hand through his hair. "Bare bones, Yondan."

"I'm a fucking idiot, all right?"

"Not news to me. What else?"

"Shit from my past came up that I shoulda told her about."

"And she found out from someone else," Beck stated.

"Yeah. She walked away from me, man. For good, I think."
What had compelled him to confess that?

"You're not gonna let that happen, D. We'll figure this shit
out."

Deacon bristled at the word *we*. "Did I ask for your fucking
help?"

"You are such a prickly bastard. But you show up to talk to her
looking like that?" He gestured to Deacon's bloodied knuckles.
"With that wildness in your eyes? She'll run. Or call the cops. And
think about it. If she walked away last night, she ain't gonna talk to
you today anyway. No matter what you do—even if you show up
with a truckload of flowers or buy out Tiffany's. Give yourself time
to figure out how to fix it."

"I hate this."

"Part of the gig with women, right?"

"I wouldn't know. I've never done relationships. Until her."

Footsteps stopped at the top of the stairs above them. They
both looked up.

Ronin's cold gaze moved between them. "Deacon. A word."

"Not in the mood to talk."

"That wasn't a request."

"I don't give a damn what it was. I said no."

Sensei's extreme displeasure pulsed through the air like a poi-
sonous dart.

Deacon caved. He couldn't go against his Sensei any more than
he could go against his Shihan. Softly, he said, "She knows," and
those two words changed Ronin's demeanor entirely.

"You told her?"

Deacon shook his head.

"Fuck." Then, "Who did?"

"My cousin Tag."

Ronin shot Beck an odd look—as if he wasn't sure he should speak freely. "What happened?"

"After she found out at dinner last night, she broke it off with me." Deacon pushed off the wall. "Look. Talking about it with you two ain't gonna change a damn thing. So can we please fucking drop it? I need to talk to her."

Ronin sighed. "Don't go to the office until I talk to Amery and find out what kind of shape Molly's in."

"That's crap, Ronin. I need to—"

"Take the rest of the day and get your head on straight. And yeah, I've had plenty of experience taking that advice myself. Besides, Amery gave Molly a Taser for her birthday. Don't give that woman an excuse to use it."

Beck groaned. "Now you're just taunting me, Sensei, with the image of Deacon twitching on the floor while Molly keeps zapping him."

"Piss off. I thought you were on my side."

"I am. But you gotta admit it'd be funny," Beck said to Deacon. Then he looked at Ronin. "Since Deacon's day is done here, I'll take over his endurance training. I could stand to get out and mix it up."

"Where you taking him?" Ronin asked.

"We'll do stadiums."

Deacon flashed his teeth. "Bring it. We'll see if you can keep up, old-timer, because I live for this shit."

"Old-timer?" Beck gave him a nasty grin in return. "You forget I trained with Sensei's Sensei for four years. Stadiums will be a Sunday walk in the park compared to that."

"If I didn't have meetings, I'd tag along to watch," Ronin said.

"Watch? Blow off your meetings, Sensei, and we'll show you how it's done," Beck challenged.

Ronin speared them both with an evil smile. "Oh, grasshop-

per. You forget I trained with *your* Sensei's Sensei. My pain threshold and stamina will make you both fucking cry."

BY the time Deacon and Beck finished ten sets of stairs in Mile
High Stadium, they were both so wet, it appeared they'd been
caught in a downpour, and they were so out of breath, they couldn't
speak. Which was exactly how Deacon wanted it.

Of course it was too good to last.

"I needed this. It's good to mix it up every once in a while,"
Beck wheezed.

"If you say no pain, no gain, I'm pushing you over the railing,"
Deacon warned.

Beck laughed. "And people say you have no sense of humor."

"I thought people said I was an asshole with no heart."

"They say that too." Beck tipped up his water jug and drank.
"So you reminded Molly of your asshole side last night?"

"Yeah." He stared at the seats across the stadium until they
were an orange blur. "I got backed into a corner. Couldn't come
out swinging, so my mouth ran unchecked."

"Huh. I'm surprised you didn't just close down. That's what I
see you do when Maddox gets under your skin during training."

"I did that too. Verbally attacked her and then silence." When
he admitted that out loud, he wondered why the hell Molly put up
with him. Wasn't the first time he'd reacted that way, and it
wouldn't be the last. "Jesus. I'm a real fucking prize, huh?"

"Give her some time, D."

"How much time? The longer I stay away from her, the better
the chances she'll think I don't give a damn about her. I know her.
Unless I can convince her I am capable of change, she'll assume the
worst and then cut me off at the knees."

"Molly has already changed you. You never would've talked to
me about this personal, emotional shit before."

"Like you gave me a choice, douche bag."

Beck shrugged. "It's how I show I care, fuckface." He drained his water jug. "My advice, for what it's worth, is steer clear of her until the weekend. She'll be an emotional train wreck for a few days. Be best if you don't hop on until she's past crazy town."

"Nice."

"Hey, I'm trying to help since you're new to the ins and outs of relationships. Her friends will rally around her. They'll listen as she calls you every name in the book, as she details your flaws to them, as she lists every time you disappointed her. Then she'll question what she ever saw in you. Her posse will offer advice, most of which she'll ignore. But she'll have time to chew over all of it before you two meet face-to-face and figure out where to go from there."

The thought of Molly telling anyone about his private pain in order to gain sympathy made his stomach churn.

No. His Molly wouldn't do that. She wasn't like other women. She'd keep this between them. Even if she walked away.

"You're quiet. Because you don't agree with me?"

"You've got a lot of advice on how women think and act, yet I ain't ever seen you out with a woman."

"You and me haven't exactly swapped life histories, Yondan. But since you asked, I'll just say, five years ago I lost my wife and my job at Black Arts within four months of each other. I moved to San Fran and reset my priorities."

"Was it sweet vindication when Ronin asked you to return to Black Arts?"

"Ronin Black turned my life upside down. Firing me wasn't as unsettling as his mistaken assumption that I'd betrayed him. He served as judge and executioner. To make matters worse, my mom works for Okada, and she can't say enough good things about the company. So I had to lie to her about my reason for leaving Black Arts. That never sat well with me. Anyway, being with House of Kenji gave me perspective I lacked. When Ronin approached me about returning, I knew things would be different."

"Why?"

"Well, because 'never forgive, never forget' Sensei Black came to me. Before, he wouldn't have lowered himself to ask for my help, say nothing of my forgiveness. He's changed. His vision for Black Arts has changed. I've changed. I have value to him now because I have other experiences to draw from." He grinned. "I just have to practice patience and remind myself not all changes have to be immediate. Some things are worth waiting for."

In Beck's sneaky way, he'd imparted the advice Deacon needed. "You sound like Ronin."

"I'll take that compliment." Beck stood. "Break's over. Ten more sets."

"I thought we were done."

"You thought wrong."

CHAPTER TWENTY-ONE

THURSDAY afternoon, Chaz pulled Molly's chair away from her desk and spun her around. Then he dropped to his knees in front of her.

"Chaz, while I'm flattered you look as if you're about to pop the question—"

"I'm about to pop a blood vessel, doll." He watched her very carefully. "I heard you crying in the bathroom again this morning."

"And here I thought noises we hear coming from the bathroom weren't a topic of conversation."

"I'd laugh if I didn't want to cry right along with you, because I know you're hurting."

"Chaz."

"What happened with Deacon?"

"We broke up."

His eyes flashed impatience. "Why?"

"I can't talk about it. But he didn't *do anything to physically harm me anywhere on my body*—paraphrased from our paralegal dropout pal, Presley."

"Good. But that still doesn't give me any idea what I can do to help you."

Leave me alone. "I'm fine."

"You're not." He took her hands. "Please. Talk to me."

Damn Chaz and his sweet concern; now she wanted to bawl again. And she thought she'd been holding it together pretty well. "I love you, and thanks for caring about me, but I . . . can't."

"You mean you won't."

"No, Chaz, I mean I *can't.*"

He kissed her knuckles. "Okay, sugar lump, I'll stop nagging you. But whenever you change your mind, I'm right there. No questions asked."

AFTER Presley, Chaz, and Amery had all failed to get through to her, Amery called in the big gun.

Ronin.

Molly had gone mute when gorgeous, mysterious, intuitive Sensei Black stopped in front of her desk on Friday morning. Even after she'd known him for almost two years, she didn't really know him. That was the way he preferred it.

He studied her for the longest time. Then he said, "Grab some coffee. Amery cleared out of her office so we can talk privately."

She shook her head.

"Molly. I'm the only person who knows all about his past."

"All of it?"

He nodded. "I know that's why you haven't talked to anyone. But you can talk to me about it."

"All right. Just . . . give me a minute."

"Take your time."

She filled her mug and meandered to Amery's office. She paused in the doorframe and studied Ronin.

He lounged in Amery's desk chair. He could've taken a seat on the couch and made this more casual, but that wasn't his style. Keeping a semblance of formality suited her. She'd be less likely to break down. She'd done that enough.

Molly closed the door behind her and settled into the guest chair across from Amery's desk.

Ronin Black excelled at the waiting game, but today he jumped right in. "Give me the basics of what you know."

"Deacon's twin brother, Dante, died in a car accident when they were fifteen. His birth name isn't McConnell, but Westerman. His family is Texas-oil rich. I found all this out during a dinner with Deacon's cousin Tag." She swigged her sweetened coffee, but the scalding liquid didn't wash away the bitter taste those words left in her mouth.

"Look, I'd be pissed too if I'd found out the way you did."

"That's your way of saying you've known all along."

"Because of my family, background checks are the norm when any new person comes into my life."

Molly raised her eyebrows. "Even Amery?"

"Even her. You can imagine how pleased she was when she discovered I'd had her investigated." He shared a quick grin.

"Where'd you meet Deacon?"

"At an underground fight in Pueblo. He'd been undefeated in the south for two years. So he was understandably pissed when I beat him."

"You whipping up on him loosened his tongue and he blurted out his life story to you?" Dammit. She hadn't meant to sound cynical.

"No. His willingness to confide in me wasn't because of me but because he was finally ready to talk to someone."

Molly didn't believe that. When Ronin Black stared at you with that piercing gaze, you had the overwhelming urge to confess every transgression, just to get him to stop dissecting your soul.

"Even at the time I knew he hadn't told tell me everything." Ronin sighed. "I'm not sure I know the whole story even now."

You don't know the whole story either, her conscience prodded her. *You left Deacon before he could explain.* She understood the mind-set of keeping your own counsel—she'd done it for years with her own family situation—but she was not in the wrong here.

"When I offered him an instructor's job," Ronin continued, "I had him thoroughly checked out."

"Deacon didn't pass his background check?"

"He passed. In fact, his record was squeaky clean. Maybe it makes me a judgmental prick, but Deacon had the tats, the shaved head, and the attitude. Guys like that don't get through life unscathed. When I asked him specifics, he told me enough to get a better understanding of him. He trusted me, and that's something I don't take lightly, Molly, because Deacon doesn't trust anyone. He keeps to himself—or at least he did up until the last year or so." Ronin paused again. "Knox and Deacon are tight and have been from day one. But even after five years of being his friend, Knox doesn't know about Deacon's past—that's how painful it is for him to talk about."

"That's what I don't get. We hadn't even been dating a week and my grandma died. He dropped everything to be with me. He could've at least told me about his brother then."

"I disagree."

Her gaze returned to his. "Why?"

Ronin studied her.

The man was scary as hell in Sensei mode.

"You were grieving. Contrary to popular belief, misery doesn't love company. Deacon telling you about his twin's death would've taken away from your grief."

"Bullshit."

He shrugged. "You say that now. But we both know if you were pouring your heart out to him and he interjected that he knew exactly how you felt, you would've been resentful."

That knocked her back a step. Was that true?

"Sounds like it was more important for him to support you, which surprises the hell out of me, to be honest." He paused. His watchful gaze gave nothing away. "Don't take this the wrong way, but you don't have the right to intrude on his grief any more than he did on yours."

Her tears fell, and she snatched a tissue from Amery's desk. "Maybe the timing wasn't right when we were in Nebraska. But we've been back in Denver for two weeks. We've spent more time together than apart. We've become intimate on levels I wasn't aware existed. The way we are together . . . I've never given over everything of myself to a man—or to anyone—like I have with him."

"And Deacon keeping his past sorrow from you takes something away from that?" Ronin asked gently.

"Yes. I realize he didn't hold a gun to my head and order me to spill my guts. I freely chose to share everything about myself and my past with him. Did I bare all because I expected him to do the same? I don't know. I guess I'd hoped it'd encourage him to open up to me. Because that's how I thought relationships worked."

"You're not wrong. That is the norm for most people."

"But not for Deacon."

"Not for me either."

Molly glanced up, surprised by the regret in Ronin's tone.

"Most people search for that special connection with someone. Guys like me and Deacon? We avoid it. Then closing down becomes such a part of who we are that we don't even realize we're doing it." His hand formed a fist on the desk. "It's incredibly hard to let go of that mind-set. And when we fuck up a good thing— which we inevitably do—it's because we don't have the emotional skill set to understand it or fix it. We've never needed it.

"That said, Deacon should've talked to you about the incident in his past that defined him. He knows that. Right now he's in an internal beat down a million times worse than any fighter he'll ever face in the ring." A faraway look entered Ronin's eyes. "I did the same damn thing with Amery. I should've told her up front about my family connection. We, too, had reached a level in our relationship neither of us expected. She felt betrayed—as she should have. I had to see the person I cared more about than life itself look at me like I was a complete stranger."

"I feel like that's what he is. And maybe it makes me self-centered to internalize this, but it hurts that he didn't tell me. It really hurts that I'm not special enough to him to know about his past. I'm just like everyone else—in the dark." Her voice caught. "And because I was so pissed off, I walked away. But as much as I hurt, I know he's hurting worse. How many years has Deacon had to deal with all of this alone? He doesn't open himself up to anyone, and that breaks my heart." More tears seeped out. "I haven't heard from him at all since this went down." And after all she'd just said, it'd be contradictory to admit that she'd expected Deacon to come after her. Like he had when she missed class. Like he had when she went to Nebraska. She'd gone to bed the night she'd left the restaurant absolutely heartsick, but she'd believed—wanted?—hoped?—that he'd bully his way into her house and try to make things right between them.

He didn't, and he won't. When are you going to learn?

"I believe given a few more weeks, he would've opened up to you. As far as him storming in here, Amery warned him if he showed his face she'd call the cops. And Deacon knows she doesn't bluff."

Her head snapped up. "Amery threatened him? Did you tell her . . . ?"

"No. She doesn't know anything about his past and nothing about what happened between you two, just that he fucked something up big-time and you're a mess." Ronin leaned forward. "That's all she needed to know to rally behind you, girl."

"See?" She sniffled. "I've got all these great friends who stand up for me and I can't talk to any of them about this. They don't understand why I won't tell them what happened."

"It's hard, but I admire your loyalty to Deacon."

That brought up something she hadn't considered. "Is he worried that in a fit of anger I'll blab his most closely guarded secret to my friends?"

"Lots of women would have." He leaned forward. "Deacon put his rage about the situation into play the next morning by beating the hell out of Micah Courey."

"What?" she said with gasp.

"Deacon nearly sent him to the hospital." Ronin's eyes gleamed. "It was fucking beautiful to watch. Ever since he came back from Nebraska, he's not been training at the level he needs to be. So when he faced Courey in full-fight mode? It was like a switch flipped inside him. Every aspect of Deacon's training throughout the last five years coalesced. He was a fighting machine. I swear Maddox was so proud he even shed a tear or two. Needham is toast. It'll be a huge win for him and Black Arts since now he'll be able to retain that focus."

Realization slammed into her. Even their fledgling relationship had been a distraction to Con Man's career. Maddox had understood that and tried to derail this very thing months ago, when he'd enlisted Ronin's help to keep Molly and Deacon apart. But this time Deacon's stubbornness had won out—he wanted her, everything and everyone else be damned. Including his fight career? He'd blown off a full training session to spend time with her on Sunday. And their vigorous, frequent sex had to take a toll on him physically by sapping his extra energy.

So Molly had handed Black Arts the golden opportunity to prove to Deacon that without a girlfriend, and the rage about that driving him, Con Man would become the fighter he needed to be.

She might be sick.

No wonder Ronin had felt the need to come here personally to explain and soften the blow.

"Molly?"

Ronin's ninja senses were unparalleled, so she couldn't let on that she knew it was over between her and Deacon. "Sorry."

His golden-eyed gaze sharpened. "About?"

"All of this drama. I hate that Amery is in the middle of it. She's got a business to run. And with me being on autopilot the past few days, I haven't pulled my weight." She snatched another tissue. "Amery deserves better. So I'll do as my grams advised. Pull myself up by my bootstraps and do what needs done. Move on."

"But that's not—"

"It's fine." Molly stood and offered Ronin a watery smile. "Thanks for talking to me."

"Molly, wait—"

She didn't hear anything else after she shut herself in the bathroom. Staring at herself in the mirror, she gave herself the mother of all silent pep talks.

This too shall pass.

You can't miss what you never really had.

Don't let a broken heart break your spirit.

Just keep swimming.

When all else fails, make a list.

The first thing on that list would be to find a new gym.

CHAPTER TWENTY-TWO

FOCUSING on Fee's birthday party for Katie Saturday night provided Molly with a much-needed distraction. She'd hauled booze, set up seating areas, spooned out dip and hummus, loaded platters of crackers and chips.

So when Katie started micromanaging the placement of the bowls of gourmet olives, Fee banished Katie to her bedroom and put Molly on babysitting duty, warning her to get ready.

"Get ready" was girl code for—*you deal with the crazy bitch when she starts strutting around in just her hot rollers.*

It sucked to be the modest one in a sea of nymphs.

Sure, in the dojo locker room Molly could strip down to her bra and panties. But strolling around buck-assed naked in front of her friends? No way. Not even if she had a killer birthday suit like the birthday girl did.

Rather than sit on the counter in the bathroom, Molly parked herself in the bedroom, barring the door, keeping Katie in, rather than keeping others out.

"Hey, jailer," Katie yelled from the bathroom. "Take a look at the outfits on the bed."

Molly wandered to the alcove housing the four-poster, lake-sized bed. Swaths of sheer, shimmery blue fabric were artfully draped across the metal rods above the mattress, creating a canopy. Her gaze caught on leopard-print fur-lined handcuffs—a pair dangled from each side of the headboard.

An image popped into her head of being locked in cuffs as a man teased her with yards of silk.

Not a man. Deacon.

Dammit. Stop thinking about him. It's over.

She focused on the clothing displayed on the pristine white comforter, as if arranged by a boutique salesperson.

The first outfit was a pale pink baby-doll dress—holy crap was it short, even with the puffy rolled layers of chiffon at the hemline. The neckline had been trimmed in white marabou. The silver stilettos on the floor were also festooned with pink fluff.

It screamed . . . retro. If anyone could pull off the sixties sex-kitten vibe, Katie could.

Outfit number two paired skinny jeans—Gucci, of course—with a shirt that started out a brilliant blue across the shoulders. The colors gradually lightened to a pale blue that reminded Molly of Deacon's eyes. The fringe mimicked the ombré look of the fabric—but in reverse. The boots Katie had picked were killer: black leather with a cuff that covered the knee and the needle-sharp heels were at least four inches.

It screamed hot and sexy. No one wore a pair of fifteen-hundred-dollar jeans better than Katie.

The last outfit had a tiny red leather skirt, a sleeveless white V-neck silk shirt, and a sequined bolero jacket in tones of red, cream, and black. The black ankle-strap heels completed the ensemble.

Katie poked her head out. "So? What do you think?"

"Does the little red number come with a cape and a bull?"

She grinned. "It might attract a certain bull rider I've invited."

"Won't Ivan get jealous?"

"I'm counting on it. But tell me what you think of the others."

"I like the fluffy pink baby doll."

"But?" Katie prompted.

What Molly knew about fashion was cribbed from two sources: *Fashion Police* and *InStyle* magazine. So she hesitated to be truthful with Katie, who attended fashion week in New York. "Well . . ."

"Spit it out."

"The shoes make the outfit boudoir wear. If you had white go-go boots, then it'd be perfect."

Katie squealed. "I have a pair of those! Can you grab them out of my shoe closet?"

"Sure." Katie had multiple closets in this mini-mansion. But the shoe closet was actually a small sitting room she'd remodeled for her vast footwear collection.

Since it'd be easy to get distracted by the shoe mecca, Molly headed straight for the boot section of the closet and found the shiny white vinyl boots on the second shelf.

Thankfully, Katie was dressed when Molly returned. Her long blond hair fell in perfect waves. She'd applied her makeup with a heavier hand—smoky cat eyes, frosted lips, blusher that accentuated her cheekbones.

"You look stunning, birthday girl," Molly told her.

"Thank you. Now that I'm getting older, I'll probably have to double up on my skin-care regimen."

"Older. Right. You're what . . . twenty-four today?"

"No, I'm a quarter of a century, baby." Katie tugged Molly into the bathroom. "So tell me about the party setup. It's killing me not to be in charge of it."

"You'll live. Tell me who you invited."

Katie's eyes met hers in the mirror. "I'll tell you who I didn't invite."

For the briefest moment Molly felt bad for Deacon because she knew what it was like to be excluded.

"Ronin and Amery won't show. Neither will Knox and Shiori. Beck will be here. Big Rig . . . he's scared of me, I think. Maddox said he'd put in an appearance. So did Fisher."

"What about Blue?"

Her pert nose wrinkled. "I didn't invite him."

"Katie, he's your boss."

"Which is exactly why I don't need him judging me on my birthday!"

"But he's Fee's brother."

"You think Fee wants Blue to see her getting wild? No. He'd sic Gil on her, to try to talk some sense into her, which is why Gil wasn't invited either. Anyway, some of my friends from high school will be here, as will others I've met here and there. It oughta be an eclectic bunch."

Jaz strolled in and gawked at the luxury bathroom. "Wow. This is . . ."

"Over the top, right? My dad had it redone last year for my birthday. I'm glad he let me talk to the interior designer, or else I'd be living in a pink palace with unicorns and butterflies adorning the walls. The man treats me like I'm seven."

"It's beautiful. The design reminds me of bathrooms I've seen in W Hotels."

Katie's mouth dropped open. "That's exactly what I showed the designer! How do you know about that style?"

"I'm in the hotel business, remember? We have to keep up with the competition. Anyway, quick question. Fee asked me where you want the gift table set up. I told her we didn't need one, but she sent me in to double-check."

Katie raised one perfectly manicured eyebrow. "Why wouldn't I need a gift table at my birthday party? Everyone knows a birthday party equals birthday presents."

Jaz blinked, as if Katie might be kidding.

Molly saved her. "I know the perfect place to set up." She smiled at Katie. "Stay here until we come and get you."

"Could you at least bring me a drink?"

"No. You can chill until the party starts. Drinking alone on your birthday sucks," Molly said.

"I hear ya there, sista," Jaz said and low-fived her.

As Molly and Jaz headed to the kitchen, Jaz muttered, "I didn't bring Katie a present."

"Oh."

"What'd you get her?"

"A gift certificate for a massage." Emmylou Simmons, a massage therapist and former friend of Amery and Chaz, still rented space in Amery's building for her massage studio. But Emmylou didn't spend much time there since she'd upped her rates and her regulars could no longer afford her. Molly considered that a dick move, but it was how the woman operated. Maybe it was a dick countermove, but since Emmylou had a serious crush on Katie, Molly knew she'd give her an extra-long massage. Emmylou touching what she couldn't have . . . Yeah, a sweet bit of revenge for the shitty way Emmylou had treated Amery.

"I'm fucked; I didn't bring a gift. I figured she'd celebrate like, oh, normal adults. Too much booze with her friends and a random hookup," Jaz said.

"Katie never does anything the way you expect her to," Molly said as they entered the kitchen.

"And that is one of the very best things about her," Fee added, licking frosting off a cupcake. At Molly's frown, she said, "What? I cannot drink on an empty stomach."

"Nice justification, Fee."

She grinned. "I rule at justification, Jaz-a-reno."

"Stop calling me that!"

"Nicknames are part of the gig, hanging with us."

Jaz looked from Fee to Molly. "Bullshit. I've never heard you guys use nicknames with each other."

Fee burst out laughing. "Gotcha, DJ Jazzy-Jaz."

"Seriously gonna kick your ass one of these days, Curacao."

"Bring it." Fee licked her thumb. "Or you could become my training partner. Then you could *try* to kick my ass every day while I prove the superiority of Brazilian jujitsu."

"Whoa, whoa, whoa," Katie said, strolling into the kitchen. "Are you trying to poach Jaz from Black Arts for ABC?"

"Hell no. You think I wanna tangle with Ronin Black?" Fee shuddered. "I was just making conversation." Her eyes narrowed. "Which you should *not* be hearing, since you're supposed to be in your bedroom."

"I'm done with that. It's better for me to greet people at the door. That way I'll be sure to talk to everyone."

"That's actually a great idea," Molly said.

"Of course it is. That way I'll get to pick a birthday fuck."

Fee and Molly exchanged a look . . . which, of course, Katie caught.

"Stop judging me. Yes, Ivan will be here. But we're not a couple. He knows it's just sex, no strings with me."

"There's no such thing," Jaz said softly.

"I agree," Fee said.

"You wanna make this the trifecta of *Katie's wrong*?" Katie demanded of Molly.

"Sorry, K. Sex always has strings, and there's bound to be blowback—and no, I didn't say *blow job*—when the free-for-all fucking ends."

"What about one-night stands?" Katie countered.

Jaz shook her head. "Hooking up for one night only is a whole different animal."

"There can be guilt in one-nighters," Fee said. "But there's a boatload more guilt in a fuck-buddy relationship. Guilt from the person who wants it to be a real relationship. Guilt from the person who can't give them what they want."

"Speaking from experience, Fee?" Katie asked.

"I learned I'm better off getting myself off with a vibrator than with a guy." When the pause lingered too long, she smirked at Katie. "So if you don't score a birthday fuck tonight, my gift will come in very handy."

TWO hours into the party, the booze was half gone and the house was packed.

Since Molly had spent most of her time restocking food and drinks, she shouldn't have noticed Deacon in the corner, watching her from the shadows. But she did.

Just pretend you don't see him.

That was lame.

Then storm up to him, slap him across the face, and walk off.

That was mean.

He deserves it.

While she debated a course of action, Deacon acted.

He stopped before her only when she held her hand up to keep him from coming closer. "You weren't invited to this party."

"So? I knew you'd be here, so I crashed it."

"You always do what you want and damn the consequences?"

"Only when the stakes are as high as they are with you."

Don't fall for his lines.

"We need to talk."

"No, we don't. Go home, Deacon." She turned and started to walk away.

"Molly," he said her name sharply.

She hated that his tone immediately had her looking at him.

Keep walking and don't look back.

"Don't."

"Don't what?"

"Shut down."

"If anyone is shut down, Deacon, it's you." Against her better judgment, she retorted, "While I understand you have reasons for keeping secrets, I don't have to like it, let alone accept that's part of the deal with you."

"Don't be like this."

"Be what? Rational? I don't know why I ever thought this would . . ." Molly looked away. "Your past isn't the biggest—or even the only—hurdle between us, Deacon. You know that. Now I know that. We shouldn't have pretended otherwise."

"Molly. Babe. Look at me."

The instant their eyes met, she felt the pull between them. And he knew she still felt it.

"One hour. Give me one hour to tell you everything. No bull-shit. No holding back."

Don't give in.

"If you want to walk away after that, I won't stop you."

She felt herself caving. If nothing else, this might give her clo-sure. "All right. Tomorrow at eleven. At Snooze."

Deacon shook his head. "Not in public. And it has to be tonight."

"Where?"

"At the dojo."

She needed to be in a place where she felt confident and in control. She shook her head. "At my office. I'll meet you there in an hour."

Deacon watched her very carefully. "You'll really be there?"

"You worried I'll stand you up like you did to me?" When he didn't respond, she said, "I'm not a 'paybacks are a bitch' bitch. If you don't know that about me, Deacon, maybe we should just forget this—"

"No." Then Deacon's hands were gently framing her face. "I'm fucking this up. Story of my goddamn life. Just . . . please. Give me a chance."

The cool detachment she expected to see in his eyes wasn't there. She could feel his arms shaking and he didn't try to hide it.

"I'll be there."

CHAPTER TWENTY-THREE

DEACON drove his motorcycle to Hardwick Designs and parked it in the alley next to the back door. Then he walked around the block—twice—looking for Molly's car.

No sign of it.

You fucked this up, played on loop in his head.

When he stopped at the main office door and didn't see lights on inside, he had a very real fear that Molly hadn't shown up.

Fuck. Was he so far gone with wanting her that he'd drunk himself into a stupor and was dreaming he'd crashed Katie's birthday party so he could talk to Molly?

No. He'd really been there. So had she. He'd watched her for an hour before she'd noticed him.

And he hadn't imagined the flash of pleasure in her eyes at seeing him. It'd been brief, but it'd been there. So he had the foolish hope that all wasn't lost with her.

Still, he held his breath when he pushed on the door. It opened, the bell jangling to announce his arrival.

Molly wasn't waiting for him, but he heard her rustling around in the back.

Probably looking for her Taser.

The sick thing was? He'd *let* her tase him if it'd start them talking again.

Nervous, he paced in the reception area.

Molly sauntered past him without a word, relocked the front door and reset the alarm.

Although she still wore her party clothes—a low-cut western shirt that showcased her rack and a frilly skirt that hugged her ass— she'd kicked off the pink and army-green camo combat boots.

Seeing her relaxed stance, her feet bare, her hair up in a ponytail, almost had him falling to his knees. This was his Molly.

"I thought we could talk out here. The couch is more comfy than the office chairs."

Deacon doubted he could calmly sit and discuss the total destruction of his life as he'd known it. "I don't even know where to start." He rested his hands on the top of his head and blew out a long breath. "Fuck that. I do know. What'd you tell me to do the first time I fucked up and couldn't remember what to say? I needed to hit the high points?"

"You remember that?"

"I remember everything you ever say to me, babe. So . . . here goes. I'm sorry for bein' an asshole to you at the restaurant. I'm sorry that I embarrassed you in front of Tag. I'm sorry that you felt you had to run from me. I'm sorry that I said bullshit. I didn't mean to hurt you. I'm sorry that I had to wait five fucking days before I could talk to you."

"Why did you wait?"

"Besides Amery and Ronin forbidding me from coming here or approaching you at Black Arts? I had to get up the courage. Fee told me about Katie's party and dared me to crash it."

"And you can't resist a challenge."

"I can't resist you. You are the only reason I went. I wanted a chance to make this right."

"Why?"

Because I fucking love you.

"Because I lost everything when Dante died and I ran away." Deacon found the balls to look at her. "I realized I was about to lose everything again, and this time I'm staying put."

"Deacon."

"I'll tell you everything. Even things I've never told anyone."

"Not even Ronin?"

"Not Ronin. Not my dad." Before Molly could ask, *Why are you telling me?* he said softly, "Some of it is so ugly I didn't want to think about it, let alone tell anyone about it."

She didn't say anything to that—but what could she say?

So he soldiered on. *Take a deep breath. You can do this.*

"The condensed version is when I was fifteen I was in a car accident that killed my twin brother and also my girlfriend. I was driving. It permanently fucked up my life to the point I left home."

When Molly remained quiet, he knew she was letting that sink in before she spoke. "Is that why you changed your name?"

"No. That's another part of it. Just . . . I need to start at the beginning." Deacon faced the window, bracing his hands on the ledge. "I don't know what the hell my parents were thinking, naming identical twins Deacon and Dante. No one could keep our names straight, let alone our personas. Then again, most of our life we didn't have separate identities. We had a singular moniker—the Westerman twins."

"Did that bother you?"

"Not that I remember. We were a package deal until high school. Dante was a fucking brain and got into all the advanced-placement classes. I was a jock. He claimed he lifted weights and ran with me because he didn't want to be seen as the weaker twin, but the truth was we preferred spending time together. We were more than brothers; we were two halves of the same whole. But we were always competitive. So it pissed me off that smooth-talker Dante kissed a girl before me. The smug fucker bragged about meeting her under the bleachers for make-out sessions. Since few could tell us apart, I showed up pretending to be him."

"No. You didn't."

"Yeah, I did. For a week after that, everyone could tell us apart since I had a black eye. He ensured I wouldn't be kissing any girls either, since he also gave me a fat lip."

Molly laughed softly. "Sorry. I shouldn't laugh, but you deserved it."

Deacon allowed a smile because the sharp pang of loss was bearable for a change. "True. Dante wasn't a fighter, but that didn't mean he didn't know how to throw a punch."

"So you two together were the brains and the brawn of the Westerman family?"

"Tag told you that our granddad started the family oil business. Granddad expected his sons to learn the ropes from the ground up. Our dad expected the same from us. The summer after our freshman year, we were sent to our uncle Jesse's ranch. He had a dozen working oil rigs on his place, so we learned to read them like real oilmen. Dante was more interested in the science side of the oil business—engineering and the geological aspect. He studied. I did the dirty work and ran wild. I raced dirt bikes, cars, horses, tractors, you name it. Even then it was obvious to everyone in the Westerman family that Dante would head up JFW Industries—which is now JFW Development—one day."

"Was your dad happy his son would follow in his footsteps?"

Deacon shrugged. "I guess. He sent us there for two summers. While Dante came back full of ideas about future business-development plans, I came back rougher around the edges, which infuriated our mother. She obsessed about 'my station in life,' constantly berating me about acting like an heir to a multimillion-dollar business, not like a roughneck running the rigs. Dante could do no wrong in her eyes. He had a way with her. Hell, he had a way with all the girls. So it wasn't just his looks that had girls flocking to him. We were identical, and girls weren't falling all over themselves to get with me like they were with him."

"So neither of you tried to look different and set yourself apart from the other?"

"Nah. I imagine we would've done that at some point, but we never got the chance."

Molly's bare feet shuffled across the carpet as she moved into his peripheral vision.

"The first week of junior year, I started dating Cassidy, much to everyone's surprise."

"Why?"

"She was a year older than me. A good girl. She'd been designated class sweetheart three times. I wasn't a bad boy." He shot her a quick look. "No tats, or a motorcycle, or shaved head at that time. But I'd gotten into trouble for fighting. She didn't care. Before too long I was spending all my time with her, but Dante was cool with it. He always said, *Brother, I got my own deal going on. Don't worry about me.* But I did. I never wanted him to feel left out."

Maybe if you would've left him out, he'd be alive today.

"Anyway, that fall Cassidy was elected homecoming queen. I escorted her to the football game and took her to the dance. Since Dante didn't have a date, he went to a party out in the boondocks. When Cassidy and I got there after the dance, Dante was drunk—not the norm for him. Usually Cassidy didn't drink either, so I didn't think anything of it when she went off with her friends. I stayed by the bonfire, listening to Dante's drunk talk about a girl I'd never heard of. A girl he claimed he'd been having sex with since school started, which made me so mad . . ."

"Why?"

"Because he always told me everything right away. And he'd kept something that goddamn important from me for two months. So I'm grilling him about it, scheming on how I can get Cassidy in bed to even things up with my brother." He closed his eyes. "That's how I spent my last hour with him. Bein' mad at him for losing his virginity first. Bein' mad at him for pulling away from me because I knew that was the start of us having separate lives."

"So did you leave him there so you could nail the homecoming queen?"

He snorted. "No. I didn't lose my virginity until I was nineteen. I just . . . I had no interest in sex. That'll make more sense later. Anyway, Cassidy stumbled back to the bonfire totally hammered. So I had to deal with my drunken brother and my drunken girlfriend." Deacon turned around and looked Molly in the eye. "I hadn't been drinking. Period. Not a fucking drop."

"You must be making that distinction for a reason."

He nodded and turned back toward the window. "The party was thirty miles out of town. When I realized it was two a.m. and we'd missed our curfew by an hour, I debated on whether to even go home or just stay at the campground, but it started to rain. So I poured the drunken duo into my truck, with Cassidy sitting in the middle. I told them to buckle up, but I'd been too focused on the fog rolling in to double-check if they'd listened to me. By then they'd both passed out anyway."

He clenched his fists. "I don't even know how it happened. One second the truck was on the road, and the next it spun out of control, plowed through the ditch, and headed straight for a tree. The impact knocked me out. When I came to, I didn't see Cassidy or Dante. I thought they'd gotten out. Everything was hazy. I noticed the windshield was gone. In the headlights I saw Dante suspended in midair outside the truck and Cassidy's legs on the hood. I couldn't see the rest of her." The immediate sick feeling threatened to choke him. He swallowed the bile and kept going, wanting to get through this. "Later I learned Dante had been thrown into a barbed-wire fence and had died instantly. Same with Cassidy, only her body hadn't made it past the hood.

"I don't remember the ambulance guys pulling me out. The

impact with the steering wheel had broken two of my ribs, punctured my lung, and caused internal bleeding, requiring emergency surgery. So I didn't actually wake up until almost forty-eight hours after the accident. My first conscious thought was *Dante is dead*."

Needing a moment, he paced to the end of the reception area and looked out the window covered in metal safety bars. That reminded him of where everyone in town had wanted him after the accident.

Molly's arms circled his waist, and she rested her face between his shoulder blades. She didn't say a word, just gave him the strength to go on.

"As if it wasn't bad enough I'd been driving the vehicle that killed two people, because we'd been at the party, rumors were going around town that I'd been drinking."

"But didn't the hospital test your blood-alcohol level before you went into surgery?"

"Yeah. The hospital staff, the cops, and EMTs knew I had a zero blood-alcohol level. But the rumor was since my family had . . . influence, they'd paid off the officials to hide the fact I'd been driving drunk."

"Omigod. That is awful."

He closed his eyes. "The entire town thought I should be in jail for manslaughter. More rumors circulated that Cassidy's parents planned to sue us. Not that it was an option, since Cassidy's parents received a copy of the accident report, including their daughter's blood-alcohol level and that she hadn't worn a seat belt. Her parents only added more speculation when they banned me from Cassidy's funeral. I was a pariah."

Her tears dampened the back of his shirt. "Deacon. Stop. I've heard enough."

He spun around and forced her to look into his anguished eyes, to really see him, to see what this had done to him. "No, goddammit. You were willing to kick me to the fucking curb because I kept this from you, so you damn well will hear every bit of it. All the way to the bitter end, because, babe, it gets even uglier."

Embarrassment flared in her eyes before she glanced down. "Okay. Finish it. But I can't . . . look at you while you're telling me."

"Why not?"

"Because I'll be so focused on how I can be there for you now that I'll miss what you went through then." Her tears landed on his hands. Then she tenderly kissed his scraped and scabbed knuckles. "I'll listen to whatever you want to tell me whenever you're ready. And I'll be right here for you when you're done."

It took a moment to find his balance. "My parents were lost in grief. I was filled with guilt and anger and loneliness like I'd never known. I didn't go back to school as I recovered from my physical injuries. Two months after the accident, when I couldn't take the rage anymore, I went out and picked a fight with the biggest, meanest motherfucker I could find."

"Where'd you find him?"

"Biker bar. Guy beat the fuck out of me. But during the fight I figured out that's where I could channel my rage to block out my grief. Fighting became my coping mechanism."

"It still is, isn't it?"

"No. Now I fight because I'm good at it. But Jesus fuck. I couldn't get away from myself or my family connections or the accident. As if being sprawled on the ground, eating dirt, bleeding, and sobbing like a fucking girl wasn't enough"—he paused to swallow—"some asshole in the bar recognized me."

"No," she breathed.

"Oh yeah. The douche fucker worked for my old man and called him."

"What happened?"

"My dad showed up, loaded me in his car, and took me home. Then he disappeared for a few days. Without him as the buffer, my mother didn't have to hold back."

"This is the ugly part, isn't it?"

Yes. This was his private shame.

"Deacon. You have to believe I'm the last person who'd ever sit in judgment of you."

"I do believe that, which is why I'm here pouring my guts out and not hiding in the bottom of a bottle of Jäger at the strip club at the thought of losing you."

She squeezed him hard. "Tell me."

He had to force the words out through gritted teeth. "My mother told me she wished I had died instead of him."

Molly's distressed gasp sliced through him. She ducked under his arm and plastered herself to the front of his body, her shoulders heaving as she tried to muffle her sobs against his chest.

Deacon's heart turned over then, at having this beautiful, sweet, loving woman here with him, crying for him. It loosened the lump in his throat so he could go on. "I was devastated." The isolation his mother had caused with her words had tainted everything in his life and had haunted him for years. As he'd grown older he'd understood them for what they were, but the broken child in him couldn't forgive her or forget.

Molly continued to sob as if her heart had been split open.

He wiped the tears from her cheeks. Then he pressed his lips to her forehead. "I left shortly after that."

"Left? Where'd you go?"

"Everywhere. And nowhere. I was dead inside. I changed the way I looked—shaved my head, started getting tats—so I wouldn't be reminded of him every time I looked in the mirror." He'd obliterated the image of who he'd been so completely that it pained him to admit he couldn't remember what he—they—used to look like. Dante had been a disembodied voice in his head for so long, not a physical presence, that was how Deacon remembered him.

"But you were fifteen," Molly said. "How did you support yourself?"

"I turned sixteen two weeks before I left. I'd taken a couple hundred dollars out of my bank account before I took off. I washed dishes or worked as a janitor for cash under the table. Menial-labor jobs ensured I wouldn't have to interact with anyone. I moved around a lot. I had no interest in anything—sex, women, booze, or drugs. The only thing I cared about was bulking up so when I turned eighteen I could start fighting. I found a sketchy dojo that offered to train me in jujitsu. The underground fight scene is illegal, so I had to keep traveling farther away to find decent opponents."

"How long did you stay away from home?"

"Almost five years."

"Did your family look for you?"

"At the time I didn't care. I legally changed my name a week after I turned eighteen."

"Why did you ever go back?"

He rested his chin on top of her head and closed his eyes. "I heard that my dad had a heart attack. By the time I'd found out—I don't remember how that crossed my radar—it'd been a couple of months, so I knew he wasn't dead. I showed up at his office. With the extreme change in my appearance, the receptionist refused to believe I was Bing Westerman's son. We argued, and he came out of his office to see what the commotion was about."

Deacon paused, letting the memory from that day solidify. His father had run toward him. *Run.* In his three-piece suit. And he'd wept. Openly. Repeatedly.

"What happened?"

"He hugged me. I . . . It'd been a long time since I'd had anyone touch me not out of anger, so I balked. Then he said, 'Lemme have a look at you, son.' I'd grown two inches, packed on forty pounds—mostly muscle—shorn my hair, and inked my skin. I honestly hadn't expected him to recognize me."

"What did he say when he finished inspecting you?"

" 'You erased all traces of him, didn't you?' "

"Whoa. Did he mean you'd erased the old you? Or that you'd erased any resemblance to Dante?"

"Both, probably. I didn't ask. Then, before it got even more awkward, he asked me to lunch. He took me to a chain barbecue joint, not the hole-in-the-wall place by his office he'd always taken us to before." Us. God. He'd forgotten how much Dante had loved barbecue. "Anyway, I figured he'd taken me someplace where no one knew him because I embarrassed him. I made up my mind to leave right after lunch. He sensed my intention to bolt and told me he brought me there because after not seeing me for almost five years he doubted he'd taste the food anyway, so he might as well eat crap."

"He sounds like a sweet man."

"He can be at times." And that did mark a big shift in their relationship. "We stayed in that booth for four hours and talked. I refused to see my mother, although I agreed he could tell her that I was all right." Deacon's throat felt scratchy. "Molly, darlin', I need to get a drink."

"I wondered if you needed one. I've never heard you talk so much."

He retreated to the break room and drank a full glass of water. Then he stared at the empty cup for several long moments. How much more did she need to know?

His brother offered advice. *All of it. No sense in giving her the CliffsNotes version now.*

Dammit, Dante. Talking about you makes me miss you.

Well, I was the cooler twin, so I can see why. But you have the chance to let her fill part of that void I left. Figure this shit out, bro, so you can move on.

But if I move on, will you too?

No answer.

Deacon returned to the reception area and resumed his place in front of the windows.

"Better?"

"I guess."

"Do you want keep going?"

"There's not that much left. By the end of our lunch, Dad asked me to come to work in the family business. He offered to hire a trainer to help me advance to the next level in cage fighting."

"What did you say?"

"No, thanks. I didn't need him or his money, and I'd do it on my own like I'd done everything else in my life." That's when Dante's voice had overtaken his thoughts. Telling him that their father shouldn't have to pay forever for their mother's words, which had driven him away. "It fucking killed me to watch every bit of happiness drain from his face. So I agreed to work part-time. I found a gym and a dojo. The guy running the gym also pro-moted legitimate fights. I gradually shifted my focus fully to my training."

"Is that when you fought Ronin?"

"He told you that, huh?"

Molly moved in to stand next to him. "He mentioned it was an underground and unsanctioned fight."

"I'd started doing both and participated in enough amateur bouts to qualify as a professional fighter. After I returned to Texas, I reached second-degree black belt level and became a certified kickboxing instructor at the gym. I also added Muay Thai to my training regimen."

"So Ronin snapped you up for Black Arts?"

Deacon turned toward her. He touched her sweet face before he tucked an escaped tendril behind her ear. "More or less. I agreed to Ronin's six-month trial period, and I've been there ever since."

Then Molly wrapped herself around him.

He closed his eyes. He wanted this—a life with her—more than anything in the world.

"Thank you for telling me. Not just what happened when you were fifteen, but all the choices you made in the aftermath."

"How do we move on from this?" Deacon swallowed the fear crawling up his throat when Molly didn't immediately answer.

Then she chased all those shadows and fears away by simply laying her hands on his chest, over his heart. "We promise to be open with each other about everything. Big and small." She offered him a watery smile. "I know you claim you don't like to talk about shit."

"Claim? Babe. I *don't* like dissecting every damn thing."

Her eyes narrowed.

Shit. "Well, except the important stuff."

Molly banged her forehead into his chest in mock frustration.

Deacon kissed the top of her head, drawing strength from the fact Molly was here. Touching her, holding her, breathing her in . . . gave him the push he needed to do this. No matter how hard his heart raced. He slowly moved his hands up her back, tugging on her hair to get her to look at him. Those beautiful brown eyes locked on his and provided the courage for him to say what he needed to. Curling his right hand beneath her jaw, he whispered, "I love you."

If he hadn't been holding on to her jaw, it would've dropped.

"I never understood what that meant. Now every time I look at you, I know."

Tears pooled in her eyes. "Deacon."

"I didn't say it because I'm trying to manipulate you into forgiving me faster. I'm telling you because I feel it. Fuck, do I ever feel it for you. Even though I let you in more than I've ever let anyone else, I still held back." He swept his thumb across her trembling lower lip. "No more holding back with you. I wanna be the man to give you everything you need. I say that and I know how goddamn selfish it sounds, because you're so fucking perfect and you deserve more than a broken man like me. But dammit, when I'm with you I feel . . . whole again."

Molly was so freaking beautiful with that light glowing from within her reflecting back at him. "Was that hard to say?" she asked so softly he barely heard it.

"Terrifying."

"I can tell. You're shaking."

"I spent the last five days worried that I'd lost you. I'm standing here, touching you, and I'm still freaked the fuck out that it's too little, too late."

"It's not. I hurt for you. I know that sympathy or empathy pisses you off, but I ache thinking about how closed off you've been when you've got so much to give. So much more than you're even aware of. And that of all the people in the world you could've fallen for, you chose me."

"My *heart* chose you, babe."

Molly cried harder. "I've never had anyone love me, Deacon. I'm as scared as you are. I don't know how to do this—how to give it back either."

That admission floored him—which just proved they had a lot to learn about each other. "So we're both kind of a mess, huh?"

She sniffled. "I guess that makes us a good match."

"It makes us a perfect match." Deacon gently wiped her tears. Then he kissed her, just a soft press of his lips to hers, more promise than passion.

"Come home with me." He slid his hand back to run his fingers through her hair. "I need you in my bed."

"Just to sleep?"

Fuck no. "For tonight? Yeah. If that's what you want."

"And then tomorrow?"

Deacon pulled her hair hard enough to get her attention and see heat flare in her eyes. "Tomorrow morning you wake up with my face between your thighs. After I make you come twice, then I'll fuck you as many times and in as many ways as it takes for you to believe I am the only man you'll ever need."

"You are that man. I just hope I'm enough for you."

"You already are." This time Deacon let his kiss linger. "Leave your car here and ride with me. I don't want to be away from you for even the length of the drive."

"I'll leave my car at my apartment. We'll need to stop at my place anyway so I can get my stuff." Molly poked him in the chest when he started to argue. "And before you give me the typical Deacon *you don't need to wear clothes when you're around me, babe,* I assure you, I do need my bathroom stuff."

She was so freakin' cute when she got bossy. "I have bathroom stuff for you."

Her gaze moved over his bare head. "Says the man with no hair, so he has no need for shampoo or conditioner. And I doubt you'll let me use your razor."

"Hilarious. But I bought you all the same shit you have in your bathroom and stocked it in mine."

"When?"

"After you went to work I took a picture of all the makeup crap you left out on the counter and the bottles in your shower. Then I went to CVS. The chick who helped me even offered a few suggestions for other things you'd probably want." When Molly continued to stare at him, he bristled. "What? It wasn't like I used any of it. All that junk is still in the bags, so if you wanna return it—"

She placed her fingers over his lips. "Shut up, you sweet, babbling man—which is not something I ever thought I'd say to Deacon McConnell."

He lifted his eyebrows.

"I love that you did that for me. You pay attention to me. I've never had that either." She bit her lip when it started to wobble. "Thank you."

Molly hadn't moved her hand, allowing him to talk, so he puckered his lips to kiss her fingers.

Her eyes softened. "So you cleaned out a drawer for me. That's a pretty big step."

Not as big a step as saying I love you. "I'd hire a moving company and move all your stuff into my house tonight if I could. But you'd accuse me of bein' high-handed."

"I'm not ready for that step." She brushed her lips across his. "Yet. And you're not ready for the explosion of 'floral vomit' that composes my stuff either."

He smiled. "True dat." He touched her cheek. "But I will push for you moving in with me, sooner rather than later."

"To prove that you're serious about me."

"I already told you I love you. Doesn't get a whole lot more serious for me, babe."

Molly retreated, and Deacon forced himself to let her.

"We can go out the back."

She locked up, immediately noticing his motorcycle in the alley, and shook her head. "No way."

"Molly—"

"No. I'll follow you." She paused. "Although I bet you drive this thing so fast my poor Subaru couldn't keep up."

He shrugged and snagged his helmet. "It's why I bought it. This model leaves Ronin's bike in the dirt."

"Of course you guys race."

"I can't beat the hell out of him in the ring, so I gotta beat him at something." Letting the helmet dangle in his left hand, he set his right hand in the small of her back and said, "Where'd you park?"

"Around the corner. I'll be . . ." She looked up at him. "Oh, stop growling. I'll be happy to have you escort me to my car so the boogeyman doesn't get me."

"Good answer." When they reached the sidewalk, he said, "I'm proud as hell that you can protect yourself, Molly, but I hope you never have to prove it."

"I know." She stood on tiptoe and kissed him. Really kissed him like he'd been dying for all fucking week. Although Molly hadn't repeated the words back to him, Deacon had to have faith and patience that she would.

CHAPTER TWENTY-FOUR

DEACON beat Molly to his place by ten minutes, giving him enough time to clean up the shithole he'd been wallowing in since Tuesday night.

In an attempt to get things back to the way they were, maybe even back to normal, he ordered a healthy pizza and she picked out a movie on pay-per-view. They curled up together on the couch.

He breathed a major sigh of relief that she hadn't pushed him to talk more. Everything Tag had reamed him about over fucking voice mail the morning after the dinner was true—Deacon was emotionally stunted and he lacked the skills to move forward. But that didn't mean he couldn't learn those skills when so much was at stake. The change wouldn't happen overnight. It'd take time for him to figure out how to open up to her. Something she seemed to understand.

When bedtime rolled around, Molly insisted on putting away all her new stuff. The woman had actually teared up while holding a bottle of her shampoo.

Fuck. He'd never understand women.

Finally, after forty-five minutes passed, he'd had enough. Just as he was about to drag her ass into his bed, she wandered into the bedroom, rubbing lotion on her hands.

"About damn time," he groused.

"After all the crying I've done this week, especially tonight, I had to put cold packs on my eyes or they'd be so puffy tomorrow I wouldn't be able to see."

"Strip and get in here next to me."

"Deacon—"

"I'm not gonna jump you. But sleeping naked together is our thing."

She smirked. "It is?"

"Yeah, it is." That wasn't as hard to admit as he'd imagined.

She clicked off the bedside lamp.

He could barely see her getting undressed. "Babe. It's a little late to be shy with me."

"Not after I consoled myself with ice cream this week. And then I didn't go to class to work it off, so I'm feeling poochy." Molly lifted the covers and dove in.

Deacon immediately hauled her against him. "Tell me where you're feeling poochy so I can feel you up and give you a second opinion."

"Omigod, *no*, I am not telling you that." She tried to push him away. "Geez, Deacon, it's embarrassing enough that I even told you I wallowed in sugar."

He rolled on top of her. "Don't slam yourself. I hate that shit. You're a fucking goddess."

"Get off me."

"She says as she clamps her hands on my ass, holding me in place," he said with a grin.

"I love your body." Her hands glided up his back.

Just the body? What about the man inside it?

Deacon kissed her, trying to focus on what he could control.

"You really want me to move off you?" he murmured against her lips. "Or do you want me to start moving on you and in you? Fast and hard. Or maybe slow and sweet."

"I'm holding out for the wake-up call you promised me."

He pressed an openmouthed kiss to his favorite spot on her neck. "Remind me again what that was?"

"Your tongue on my pussy, making me come twice before you fuck me."

"I love it when you talk dirty." He nibbled on her earlobe. "Say something else."

"We're supposed to be going to sleep, not making each other horny."

"I only have to look at you and I'm horny."

She slapped his ass. Hard. "Off."

Deacon rolled to his back but tucked her body against his. He'd missed this. The warm, soft comfort of her next to him.

After a while, when he sensed her restlessness, he said, "What?"

"You told me the bad stuff. Tell me something good. About your brother."

His usual *why would you care* response didn't come. He had to accept that now that Molly knew about Dante, she'd want to know more about him.

"Dante and I had exact opposite tempers. I'd get enraged and come out swinging. His anger was a slow burn. The longer it simmered, the hotter he got. So when he finally hit the boiling point, he blew like a volcano."

"Did you two ever get into knock-down, drag-out fights?"

"As kids? Nah. We had our moments, but they were rare. When we got older, we had different interests but we had the same opinion on most things." He paused, and the memory came rushing back. "Except this one time, when we were thirteen . . ."

When he finished the story about Dante, the armadillo trap, and the gross of bottle rockets, he had Molly laughing.

It'd been a long time since he'd thought of that. Of the good times and not just the loss of them.

DEACON shouldn't have been surprised by the nightmare.

One of the main reasons he didn't talk about the accident was his subconscious came back to bite him in the ass and made him relive it in his sleep too.

It started differently, but it always ended the same way. This go-around, his fucked-up psyche put Molly in the front seat between him and his brother.

An animated Molly flirted with Dante—who for the first time looked exactly like Deacon at his present age. Deacon had no feelings of jealousy, just relief that his brother approved of his girlfriend. Because god knew Dante hadn't liked Cassidy.

But when he reached the part of the dream where the tree loomed ahead, the knothole mouth that screamed was Molly's mouth. When he turned to look at Cassidy passed out in the middle, it was Molly sailing through the windshield.

He screamed and bolted upright in bed.

Then Molly was in his face. "Deacon."

"You're alive." As soon as he said that, he had to look away out of embarrassment.

Of course she's alive, you dumb fuck.

"Look at me."

He shook his head.

"This is why you don't talk about the accident." She set her hand on the back of his sweaty neck.

Her cool fingers stroking his fevered skin settled him a little.

"You had a nightmare like this in Nebraska. That afternoon you made me sleep. When I woke up, you were gone. I thought I'd heard a scream, but I figured I'd imagined it."

"No, you didn't. That one was particularly bad. And I needed . . ." *To get away. Like I do now.* When Deacon scooted toward the edge of the bed, intending to escape, Molly threw her leg over his hips and forcefully pushed him flat on the mattress.

"Lie still."

"Molly—"

"It's my right as your lover to touch you in passion and in pain." Her hands journeyed down his chest. "You're in pain, Deacon. Let me give you something else to think about."

Her silky hair trailed down the center of his torso, following in the wake of her kisses. She took his soft cock in her mouth, sucking and tonguing the flesh until it began to harden.

It didn't take long for his cock to become fully erect with the expert way she worked him over.

Her hair was a curtain masking his view. He snagged a handful of the dark tresses and yanked to get her attention. The wet warmth surrounding his dick disappeared. Her gaze met his.

Deacon said, "I want to watch you."

She circled the rim of his cockhead with her tongue and lightly suckled. Then she brought his shaft into her mouth slowly until the entire length was buried deep enough the head touched the back of her throat. She swallowed once.

He groaned. "Jesus. That feels so fucking good."

Then Molly released him in that same leisurely manner until his dick was wet, throbbing, and entirely out of her mouth. "I know you like to watch me blowing you. But this time I want you to close your eyes and let me have my way with you. Do nothing but feel how much I love touching you like this."

Like he'd ever say no to that. Deacon traced the edge of her jaw down to her chin, moving his fingers to outline her lips, which were so close to his cock he felt her fast breath teasing the wet tip. "Okay."

A secretive smile curled those full lips. She placed one hand in the center of his chest and pushed until he was flat on the mattress. Her hair fell, covering her face.

But then the heat and suction returned, and Deacon gave himself over to it.

Molly's hand jacked his shaft, rising up with hard pulls to meet her tight, wet mouth sliding down. Every few strokes, her fingers would drop between his legs to fondle his balls. Or to rub the section of skin between his sac and his asshole.

It should've embarrassed him, how much he liked that touch. But it made him even hotter that no part of his body was off-limits to her, the same as every inch of her was his to taste and touch.

Coherent thought morphed into silent pleas for her not to stop. His body jerked. His hips shot up. Goose bumps erupted when she paused to plant wet kisses on the insides of his thighs as she raked the outsides with her fingernails.

He fucking loved it. She understood he didn't need a sweet and reverent blow job. He needed urgency, a tiny spark of pain, and being reminded that she'd taken control.

He yelped when she squeezed his balls.

He fisted his hands in the sheets and not her hair when she deep throated him.

He whimpered at the wet lash of her tongue over his anus.

Molly had him so wound up—belly muscles quivering, quads as tight as if he'd performed a hundred squats that even his freakin' knees were sweating by the time she unleashed his orgasm. Her cheeks hollowed as she sucked every hot spurt, her fingers loosely circling his shaft as she stroked and the tip of her finger swirling around his anus.

Deacon tried to hold on, tried to remain cognizant, but the pleasure swamped him and he gave in to it. Then sleep beckoned, and he couldn't ignore the summons.

The last thing he remembered was Molly snuggling into him with a softly whispered, "Let's hope your dreams are much sweeter now."

CHAPTER TWENTY-FIVE

BEING naked in bed with Deacon defined decadent.

Being naked in bed with Mr. MMA brooding badass after he'd poured his heart and soul out to her, confessed his love, and then proved it, oh, twice? Downright heavenly. Her body, throbbing from Deacon's very thorough attentions, the heat, the weight, the scent of him all over her . . . She knew there'd never be another man for her.

Deacon bent down to nuzzle the side of her breast. "You trying to get me hard again with that sound?"

"What sound?"

"That sexy little hum you make when you're thinking about us fucking."

"Does it bother you?"

He didn't look up when he said, "It's the hottest thing I've ever heard."

"Better than when I make that *sexy little fucking moan* you get crazy possessive about?" she teased.

"You make soft need-you noises when I start to touch you. You make desperate-to-come noises when I'm inside you. But that little hum I hear *after* I've fucked you? It lets me know you're still thinking about me fucking you."

"Hmm."

"What?"

"Will it get your back up if I say that's sweet?"

"I ain't sweet, babe. Not fucking ever."

Wrong. But she'd keep those moments to herself. When she caressed the smooth line of his head, down to the back of his neck, he sighed. His reaction to her touch was one of the sweetest things ever.

"You still seem tense. Want a back rub?"

Deacon raised his head. "You'd do that?"

"Let's see . . . putting my hands all over this body, an outstanding example of masculine perfection? Damn. Such a chore. What was I thinking? I rescind my offer, because touching you would totally suck."

"You wanna suck me too, I'm good with that. Because, babe, you are *very* good at that."

"Thanks. Roll over." Molly shifted and slid down to straddle his naked ass. Maybe she should try to keep some of her weight off him by balancing on her knees. Nah. He'd notice and chew her out for her body-image issues, so he'd just have to suffer if she squished his dick.

Before she dug her fingers into his muscles, she ran her hands across the broad expanse of his back. She'd seen his tattoo before, but she hadn't studied it this close.

The angel's wings spread from one shoulder to the other and stretched down to his hips. The feathers faded from black to gray. The detail was breathtaking, utilizing his skin as part of the shading, which accentuated the solid lines. When he moved, his muscles gave the ink fluidity.

His arms were in a blocky U shape against the mattress. She

noticed the symmetry between the tats on his arms with the one large piece on his back. Two thick black bands circled both of his biceps and were connected with what looked like a DNA chain. From that point down, the designs on each arm were different. He hadn't gone with full sleeves—not yet anyway. These tats weren't strictly shades of black, but bold colors interwoven in the chains and scrolls, creating patterns and yet total chaos.

"You're quiet."

Molly traced a spiral of green that looked like a fern frond beginning to unfurl. "Just admiring your ink." She leaned forward and pressed a kiss behind his ear. "It's beautiful."

"Not everyone thinks so."

"Does anyone who's not in this bed matter?"

Deacon didn't answer.

His silence didn't bother her. Because she knew his initial knee-jerk reaction was from defending the art on his body. And it pained her to admit, but at one time she'd been judgmental about men and women who sported tats. She hadn't understood the beauty in personal expression until she'd gone to college. Her roommate had decided to mark the pivotal points in her life with ink as a daily reminder of life's joys and sorrows.

Molly hadn't gotten quite brave enough to do that. "Can you tell me what any of them mean?"

"The angel's wings . . . That artist I told you about who did the art in my living room drew them for me. I had the outline of the tat started on the one-year anniversary of Dante's death. Every year I added more until it was finished. Since then I've had sections of it re-inked every year, so I . . ."

"So you don't forget the pain and suffering you went through on that day and what you lost."

"Jesus. How did you know?"

"I didn't. Not for sure."

"You scare me," he said softly.

"I know. But you're not alone in your fear, Deacon. I feel it too." She scooted down and pressed the cradle of her hips to the base of his buttocks. Molly rested her cheek between his shoulder blades and stretched her arms out on top of his.

Deacon exhaled heavily. "I like that, babe. Don't move."

That simple body-to-body contact gave them both something they needed. Comfort. Trust. A different way their bodies could feel connected as one.

Molly dozed off when she heard Deacon's soft snores.

Fingers threading through hers roused her.

"Sorry. I didn't mean to fall asleep on you."

"Now I understand why you like having my weight on you."

"I'll bet your legs and ass are tingling."

"Nope." He reached back and smacked her ass. "Get cracking on that back rub, woman."

She straddled his butt and started pressing the heels of her hands to the base of Deacon's neck. Within a minute or so of her digging her thumbs into his flesh, he released the tension and melted into the mattress.

After a bit she said, "Not to be crass, and I'm not asking for specifics, but I was surprised to learn that your family is rich. Does your family have a long history in Texas too?"

"No. The Westermans are new oil, which is completely different from old Texas oil."

"Um, isn't all oil . . . old?"

He laughed. "Our family story is along the lines of the Clampetts of *The Beverly Hillbillies* and not the Ewings of Southfork. When I returned to Texas after bein' gone for almost five years, my dad told me I had a trust fund. But he wasn't sure if changing my name affected my claim on it. I had to meet with Granddad. Jesus, he was a scary man."

"Was he upset you changed your name?"

"Not after I told him why I'd done it. It helped, I think, that I took Uncle Jesse's surname. Uncle Jesse was my grandmother's brother, and Granddad respected the hell out of him."

Molly dug her thumbs alongside his spine, above his buttocks. "What happened?"

"He freed up the money, but the stipulation was that I got put on the JFW board. Then he informed me that Dante's trust had become mine as well. After living hand-to-mouth for years? I almost passed out when they told me the ridiculously high amount in the account. And I don't talk about it because what I'm worth ain't nobody's business."

"Your financial worth isn't your true worth to me, Deacon."

"I know that, babe." He slowly raised his head and looked at her. "And I fucking love you for saying that."

"I wouldn't have said it if I didn't mean it." She shifted to the side so she could look into his face. "But I need some idea if you're talking about a trust that allows you to buy first-class airplane tickets without checking the price? Or if you just buy the damn airplane."

"JFW has several planes. We're not talking an Okada level of money—either for the business or the family. But my eight-figure trust fund ensures I don't ever have to work as a dishwasher again. I'm lucky enough to be able to follow my dream to become a MMA champion and train full-time."

Her jaw dropped at the nonchalant way he tossed off *eight-figure trust fund*.

"Tag is my investment guy. Granddad also set up stipulations of how much money I have to take out every year."

"You don't mean a limit of how much money you *can* take out?"

He shook his head. "I have to take out a certain amount. Not that I'm complaining. With the exception of a couple of cars, I never developed expensive tastes."

"How will you ever survive until your next payout?"

Deacon appeared to be scrutinizing her for malice. Seeing none, he gestured to his apartment. "Ain't like I'm livin' at the Ritz."

"But like Shiori . . . you could live there if you wanted to."

"Yeah. But the penthouse at the Four Seasons is nicer and way more tricked-out."

She laughed. "Goofball."

He threaded his fingers through hers. "I'm happy to see your hands and knuckles have developed thicker skin."

Molly was glad he changed the subject. "Kickboxing is hell on manicures. There goes my dream of striking it rich as a hand model."

Deacon smiled—but it didn't reach his eyes.

She smoothed her hand over his pate. "What's going on in this shaved head of yours?"

"Ronin and Amery had a huge fight and broke up over money and family shit. I don't want that to happen to us."

"Different situation." But Deacon and Ronin were even more similar than she'd thought, and it spooked her, to be honest. But right now Deacon didn't need to hear her fears.

"True. But all the money in the world won't give me back my brother."

Molly kissed his cheek, her heart heavy for this man who'd lost so much. "So I hope you keep Dante alive in your memories, Deacon. Anytime you want to talk about him, feel free."

"You might regret that you offered that."

"Never. But I am slacking on the massage I offered you." She returned to her position on her knees above his butt, rubbing, pushing, and working his muscles until her hands were sore. Then she bent forward, using her tongue to trace the feathers and swirls inked on his skin.

Deacon reared up. "Dammit, Molly. Warn a guy."

"I'm gonna lick your tattoos, Deacon." She loved the taste of his skin. Salty, with the musk of sex. She loved the way he smelled. Warm, manly, with the underlying scent of clean cotton sheets. She scraped her teeth down the side of his neck and across his shoulder, absorbing his shudder like a full-body kiss. "And when I'm done with the back, I'll flip you over and work on the front."

He turned his head. "What goes around comes around. You lick me? I'm gonna lick you."

The hot, sexual warning blazing in his eyes sent goose bumps cascading down her spine.

"You play with my chest? I'm gonna play with yours."

"Why are you telling me this?"

"During the five days we were apart, I promised myself when I got you back in my bed, I was gonna kick up the kink."

Molly's pulse spiked, and she knew he'd felt it when he chuckled. Wanting him to show her that kink, she rubbed her breasts against his bare back and licked the shell of his ear. "Roll over. Unless you want me to rub my wet pussy over this hot, hard ass of yours and get myself off." She canted her hips and ground down on his left buttock.

"Fuck, yeah. Use my ass to get yourself off, because you know what that means."

What goes around comes around. I'll use your ass to get myself off.

Molly spread her pussy lips open so her clit had direct contact with his rough skin. Then she rolled up and back.

"Jesus, woman. You're wet."

"Touching you does that to me," she panted in his ear.

He groaned. "Keep doin' that. Talking dirty as you rub one out."

"Did you jack off this week when I wasn't there to keep your poor cock from suffering from semen buildup?"

"I tried to whack off. But it didn't work. I only wanted you."

"I only wanted you too." How could she already be close to coming? She began to move faster.

"That's it, babe. Take what you need."

She wrapped her hands around his biceps to anchor herself because their skin had grown slick. Her vision went a little wonky and she pressed her cheek into the curve of his neck. When the tiny pulses radiated from her clit, she rubbed harder, clutched him harder, breathed harder.

He tightened his ass cheek and she released a low moan.

When her pussy stopped throbbing, she relaxed against him and kissed the nape of his neck.

"So goddamn hot how easily you let go with me." Deacon turned his head to get at her mouth. "Your body on mine, your wet pussy rubbing on me, your breath hot and fast in my ear. You drive me fucking crazy, woman."

"Now you need to turn over so I can lick your tats on the front side." For once she scooted off him faster than he could grab her, and she laughed.

Deacon's heavy-lidded gaze and hard cock spurred her to drive him to the edge, just to see how far he'd let her go before he took over.

In her most commanding voice, she said, "Hands above your head."

He complied, his big hands gripping the slats of the headboard. But Deacon, being Deacon, didn't allow her full control. "As much as I love your mouth around my cock, that part of me is off-limits during this frontal massage."

His clipped tone indicated it wouldn't be long before the beast came out. And she couldn't wait.

So Molly ignored his edict. Keeping her gaze fastened to his, she bent her head, licking up his shaft, stopping to suck the precome from the head. He hissed a warning, so she moved up, outlining the pillows of his abs with the tip of her tongue.

When she reached the tats on his chest, she focused on mapping the lines and swirls with her mouth. Her breasts dragged along his skin, her nipples hard as diamonds. The way her heavy breasts swayed with her movements drove him crazy. At one point she swore she heard the wooden headboard slats cracking under his iron grip as he fought his natural instinct to touch her.

"Molly."

"Hmm?" She placed soft kisses around the defined line of his pectorals, creating an ever smaller circle until her lips completely covered his nipple. She lapped at the flat disk, loving how fast his hips shot up.

"Fuck."

"Like that, do you?" she said, looking up at him. Oh. Those eyes. The way they burned for her . . . heady stuff that she could put a look of need like that on his face. Molly lowered her head again. This time she used her teeth on his nipple. Scraping the surface and biting down with enough force that he bucked beneath her.

"You're in for it," he warned.

Her gaze hooked his again. "Bring it." She blew a stream of air across the wet tip, smirking at his sharp intake of breath. "You really have nice nipples, Deacon. Perfectly shaped." She sucked the whole thing into her mouth. "Very responsive." Then she dragged her mouth across the slope of his pectoral to his other nipple. Teasing it ruthlessly, making it wet and tight, then switching back and forth between both nipples until Deacon damn near couldn't lie still.

Molly shifted back, letting her hair drift over his chest, his belly, and his cock and balls. She flattened her palms on his chest and propped herself up. As she squeezed the hard muscles, she swept her thumbs across the tight nipples.

"You done?" he asked tersely.

"Maybe." She slid her hands up, following the amazing contours of his arms. When she reached his wrists, they were face-to-face, mouth-to-mouth, her abundant breasts smashed against his chest. Still feeling giddy about the heated look of lust she'd put in his eyes and the hardness she felt prodding her ass, she angled her head and traced his lips with hers. "Give me the kink you promised, Deacon."

A noise more akin to a roar than a growl vibrated in her mouth when Deacon's lips connected with hers.

He kissed her hard, his mouth consuming hers with a hunger that robbed her of breath. One hand was pulling her hair while the other curled around the back of her neck, holding her in place.

When Molly began to roll her hips against him, he brought his leg up, stopping the motion. Then he rolled her onto her back. The speed of his movement and his strength sent her pulse tripping and pushed her excitement to fever pitch again.

Deacon broke the seal of their mouths and buried his face in her neck. No sweet whispered words of reconciliation or soft kisses. No. The beast sank his teeth into the spot that could send her straight into orgasm. He pinned her down with his big body, her hair still clutched in his fist, ensuring she couldn't move as he made her crazy, dizzy, and stupid with want.

When Molly gasped his name, he moved his lips up her throat. "My turn to get off. And it's gonna get messy when I fuck your tits and come all over this pretty neck." He blew softly in her ear. "I want you wet and sticky. Covered in me—on your chest, your throat, your face, and in your hair."

Her face heated. More like her entire body flushed.

"Grab the headboard with both hands and arch your back." He released his hold on her hair and slipped his hand between her legs. "I like that your pussy gets wet from touching me. But I'll need lube, so stay put while I get it."

Deacon didn't go far. He pushed up onto his knees and leaned over to open the nightstand drawer. That put his beautiful cock almost right in her face.

And that was a temptation she couldn't resist. Angling her head closer, she parted her lips and sucked his shaft in deep, clear to the root.

"Jesus, fuck, Molly!"

She flicked her not-sorry gaze up to him. There was something so powerful and yet so humbling locking eyes with him while his cock was buried in her throat.

A wicked smile settled on his lips and he stroked her cheek. "Get me good and wet, babe. Don't suck. Don't swallow."

Her mouth watered around his girth, and she had to breathe through her nose.

Deacon watched her eyes as he toyed with her nipples. Caressing. Pinching. Twisting. Licking his thumb and index finger before he switched sides. "You have the greatest tits I've ever seen."

She hummed her approval of his compliment around his cock.

He hissed in a breath. Then he curled his hand beneath her jaw, forcing her to release his dick. "My Molly is no shrinking violet when it comes to down-and-dirty sex."

My Molly. God. She loved that. "Because of you, Deacon. You make me feel sexy and adventurous."

"You are, and it doesn't have a damn thing to do with me." After he tucked his knees on either side of her hips, he squirted a line of lube down the valley of her cleavage and zigzagged more up the insides of her breasts.

Goose bumps spread up her chest and down her belly from the cold gel.

Then Deacon forced her attention to his face. "You watch me while I've got these gorgeous tits wrapped around my cock. You see how much I love fucking this body of yours."

Molly could see it and she'd never been so turned on in her life, knowing that she could make Deacon's hands shake with how much he wanted to take her this way. "Can I touch you?"

He shook his head. "Can't touch yourself either. Once I've shot my load, you're gonna sit on my face, so I'm covered in you, just like you'll be covered in me."

Her clit pulsed in anticipation. It looked like he'd be fulfilling another fantasy today.

"Spread your legs so I can fuck your pussy if I want."

There went her chance to rub her thighs together so she could get herself off. Probably intentional on the sadist's part—not that she'd tell him that, lest he stop.

Those big hands pushed her breasts together so tightly her nipples nearly touched.

"I can feel how hard and fast your heart is beating." The hunger in his eyes gave way to ecstasy as he pushed his cock into the channel he'd created. He eased back slowly and pushed in with equal leisure, his head briefly falling back, exposing the long line of his throat.

The man was magnificent, lost in pleasure.

The pubic hair on his balls scraped over her sternum with every thrust. Deacon's hands were gripping her boobs so tightly his knuckles were white, blending in with her pale skin. He'd probably bruise her, but she would wear his marks of passion, of possession, with pride.

"Fuck yeah." He glanced down, his eyes glittering as he watched his cock disappear into her tit tunnel until the thick head popped out the top.

Molly half expected that Deacon fucking her breasts wouldn't do anything for her; she'd go along with it because this was something he wanted.

But she couldn't have been more wrong. All of him—his weight, his heat, his scent, his need—was druglike in its intensity. Her hands voluntarily immobilized added a sense of surrender. The look of bliss on his face—she might've had a mini O from that alone.

"You're—this feels so fucking perfect. I ain't gonna last." His strokes became quicker.

Sweat coated his body and a few drops landed on her chest. She wanted to lick the rivulet of sweat running down the cord straining in his neck. She wanted to rub her palms over his damp head, making them slick with his sweat and his scent.

His deep grunt of satisfaction was her only warning before the first warm spurt hit her chin. She tilted her head back, and the next jets of come dotted her neck.

Deacon slid his cock down, and the final offering splatted across her chest below her collarbones.

She looked up at him. Witnessing the pure male possession in his eyes and the sexy twist of his lips . . . In that moment he owned her.

He scooted all the way down her body and plunged his cock into her. He didn't move or thrust; he just remained still. Then his face was above hers. His tongue darted out, and he licked the come from her chin before he smashed his mouth to hers, sharing his taste and his passion for her in a kiss that left her no doubt the man loved her.

Molly's hips shot up, and she dropped her arm down to get a handful of his ass. She tightened her pussy muscles as her sex pulsed around his shaft in three short bursts.

Deacon continued to kiss her, making no effort to get off of her. But chances were good that body fluids had stuck them together anyway.

Then the crazy man rolled them. After he dislodged his cock, he pushed on her shoulders, setting her upright. "On your knees, babe, and hold tight to that headboard. I'm gonna eat this cunt until you scream my name."

"Deacon—omigod, what are you doing?" He'd slid between her thighs and pushed them apart so her wet pussy practically covered his face. He had to be suffocating.

He turned his head and bit her thigh. "If you can still talk, then I'm doin' something wrong. Lower your hips."

"But—"

He slapped her ass. Hard. "Do. It."

Holding on to the headboard gave her a sense of unbalance, so she dropped to her hands and widened her knees.

Then his warm mouth suctioned to her pussy. Deacon's sucking lips and flicking tongue worked her over to the point verbal communication became limited to "yes, more, don't stop" and a few moans and gasps.

And screams.

Yes, the man made her come so hard the first time she'd screamed. The second time . . . she couldn't make any noise at all because she'd forgotten how to breathe. The third time he'd done something with his teeth on her clit and his thumb in her ass that . . . Yeah. No words could describe that orgasm beyond *epic*.

After she'd flopped on the mattress beside him, she assumed they'd take a minute.

But Deacon's damp face and wet mouth were immediately on her nipples.

"You're obsessed with them," she said with a soft wheeze.

"I'm obsessed with you. These are just attached to you."

She reached down and stroked his sleek head. "Thank you."

"For?"

"For showing me that multiple orgasms and collapsing into a sticky pile after phenomenal sex isn't a myth."

"My pleasure." Deacon looked up at her. "This makeup-sex shit is pretty fucking awesome. But, babe, I'm hoping we never have to do it again."

"Me too."

CHAPTER TWENTY-SIX

DEACON insisted on walking Molly into the office Monday morning, so Chaz, Presley, and Amery understood they were back together.

Not that anyone would mistake the lingering kiss he left her with as anything but possessive.

Molly had poured herself a cup of coffee when Amery sidled in for a refill. "Morning, Amery."

"Morning, Molly. Got a second to talk?"

"I don't suppose you want to discuss the Wicksburg Farm account?"

"No, I don't suppose I do."

Great. "Sure. I'll be right in."

She took a couple of deep breaths after Amery walked away.

Presley intercepted her. "You don't think you and Deacon getting back together rates a phone call to me?"

"If Deacon and I had left his bedroom at all yesterday, I would've called."

Her eyes went as wide as her grin. "You're not joking about spending all day in bed, are you?"

"No."

"But things are good?"

Molly grinned back. "Very. And I promise we'll talk as soon as the boss is done grilling me." She headed straight for Amery's office and shut the door behind her.

Amery checked out Molly's outfit. Since Molly hadn't been home since Saturday afternoon, she'd paired the spare pair of black jeans she'd found in her workout bag with the sequined silver tank top she'd worn beneath her western shirt to Katie's party Saturday night. She'd finished the outfit with one of Deacon's crisp white dress shirts, knotted at the waist. "That's a funky outfit, Mol. You look good."

"Thanks. I feel good." Molly settled in the visitor's chair and crossed her legs—a move she couldn't have done a year and a half ago, before she started working out.

"Did your conversation with Ronin on Friday prompt you into giving Deacon another chance?"

Molly shook her head. "In fact, my discussion with Ronin increased my doubts about . . . everything."

"Fuck. I worried that might happen. Sensei Black isn't as attuned to emotion as he thinks he is. And sometimes he comes off as an uncaring asshole."

No kidding. "I'll be straight with you. It seemed like Ronin was warning me off Deacon."

Amery's eyes went flat.

"You're right that your man says what he thinks and damn the consequences. Maybe I wasn't supposed to take it that way, but I did."

"Do you remember exactly what Ronin said and how he phrased it?"

Molly repeated as much of that part of the conversation as she could remember. She withheld a laugh when Amery smacked her own forehead after she finished speaking.

"I know him, Molly. And he wasn't saying Deacon was better

off not in a relationship with you. He was relaying how Deacon dealt with the hurt and frustration of not being with you. In his Ronin way, he was telling you to be prepared because Deacon would be coming for you as soon as he got control."

Her jaw dropped. "That is not at *all* how I took it!"

"I know. And Ronin sort of suspected that after he got done talking to you. So he asked me to clarify a few things, but by the time he mentioned that on Friday, you'd already left for the day." Amery sighed. "I love him. The man's instincts are unparalleled when it comes to me, but I'm the exception with him, not the rule."

"Was Ronin all mental ninja with his other girlfriends?"

"No. After Naomi, women were a tool. He used them when he needed them and put them out of his mind when he finished with them."

Molly sipped her coffee. "Harsh."

"But true. I could make excuses and claim he's a man's man. He understands his instructors and his guy friends. Knox, Deacon, Gil, and now Fisher and Riggins. But he is way off base when it comes to Blue, Beck, Maddox, and Ito. He seriously fucked up with Knox and the Shihan issue." She shook her head. "That was another situation I had to explain to Master Black *after* the fact, about how wrong his approach had been with Knox. And don't get me started on how fucking clueless he was about his own damn sister." She paused and closed her eyes. "He's getting better with Shiori. And Katie. She can be annoying, but she knows her stuff. That's not something I ever thought I'd admit." She opened her eyes and looked at Molly. "But back to you. I'm so freaking sorry I sicced Ronin on you and he made it worse."

"You misunderstood. Ronin helped me—up until the point he talked about how much better Deacon fought when he was in turmoil over me. Ronin is the only one who knows that Deacon has things in his past he'd rather not discuss."

"But Deacon told you those things?"

"No. I found out from someone else. That's where my problem began. Deacon's secrets aren't mine to tell. I couldn't talk to anyone about what happened between us because the breakup was based on his nondisclosure." She groaned. "That sounded like a damn business breakdown."

"Cut yourself a break, Molly. You majored in business. It helps to put things in a context you can understand."

"I'm happy you know that about me. Anyway, Deacon made it right with me. He gave me time to settle, and then I was at a point where I could listen." Molly stared into her coffee cup. "It didn't make it any easier to hear."

"Did Deacon tell you all of it?"

Her head shot up. "Why would you—"

"Ask that? Seems like a weird question, I know. But trust me—my husband has many secrets. Just when I think I've uncovered them all, a new one pops up. I've had to accept that loving him means letting him tell me those secrets on his time frame, not mine. So is that something you can live with?"

Why hadn't Molly considered that Deacon might be keeping more from her? Because he'd come clean about the accident, his family, and financial situation?

"Hey, I'm not trying to sow seeds of discord. Far from it. I'm happy that you and Deacon found each other. But I can't help drawing the parallels between Ronin and Deacon. There's a reason they get along so well beyond their connection to martial arts."

"You mean because they're both rich?"

Amery fidgeted. "I wondered if Deacon would disclose that. And I hated that if he didn't, it wasn't up to me to tell you. Jesus, Molly. You know I know how that feels."

Ronin had hidden his billionaire-heir status from Amery, and it'd caused a serious break in their relationship that'd lasted several weeks. They'd repaired it, but Molly knew their financial disparity was still a concern for Amery. "I know it would've caused a conflict for you. But I understand that your loyalty is to Ronin."

"Thank god. I worry it might be a tricky balance between us, keeping our friendship and our business relationship, as well as our significant others' secrets. I don't want either of us to be afraid to confide in the other. I trust you, Molly, and I think you trust me."

"I do. So how did you learn about Deacon's family money? Ronin?"

She shook her head. "Deacon's father flew in for the last fight—the one you skipped because he stood you up—on the company's private jet. Not a charter, but a private plane they own. Deacon's dad didn't hide that, but he didn't brag, either. I ended up talking to him at the after-party since Deacon was with—" Amery snapped her mouth shut.

"Ring bunnies. Yeah, I know about them. Speaking of after-parties . . . the fight card that he and Needham are on is being held in Denver, right?"

"Yes."

"We haven't done promo for it."

"That's because it's not sponsored by Black and Blue Promotions. East Meets West dojo is in charge. And they throw killer parties." She grinned. "I saw Katie taking notes and digging through the garbage in her ring-girl costume to see if the hors d'oeuvres were from Costco."

Molly laughed. "She would. That woman is tenacious. And I'm glad you've gotten over whatever problem you had with her."

"Jealousy. I didn't like the way she looked at my man."

"Amery, every woman looks at your man that way because he is exquisite to look at. But the only woman he ever looks back at like that is you."

Amery sighed. "I know, right? I'm the luckiest woman on the planet."

"And with that . . . I'll get to work."

"We'll have our weekly meeting at eleven thirty. I'll order in. Let Presley know."

"Will do. Thanks."

The rest of the day sped by. Amery had brought in three new accounts the past week. And as Molly sat in on the creative brainstorming session, she realized for the millionth time how thrilled she was to work here—where her job was more than just a job and her boss was more than just a boss.

DEACON showed up at Molly's apartment an hour after she'd gotten off work. His brooding face and quiet demeanor indicated his training day hadn't gone well, so she didn't ask specifics.

While he showered, she finished making dinner. Prior to their break, she'd convinced Deacon to give her the diet he followed in the weeks leading up to a fight. Since the bout with Needham was in two and a half weeks, she knew he changed eating patterns today. She fixed ground turkey and brown rice, along with a spinach salad with non-starchy vegetables. Before bed he'd have a "dessert" shake—chocolate protein powder, almond milk, and low-glycemic fruit, like strawberries.

His clean scent reached her before he did. His bare arms encircled her, and he kissed the side of her neck. "Hey."

"Hey. Feel better?"

"Seeing you barefoot in the kitchen, wearing those raggedy-ass sweatpants and this tiny tank top, reminds me that I'm a lucky bastard."

"Aw. You say the sweetest things. Have a seat. Dinner's almost done."

Deacon rested his chin on her shoulder. "Babe. What's all this?"

Molly turned and wreathed her arms around his neck. "Fight diet starts today, right?"

"Yeah."

"So that's what we're eating. I followed the recipes exactly—no substitutions. Even the spices I used are sodium free."

"You did that for me," he stated tersely. "Without asking."

Not the reaction she'd wanted. "Yes. Don't be mad. I promise I didn't add or change anything that would—"

"Stop talking."

Her eyes narrowed.

"You don't get it. No one has ever done anything like this for me."

"Deacon . . ."

"No one. And my woman"—he rested his forehead to hers and closed his eyes—"my hot, sexy, sweet woman was thinking of me. At the end of her long workday, she went to the store, tracked down all the weird shit I'm allowed to eat, and cooked it for me. Not only that, but she tried to make it taste decent. Fuck, Molly. Do you have any idea what that means to me?"

"I'm starting to," she murmured.

"You amaze me. What you give me . . ." Deacon eased back to gaze into her eyes. "I love you. So fucking much." Then his mouth was on hers, bestowing a kiss unlike any she'd ever been gifted with before. And it was a gift, the precious way Deacon made her feel.

So give him a gift in return. Tell him you love him too.

She would. Just not right now. She twisted out of his hold. "Let's eat before it gets cold."

After he'd sat at the eat-in counter, she set the food down in serving bowls rather than dishing it up. "That's one thing I was unclear on. Serving sizes. But if you need a food scale, I have one around here someplace—"

"Babe. Sit. I've been doin' this long enough I can eyeball my portions."

"Okay. But I'll probably have to put salt on mine. That's one thing I can't give up."

Deacon frowned. "You don't have to eat this just because I do."

"I know. I just thought it'd be easier if we're eating the same meal."

He leaned over and kissed her hard.

Although Molly had tried to jazz it up, the food was still really bland. But that didn't stop Deacon from eating two helpings of turkey and rice and three helpings of salad.

As soon as they finished, he rinsed the dishes and loaded her tiny dishwasher. A domestic Deacon was a sexy Deacon.

He turned and caught her watching him. "You keep looking at me like that and you're gonna get fucked right here on the kitchen floor."

"That would be fun. Maybe later. How long are you staying tonight?"

"I thought I'd stay over." He yanked her against him. "Don't like sleeping alone anymore."

"You could always get a dog," she teased.

"Wrong. I don't like sleeping without *you*."

Deacon's need for constant physical contact between them was one of her favorite things about him. The fact he could now verbalize that need? Made her damn near giddy. "I'm happy you want a sleepover, but fair warning: I'm putting you to work first."

"What kind of work?"

"Well, last week when I needed to do something to take my mind off you and I couldn't quite make myself go check out the kickboxing programs at other gyms—"

"What? Why would you even think about doin' that?"

"Because if we were broken up for good, it would've been too hard seeing you all the time. Black Arts is your place more than it was ever mine. I thought it'd be the easiest solution."

"Nope. There's a better one." He got right in her face. "We're never breaking up again—got it?"

She smiled at his ferocity. "Got it."

"Now, what's this damn 'honey-do' list you've got lined up for your man?"

"It's not a 'honey-do' list; it's a project."

"I'm good with projects."

Were her eyes deceiving her, or did Deacon actually look happy about helping her? She grabbed his hand and towed him into the spare bedroom before he changed his mind.

Inside the room, Deacon looked at the furniture on the plastic tarp, next to the cans of paint and the sanding blocks. "What did those bookcases do to piss you off?"

"I needed to change something, and sanding the bookcases was a great outlet for my aggression."

"Was there something wrong with the bookcases that they needed to be fixed?"

"No. I just wanted to give them a fresher look."

"Fresher look," he repeated. "Babe. I don't even know what the fuck that means. If you wanted something different, why didn't you just buy it?"

Molly counted to ten. It wasn't Deacon's financial status that kept him from understanding; it was his Y chromosome. "Because I can't buy it the way I want it. That's why it's called a 'do it your-self' project. On one of the home-improvement channels, I watched a woman revamp her old bookcases, and they turned out amazing. Totally changed the look of her entire room. Since I needed a distraction last week, I started this project."

"Probably a more productive distraction than punching the fuck out of everyone who crossed your path."

Men. "Yeah. It helped."

Deacon crouched down for a closer look at the mess. "It's a woman thing, huh?"

"What?"

"Changing shit, rearranging shit, revamping shit."

"I guess. Although some guys like to do it too."

He snorted disbelief at the very idea of that.

She bristled. "If you don't want to help—"

"I do wanna help, but I gotta be honest. I don't understand why you took perfectly good bookcases and sanded the varnish off them . . ." He bent over the largest bookcase. "Jesus. Did you do that?"

"Do what?"

"Beat on this with a hammer or a chain? There are dents fucking everywhere."

"Yes, I used both, actually. It's a distressing technique that's supposed to make it look antiqued."

"Taking a hammer and a chain to oak makes it look like a psycho decided to redecorate."

"Deacon!"

He turned, his face registering surprise at her sharp tone. "What?"

"Get out. I do not need your criticism when you don't know what the hell you're talking about. I've been looking forward to finishing this project, and you will not suck the joy out of it for me."

Deacon looked confused.

"Seriously. Get out. Go watch TV or something."

"Watch the TV that's sitting on the floor because you took it off the bookcase so you could revamp it?"

"Omigod. We are *so* breaking up over this."

He laughed. "Come here."

Molly crossed her arms over her chest and glared at him.

"Fine." He moved to stand in front of her. "I'm not goin' anywhere. You get a kick outta doin' this stuff? Then I'll stand by and watch you be happy about it."

"Really?"

"Really. Can't promise I'll ever understand it. Knox even warned me about this when I helped him put up shelves in the baby's room." He smirked. "It was a design idea Shiori saw on one of the home-improvement shows. Knox threatened to put a block on those channels. But for all his bitching, he still did it. He calls them 'honey-do-me' projects; if he gets them done, he gets to do his wife."

"Cynical."

"But true." He touched her nose with his. "And I'll bet you look really fucking cute covered in paint." His eyes lit up. "Please tell me you wear them cutoff overalls and no shirt when you're painting."

"No, pervert."

"Probably a good thing. If I see you dressed like that? I'd drag you off to bed for hours."

"Make yourself useful and flip these bookcases over so I can paint the backs."

"They're already painted. And no offense, babe, but I noticed you missed a few spots."

Molly beat her head into his chest with mock frustration. "I sanded that paint off on *purpose*. So how about you are the muscle in this project, while I handle the artistic side."

THE next morning Deacon left for the dojo early—after offhandedly mentioning they were having a "couples" dinner thing or "some such shit" with Knox and Shiori this week.

She headed into the extra bedroom and checked out the fruits of her labor. For the bookcase base color, she'd chosen a soft sage green. She'd painted over that with a coat of white stain, wiping most of that off, so the green was visible beneath. Then she'd sanded random spots. Last night she'd added the final coat, an opaque gray varnish that dulled the paint into an antique patina. The gray tone settled into the dents and pits, creating tiny dark spots so the piece really looked old. It'd turned out awesome.

She wandered toward the kitchen to refill her coffee and

stopped in the living room. Deacon might not appreciate the country-cottage look of her living space, but she loved it. After growing up with bare walls and just the basics, she never took for granted that she could express her personality through the home she'd made for herself.

She'd placed two mismatched oversized chairs, one covered in rose chintz and the other in sage-green velvet, opposite the tufted sofa, done in a floral pattern composed of shades of pink and green. Between the couch and chairs she'd positioned a pine coffee table she'd refinished with a reverse-crackle glaze—her first DIY project. Directly behind the chairs was the space for the large bookshelf. She'd culled a few things from her grandmother's house over the years, an antique birdcage, some funky botany prints she'd found in the closet, and a wooden vase her grandfather had carved—all items she proudly displayed.

So she liked her private space frilly and girly. Mr. Big Bad MMA didn't look as out of place in her space as she'd imagined.

CHAPTER TWENTY-SEVEN

AFTER a grueling week of training, work, and hours of makeup sex, Deacon and Molly showed up late to Diesel on Saturday night.

Their friends gave them a rash of shit about that. Maddox had even gone as far as checking Deacon for hickeys. Good thing they couldn't see Molly's tits, because she had three or four red marks on each breast.

All the chairs around the table were full. Maddox, Beck, Ivan, Sergei, Fisher, and Blaze were all there, plus Blue and Gil. Even Riggins had put in an appearance. Katie, Fee, Presley, and Jaz sat at the other end of the table.

When Molly tugged her hand from his to join the ladies, Deacon hauled her back. He whispered, "Ten minutes with them and then I want you with me."

She stepped in front of him and rolled her eyes. "Why don't you just get a leash?"

Deacon placed his mouth on the pulse point in her throat. "Because I haven't found a collar yet that won't mark up this pretty skin."

Her breath caught. Then she slapped her hand on his chest and tried to push him back. "Not happening. Ever."

"Then you'd better have this luscious ass parked on my lap in ten minutes, hadn't you?"

Deacon snagged a chair from the table behind them, spun it around, and straddled it. "What's up?" he said to no one in particular.

"Maddox has chick problems," Ivan offered.

"Then why aren't you sitting there"—Deacon pointed to the women's end of the table—"whining to them for advice?"

"Fuck off, D." Then Maddox tipped his beer bottle to Ivan. "You too, Ruskie."

Beck stretched his arm across the back of the booth. "I'd take your problem any day, Mad."

"Me too," Blue added.

"It's not that kind of chick problem, you dipfucks," Maddox said with a scowl.

The waitress showed up. Deacon ordered water for himself after he saw Katie had poured Molly a margarita from the pitcher on the table so he knew his woman was taken care of. "So what else did I miss? Spare me the chick-problem drama."

"Says the guy getting laid regularly," Beck complained.

Deacon shot Molly a quick glance and allowed a smug smile.

"There's an exhibition next weekend in Los Angeles put on by *International Mixed Martial Arts* magazine. The PR person has asked if we'd supply a fighter."

"That's unusual, isn't it? And late notice."

Maddox shrugged. "It's a calculated move, a callout by TGL, my former employers. I've been with Black Arts for a year. Guess we've been a little too low-key for their comfort."

"Does Ronin know about this?" Deacon asked.

"Yeah. He sees it for what it is." Maddox looked at Deacon. "It'd be a bad move to put you or Ivan or Sergei in the ring at the expo. You all have big fights coming up in two weeks. Which TGL knows. This is a test to see if we've been keeping other fighters on our roster out of the spotlight."

"Think we've got a ringer or two, do they?"

Maddox nodded.

Deacon glanced at Blaze. No doubt he was a ringer. The guy had huge amounts of talent, but skill didn't matter when he burned himself out midway through the second round. So he'd undergone different conditioning exercises to increase his aerobic threshold, and he'd been learning how to keep energy in reserve. But he was a good six months out from testing that in the ring against a real opponent.

"What's your gut instinct?" Gil asked Maddox.

Several long moments passed before Maddox spoke. "Go one better than just supplying a fighter. Have Black Arts MMA and Black and Blue Promotions create a big splash. Put Katie in charge of a PR blitz, with Hardwick's help. Host a party, displaying *all* of our fighters and *all* the jujitsu instructors from Black Arts and ABC. It'd be a perfect opportunity for Sensei Black to talk about his recent association with the House of Kenji and remind everyone how Black Arts MMA was born out of a respected dojo, steered by a highly respected master with an eighth-degree black belt."

Dead silence stretched across the table. Even the ladies had stopped gabbing.

Finally Blue grinned. "That's a fantastic idea. Who else have you told this to?"

"Ronin and Amery."

"They're on board?" Deacon asked skeptically.

Maddox looked at him. "One hundred percent. Shocked the shit out of me too. In fact, it was Ronin's idea we meet here tonight. He wants our input. We'll have a formal meeting with everyone tomorrow."

"You want both Katie and me taking notes tonight?" Molly asked.

"Yes. That way we'll have all the bases covered when we pitch the final proposal to Master Black."

Concern pinched Molly's brow before she said, "Shouldn't Amery take the lead on this project?"

"She told me that as Ronin's wife she'd be in a different role at the event. This will be Katie's deal—and yours—to create a workable plan on short notice. The fight expo is one week from tonight."

Then everyone started talking at once. Between the noise level in the bar and the increasingly loud discussion at the table, Deacon couldn't decipher anything. He put his fingers in his mouth and released a shrill whistle.

All eyes zoomed to him.

"Before y'all get into the gritty details of the dog and pony show, I wanna know if we're bringing a fighter. And who that's gonna be."

Maddox glanced across the table. "Fee will be representing Black Arts. TGL won't be expecting that, and they'll have to scramble to find a female fighter."

Gil gaped at Fee. Then he let loose in Portuguese. One didn't need to understand the language to know that Gil was chewing Fee's ass.

When Fee stood, yelling back at him, holding her drink aloft as if to toss it in Gil's face, Blue intervened—physically and verbally.

They both shut up.

Then Blue looked at Maddox. "Sorry for the interruption. ABC is honored you've chosen Sophia to represent the Black Arts MMA program."

Deacon needed a shot of Jäger. No one noticed when he headed to the bar. He'd been in Diesel enough times that Shoshanna, the weekend bartender, had the shot poured and in front of him before he ordered.

"Thanks."

This great plan of Maddox's had taken Deacon by surprise. While having Fee fight would be a novelty, it wasn't the least bit representative of Maddox's new fighters.

What got his back up was the suspicion that Maddox wasn't confident enough in any of his fighters to showcase them. Ivan had finally won enough matches to reach professional status. So out of the five fighters on Black Arts MMA roster, only Deacon and Ivan had the fight records that'd interest one of the major MMA fight organizations in signing them.

In the year since Maddox had been hired to revamp the Black Arts MMA program, it didn't seem he'd done as much as he should have. Deacon knew that Ronin had re-upped Maddox's contract for another year. What had Maddox done to earn it?

Normally he didn't think about this crap. It wasn't his job to critique Maddox's job performance. As long as Maddox worked with him and Deacon kept winning, the rest shouldn't matter.

"Whatcha thinking about so hard?"

Deacon jumped. Christ. He hadn't even heard Beck approach him.

"You look guilty. Ah. You're just away from Maddox's scrutiny so you can indulge in a shot."

"Yep." He pointed to his shot glass. "Want one? I'm buying."

"Jäger? Sure."

Deacon caught Shoshanna's eye and signaled for another. He figured Beck had followed him for a reason besides monitoring his alcohol intake. "I wouldn't think as Shihan that you could skip helping plan this blowout."

Beck snorted. "Maddox will do what he wants. Ronin has the final word. My input is just noise—unless Maddox does something that conflicts with Black Arts martial arts philosophy."

Shoshanna set the shot in front of Beck with a smile. Usually she scurried off. But tonight she leaned over the bar, gifting Beck with an eyeful of cleavage. "You spoken for, too, sugar?"

"Not tonight."

"You flexible?"

"If you mean whether I'd be interested in waiting around for you until after closing time, the answer is yes. If you're asking if my body is flexible?" He took a slow sip of his shot. "For that one, sugar, you'll need a hands-on demonstration."

She smiled. "I'm off at eleven."

"I'll be here."

Beck's eyes were glued to her ass as she sashayed to the other end of the bar.

"Doesn't seem like *you've* got chick problems, Shihan."

"That was for your benefit." Beck smirked. "Shoshanna has had firsthand demonstration of my flexibility several times in the past few months."

"You dog."

"A hot chick offers me a bone, I'm gonna take it."

Deacon held his glass up to toast Beck's words of wisdom. "So what else is going on?"

"Between us?" Beck glanced over his shoulder. "As dojo GM, it's my job to check the security logs. In the past three months, Maddox has logged in at various times on Sundays—never at the same time. The camera feed is off on that day, so I can't see what he's been doing."

"Maybe it's personal time for cardio and weight training?" Deacon offered, remembering the times he'd run into Maddox on Sundays.

Beck shook his head. "I monitor the machines. No activity those days."

"Have you asked Maddox about it?"

"Not yet. I only received the quarterly security logs last week, which is what tipped me off."

Deacon studied him. "What's your gut feeling?"

"Maddox is training someone privately. Maybe a couple of someones. So he's not hiding it, but he hasn't mentioned it to me or Ronin."

"You sure Ronin doesn't know? Because the man is as close-mouthed as they come."

"Not more closemouthed than you, Yondan—that's for damn sure," Beck said dryly. "Anyway, if Ronin knew, he'd tell me, even if Maddox asked him to keep it to himself."

"True." He paused. "Who do you think is getting free training? Courey?"

"Maddox never was sold on bringing him on board. He used him to taunt you. Then you beat the fuck outta him and Courey lost his usefulness."

Deacon hated the stupid games Maddox played in the name of kicking performance up a notch. "Then who is he training?"

"Fee."

"Fee? Seriously? But why hide it?"

"Because Ronin doesn't want to invest Maddox's time starting a women's MMA division. But Maddox has been scouting female fighters for years—before it became the cool thing to do. He can't ignore that Fee has all the right components to make a big splash in women's MMA."

"Did you know about this exhibition before Maddox sprang it on us?"

Beck shook his head. "Maddox and I are respective of each other's roles at Black Arts. We're two division heads answering to the CEO. So after his announcement just now? I looked up the event on my phone. Guess who else is slated to attend the event besides his former employer?" He paused. "The scout for the UFC's women's division."

"Seriously?"

"Yeah. So there's some kind of weird politicking at play with

Maddox and TGL. I don't like it. Especially if Ronin doesn't know about it. The last fucking thing Sensei needs is to look like an idiot who doesn't keep tabs on his trainer."

"No kidding." Deacon realized Beck had the same intuitive nature as Knox, and that was exactly what Ronin needed. Sensei wasn't an easy man to work for—and he was glad Beck had Ronin's back. "Think Blue knows?"

"It pains me to say this, because I don't wanna come across as a goddamn busybody, but it is my job to know everything that goes on in the building. Fee moved in with Katie so Blue *couldn't* keep tabs on her outside of the dojo."

"Then Blue wouldn't know she'd been spending her Sundays training." Deacon groaned. "Jesus. *As the Dojo Fucking Turns,* eh?"

"Apparently. As long as I'm on a gossip-girl roll, what if Maddox and Fee are hooking up in addition to meeting for secret training sessions?"

Deacon stepped away from the bar. "And with that . . . I'm done." He patted his crotch. "Whew. For a second there, I worried my dick had turned into a vagina during this conversation."

"You are a fuckwad."

"No. I'm a man who's damn proud of my Y chromosome." Beck laughed.

Thankfully they were wrapping up the PR/party/event plans when Deacon and Beck returned. As soon as Molly acknowledged him, he tapped on his watch. He mouthed, *Been forty minutes, babe.*

She mouthed back, *You'll live.*

Not the answer he wanted. He stood and reached for her. "Enough business talk."

"But, Deacon, we need her input," Katie said.

"Nothin' will be decided tonight anyway, so it can wait. I can't." Without another word, he towed Molly away from the table and around the corner. He pressed his hands by her head above the wall.

"What's this? I thought you were taking me to the dance floor."

"I can't dance to this shit."

"You're in a mood."

"One that's rapidly turning into a bad mood," he said brusquely. He curled his hand around the back of her neck. "I wish we'd stayed in bed. None of this crap that's goin' on has anything to do with us."

"You are wrong about that, because this time next week we'll both be in LA." Molly hooked her fingers in the belt loop of his jeans and tugged until their bodies were closer. "But why the bad mood? You expected to be Black Arts MMA showcase fighter?"

"No. Just some stuff Beck said got me to thinking."

"Maddox's big announcement got all of us thinking too, that he and Fee are more than trainer and trainee. Not that Fee has ever hinted at anything in that direction."

"Fee and Maddox? In a relationship and shit? Never gonna happen."

His declaration seemed to annoy her. "And how are you so cocksure about that?"

"One, because Maddox was married to a Brazilian woman and he'd never put himself through that hell again. Two, Gil."

"What's Gil got to do with it?"

"Babe. Think about it."

"Don't *babe* me. And since when are you so perceptive about relationships and shit?"

Such a smart mouth. "Don't need to be perceptive when I've got eyes. Gil and Fee have been dancing around each other longer than we ever did. It'll come to a head one day—sooner rather than later. And I hope I'm a fuck of a long way away when that happens."

"I never thought of that. I'm surprised there isn't more hanky-panky going down between the instructors and students at Black Arts and ABC."

Deacon lifted his eyebrows. "Hanky-panky? Is that what we got up to in the training room?"

Molly offered him a sultry smile. "That was too hot to be mere hanky-panky."

"So define hanky-panky, literal girl."

"Dry humping on the mats. Oral sex in the stairwells. Hand jobs in the—"

He smashed his mouth to hers, stopping the flow of dirty scenarios. Damn teasing woman knew it'd get him hard.

She laughed against his lips.

"Speaking of hand jobs," he murmured against her throat. "I haven't forgotten our game of 'get off, get gone.' I know it's my turn."

"With as often as you've been fucking me since our reconnection? I don't see when you would've had time."

"And there's that dumb 'twelve-hour no payback' rule," he complained.

"That would've been a problem for you this week, stud. How you've had energy to fuck me stupid morning and night with as hard as you've been training? I thought I might not see you much. But you proved to be a man of many talents and outstanding physical stamina. I'm lucky." She pecked him on the lips. "And a little sore."

His concerned eyes met hers. "Have I been too rough?"

"I would tell you, but you haven't been. You've just been insistent, and I'll never complain about that. I love the way you look at me. I love the way you touch me. I love that you're obsessed with showing me how you feel about me so I don't doubt what's between us. I really love your kinky side, because it unleashes mine." She slid her hands up his chest. "But we have no choice but to take a break because I bled that last time."

Guilt and shame punched him in the gut. "I fucked you hard enough to make you bleed?"

"Don't look so horrified. I got my period. That's all."

Relief rolled through him, followed by utter cluelessness. "So, uh, yeah. Cool." *Cool? Really dumb-ass? You think it's cool that she's bleeding out her cooter?*

"Deacon. I know you've never had a girlfriend, so you haven't dealt with this before, but it's not a big deal. Five days and it'll all be over."

"Five days?" he repeated. "Seriously?"

"Five days out of *every* month."

Holy fuck.

"Are you worried I'll turn into a raging bitch?"

"Fuck no." He locked his eyes onto hers. "But do I need to stockpile chocolate and Kleenex?" He paused when a feeling of panic welled up in his chest. "You ain't expecting *me* to go to the store and buy Tampax, Midol, and that feminine-product shit for you, right?"

She briefly closed her eyes. "I swear I'm gonna look on eBay to buy the filter that your mouth is missing."

"Ha-fucking-larious." He got right in her face. "Bottom line: What's this mean?"

"It means we'll have to come up with something to do other than fuck for the next five days."

"That's it?"

"Pretty much."

"Cool." Deacon smiled. "So you up for hitting the honky-tonk for a little two-steppin'?"

Her brown eyes glittered. "Babe, I don't even know what the fuck that means."

God, he loved this woman. "Don't worry. It'll be fun."

CHAPTER TWENTY-EIGHT

MOLLY couldn't believe she'd be in Los Angeles in less than an hour.

Everyone else was cynical about flying, complaining about flight delays and the headaches of travel, but Molly thought it was really freakin' cool she could hop on a plane in Denver and be in California in two and a half hours.

The days leading up to the last-minute LA trip had been crazy. Amery and Ronin had flown out Thursday morning with Knox, Shiori, and Nuri on Okada's private plane. Thursday night Katie, Maddox, Fee, Blue, Gil, Sergei, and Ivan had flown on Max Stanislovsky's private jet. Molly and Presley had joked about being forced to fly "commercial" in lowly first class.

They were the last ones to travel, along with Deacon, Beck, Blaze, Fisher, Jaz, Riggins, Zach, and Jon-Dean.

Black Arts would have an imposing presence at the expo.

Tonight was the big party sponsored by Black and Blue Promotions. According to what Amery had told her, Black Arts MMA and Black and Blue Promotions had spared no expense for this trip. They'd booked an entire wing in the swanky hotel next to the convention center where the expo was located.

Since Deacon had slipped into his normal, brooding persona on the flight, Molly looked out the window and tried to imagine what the next three days had in store for her. She and Presley had obsessed over what to wear to the big party. Finally Chaz had come to their rescue and taken them to Natasha's, an exclusive boutique with vintage—aka used—designer clothing.

While Molly hemmed and hawed over the prices of the outfits, Chaz had reminded her they were called "special occasion" dresses for a reason. Not only that, but she had to look professional from the moment she stepped on the plane. Chaz had assured both her and Presley they could get by wearing a smart pantsuit while they helped finalize party preparations.

"Why so quiet, babe?" Deacon asked.

"Just following your lead, babe."

He kissed her cheek. "Smart-ass."

"Maybe I should ask what happened to your good mood."

Deacon snagged her hand and played with her fingers. "My dad called."

"I wondered who was calling so early."

"He forgets about the time change."

"What did he want?"

"To tell me he won't be at the Needham fight."

Her heart sank for him. "What? Why not?"

"Evidently Julianne has to have surgery."

"On a Saturday?"

"No. She's having it Friday afternoon. She needs someone to stay with her, and she insists on it being him."

"Deacon, I'm sorry. That sucks."

"Yeah, well, it's not like I can tell him not to be with his wife." Deacon looked at her. "You'll be there."

"Of course. I'll be wearing my CON MAN ROCKS MY FUCKING WORLD T-shirt."

His lips twitched.

"Is there a chance Needham will be at this expo?"

"Don't care. It'll be interesting to see where Maddox found practice space for us. Since he insists on closed practices."

"This close to a fight, it's gotta be a full training facility, right?"

Beck turned around in his seat. "I know where it'll be. It's one of two places."

"Where?"

"House of Kenji has two affiliated dojos in LA. It's private membership, so no public-access issues."

"Makes sense."

"I've taught in both places. Top-of-the-line facilities."

Molly listened to them talk. Her focus wasn't on Deacon for a change, but on Beck. The man was deceptively good-looking. At first glance he didn't appear to be anything special—not like the immediate, visceral punch of Deacon—but upon a more thorough examination, the man had it going on. A narrow face that broadened into ruggedly handsome when he smiled with those full lips. Wide green eyes that imparted tranquility. A flat nose—she'd yet to meet a fighter or a martial arts practitioner who hadn't broken their beak at least once. Like any man whose livelihood depended on the strength and condition of his body, Beck's physique could inspire female fantasies. But the most striking thing about him was his hair. The most glorious color of red—not orange, but cinnamon colored, with darker strands of mahogany, gold, and auburn. He wore it long—long enough to pull back and create a ponytail at the nape of his neck.

"Molly?" Deacon prompted.

Dammit. Hopefully he hadn't noticed her study of his Shihan. "Sorry. I've got a million things on my mind. What did you say?"

"I'll be at the hotel more than Deacon since he's training, so if you need anything, call me."

"Is this a Deacon-approved offer?" she half joked. "Because he tends to get snarly if other men offer to help me. Or look at me."

"Like I didn't know that," Beck said dryly.

"He's the only one of any guys here besides Ronin and Knox I'll trust you with," Deacon said.

"Gee. Thanks for the vote of confidence. There goes me banging Sergei in the utility closet."

"Not even funny, babe."

Beck turned around.

Molly looked out the window. Sometimes Deacon overwhelmed her.

"Why'd you turn away from me?" He set his hand on her thigh.

"I'm hoping to get a glimpse of the ocean."

"Really."

"Really. I've never seen the ocean. Seeing it from the plane might be my only chance."

"Molly, look at me."

"I don't want to. So just . . . go back to not talking to me."

"You're mad."

"Mostly confused."

"About?"

"About why you say stuff like *He's the only one of the guys here besides Ronin and Knox I'd trust you with*. You have this crazy idea that all men lust after me, when it's not even remotely close to true. If I even talk to another man—or heaven forbid a strange man talks to me—you turn into Deacon the Beast." She paused. "I like Deacon the Beast in bed. I like Deacon the Beast in the ring. But I don't like Deacon the Beast glaring and throwing down ultimatums at me and at his friends. Do you really think I'm looking at any of them when I could be looking at you? Do you really think when I'm out in mixed company I'm checking out other men as a possible replacement for you? I want you. No one else. The fact that I have you? I wouldn't fuck that up. This—you mean too much to me."

Deacon kissed her shoulder. Then he stretched across the seat and kissed the side of her throat. "I fucking love you. I know it makes me a goddamn beast when I think of some guy trying to get to you like I get to you."

"Not gonna happen."

"Promise me."

"I promise."

Molly dozed off for a while after that, and when she woke up, she saw Deacon staring at her.

"Hey, beautiful. We're about to land. Look out the window."

There it was. The ocean. "It looks so calm."

He chuckled. "Trust me. It's not."

She stared until the plane banked and all she could see were buildings and freeways.

Welcome to LA.

RONIN had sent two vans to bring them to the hotel. And since he'd rented so many rooms, the assistant manager escorted them all up to the twenty-second floor and handed out keys.

The hotel was classy, done up old-glam Hollywood style. Mirrors, crystal chandeliers, marble, tones of gold, cream, and black. So she didn't know what to expect when Deacon opened the door to their room. She stepped inside a suite. Glass windows overlooked the city. The space had a living room with a fireplace—in Los Angeles? And a wet bar, a dining room, a kitchen, a half bath. She headed down the hallway to the double doors and opened them to find a luxurious bedroom. A four-poster canopy bed on a platform, another sitting area, a full entertainment system. Another set of double doors led to a bathroom with a glass shower, a whirlpool tub, and his and hers vanities.

Deacon hadn't come along to explore the space. But when she returned to the living area to gaze out the windows, he came up behind her and wrapped her in his arms. "So? What do you think?"

"I think it's the nicest hotel I've ever stayed in."

"It is pretty swanky. Good thing Ronin can afford it."

"Did everyone get suites?"

She felt him smile against the side of her neck. "Nope. Everyone got their own room. Since we're sharing, I told Ronin putting us in a suite was still cheaper than paying for separate rooms for us."

"Clever."

"Gives me lots more places to fuck you than just in a bed."

"Speaking of . . . there's a note on the bed addressed to both of us."

"A personalized hotel welcome, I'm betting."

"No. It's in Amery's handwriting." Molly clasped his hand and towed him into the bedroom. She ripped open the sealed envelope, pulled out the card, and read:

> *Molly and Deacon~*
>
> *Glad to have you here, but don't get too comfy after you check in. Maddox is sending a car for Deacon and the other fighters right away. Molly, we're in the Monroe Ballroom on the first floor. Come down as soon as you can.*
>
> *A~*

"There goes my plan for a quickie."

"Use your sexual frustration to hit harder during training today."

Deacon kissed the back of her head. "Good plan. Let's head back down."

The keycards were in holders on the catchall table by the front door. He handed her one and tucked his inside his front pocket.

While they waited for the elevator, Deacon caged her against the wall so they were face-to-face. He had that fierce look in his eye.

Her belly jumped. "What?"

"Plan on bein' naked the moment we get back to the room tonight. Plan on bein' sore tomorrow, because I'm gonna fuck you on every horizontal surface."

"You trying to get me wet and horny right now?"

"Yep. Figured it was only fair, since I'm hard as fucking concrete after seeing how hot your ass looks in those pants as you bent over to get your purse."

The elevator dinged.

When Deacon pushed back, Molly saw Presley standing behind him, wearing a huge grin.

"Hey, guys."

"You get a note with instructions too?"

"We all did. Beck is in the room next to mine and Ronin wants him at the dojo, so he said not to leave without him."

The elevator door closed.

No one got in the car until the eighth floor. An inked bruiser wearing workout clothes stood in the middle of the car.

Deacon stiffened beside her.

The man's eyes and Deacon's met in the mirror. He scowled. "Whatcha lookin' at?"

"You weren't that bulked up the last time we met in the ring, Twitch. What are the chances you'll pass a drug test this time?"

"Con Man. Thought you dropped off the face of the earth. Haven't heard nothin' about you in a long fuckin' time."

"Same goes."

"Probably 'cause I don't go by Twitch no more."

"Yeah? What's your ring name now?"

"Bulldozer."

"Tyrese 'Bulldozer' Witchell? Who came up with that mouthful?"

"My publicist. She said I needed a name with impact. Nothin'll knock you down faster than a bulldozer." He punched his left palm with his right fist as a demonstration.

Wow. This dude was the poster child for big and dumb. Molly didn't dare look at Presley or they'd both laugh.

"You here for the expo?" Bulldozer asked.

"Just as support for my club and my dojo. I'm not fighting. What about you?"

"The UFC is scouting me for their light heavyweight division."

"No shit?"

"It's basically a done deal." He gave Deacon a pitying look. "Some of us have what it takes. Most of you don't."

The elevator doors opened. Bulldozer lumbered out.

"You have real winners for friends, Con Man. I'm hurt you didn't introduce me," Presley said with a pout. "The tat on the back of his neck said *No Regerts*."

"No way," Molly said. "Did you take a picture of it?"

"Of course. Hello, Instagram."

"Elvis, you're tempting me to call him back," Deacon drawled. "I'd never stand in the path of true love."

"Omigod, Deacon made a joke!" Presley clapped. "Wait. Will they kick you out of the badass club for that?"

"I'm the president. They can't kick me out."

"Two jokes in one day? Maddox is so gonna ream you for drinking on the plane."

"I haven't been drinking, but I sure can—"

"Give me one second," Molly said, dragging Deacon around the corner of the elevator bay.

He pushed her against the wall and kissed her until she couldn't breathe. "Miss me today, babe."

"I will."

"Can't wait to get you alone tonight."

"I can't wait either." Would sex in a fancy hotel be off-the-charts hot?

With Deacon? Guaranteed.

Molly wasn't really paying attention to where she was going when they turned the corner and a freight train slammed into her. She would've hit the marble flooring if not for Deacon catching her.

"You all right?"

She nodded.

Then Deacon went after the guy. "Hey, Grape Ape."

The big dude, in an ugly purple shirt, stopped and turned around. "What?"

"You damn near knocked my girlfriend over and didn't stop to see if she was all right."

"So?"

"So, get back here and apologize to her for bein' an inconsiderate dickhead."

Molly thought about ducking behind the palm tree.

The man said, "Make me."

"Jesus, what are you? Five?"

The guy turned away.

"Fine." Deacon grabbed his arm, twisted, and the Grape Ape dropped to his knees. "A. Pol. O. Gize."

"Shit. Fuck. Let me go."

"A. Pol. O. Gize. Fuckface. Now."

"Ah, sorry, lady."

"And?" Deacon prompted.

"And your boyfriend is a fucking psycho." He glared up at Deacon.

Deacon bent down and whispered in the guy's ear before he let him go.

"What did you say to him?"

"Gave him some advice."

"I don't wanna know, do I?"

"Probably not. I used bad words. I think he wet himself."

Molly laughed and whispered, "My hero."

"Deacon! Come on."

"Gotta go, babe." He kissed her quickly. "Later."

Presley looped her arm through Molly's and directed her down a long hallway. "While you were sucking face, I found out where the ballroom is."

"Thank you."

"*Soooo . . .*"

Molly groaned. "No conversation ever starts well with your drawn-out *soooo*."

"I overheard what Deacon said to you at the elevator. I won't repeat it, but damn, girlfriend, why are you not up in your room banging that man like a broken screen door?"

"Work. Same as him. Trust me. If the man could've gotten us both off in the five minutes we had in the room, he would've tried."

"As Chaz says"—she mimicked his singsongy tone—"*hate you.*"

"I know we're here because of work, but none of the single Black Arts guys trips your wires?"

"The hottie known as Riggins? Yes. But he looks at me like I'm a freakin' science experiment, which means he doesn't date chicks with ink."

"Or maybe it's the colored hair. Or the piercings. Or the scars," Molly offered.

"Whatever. I'd love to have my hands on Big Rig's perfect ass while he's pumping into me, but that ain't happening. So moving on . . . Ivan is hot, like hard-core hot, but he and Katie have that fucked-up thing going on, and then there's some family business stuff with his dad I'm not cool with. At all."

Molly frowned. "You mean the fetish club?"

"No. And if you don't know, it's not my place to tell you."

Weird answer. "How about Fisher?"

"He's built and sweet, but he'd fall in love with me, want to get serious right away, propose, and expect me to start popping out babies. He's that kind of guy, and I'm so not ready for that."

"Beck?"

"Now, him I like. Bet he uses that Zen attitude to fuck like an animal. But he's distracted this trip. Blaze is a baby. It's not my job to break them in."

"I'm guessing it's the same story with Zach and Jon-Dean." Molly looked around. Why hadn't they reached the room yet?

"But I'd do Maddox. He's got that nasty/sweet temperament. And those fucking eyes of his. I'll bet he's got some hard-core stamina. I'd be curious to see what size motor he's running in those coach's shorts."

"Maddox is, like, fifteen years older than you."

"Nope. He's *nineteen* years older. And that, my friend, just means he'll have perfected killer moves in bed." Presley stopped. "Shit. Are we lost?"

A loud whistle rent the air.

Katie waved at them from the very end of the hallway. "Down here!" When they reached her, she said, "You're just in time."

"For what?"

"For the super-secret Operation Jealous Hag."

"I'm in," Presley said without hesitation.

"Good. Because you're the other one he wants."

"Who?"

"Maddox."

"Katie, have you been drinking?" Molly demanded.

"No! This is my big chance to get Black and Blue Promotions noticed in the industry. I will be stone-cold sober until I'm back in Colorado."

"Okay. So what's Operation Jealous Hag?"

"It's best if Maddox explains."

That's when Molly noticed Maddox sitting at a table by himself, lost in thought.

Katie whirled around and walked backward. "This operation cannot go beyond the five of us, okay?"

"Five? I count four."

"Fee's included in this for obvious reasons."

Obvious to who? Molly wanted to ask, but didn't.

"Amery is with Ronin and some House of Kenji people, so we've gotta make this fast before she gets back."

Katie sat next to Maddox, and Molly and Presley took the chairs opposite him.

"What's going on?"

"Basic story? Nasty divorce with my ex, Rox. I've been lying low in Colorado, building the Black Arts program. Now that we're launching it, Rox will be here to see how I'm doing—not just professionally."

"His ex-wife is Gil's sister," Katie interjected.

Maddox raked his hand through his hair. "So I've got a plan. Each night I'm here, I show up with a different gorgeous woman on my arm. My ex sees I've moved on, and I can watch her choke on her jealousy." His gaze flicked to Katie. "Katie is my date for the party tonight." His focus moved to Presley. "Are you willing to be my date tomorrow night after the fight?"

"Sure, but I'm not exactly the kind of woman that other women are jealous of."

"Wrong. You're young, hot, and edgy. You're everything she never was and will never be."

"While that bullshit flattery might work at the country-club bar on a forty-year-old divorcée on a Friday night, it won't work on me." Presley stood and placed her palms on the table, angling toward him. "Why would I be interested in you? I'm twenty-six, baby. You're forty-five. What's the pull between us? Convince me that you're equally ready to play a part in this and I won't just be standing by your side looking . . . young, hot, and edgy."

Way to throw down the gauntlet, Pres.

Maddox stared at her long enough for it to be uncomfortable for everyone. Then he rolled to his feet in a sensuous move like a jungle cat about to pounce. His measured gait as he strolled toward Presley hit the sweet spot between predatory and constrained.

Molly couldn't get over the change in Maddox's demeanor. He'd gone from disheveled to disarming in a slow blink of his long black lashes. He looked as if he'd spent all night fucking hard in bed, but he didn't have the aura of a satisfied man; instead he looked hungry. Wild. Greedy. Like a man who hadn't gotten enough and was back for more.

He moved in behind Presley, who'd pushed herself upright. "The pull between us is sexual. A man of my experience can get you addicted to my touch, baby." He trailed his fingers across the bare section of her shoulder. "Very addicted."

Presley visibly trembled.

"Every time I look at you, you know I'm imagining all the wicked things I can do to your hot little body and make you beg me for more. Beg me in that sexy bedroom voice of yours. I'll demand what's mine anytime, anyplace. And you'll say yes to me without hesitation." He slid his hand up the back of her neck and grabbed a fistful of her hair. He pulled it hard enough she gasped, but she didn't try to escape when he used his hold on her to maneuver her face next to his. "Couples look at us and want to be us. Not because we're rich or powerful. Couples will envy us because of that zing of sexual need that radiates out from us. They'll imagine us fucking, Presley." His voice had dropped to a raspy whisper. "They know even their most vivid imaginations won't do justice to how hot and dirty we are behind closed doors."

After his hand fell away, Presley looked as if her knees might give out.

Breezily, Maddox said, "Did that convince you?"

"Uh."

One-word answers weren't Presley's style, so Molly knew her friend was rattled. She stood and stepped in. "Interesting demonstration of your ability to fuck with people's heads, Maddox. I'd be impressed if I hadn't already known that's how you achieve results with your fighters."

Maddox leveled a death glare on her, but it wasn't nearly as intimidating as Deacon's.

"Here's what I think. You'd be better served to have *one* hottie on your arm all weekend. If your ex sees you surrounded by a bevy of beauties, she'll know you're overcompensating. She'll either think, *That loser is still stuck on me,* or, *Good riddance to that dog.* But if you're openly devoted to one much-younger lady? That'll get to her. Eat at her. She'll wonder what she could've done differently to keep you. She'll wonder if people are feeling sorry for her because you're so much happier with a newer, hipper model. She'll have a really shitty weekend."

Maddox stared at her for another ten seconds. Then he said, "Damn, woman. You are scary mean. No wonder you and Deacon make such a perfect couple."

Molly curtsied and Maddox laughed. Then she faced Presley. "Your choice whether you're playing the part of Maddox's one true, sexy lady love. It just can't interfere with our main reason for being here, which is to make *Amery's* life easier. So how about before you commit to anything, we talk to the boss?"

That snapped Presley out of it. "You're right." She flashed Maddox a cheeky grin. "You had me convinced about us having smoking-hot sexy times. Too bad it's all for show, huh?"

His eyes cruised over Presley with genuine heat and regret, which had Presley trembling again. "Yeah, roller derby girl, too bad." Maddox looked at Katie. "So are you playing the part of my one, true, sexy lady love?"

"That will seriously curtail me getting any tail—and there are fine ones all over the place." Katie's playful grin vanished. "Seriously, this is my chance to network and get the latest gossip in the world of MMA. That'd be hard to do if I have to be plastered to your side the next two days and nights, pretending I can't wait for you to fuck me."

"Hmm. It appears your choices are piss off Ronin or piss off Amery," Molly said dryly.

Maddox's gaze zoomed to Presley. "I'll be in your room an hour before the event so we can get a few personal things squared away."

"Cool."

As soon as he was out of the room, Katie said, "You're solid under pressure, Presley. If Maddox had verbally seduced me like that? I would've been on my knees."

Presley waved her off. "All talk. Action is what counts. But if he can bring the fire, baby, I'll bring the gasoline."

Amery strolled in. "Hey, you're both here. Great. Let's get started."

CHAPTER TWENTY-NINE

GLAD-HANDING, smiling, schmoozing—acting all friendly and shit?

Not Deacon's scene. At all.

Maddox had told Deacon he could get away with some of his typical "brooding, mean motherfucker" attitude. Deacon thought the people who expected him to be approachable, nice, and chatty needed to have their fucking heads examined. He was an MMA fighter. He punched people in the face for a living.

He was not happy he had to suffer through this industry party without Molly by his side. He'd known she'd have work responsibilities, but it looked to him like Molly and Katie were doing all the work while Presley was hanging on to Maddox as arm candy.

But Presley had nothing on the hot and sexy way Molly looked. The woman killed it in a knee-length, flesh-colored dress. It was modest enough to be professional, but the material clung to show off her feminine shape. A black lace band stretched across the dress's deep V-neck, masking her abundant breasts. At least he wouldn't have to punch any perverted fuckers for staring at her great tits.

By the time he'd returned to the hotel room after training, Molly had been gone. As soon as he'd opened the door to their suite, the sweet, floral scent of her lotion had hit him. Although his body hurt like a bitch and he debated on crawling to the shower, his cock immediately rallied, eager for a workout. It'd been damn near a week since he'd done anything more than kiss his woman. They had serious making up to do.

Riggins leaned closer and muttered, "I need a drink."

"You and me both."

"Want me to bring you something from the bar?"

"Can't."

"Right. You're a week out from the fight. Bet you're hungry too."

Deacon's gaze sought out Molly. "You have no idea."

Riggins chuckled. "For food, horndog."

I'd be just fine feasting on her for hours.

"You missed the run-through earlier."

"Run-through. Like a . . . ?"

"Dress rehearsal for Ronin's speech."

"Yeah, sorry I missed that." *Not.* He sighed. "Fill me in so I'm not up there scratching my balls, clueless about what's what."

Riggins went into a far deeper explanation about who was supposed to stand where and who was taking the mic and why than Deacon needed. When Deacon said as much, Riggins shrugged. "It's my job to be a detailed-oriented guy."

They watched as an agitated Beck approached them.

"What's up?"

"My fucking blood pressure."

"Why?"

"Sensei invited the candidates I'd suggested for new Black Arts instructors to come to the expo. They're all here."

"So? Isn't that what you wanted?"

"I did not expect to be conducting interviews at fucking midnight tonight with zero advance notice," Beck snapped.

Whoa. Zen-man had his gi in a knot. "That's what Ronin asked you to do?"

"Ronin hinted at that. He didn't come right out and say that's what is gonna happen after this shindig. And now Sensei is surrounded, and I sure as hell won't interrupt his leagues of admirers to get clarification."

Deacon crossed his arms over his chest. "I know you were Black Arts' Shihan before Knox, so you've dealt with Ronin's you-ought-to-be-able-to-read-my-fucking-mind behavior before. Yes, he's your boss and what he says goes. But call him on his shit, Beck, if you don't agree with him."

"Who'd you arrange to meet tonight before the last-minute interviews were hinted at?" Riggins asked.

Beck's gaze moved to Riggins. "An old friend. But that's not what this is about."

"You sure?"

"No." Beck ran his hand through his hair again. "Fuck. How'd you know?"

Riggins shrugged. "There seems to be all-around confusion on what this trip is really about. It's business. Period. Interpersonal shit shouldn't take priority. Knox and Shiori, Ronin and Amery, and I are the only ones who understand that."

"What the hell are you talking about?"

"Beck is pissed for having to back out of a hookup because Sensei needs him to do his job. You are eye-fucking Molly, and I expect to see you two sneaking off to a coat closet as soon as the speeches are done. Maddox is parading around with Presley, a chick half his age, to make his ex–old lady jealous—and I ain't sure that's not the only reason we're here in LA. Jaz is hiding in her room like she's afraid she'll run into someone she knows. Then there's Fee and Gil, who are constantly arguing about something that happened between them five years ago that has nothing to do with her ability to fight."

"Wait. You speak Portuguese?" Beck said.

"Yeah. I also speak Russian. So I know that Max Stanislovsky lending Ivan the company plane had some strings attached. Haven't you noticed both Ivan and Sergei have been on their phones nonstop? They'll disappear as soon as this gig is over to do whatever Max asked them to." He gave a head jerk to Katie. "Hot stuff over there is doing a great PR job, but she's doing a piss-poor job ignoring Blue, since his whole purpose for being fawned over by female BJJ devotees is to get Katie's attention. Zach and Jon-Dean are doing a stellar Beavis and Butt-head imitation as a couple of rubes in the big city. Then there's Fisher and Blaze, who've already been suckered by the advances of the hot chicks I suspect are working for TGL to get the inside scoop on the Black Arts MMA program from the weakest links."

Deacon and Beck both stared at Riggins with their mouths hanging open.

"What?"

"*What* is exactly right. Dude. In the last six months I've barely heard you string two sentences together. And then you rattle off all that like we're idiots for not seeing it?"

"Well, you are. It's really freakin' obvious."

Deacon got in Riggins's face.

The man didn't even blink. Or flinch.

"Who are you?"

"I'm a simple EMT who enjoys jujitsu and people watching."

"Bullshit. Tell me."

Riggins's sharklike smile sent chills up Deacon's spine. "If I told you, I'd have to kill you." He pushed off the wall. "Now I really need a damn drink." And he walked away.

Beck looked at Riggins's retreating back. "Ever get the feeling you've been completely wrong about someone and it's about to bite you in the ass?"

"Yeah. I used to think Ronin was the scariest motherfucker in the dojo. No more."

Ronin and Amery were gathering the Black Arts crew.

Beck said, "Come on. Showtime."

The instructors were lined up in the first row on the stage, behind Ronin. The fighters and Katie were in the back row.

The three hundred people in the room actually quieted down when the head of PR took the podium.

"Good evening, everyone, and welcome to the *International Mixed Martial Arts* magazine MMA expo!" Polite applause. "This kickoff party is sponsored by Black and Blue Promotions and Black Arts, based out of Denver, Colorado. Rather than read the impressive list of instructors and fighters associated with Black Arts, I'll introduce Sensei Ronin Black, eighth-degree jujitsu master, who owns and operates both businesses." She faced him and bowed. "Hachidan Black, the floor is yours."

Thunderous applause echoed throughout the space. "Thank you." Ronin faced the audience and began to speak.

The man, for being borderline antisocial, was a compelling speaker. After he hit the high points of his speech, he started introductions, beginning with ABC, the role Blue had in ABC and Black and Blue Promotions, and then ABC's instructors.

Next he introduced the Black Arts instructors.

Deacon watched the growing buzz rippling through the crowd as they heard the impressive credentials of those affiliated with Black Arts.

Then came time for Ronin to turn the microphone over to Maddox. "Last year Black Arts was able to bolster its fledgling MMA program by hiring the best trainer in the business. Maddox Byerly."

Maddox whispered to Ronin and clapped him on the back before he spoke. "It's been a humbling experience to work with that man day in, day out. Sensei Black lives the philosophy he teaches. He has the highest standards, not only for his instructors and students, but for anyone who is affiliated with Black Arts in any way. As Hachidan Black mentioned, Black Arts had an existing MMA program before he handed me the keys to the training room. I inherited a small but powerful roster of fighters. Let's start with the ladies. Or should I say *lady*—the lone female MMA fighter on our roster—who is representing Black Arts tomorrow night at the expo. She is a third-degree black belt in Brazilian jujitsu, she is an instructor at ABC, and her smile is nearly as deadly as her arm bar. I present Sophia 'Stinger' Curacao."

Wild applause and wolf whistles as Fee stepped forward and waved to the crowd.

"Our MMA middleweight fighter is a third-degree black belt in jujitsu, an instructor at Black Arts, a Muay Thai devotee, a championship kickboxing contender, and a former wrestler. His professional record, in the past three years, of thirty-eight wins and two losses speaks for itself. Let's hear it for Deacon 'Con Man' McConnell!"

Equally loud applause rippled through the room.

Rig and Knox moved aside so Deacon could step forward and wave to the crowd.

Then Maddox went on to introduce the remaining roster and the training specialists, mentioning Ito—the only instructor who'd opted not to come.

During the introductions, Deacon scanned the crowd for Molly. He saw Amery in the front row. Presley stood off to the side. But he hadn't seen Molly since he'd first walked in.

Where the hell was she?

"Thank you, everyone, for your attention," Ronin said. "If you have any questions about Black and Blue Promotions or Black Arts, there are brochures on the tables with contact information. Enjoy the rest of the evening."

Thank fuck he could get out of here now and find his woman.

A hand landed on his shoulder. "Before you run off, I think I can convince both Smackdown and Bellator to send reps to the Needham fight next week. I'm meeting with them tonight."

Deacon scanned the crowd for Molly's shiny brown hair. "So?"
Maddox stepped in front of him. "So, show a little enthusiasm."

"Why? These guys get a fighter all fired up, thinking their life
is about to change. Then the organization 'forgets' to send a scout.
I've seen fighters devastated because some dude in a suit wasn't ring-
side. I don't put my faith in anything besides my ability to fight."

"I want this shot for you, Deacon. You deserve this more than
any man I've ever known. Lots of fighters have the skills to get to
the top, but you, my friend, have the heart of a champion." Maddox walked off, leaving a dumbfounded Deacon staring after him.

He turned around and two women—a blonde and a brunette—
blocked his path. They were too classy to be ring bunnies. Had to
be strippers.

Sounded like someone—likely those TGL bastards—had done
their research on him.

Too bad they'd done it prematurely.

"Hey, aren't you Con Man McConnell?" the brunette asked.

"Yep."

The brunette hip checked the blonde. "I told you it was him!"

"We're big fans of MMA," the blonde said.

"Go to a lot of fights, do you?"

"All the time."

Deacon gave them each a cool once-over. "You ladies ring
girls?"

"What?" the brunette said.

Bingo. These women didn't know shit. He locked eyes with
the blonde. " 'Pour Some Sugar on Me.' "

She blinked and then rolled her hips forward. "I'll do anything
you want me to, sugar."

"No, that was your stripper song, wasn't it? Bet you had crys-
tals on your tasseled pasties and your G-string. Bet you dumped
water down your body and played with your nipples as you humped
the pole on your knees."

The brunette turned wide eyes on the blonde. "Misty, he's seen your act!"

Deacon laughed. "I've seen lots of acts, and I see right through yours, ladies. Word of advice. MMA is one place where you can't fake it. Real fans, fighters, and promoters will laugh you out of the room. And if you don't want people to know you're a former stripper? For fuck's sake, don't dress like one." He stormed off and made it fifteen steps before he saw Molly.

She leaned against a pillar, her arms folded over her chest.

He erased the distance between them. He pressed his lips to hers and snaked his arm behind her to pull her close. "Where the hell have you been, babe? Goin' crazy without you."

"Seemed like you were making very important contacts."

He buried his face in her neck. "You look stunning tonight. I saw you across the room in this amazing dress, and it fucking killed me that I couldn't get to you to tell you that until now."

"Sweet man. And what were you telling the ring bunnies?"

"Not ring bunnies. Strippers. I told them to do their research before trying to pass themselves off as MMA enthusiasts."

She laughed. "Of course you can differentiate between normal women and strippers." She twined her arms around his neck. "How did everything go today?"

"Training was brutal. But standing around pretending I give a damn about any of this stuff was sheer hell. I would've rather trained another four hours than deal with this." Deacon didn't mention Maddox's meeting with the fight organizations. No reason to get his hopes up. He planted kisses up her throat. When his lips reached the corner of her mouth, he paused, letting their breath mingle, keeping her on the edge.

"Kiss me."

"It's not your mouth I wanna kiss right now."

She swayed against him. "Let's go to the room."

"I'm playing the 'get off, get gone' card."

"No," she breathed.

"Uh-huh."

"But that's not fair. We haven't had sex for almost a week! We could be fucking all night long in our luxury suite!"

"You'll survive without my cock for another twelve hours," he rasped against her ear. "Think of how fast and hard we'll go at it the first time. Your skin will have friction burns."

"Deacon."

"Game starts now, babe." He kissed her quickly and clasped her hand. He'd noticed a door tucked between the empty banquet rooms. If they were lucky, it'd be unlocked.

Molly's heels made little sound as he hustled them down the hallway.

No one stopped them. He doubted anyone noticed them. Still, he forced himself to slow down. Once they reached the door, he shot a quick look up and down the hallway before he tried the knob.

Unlocked. Halleluiah.

His cock was already half hard and he willed it to stand down. But his body always reacted to the nearness of hers. Everything jumped into overdrive; his blood pumped faster, his breathing turned ragged, sweat dotted his head, neck, chest, spine, and groin.

Light from the street shone into the small space. No chair or table in here, so he'd have to improvise.

Deacon pushed her up against the door.

"What is it with you and doors?" she murmured.

"You're right. I've got something much better in mind."

"Me and my big mouth."

"Gimme that big mouth." Deacon curled his hand beneath her jaw, holding her in place as he kissed her with the passion he'd had locked inside all damn day.

Molly opened for him fully, making the sweetest groan in the back of her throat when his tongue slid against hers.

He tasted, teased, explored. Her passion was such an innate part of her. He basked in her immediate and unwavering response to him. Anytime. Anyplace.

She pressed her hands against his chest and emitted a whimper when he tugged her hair, changing the angle of her head to take the kiss deeper yet, straight into the heart and soul of her.

When she began bumping her hips into his, he broke free from the consuming kiss. "Feel like I haven't done that in days," he panted.

"You haven't."

"Been neglectful of my woman's needs." Deacon brushed his lips over the shell of her ear. "Turn around."

"You can't fuck me," she warned.

"Not even with my mouth?"

"Oh." She turned around so fast she smacked her forehead into the door. "Ouch."

Deacon slowly inched her dress up her thighs, rucking the silky fabric around her hips. "Nice ass. I wanna see it. Take off your panties."

Resting her cheek against the door, she hooked her fingers into the scrap of satin and rolled them over the curves of her thighs.

When they were at her knees, Deacon twisted the material around his palm and ripped them off.

"Deacon!"

"What? You hate wearing wet panties." He rubbed his mouth over the back of her head and his groin into her ass. "By the time I'm done feasting on your cunt, babe, your sweet juices will be running down the insides of your thighs."

"I think I just came."

He chuckled. "Spread 'em wide. Hands on the door. Nope. Lower. Lower." Then he took her hands and put them where he wanted, so they were just below the level of her hips. "Perfect." He adjusted his dick before he lowered to his knees. "Fuck yeah. That's what I'm talkin' about." Her sweet pink pussy was at mouth level.

"Omigod, Deacon. No. I can't. This is too—"

"Exposed?" He licked her slit, then wiggled his tongue inside her opening and pulled back out. "You worried I'll be up close and personal with this sweet little asshole?" He swirled his tongue around that tight rosette and Molly made a noise he'd never heard from her. "I'm gonna lick, bite, and suck on this tiny pucker, and then one day soon I'm gonna fuck it. Hard."

"I love your dirty talk."

"You love my dirty actions even more."

He abandoned his plan to build her up slowly. He opened her up and set his mouth on her, eating at the hot flesh until he felt her blood pumping faster. Until his face was glazed with her essence. He loved this. He could do this all fucking day.

"You're too good at this. I'm already close."

Deacon changed the angle of his head, sliding his tongue down to her clit. Teasing it with soft lashes, pausing only to suck directly on the nub.

Her moans escalated. Her legs began to tremble.

"Fuck, babe. You needed this. Bad. Give it to me." He lapped at her, still holding her wide-open so he could engulf all of her pussy with his hungry mouth.

Molly released a muffled scream against her biceps as her orgasm blasted her with long, hard pulses. He drew the pulsating flesh into his mouth, his lips sucking in cadence with the throbbing of her clit.

In the aftermath, Deacon placed soft kisses around the swollen tissues and backed away, his own breaths sharp and shallow.

As he rolled to his feet, he trailed his fingertips over the backs of her legs, from just inside her ankle bones, up the muscles in her calves, the creases behind her knees, the inner skin of her thighs. He unrolled her dress, watching the fabric swish as it fell into place.

She still hadn't said anything.

So he kept touching her. Gliding his hand up her side to palm her tit. Squeezing the soft weight, then pinching the tip of her nipple. Reveling in the fact this woman was his. "Molly."

She walked her hands up the door and slumped her spine against his chest. "Have I ever come that fast before?"

"That I've seen? With your vibrator. I like to take my time." He kissed the side of her throat. "Until I don't."

"You rocked my world, Deacon."

Tell me you love me.

Made him feel needy and pathetic, but he was; he needed to hear those words from her.

Deacon's stomach growled.

"The real world intrudes. Should we grab some food before we head up to the room? I imagine you have to be at training early tomorrow."

"Way too early. But Maddox will be focused on Fee."

She turned around. "Did Fee meet with any fight organizations tonight?"

"No. The only one doin' anything with female fighters is UFC, and they're sending a rep tomorrow night."

"I won't get to sit with you at the event, will I?"

"'Fraid not. The whole thing will last maybe four hours. Then I'm free to lock us in our hotel suite and do raunchy things to you."

"What kind of raunchy things?"

Deacon nuzzled her neck. "The four-poster bed will be great for bondage." His mouth meandered to the spot below her ear. "The bench looks good for spanking." He blew in her ear. "I'm still thinking on whether the couch or the rug on the floor will be softer on your back as I'm fucking your tits."

Molly tipped her head back and looked at him. "Too bad about that pesky twelve-hour rule I offered to let you break. Because, babe, I would've let you do every single one of those things to me tonight." She smiled and leaned forward to bite his lower lip. "Twice."

"Evil woman. Let's go."

He snatched up her underwear and balled them in his pocket.

"So are we going to eat?" she asked.

"Nah. Not hungry."

"Deacon. I heard your stomach growling. What have you had to eat today?"

"Two protein shakes. A chicken and rice bowl. Two protein bars. And pussy." He smirked. "The last one was very satisfying, so I'm good."

CHAPTER THIRTY

MOLLY survived the whirlwind weekend in LA.

Deacon had been gone Saturday morning when she'd woken up. She knew Maddox wasn't working with him because Maddox was right there, every damn time she turned around. Groping Presley, who didn't seem to mind because she was groping him back with equal enthusiasm. According to Katie, the hand-holding, ass-grabbing couple had run into Maddox's ex-wife half a dozen times and the woman was beside herself with rage and jealousy, so Operation Jealous Hag had been a resounding success. But Molly had been so busy she hadn't gotten the particulars from her friend— which was odd, given Presley was notorious for oversharing.

Maddox had cornered her after lunch. "I need you to do me a favor tonight."

"What kind of favor?"

"I need you to steer clear of Deacon for at least an hour after the fight. He's not officially meeting with Smackdown or Bellator, but he has to appear interested. And we both know he'll blow off these guys . . ." *If there's a chance you'll be blowing him* went unsaid.

"I don't know where you've received the mistaken impression that I have *any* control over Deacon, Maddox," she retorted.

"Christ. Don't kid yourself. Would you please just help me out here? You want what's best for Deacon and his career, right?"

"No. I want him to fail spectacularly because he's so much fun after he loses." *Tone it down, Mol.* She counted to ten. "Of course I want what's best for him."

"One hour. That's all I'm asking."

"Fine. He'll assume I'm working anyway."

"Good." Maddox's eyes turned hard. "Where the fuck is Presley?"

"Amery has her doing something. Why?" Wasn't Maddox supposed to be with Fee all day before the big fight?

"I'm buying a chain for that girl to keep her by my side." He leaned closer. "You cannot leave. My ex is across the room and I've managed to avoid being alone with her."

Molly saw the chance and took it. "I'll stay with you. In return, I want to know everything about these fight organizations that are looking at signing Deacon."

Thirty minutes later Molly knew Maddox had spilled more than he'd intended. But she also realized Maddox had assumed Deacon had told her way more than he had.

So Deacon's claim that he'll tell you everything lasted what . . . ? Two weeks?

She couldn't ask Deacon specifics since prior to the fight she'd seen Deacon for ten minutes—five of which he'd spent fucking her brains out up against the glass shower door. Then he'd bailed after blowing her circuits with a soul kiss.

She'd sat with the Black Arts crew during the exhibition. The fighters were seated in a different area of the arena, so Molly wondered if Deacon was making the "connections" Maddox had been harping on.

After the exhibition ended—Fee easily won her fight—Molly returned to the hotel with Beck, some guy named Gunnar who used to be an instructor at Black Arts, and Riggins. She skipped the after-party, and Riggins insisted on escorting her to her hotel room.

She poured herself a rum and Diet Coke and stared out the window at the glittering lights of Los Angeles. Molly didn't know how much time had passed before she heard the door open. Her heart immediately beat faster. She saw Deacon in the reflection of the glass before he wrapped himself around her.

"Hey."

"Hey."

"You left right after the last fight," he murmured against her neck.

"Since Beck was leaving, I caught a ride. I knew you'd be along when you finished."

"Babe, what's goin' on? You seem sad."

"I'm not. I was just thinking about how cool it would've been to see the ocean." And Molly felt stupid for her hope that Deacon might've planned to surprise her with a romantic, late-night trip to the beach. But he didn't do romance. Not for some macho reason, but simply because romance didn't cross his mind. Sex did. So he wooed her and wowed her with sex.

And that night Deacon had introduced Molly to the joy of bondage. He'd tied her spread-eagle to the four-poster bed and fucked her for an hour. Then he'd bent her over the couch and spanked her—more tease than pain—and fucked her for another hour. Then he'd ordered fruit and ice cream from room service, spread her out on the bar, and used her body to create a sundae.

Just thinking about the contrasting sensations of his hot mouth and the cold ice cream on her body made her tremble. She could admit that Deacon licking and sucking on her everywhere—from her earlobes to her pinkie toe—had been romantic. In a Deacon-like way.

A shout startled her out of the memory, and she looked around the arena, wide-eyed, remembering where she was.

Right. Fight night had finally arrived.

The week following their LA trip, Deacon had been scarce. When they were together, he was sleeping or obsessively watching fight tapes.

Molly let him be.

Then he'd shown up at her apartment at two a.m. last night, looking exhausted and worried. "I couldn't sleep," he said. "I don't like to sleep without you. I hadn't realized until tonight how much I fucking hated that this week."

She'd stripped off her pajamas and crawled into bed with him naked. Almost as soon as he'd wrapped her in his arms and whispered, "Love you, babe," he'd fallen into a deep sleep.

Her sweet, snuggly man had been gone this morning when she'd awoken. But he had texted her:

THNX 4 last night. I ♥ U

Might've been silly, but she'd looked at it several times during the day.

Now here she was, waiting to watch her sweet, fierce lover prove his prowess or get pummeled.

Black Arts had a reserved-seating section in the front three rows behind the judges' table. Molly would've preferred to sit someplace else, but Deacon insisted she sit close enough that he could see her when he entered the ring.

So while the Black Arts section was full, none of her cohorts was in the area—most were at the back of the house with the fight crew. She wondered how different the night would've been if Deacon's dad were sitting beside her.

The blond ring girl—who resembled Katie—sashayed around the outside of the ring. Katie had hung up her teeny black boy shorts and cleavage-baring sports bra after the success of the event in LA. Katie was a smart woman; most people underestimated the size of her brain when faced with the size of her chest.

Presley slid into the empty chair next to Molly. "Hey, ho-bag."

"Hey, Pres. I wasn't sure if you'd make it."

"Wouldn't miss it!" She leaned in to whisper, "But who are the smarmy suits in the front row? They eyed me like a tasty burrito. It was creepy."

Presley had cultivated a retro edgy look that fit in with the fight crowd. She'd tied a thin animal-print scarf around her neck. Her square-necked blouse was the same fiery red as her lipstick. To complete the outfit, she wore dark denim vintage pedal pushers and a pair of black and red checked patent leather platform pumps. The only aspect that didn't fit with the pinup-queen image were the tattoos running down her arms and the lip, nose, and eyebrow piercings.

"You done staring at me?"

Molly rolled her eyes. "Yes. Now I see why the guys were drooling over you. Sometimes it's hard to be the friend of such a bombshell."

"Ha. Answer the question. Who are those guys?"

"Scouts for Smackdown. They're the up-and-coming MMA fight company."

"What're they doing here?"

"Checking out Maddox's roster. Rumor is they're looking to sign new fighters."

"What does that mean for the guys who get signed by them?"

"Their fight career is dependent on the company who owns their contract. The organization sets up the fights and closely monitors the fighter's life—inside and outside the ring. Everything from training, to public appearances, to televised fights, to endorsements."

Presley frowned. "Why would anyone sign on for that?"

"Money. Prestige. Recognition. Advancement in the sport. If a fighter isn't signed by one of the major fight organizations, they'll never get a shot at fighting the best in the business. Even getting ranked in the top twenty in their weight division is a boost in visibility. Their win-loss records are crucial to moving up in the rankings for the right to fight for the title." Molly gave her friend a sheepish smile when she realized she'd been babbling. "Yeah, I know way more about this than I should."

"You're involved with a fighter and our boss is married to a fight promoter. I'd be disappointed if you *couldn't* spout all that off at the drop of a glove." She grinned. "Thanks for the insider's look."

"You're welcome."

Deacon's fight was last—at least two hours from now. Of the ten bouts on tonight's card, only three interested her—Deacon's, Ivan's, and Sergei's.

She considered hitting the concession stand for a chili cheese dog. But that would add at least an hour to her cardio tomorrow. Since she'd started dating Deacon, she'd been more consistent in her own workouts.

"You keep sighing, Mol. You okay?"

"Just nervous for my man. So I'm glad you're here."

Presley gave her a shoulder bump. "Let's have a cocktail."

"Yes, please. Something fruity and girly to cut the testosterone clogging the air."

"Be right back."

Ivan fought the third bout and outmaneuvered his opponent in the first minute of the second round.

Molly watched the Smackdown guys talking among themselves. What was their criteria for choosing a fighter? Raw talent? Carefully honed skills? A murderous look in the eyes?

The next two matches featured fighters they didn't know. So Presley filled her in on Divas gossip.

When Sergei's fight started, they cheered loudly—bolstered by their drinks. The fighters were evenly matched and the fight lasted until the third round, when Sergei forced his opponent to tap out.

"I forgot how much fun this was," Presley said.

"Booze helps immensely."

Presley held her "yard" of frozen margarita up to Molly's in a toast.

"Although this is sort of the same vibe as at a roller derby match," Molly pointed out.

"But I'm in the zone then. I'm part of the event, not part of the crowd. Totally different vibe for me."

When the second to last fight ended, butterflies took wing in Molly's stomach. Her leg started to bounce up and down. She might be sick. "I have to go to the bathroom."

"I'll come with you."

"No. That's okay."

Presley got nose to nose with her. "You can't go back there and hug him for good luck. And you can't hide in the bathroom, either. My job as your friend is to make sure you're where you're supposed to be, get you liquored up, and hold your hand if needed."

That's when Molly knew. "Maddox made you come here."

"No, Maddox *asked* me to be here for you. Which I happily agreed to. Now, we'll hit the bathroom quickly and be back in these seats before Deacon makes his walk to the cage." Again she peered into Molly's face. "You do understand the importance of him seeing you here, cheering him on, right?"

"Yes." But how did Presley know that?

With the long line for the bathroom, they made it back to their seats just before the lights dimmed.

"What's Deacon's walk-in arena song?"

Molly drew a blank. "I have no idea."

Everyone was on their feet when the lights went out. Molly stood on tiptoe, straining to get that first glimpse of Deacon.

The music started and blasted through the speakers.

Presley started laughing.

"What is it?" Molly yelled over the music. "I don't recognize the song."

"'Bleed It Out' by Linkin Park." She laughed again. "I swear I thought he'd have 'Sweet Emotion' by Aerosmith—you know, since he doesn't show any emotion ever. Ironic, right?"

Molly smirked because Presley was dead wrong.

"Ooh, here he comes."

Maddox, Ronin, Knox, and Beck followed behind Deacon. When he shed the robe, revealing his gorgeous back tattoo, Presley sucked in a sharp breath.

"Beautiful, isn't it?"

"Yeah. And the tat ain't bad either."

Molly slugged her.

The ref patted Deacon down, checking his gloves, his fingernails and his mouth guard. He smeared Vaseline on Deacon's face and then signaled Deacon was good to go.

Deacon didn't hug any of his instructors. He turned and scanned the crowd until his gaze landed on Molly.

The only change in his don't-fuck-with-me demeanor was a long breath he exhaled. He turned, took the two steps up to the cage, bowed, and entered the ring.

The lights cut out again.

Molly dropped back into her seat. She wasn't standing to be a good sport for the man who'd trash-talked her man.

Needham walked in to "SexyBack" by Justin Timberlake.

What a fucktard. Deacon oughta whale on him for that alone.

Presley didn't sit until Needham dropped his robe. She shrugged. "He needs to lay off the Muscle Milk."

Needham walked into the ring.

The crowd quieted down only when the announcer started talking.

"Ladies and gentlemen, welcome to your main event of the evening! This MMA middleweight division features the challenger, in the blue corner, wearing black trunks, with a professional record of twenty-eight wins, two losses, and an amateur record of thirty-four wins and zero losses. Weighing in at one hundred and eighty-five pounds, he stands six feet, two inches and trains out of the Black Arts dojo, Denver, Colorado . . . Deacon 'Con Man' McConnell."

More boos than cheers rang out.

"In the red corner, wearing white trunks, with a professional record of seventeen wins, four losses, weighing in at one hundred and eighty-eight pounds, he stands an even six feet and trains out of Baker's Gym in Kansas City, Kansas . . . Jeremy 'Don't' Needham!"

"That is a stupid fucking ring name," Presley said. "Why doesn't Needs-His-Ass-Kicked have an amateur and a pro win–loss record?"

Molly relayed Deacon's explanation about a professional amateur status.

The ref called both fighters in and explained the rules. The guys touched gloves and returned to their corners.

Okay. Here we go.

OKAY. *Here we go.*

Deacon moved his head side to side. He stretched his arms up and out. Then he faced Maddox.

"D. You got this. You've trained your ass off. You know his weak spots. But better yet, you know your own strengths. He doesn't stand a chance."

When Deacon looked across the cage at Needham, sneering at

him, Dante's voice jumped into his head, shouting, *Release the hounds!*

Such a fucking smart-ass, bro.

Hey, that motherfucker is blocking you from reaching that next rung on the ladder. It's your time. Take it.

The referee signaled the start of the fight.

Needham practically pranced into the middle of the ring first, taunting him.

Deacon purposely lumbered forward, taking left-side fighting stance. That allowed him to cue up his right fist and leg.

Needham swung and missed.

Deacon's kick landed on the outside of Needham's quad. Twice in rapid succession.

A couple of Needham's blows came close to landing, but none connected. In a moment of bravado, he used a left uppercut.

That knocked Deacon back a step.

Shake it off.

Deacon utilized a jab to the gut to get Needham to lower his hands. In the split second he did that, he saw his opening and took it. He threw a right cross at Needham's jaw.

Needham's head snapped back. He opened his box stance just far enough for Deacon to use a powerful straight punch, right to Needham's solar plexus.

The man crumpled to the mat.

Deacon didn't waste a single opportunity. He landed a couple of kicks before the ref called the match. He squinted at the clock. Official time: 1:43

Fuck yeah.

The ref officially raised Deacon's hand as the winner.

If there was positive crowd noise? He didn't hear it. He stormed over to the side where Molly would be, but Riggins intercepted him.

"On the chair. Now."

Deacon removed his mouth guard. "He got one fucking hit in. That's it. Didn't hurt. Look at me. I'm not even winded."

"Fight rules state you get checked out in the ring immediately following the fight. Either I do it or their goons do. Choose."

Deacon sat.

"You looked good."

"No, this looked like a fucking setup."

Riggins shook his head. "You can't even be happy that you got a KO halfway through the first fucking round?"

"No. This was supposed to be my big fight. Needham was no match for me."

"So? *He* looks like a chump, not you."

Deacon snatched the water bottle Maddox held out. After he drank, he locked his gaze to his trainer's. "I wanna talk to the Smackdown guys. Now. Set it up. If they can't be bothered to make time for me, there's no fucking way I'll ever sign on with them."

"I'll let them know."

"You're done," Riggins said.

As soon as he was cleared, he jumped up and went to the netting, looking for Molly.

The crazy-assed woman climbed onto the edge of the cage. "Hey. You won."

Deacon grinned and kissed her through the netting. "Yep."

"Now what?"

"I have a meeting. Don't know how long it'll take. Will you wait for me?"

"Like you have to ask."

His eyes narrowed. "Wait with the Black Arts crew. I don't want you by yourself."

"Would it be better if I waited for you at the after-party?"

"Babe. We're not goin' to the after-party." He kissed her again.

"We're having a private party for two." Maddox shouted at him. "Gotta go."

DEACON showed up for the meeting with the Smackdown guys still in his fight gear, except he'd slipped on a Black Arts hoodie.

Three guys in suits sat across from him and Maddox.

"Great fight, Deacon. You show outstanding promise."

"That fight was bullshit and you know it." Deacon let his gaze move between the men. "Is that the kind of talent Smackdown has on its roster? Needham? Courey? I've beat the fuck outta both of those guys now. So which washed-up fighter are you gonna put me in the ring with next?"

"Washed-up?" Lars Turkin, the Smackdown talent manager, repeated.

"Yeah. Look, I've been waiting a long time to sign with a fight organization."

"Is it true you turned down a UFC contract?"

"Yep." Deacon felt Maddox looking at him. Oops. He'd forgotten to share that. "I'm a fighter. I want to fight. Not once a fucking year, either. That was my issue with them. That's why I decided to talk to you. From what I'd seen, you let your fighters fight, not just train to fight for some big TV event once a year."

"That's where we intentionally set out to be different from the UFC," Lars said. "They think they're signing the best-of-the-best fighters, but then they only put a chosen few to the test because of policy and politics. We want a guy like you, Deacon, who's been toiling in the trenches for years, who blows onto the scene and beats the piss out of everyone in your path."

Deacon grinned. "No surprise that appeals to me."

Lars smiled back. "Good. At least we're on the same page there."

"Tell him," the CEO, Jim Fichter, urged.

"We're in talks with Bellator to have their belt holders fight ours."

"Seriously?"

"We know that when anyone hears the words *mixed martial arts*, they immediately think of the UFC. And the UFC has effectively killed any competition by simply buying the damn organizations like Strikeforce and WEC. Some of their titleholders keep the titles for so long because they're not allowed to fight anyone that might be a true challenger."

"And yet they continue to dominate the MMA world."

"We are trying to change that. Bellator has managed to avoid a buyout. They've got the TV contracts, they've got great fighters, but they need a bigger pool of challengers. That's where we come in. Combining forces, creating a new championship level and yet retaining individual championship belts for our organizations, gives us an edge and makes it interesting for the fighters and for the MMA fans."

No argument there. "When is all this Bellator-Smackdown lovefest gonna happen?"

"We're working out the details, but we hope to make the announcement in six weeks and get the fights scheduled in the next six months."

"Sounds interesting," Maddox said. "But where does Deacon come in?"

"On top. If he signed with us, we'd expect him to put his money where his mouth is." Lars grinned. "He complained that fighters under contract don't get to fight? We'd put him to the test four times. Con Man beats our top four guys in his division, he'd be in contention to fight a Bellator champ in a televised bout."

Maddox's eyebrows rose. "That's a pretty hefty fucking carrot to dangle."

Lars leaned forward and looked at Deacon. "You are the real

deal in MMA. You are exactly what Smackdown needs. Sign with us and we can get you real challengers—not guys like Needham and Courey, who are good, but not good enough to reach the highest level."

"I appreciate y'all agreeing to meet with me. I'm not playing hard to get when I say I need a little time to weigh my options."

"Understood."

The older guy on the end, who hadn't said anything, finally spoke. "You mean what you said about fighting any of our guys at any time?"

Deacon squinted at him and recognized him as Dan "the Destroyer" Destin, one of the first MMA fighters who'd spoken out against the popular World Federation–style wrestling. He challenged martial arts fighters to do something "real" that was entertaining because of skill and training, not showmanship and stupid costumes. "Yes, Bob, I mean it. You got a fighter in my division who needs an opponent? I'm there."

"Even if it's next week?"

"Yep. I'm in fighting shape and I wasn't even fucking winded after Needham, so I'm ready for a challenge."

Bob nodded. "Then we'll be in touch."

Deacon shook hands with everyone and left the room.

Maddox caught Deacon in the hallway. "That throwdown is gonna come back and bite you in the ass."

"Good."

"You going to the after-party?"

"Not on your fucking life. Had enough of fighters, promoters, trainers, and fans for one night."

WHEN Deacon walked into the locker room, he headed straight for Molly. He pulled her body against his and took her mouth in a kiss that left no question how he felt about her.

True fucking love. Body, heart, soul.

And he didn't give a good goddamn who knew it.

As he continued to kiss her, falling deeper into the place where urgency met peace, she forcibly ripped her mouth free from his.

"Dammit, Deacon. Quit mauling me. We are not alone," she whispered.

He looked over his shoulder. Beck and Fisher both smirked at him. "Beat it," he said, and turned back to Molly, stalking her until her spine hit the locker bay.

"You're welcome for us keeping an eye on your girlfriend," Fisher said, making kissing noises as he passed by.

Beck clapped him on the back. "See you next week."

"Lock the door behind you."

"Deacon!"

Beck laughed and said, "Will do."

"If you keep everyone from coming in here for the next fifteen minutes, I'll sign over my Jiggles VIP pass to you for the rest of the year."

"Done." The door slammed.

Molly was gaping at him.

"Like you didn't know I was gonna fuck you as soon as possible." He dropped his mouth to her neck and sucked. "Fighting makes me horny, babe. Winning a fight? So much adrenaline pumps through me for hours afterward that I can probably go all damn night."

"Probably?"

"Let's get the first time outta the way now."

"And once again he fucks me against a door," she deadpanned.

"Is that a challenge?" he said, after he slipped the last button free on her blouse.

"So what if it is?" she whispered in his ear.

"I'd say I'll take it. And it's time you fulfill one of my fantasies."

She went still. "I'm not up for a surprise ass-fucking in a boy's locker room. That's a little too, 'Hey, bend over for the soap and squeal like a pig' clichéd for my liking."

"Christ, woman. The shit you say sometimes." Deacon groaned. "I'm not gonna fuck you in the ass tonight, especially not after that visual. And that ain't even close to one of my fantasies."

"Oh." She slid her hands under his hoodie. "What's your fantasy?"

"Turn around and strip."

She hesitated.

He curled his hand beneath her jaw. "I'm on edge. I need to fuck you. It's like a . . . compulsion. I can't move beyond that, and I don't even wanna try. I need that release. I need you." He closed his eyes. "Please. Give me this."

"I'm yours, Deacon. I'll give you whatever you want." She paused, and her lips met his. "Because I love you."

His eyes flew open.

"I know you'll want me to say it again, so I will. I love you. With my heart and soul. With my entire being down to my bones. I've been trying to find the perfect time to say it to you. So it's not very romantic, saying it in a stinky locker room—"

"It's fucking perfect." With the storm rising inside him, his answering kiss was surprisingly gentle. Then he said, "I need you to strip really fucking fast now."

He ripped off his clothes and set his supplies on the bench.

When he saw Molly had completely bared herself to him, he moved in behind her, pressing his chest to her back. "My beautiful Molly."

She grabbed his wandering hands and placed them on her tits.

"Come here. Let's have some kinky fun." After kissing the back of her neck until gooseflesh broke out and she started to squirm, he pulled her over to the portable heavy bag. He draped the towel around his neck and picked up the cloth jump rope from the bench. "Wrists together."

"You weren't kidding about kinky fun."

"I never kid about that." Deacon looped the rope around her wrists in a hojojutsu quick tie. "Hands above your head."

Molly watched him with lust-filled eyes as he tied the rope around the chain holding the heavy bag so the chain bore her body weight and not her wrists. Her pulse beat erratically in her throat. Her chest rose and fell with her rapid breathing. And she kept licking her lips—a sure sign this fantasy of his turned her on as much as it did him.

With her back against the canvas, he lifted her left leg and wrapped it around his hip. His hands were shaking so fucking hard, it took an extra moment for him to get his cock lined up.

So when his fingers connected with the creamy wetness between her thighs, he groaned and rested his damp forehead on her breast. "Fuck, woman. I can't . . ." *Breathe. Calm down. Find control.*

"It's okay. Release the beast. He won tonight. He should get to celebrate."

"However he wants to take you?" he asked with some skepticism.

"Yes."

The beast roared.

Deacon clamped his hands on the backs of her thighs and lifted her. Then he spun her around so she faced the heavy bag.

She immediately squeezed her legs around it and wiggled frantically. "I can't hold on—"

"Babe, stop fighting. Let the chain hold you on the top. I've got your bottom." He slipped the towel between her pussy and the canvas. Then he bent his knees and impaled her in one vicious thrust.

Molly gasped.

Deacon attacked the nape of her neck and the slope of her shoulders while he fucked her without pause. He bit, sucked, and kissed every inch of her skin from her hairline to the center of her spine.

Sweat poured from him, and he fought for breath—he exerted more energy fucking her than he had during the fight. He rocked his hips up hard on every thrust, pushing her clit into the towel. Faster and faster until she started to thrash and whimper.

"Please, Deacon."

He found the spot that sent her into orbit and scraped his teeth over it. When he felt her cunt muscles tightening, he sank his teeth in.

Molly bucked wildly, forcing him to dig his fingertips into her legs to keep her from dislodging his cock as she came violently.

He eased up when her climax abated, but he knew he'd left bruises.

Good. They'll match the bite and suck marks on her back, the beast snarled.

A few more brutal thrusts and Deacon reached the end of the climb. Despite the frenzied need of the beast and the insatiable way they'd fucked, Deacon came in utter stillness. His cock jerked against those hot pussy walls, while her contractions milked his orgasm, his mouth open, his breath stalled as he heard her whispering, "I love you, I love you, I love you," until he was completely spent.

It was the single most perfect moment of his life.

But when the harsh pants of pleasure faded, he pulled back in his mind, as guilt of his animalistic treatment of her began to assert itself. He pulled back in body, keeping his eyes closed against the evidence of his mindless passion and thoughtless treatment of the woman who meant everything to him.

"Don't," she said softy, bringing his attention back to her. "Don't apologize. Don't feel guilty. I love you. All of you. I wanted this, Deacon. I wanted you. Please don't take anything away from this."

He lowered her legs to the floor.

Molly spun around on her own as he unhooked her hands.

"Look at me."

Their eyes met. What he saw there . . . love shining in her eyes . . . *that* was the perfect moment.

Molly stood on tiptoe to fasten her mouth to his. With every sweeping stroke of her tongue, every teasing glide of her lips, she gave him—and the beast—peace, approval, and acceptance.

That was worth more than any fight he'd ever win.

CHAPTER THIRTY-ONE

DEACON'S dad had called an hour after the intense locker-room rendezvous. Deacon had still been high on that, lazily sated, as they drove to his apartment. So he'd answered his cell phone without conscious thought. Then, after Deacon told his dad he'd won the fight—his father must've sensed his son's distraction—he'd issued an invite to Texas to both of them to celebrate and Deacon had agreed to fly down. But Molly knew Deacon would've said anything to get his dad off the phone.

Once they were inside the apartment, they'd lost themselves in each other for the next twelve hours. The world outside Deacon's bedroom ceased to exist.

So Deacon hadn't realized the implications of what he'd agreed to until the next morning. His father had called again to confirm a family dinner on Thursday night. Then Tag had called an hour later. They'd had a cryptic conversation about contracts, buyouts, investment portfolios and mergers that she'd tried not to listen in on. Deacon ended the call, swearing he wasn't backing out this time and he'd be there.

He'd booked the tickets, she'd overpacked, and now here they were.

In Texas.

After checking into the hotel, Molly started to get ready to meet Deacon's family. She smoothed her hands over her hair and checked her appearance. The fawn-brown dress might be too fall-ish for the middle of summer, but she always felt confident in it. The fabric hung perfectly, not too clingy, not too loose. The wide tweed belt cinched at the waist created an hourglass shape.

As she applied the last coat of mascara, she saw Deacon leaning in the doorjamb, his face unreadable.

"You ready yet?"

"I'm sorry I'm taking so long. I'm nervous."

"Darlin', you got no reason for nerves."

"But this is a big step for me to meet your family." She reached for a tube of peach lipstick.

He sauntered forward. "You're wearing your hair like that?"

Molly's eyes met his in the bathroom mirror. Then she gave his usual—and far too casual for a formal family dinner—sleeveless T-shirt and jeans a pointed look. "Since when do you care about my clothing or how I wear my hair?"

Deacon grabbed the section of loose curls hanging to the top of her right breast and swept it back over her shoulder. "When it's up, I can do this whenever I want." He placed an openmouthed kiss behind her ear. "And you know how much I love pulling your hair, because, babe, it gets you so freakin' hot."

Gooseflesh had erupted at the first touch of his warm mouth to her skin. "Deacon, stop molesting me or we'll be late."

"Don't care." His soft exhale made the fine hair on the back of her neck stand up. "You smell so fucking sweet, my Molly."

She went gooey-kneed when he called her *my Molly*. It took a ton of willpower to shift away from him, but she did. "I need a few more minutes. Alone," she stressed. "Then we can go."

Deacon gifted her with one last love bite before he exited the bathroom.

She pressed her hands flat against the counter and leaned forward to level her breathing. The man could rile her up in no time. She didn't need to look like she'd been well fucked—or worse, horny as fuck—when meeting his parents for the first time.

Breathe. You can do this.

She swiped deodorant under her arms, hoping to hide her nervous sweat.

When she walked into the hallway between the living area and the bedroom of the hotel suite, she saw Deacon staring out the window with his back to her. He was on the phone. "Not what I needed to hear, Maddox. No. Fuck that. We did this song-and-dance bullshit last weekend. They know what my fucking terms are." He paused and braced his hand against the window. "Fighting for a living ain't my only option. Make sure that's understood." He went silent as Maddox spoke. Then he said, "That's why I'm here. I'll listen to what they have to say. I'm not making any decisions without discussing it with—"

Evidently Maddox had cut him off. Molly wasn't sure any of this conversation was for her ears—but what had Deacon meant when he'd said *fighting for a living ain't my only option*? Had his family offered him another job? Who would he discuss the decision with?

Highly unlikely it's you.

Annoyed by that thought, she slammed the door to announce her arrival before she returned to the living room suite.

Deacon had turned around to face her. "Look, I gotta go. Yeah." He scowled. "Whoa. I didn't ask to hear about your stupid love life, Mad." He waited as Maddox explained. Then, "Dude, seriously? Hasn't your monthly pass to bang town with Grandma Moses expired yet? Uh-huh. Well, you stick your nose into my personal business all the damn time, so here's my advice, asswipe. Cut her loose. ASAP. Later."

Molly raised an eyebrow after Deacon hung up. "Bang town? Do I even want to know?"

"Babe, *I* didn't want to know, but that didn't matter, because he blathered on about it anyway. What *is* it with people sharing shit like that with me? Like I'm suddenly Dr. Love or something."

Molly bit back a smile. "What's going on?"

"Maddox is fucking this woman named Alicia, who is fifteen years older than him. She's got hard-core insecurity issues, and she's as psycho as his ex-wife. Dude has the worst taste in women. Anyway, the last thing he needed was her showing up in LA."

"I didn't see him with anyone besides Presley. Was she at any of the events?"

"No. She didn't get a pass and she was pissed off about it. Big, ugly fucking scene." His eyes narrowed. "Presley didn't tell you about it?"

"Presley and I don't tell each other everything."

"Thank fuck for that. Anyway, I saw Maddox and Presley sucking face. So did Alicia. I figured it was part of that PR thing you guys came up with to stick it to his ex."

Come to think of it, both Presley and Maddox had acted weird on the way back to Denver. But asking Deacon to further speculate what might've happened . . . He hated gossip.

Deacon stalked forward and grabbed her hand. "Let's go. The faster we get this over with, the quicker we can come back here and make up for lost time."

"What lost time?" she said as he towed her out of the hotel room.

He poked the down button at the elevator before he crowded her against the wall. "The alone time we're losing in our hotel room with all furniture I wanna spread you out on and bend you over."

Liquid heat flowed from the burning brand of his lips on her neck in a straight line between her legs.

The elevator dinged and the doors slid open.

She set her hands on his pecs and pushed him. "We'll pick this up later."

He kept a hand on her in the elevator. And in the rental car. The tension she expected from him was strangely absent. Rather than ask why he wasn't wound tight, she tried to mimic his "it's cool" attitude. She'd started to congratulate herself on handling her nerves so well when they pulled up to what looked like a security checkpoint outside a residential area.

Deacon rolled down the window.

"ID please," the guard said.

He pulled out his wallet and passed over his driver's license. "We're guests of the Westermans."

The guard scrutinized his ID. "You've been here before?"

"Only twice."

That surprised her.

"You know where you're going, then. Have a good evening, Mr. McConnell."

"Thanks."

Deacon turned into a driveway hidden between a row of shrubs and scraggly bushes that looked out of place in such a pristinely landscaped environment. Once the tree tunnel opened up, her mouth fell open. A stone, glass, and brick mansion rose before them like a monolith.

He parked in the circular drive, his rental car out of place with the Lexuses, Mercedes, Audis, and Range Rovers—until she reminded herself that Deacon did, in fact, own two vehicles that would blend in here. He glanced up at the structure and shook his head. "Can't believe Dad agreed to this monstrosity."

"You've only been here twice?"

"They moved here after I left home. I crashed in the guest room for a few days before Granddad's funeral. Then, when the shit went down with my aunt Suzette, I stuck around only because

Dad was a mess and Julianne was worthless." His gaze was heavy with disgust. "I hate this place."

Molly had wondered if Deacon had been invited to stay with his folks and he'd declined. "Why?"

"It ain't home to me, and it never will be."

She reached for his hand on the console. "So we're both without a place to call home."

Deacon started to say something but changed his mind. Instead he brought her hand up to his mouth and kissed the inside of her wrist.

She waited until Deacon came around to help her out of the car. He kept his left hand around the back of her neck—an obvious sign of propriety, but the heavy weight of his hand reassured her.

After he rang the doorbell, she tensed up. He pressed his lips to her temple. "Babe, gotta remember to breathe. Only time I want you breathless is when I touch you."

The door swung inward, cutting off her retort.

Molly half expected a tuxedoed butler. But the man in the doorway wore gray trousers, a gray and white pin-striped shirt, and a big smile. Molly noticed a resemblance between him and Deacon, but the man foiled her scrutiny by forcing a hug on Deacon.

"Son. Good to have you here."

No positive response from Deacon.

He disentangled himself and brought Molly forward. "Dad, this is Molly Calloway. Molly, my father, Bing Westerman."

Molly offered her hand. "Pleasure to meet you, Mr. Westerman."

"Call me Bing. Please." He clasped Molly's hand in both of his and held on. He studied her more intently than she'd anticipated, and she found herself leaning away, into Deacon. Bing caught himself and retreated. "Come in. Everyone has gathered in the lounge before dinner."

Of course this house had a lounge. Probably the butler did double duty as the bartender.

Molly didn't have time to check out the foyer beyond seeing the marble floor beneath her feet, the enormous sparkling chandelier above her head, and the two grand staircases that curved up to the second story. Her initial impression? This kind of wealth meant never stepping foot in IKEA.

Bing led them into a room straight out of an English manor—a wood-paneled, thickly carpeted lounging area where men played billiards, smoked cigars, and swilled expensive spirits while plotting to run the world.

"Stay by me," Deacon murmured.

They stopped in front of a hand-carved, L-shaped bar with club chairs on one side and a brass foot railing down the other side. Bing stepped behind the partition. Looked like he was the butler and the bartender. "What would you like to drink, Molly?"

"She'll have the same as me. Jameson Select on the rocks with a splash of soda."

Molly thought it best not to correct Deacon and ask for rum and Diet Coke.

When Bing smiled and turned away to fix their drinks, Deacon put his mouth to her ear. "Dad is a shitty bartender. Makes drinks three times stronger than they should be. The Jameson is high-end, so he'll be stingy with it—trust me."

"But I'm not a whiskey drinker."

"Good. Then there's no chance you'll get hammered and my family will take advantage."

"They'd do that?"

"In a fucking heartbeat, babe." He kissed the hollow below her earlobe. "They're cut from the same cloth as your cousins."

A more expensive cut of cloth to be sure, she thought tartly.

"Deacon, aren't you going to introduce me to your friend?"

A command cloaked in a honeyed drawl was still a command.

Deacon didn't turn around, and Molly didn't see a smile on his lips or in his eyes. "I figured introductions could wait until we had our drinks."

"Very well. I'm pleased you retained something from the etiquette classes I sent you to."

Wow. He'd just blown off his mother.

Conversation buzzed in the room, but Molly kept her focus on Bing, as he used an industrial soda dispenser to add bubbles to the amber liquid in the crystal glasses.

"Here you are." Bing popped a tiny blue straw in each glass.

"Thanks, Dad."

"Need me to run interference with your mother?"

"No. I can handle her."

"I wasn't worried about you, son."

Molly sipped her drink and wished she could've slammed the entire thing when she finally noticed the people openly gawking at her.

Deacon draped his arm over her shoulder. They made their way toward a rail-thin brunette with big Texas hair, who was stylishly dressed in a pantsuit the soft hue of pink champagne. "Molly, meet my mother, Julianne."

Molly thrust out her hand. "Thank you for inviting me into your home, Mrs. Westerman."

Her pale blue eyes, as frosty as her son's, inspected Molly head to toe. The woman didn't look a day over forty. She briefly took Molly's hand. Then her gaze moved to Deacon. "Will you make introductions, or shall I?"

With his drink, Deacon gestured to the blond woman next to his mother. "I'll do it. Molly, this is my aunt Annabelle Wick— Julianne's sister—and her husband, Derek."

Derek offered his hand and muttered, "Our son, Warren."

Then he gestured to a gangly teen sprawled in a cozy seating area, who didn't look up from his cell phone to acknowledge either of them.

Deacon pointed to the next couple. "This is my uncle Clark Westerman and his wife, my aunt Sissy—they're Tag's parents."

"Lovely to meet you," Sissy said.

"Aunt Suzette," Deacon said coldly to the dark-haired woman who'd slithered between Clark and Sissy. "I didn't expect to see you here."

"Of course I wanted to be here to welcome your new girlfriend." Suzette offered a slim, bejeweled hand. "I'm Suzette Atherton. Deacon's aunt. This is my husband, Leonard." He was so tall he had to crouch a little to shake her hand. Then Suzette said, "And this is our son, Clive."

A good-looking, dark-haired man close to Deacon's age, overdressed in a three-piece camel-colored linen suit, ambled closer with obvious reluctance. The slight sneer twisting his mouth lessened his attractiveness. His blue eyes, a shade darker than Deacon's, scrutinized Molly for what seemed an eternity.

Deacon's fingers tightened on Molly's. "Clive. Are your mom and dad paying you to put in an appearance?"

"Of course I wasn't invited, but when has that ever stopped me? My curiosity overruled the potential boredom of this family dinner. But now I think"—he shot Molly an unreadable glance—"it will prove to be a very interesting evening."

How was she supposed to survive this? They were all looking at her like she was a green-skinned alien.

Bing cut through the group and stopped in front of Deacon, clapping him on the shoulder. "Tell us about your next fight."

"He doesn't know who he'll fight next," Warren said from the sitting area.

So the boy could speak.

Deacon faced him. "Actually, being that the fight with Needham ended so fast and I'm still in fighting shape, I'm fighting Duke Watson next weekend. His original opponent is out with an injury."

Molly forced herself not to react. So soon? Why had he dropped this bomb in front of his family? Was she supposed to act like she'd known?

"Duke Watson is tough. Tougher than his record indicates. I'll bet he's not about to have a four-course French meal, regardless of who he's fightin'," Warren drawled.

Deacon moved closer to his cousin. "Yeah? According to Watson's PR team, he eats nails for all three meals anyway."

Warren snorted and didn't look up from his phone. "And his press team swears he drinks the bitter tears from his enemies to wash it down."

"Watson likes to think he's invincible. I'll prove him wrong." When Warren didn't respond, Deacon said, "You a fan of Watson's or something?"

A blushing Warren looked up at Deacon with worshipful eyes.

That's when Molly knew she'd found an ally in this family. She sidestepped a stunned Deacon and sat across from Warren. "I believe Warren is a fan of yours, Con Man."

Warren blushed harder.

"That's cool, Warren," Molly said with a grin. "I'm a big fan of Con Man too. Have you seen him fight live?"

He shook his head. "Just on YouTube."

"It's scary. When he fought Needham last weekend, I thought I might throw up when he took that hit."

"That was the only hit Deacon took," Warren reminded her.

A serious fan, then. "The first time I watched him fight, he used this beautiful spinning back fist to knock out his opponent. So I asked him to show me how to do it in his kickboxing class the next week."

"Did he show you?"

"No. He made me run through all the punching and kicking drills two extra times for even asking him."

Warren completely charmed her with a shy, crooked grin. "So he's a hard-assed teacher?"

"You have no idea."

"You take jujitsu too?"

"Nope. Just kickboxing. It's therapeutic to pound out my frustrations a few times a week."

Deacon set his hand on Molly's shoulder. "That's where we met. It took her a while to agree to go out with me."

"Only because you tried to kill me first." Damn. Given his history . . . wrong thing to say. She quickly backtracked. "I've got a much higher aerobic threshold now. I don't start wheezing the first minute of class."

"I'd probably be wheezing too," Warren said. "I don't need an aerobic threshold for golf."

"You golf for fun? Or on your school team?" Deacon asked.

Molly couldn't get over Deacon's interest in his cousin. He had a puzzled look, almost as if he'd never seen him before. And he was being . . . chatty with a teenager. Very odd behavior.

"Warren is ranked a top-twenty player for high school golf for the state," his father inserted proudly.

"He's already garnered the attention of some top scouts from Ivy League colleges."

Warren scowled. "*One* scout, Ma. Don't make it out to be something bigger than it is."

"Watch your tone with your mother," his father warned.

"Geez, don't act like I'm something special in front of Deacon! He's a professional athlete. He'll probably fight for the world title in the next couple of years. The world title!" he repeated with awe. "That's impressive. Competing in the Texas high school state golf tournament doesn't compare."

"You're right. Fighting uses brute force versus the skill and finesse used in golf."

Warren glared at his mother. "What is wrong with you? Why would you say something like that when it's not true? Deacon is one of the best fighters in MMA. He's trained for years to learn the skills to take him to the top. I don't get why none of you ever talk about all he's accomplished. He's the shit." Embarrassed by his outburst, he dropped his angry gaze to his phone.

Silence.

Molly kept her mouth shut even though she sided with Warren. Deacon *was* the shit. He'd made a name for himself and he'd done it on his own. There should be a lot more family pride than the minute amount she'd seen. She'd bet a cool Benjamin that Warren's folks had no idea before tonight that their son followed his cousin's fight career.

"I believe it's time to make our way to the dining room," Deacon's mother trilled.

Molly didn't speak to Warren until the room cleared out. "Deacon is an amazing fighter. And I'm glad there's at least one person in his family who recognizes that. Thank you."

Warren looked up at Deacon. "Sorry. Didn't mean to put you on the spot."

"You didn't."

"I wasn't supposed to come tonight, but I just had to meet you. I'd give anything to watch you fight," he blurted out.

Deacon grinned. "Yeah? I can get you a VIP ticket; you just gotta get to the event." He flicked his gaze over Molly's shoulder. "I imagine my dad will come to the Watson fight since he missed the Needham fight. See if you can't hitch a ride with him. He's probably taking the JFW company plane, so you wouldn't have to shell out for airfare."

"Oh, man. Seriously? That would be so freakin' epic!"

"I'd wait to ask. Doesn't seem like your folks are down with your interest in MMA."

It seemed more like Warren's parents weren't down with his interest in his cousin. Why?

"Move it, Deacon," Bing said sharply. "Your mother went to a lot of trouble to plan this meal."

Molly noticed Bing hadn't said *cooked* this meal.

Be nice. The woman just had surgery.

But given what she knew of Deacon's mother? It'd be a struggle to be civil to the woman who'd caused her man so much pain and suffering.

Deacon took hold of Molly's hands and pulled her to her feet, then towed her behind him down a hallway.

Molly's nerves returned when they entered the large dining room with a long table that could comfortably seat fifty. But all the dinnerware was laid out at one end. Two uniformed servers remained at attention.

"Down here." Deacon's father waved at him.

With only one empty seat across from Deacon's mother, that put Deacon on his father's right side but no place for Molly to sit.

Please don't abandon me.

Deacon paused behind the chair, pointedly looking down at the seat his aunt Annabelle occupied.

How could the woman act so unaffected by Deacon's steely-eyed stare? Molly had nightmares about him looking at her with such disdain.

"Annabelle, I think what Deacon is too tactful to ask is if you would mind moving so he can sit by Molly?"

Tactful—not a word often attributed to Deacon. She bit back a laugh.

"Of course. I should sit next to Warren so he doesn't get it in his head that golf is lame. An excellent golf game equates to excellence in the business world."

"No wonder Deacon never had a head for business; his golf game was dismal," Clive said behind them.

Luckily, Annabelle's husband still held the seat to her right, so Clive had to sit elsewhere. Molly smiled at Derek and waited for Deacon to pull out her chair. When she looked around, she noticed Deacon's gentlemanly behavior surprised his family. Why? Did they think because he was a tattooed fighter that he'd forgotten his roots or even common courtesy?

Don't glare at them for their ignorance where Deacon is concerned, or you'll be glaring at them all night.

She checked out the beautifully arranged table. Three plates of graduated sizes made up each place setting. The plates had wide silver rims, a four-leaf clover at the top, and a fancy scripted *W* at the bottom. The two forks, two knives, and two spoons were real silver. The bright purple silk napkins matched the tiny vases of fresh flowers centered above each place setting. Baskets of bread and pats of butter in the shape of flowers were scattered down the center of the table. Obviously a lot of planning had gone into the presentation of the table, so Molly wondered if the food would be as impressive. What if they served a fish mousse or something she couldn't choke down?

Deacon nudged her and she looked up at him. "Julianne asked you a question."

"Pardon?"

Julianne flashed her a brittle smile. "Wine?"

"No, thank you."

"Deacon, you're sure you can't have even one glass? This is an excellent Malbec." Julianne held out her glass for Bing to refill.

"He has a one-drink limit when he's in training, remember?" Bing said.

"Oh, right. Never mind. I'll drink your share."

"You don't have alcohol restrictions while taking medication after your surgery?" Deacon asked.

"Not for such a minor procedure," Derek said. "Julianne was only in the surgery center for an hour. She could've still made her four-o'clock tee time."

Deacon stiffened beside her. Silence distorted the air—a more disturbing sound than if someone had been screaming. After a moment, Molly squeezed Deacon's thigh beneath the table. He immediately leaned over and placed his mouth on her ear. "I'm done with this bullshit. We're outta here as soon as the dessert plates are cleared."

Her heart broke for him. His mother continued her manipulative ways even now, forcing Deacon's father to miss his son's fight.

"I realize you're a doctor, Derek, but it was a bit more involved than that," Bing corrected. "Deacon, your mother—"

"Don't wanna hear it," Deacon said curtly. "Are we eating or what? Because if you're gonna drag this damn dinner out another couple of hours, we'll leave now and hit McDonald's on the way back to the hotel."

"McDonald's?" His mother sniffed. "You still go for the low blow. But by all means, if you'd rather eat processed garbage than the food prepared by our chef, feel free to leave."

Deacon looked at his father. "I tried. But I'm done." He pushed his chair back. After he stood, he pulled Molly's chair out and offered his hand to help her to her feet.

Molly didn't make eye contact with anyone as they left the dining room. She just clutched Deacon's hand as he dragged her through the maze of hallways and out the front door.

Deacon didn't say a word for fifteen minutes after they left his parents' house.

They didn't hit the McDonald's drive-thru.

They didn't return to the hotel.

He just drove.

When her stomach growled, she'd had enough of suffering in his oppressive silence. "Deacon."

"Not now."

"Yes, now. I know you're upset—"

"I'm beyond fucking upset, Molly."

"Which is why you need to stop this NASCAR speed drive through the Texas countryside and take us back to the hotel."

The muscle on the right side of his jaw ticced. His knuckles glowed white in the bluish lights of the dashboard.

At the last second, he took the next exit. He pulled into the gravel parking lot of an abandoned gas station. As soon as he'd killed the engine, he bailed out and sprinted up the rise of a small hill.

Molly quietly climbed out of the car, keeping her arms folded over her chest to ward off the sudden chill that owed nothing to the weather. As her leisurely stroll brought her closer to him, her eyes drank in everything that was Deacon. The tight T-shirt that showcased the tattoos on his arms. The jeans that molded to his perfect ass and long legs. The shiny top of his bald head, which reflected the sun's fading rays. Given his spoiling-for-a-fight body language— booted feet braced wide, hands on his hips, shoulders thrown back—she should've retreated.

But she couldn't let him revert to this closed-down behavior after dealing with his family. And she wasn't about to stand ten paces behind him, waiting for his acknowledgment.

Molly marched forward and planted herself in front of him.

His volatile blue eyes met hers.

"Talk to me."

The wind kicked up, blowing her hair all over her face. Before she could bat it aside, Deacon trapped the strands against her head, cradling her face in his hands. "I hate it here. I don't know why the hell I agreed to come. Nothing any of them can say tonight—or tomorrow—will change my mind."

"So this wasn't just a social visit?"

"No. There's a JFW board meeting tomorrow."

Why hadn't he told her about the meeting? Or the upcoming fight? Hadn't he promised he'd be open about everything? Instead it seemed he'd kept her in the dark. On purpose?

"I usually skip the board meetings. I'm a token anyway, unless there's something to vote on. That's why Tag flew to Denver. To try to convince me in person."

"Convince you to do what?"

"To side with him and force a vote in the very near future about the future of JFW. Tag and two shareholders want to sell the company. Our fathers and Clive don't."

"Do you know what you're going to do?"

Deacon shook his head. "It's really complicated, which is why I've avoided it."

"Do you want to talk about it?" She paused. "*Can* you talk about it?"

"I don't know what good it would do." He closed his eyes. "Dammit. This is the kind of stuff I'm supposed to share with you and open up about, isn't it?"

At least he recognized he'd screwed up. "Not if it's against the corporate rules. I don't need to know specifics. But I had no idea you had this turmoil on your mind in addition to all the fight stuff."

"That's because I'm a shitty boyfriend."

"No, you're used to going it alone. But you don't have to do that anymore, Deacon. It's up to me to remind you that I'm here for you. Just like you reminded me in Nebraska."

Deacon kissed her, except not with the raw passion she expected. But that didn't mean the kiss didn't pack a wallop. He rested his forehead to hers. "And it's up to me to take care of my woman. Feed you."

"Since we're in Texas, I expect you could find a Tex-Mex place to your liking."

"That I can do."

CHAPTER THIRTY-TWO

AFTER last night's fiasco with his family, Deacon hadn't been in the mood to do anything. He hadn't wanted to talk. He'd barely eaten anything at the restaurant. When they'd returned to the hotel room, Molly started sawing logs as soon as her head hit the pillow.

He'd been too full of restless energy and anger to sleep. Since he'd be fighting again in a week, he needed to do a full cardio workout and fit in as many conditioning exercises as he could—even without the proper equipment. So he'd hit the hotel workout room and spent the next few hours trying to quiet his head.

Then, this morning, he'd woken Molly up in his favorite way, his face between her thighs. Afterward he'd made love to her slowly, sweetly, dragging it out as long as possible. Touching her everywhere. Being touched in return. Whispering promises and words of love. Feeling such a deep connection to her here in this place that he'd purposely disconnected from.

Then he'd left her exhausted in bed, the keys to the rental car by her e-reader so she wasn't stuck in the hotel all day.

Deacon donned his workout gear and ran the ten miles to the

JFW office complex. Showing up at the meeting sweating and looking like a fighter made the statement he'd wanted it to make.

His dad and uncle hadn't been happy about his unprofessional appearance.

Tag just rolled his eyes.

The opposing sides made their pitches, Tag for selling the company, breaking down the costs of doing business alongside the heavy losses sustained since the price of oil had started a downward spiral from lifetime highs. Deacon's dad gave an impassioned speech about the long history of the oil business with the continual fluctuations in demand and not giving up during hard times.

Currently Bing, Clark, and Clive were against selling. Tag and a pair of board members were for selling. Deacon's vote—when it came to that point—would be the swing vote.

No pressure.

During the late lunch, Deacon made it clear he wouldn't be railroaded into making such a big decision on such short notice. At that point the tension in the room lessened. But Deacon's agitation returned when his dad told him he'd scheduled a JFW soiree, with all the key employees, at the Barclay Country Club for this evening, and attendance was mandatory for all board members.

The meeting adjourned. Running another ten miles might kill him, but at least Maddox couldn't accuse him of slacking on his cardio training.

Molly wasn't in the room when he returned. The car keys were still on the dresser. He fought his instinct not to look out the seventh-story window, but he managed to hold off the resulting dizziness long enough to see her sitting poolside with her e-reader.

He showered quickly and went to her.

She looked up and welcomed him with a big smile that lit up his entire world. "So, how was the corporate world today, dear?"

"Sucky."

"I've been lounging." She stretched. "I slept in after a vivid dream that this hot, sexy muscleman completely ravaged me. His stamina was unreal. He fucked me for two hours, in four positions, and made me come six times."

Deacon picked up her bare foot and kissed her instep. "Babe. I fucked you for one hour, in two positions, and you came three times."

"Who said it was you? Maybe I found alternate entertainment."

He growled.

"You did leave me to my own devices without much warning." Molly leaned closer and nuzzled his whiskery cheeks. "No one's hit on me today, if that worries you."

"I wasn't worried, 'cause you'd hit back."

"I learned from the very best."

"And I left you to your own devices because I thought you'd rather fend for yourself than have me set up a shopping and lunch date with Julianne."

"I oughta blow you for that sweet consideration."

Deacon took her hands in his. "I wish I could say I'm not busy right now, but we need to talk."

Molly's eyes turned wary.

"There's a JFW dinner and cocktail thing tonight at the country club. It'll be boring as fuck. But I have to go."

"Do *I* have to go?"

He sighed. "No. But because I'm a selfish bastard, I'd like it if you came along with me. You'll be left to your own devices a lot tonight, so I'd understand if you skipped it."

"How long do we have to stay?"

"I don't know."

"What else?"

Deacon hesitated and decided to just come right out with it. "Maddox called again."

An even warier look darkened her eyes. "It must be a pretty important issue for him to interrupt your family time."

Family time. He snorted. "This last-minute fight with Watson concerns him."

"It concerns me too, because I didn't know you were planning on fighting again so soon." She paused. "Have you spoken to Riggins about the physical demands of back-to-back bouts? Especially since Ronin had concussion issues last year?"

It was so fucking weird, talking to her about this stuff, because he never discussed his health and career issues with anyone. It'd always been easier to keep his own counsel on everything. "Riggins said since Needham didn't put a mark on me I'm in better-than-average shape to fight again."

"So why the call from Maddox? He doesn't want you to fight now?"

"Maddox knows what's at stake. He knows I *have* to fight. He wants to send me to training camp here in Texas with a trainer named Vasquez, who coached Watson up until last year. If there's anyone who can give me an edge on how to beat Watson, it's his former trainer."

"When would you go?"

Deacon framed her face in his hands. "That's the thing. I wouldn't go back to Denver with you. I'd go to Laredo."

"Until the fight?"

"Would you have a problem with that?"

He watched her struggle with how to answer. "Just that I'll miss you."

"You could come with me."

"Since I've been jet-setting to LA and Texas, I think you've forgotten I have a job. We're gearing up to start three new major campaigns. I keep expecting my phone to ring when Amery actually looks at the schedule."

"This is the sucky part of life with a fighter, Molly. There will be times—"

She pressed her lips to his. "I know. I just didn't think it'd be this soon."

"Let's go upstairs. Sounds like I left you wanting this morning. I have an hour, two positions, and three orgasms to make up for."

MOLLY didn't like that Deacon had sprung another surprise on her.

Within a few minutes of their arrival at Barclay Country Club, Bing had whisked his son off, leaving her in a banquet room with strangers. Deacon's mother hadn't come over to say hello, even when she knew Molly wouldn't know anyone.

People looked at her curiously but didn't offer a smile in greeting.

Fuck it. She smiled at them anyway.

The finger-food buffet didn't look appetizing, so she opted to drink her dinner. At the bar, she ordered a shot of tequila and downed it. Then she ordered a rum and Diet Coke. Drink in hand, she looked around the space, trying not to feel like the unpopular girl in the junior high lunchroom, desperate for a place to sit.

Face it. Life is like that. No matter how old you get.

Thankfully, the room had windows. So Molly was able to focus her attention outward, as if she'd never seen such an impressive expanse of green for a golf course.

Her thoughts bounced all over the place, but they always returned to her man. How he was faring since he hated this kind of social situation.

You sure he hates it? He seemed pretty damn comfortable with it.

No. Molly knew he'd rather be anywhere than here.

A feeling she was very familiar with. Especially right now.

After an hour passed, she wondered if Deacon would notice her absence if she hailed a cab and returned to the hotel.

Tempting to try it.

Needing a change of scenery, Molly slipped out the serving staff's door. But she kept her cell phone in hand, in case she had to fake taking an important call.

Once she'd stepped into the nearly deserted hallway, she could breathe normally again. She tucked her phone into her skirt pocket and turned in the direction opposite the main entrance. Since she seemed to have all the time in the world, she peeked in the windows of the other private banquet rooms. Some were occupied and some were not. Luckily, she'd checked the name of the room she'd just left or else she might've gotten lost. All the faces were unfamiliar, so she wouldn't have known if she'd stumbled into the wrong party room.

It freaked her out that the people in the rooms looked exactly the same. Women smartly dressed, makeup understated—she knew it took a ton of effort and concealer to pull off the "natural" look. The men were in sport coats, beneath that, candy-colored polo shirts that didn't look good on any man, let alone the senior set.

Deacon had grudgingly dressed in clothing other than jeans and a T-shirt. Several pairs of appreciative female eyes had checked him out when they'd walked in. He had epitomized cool, suave, and mysterious in a light gray polo, charcoal-toned dress pants, and a black linen sport coat. He looked nothing like the other country-club clones.

She saw a tiny sign that said LADIES' POWDER ROOM—no gauche wording like *bathroom* at the Barclay Country Club. After she stepped inside, she stopped.

Oh wow. This place was straight out of the 1980s, with a mauve and gray color scheme. A long countertop held an assortment of beauty items. A cushioned stool had been tucked under the counter—possibly for a powder-room attendant?

She turned a corner and discovered a lounging area. With no mirrors or sinks, it seemed a waste of space. She lowered onto the chaise and almost bounced upright again. Talk about springy. She bounced a couple more times and grinned. This could be a fun place for a quickie. If she could ever find her wayward boyfriend.

Closing her eyes, she pictured them sneaking in here—hot and wild for each other. They'd undress only enough to serve their need for instant connection and release.

She'd push Deacon on his back on the chaise. The intensity in his eyes when she rode him always got to her. Would they be mouth-to-mouth, kissing frantically, swallowing each other's groans? Would Deacon have his big hands around her hips, guiding her movements? Or would he twine her hair through his fingers, forcing her gaze to remain on his face as he manipulated her clit?

Need surged through her. When she and Deacon were body to body, he made her feel beautiful, sexy, wanted, and loved. How she wished they could return to the hotel and shut out the world like they had this afternoon. Another curl of heat unfurled as she remembered Deacon's near desperation to be inside her and how thoroughly he'd reminded them both of their intimate connection.

The door swung open, and female voices sliced through her solitude.

Molly stayed put. She was here first. Maybe they wouldn't stick around long and she could go back to brooding in silence.

"Love your shoes, Julianne," a woman gushed.

Great. Of all the people it could be, it had to be Deacon's mother.

"Thank you. Lola, my personal shopper at Neiman's, is a godsend."

"So what were you saying before?"

"Oh, just that I don't understand why he brought her to this JFW dinner. It's not like he's paying any attention to her."

"I've seen Bing herding Deacon around," the other woman said. "What's he up to?"

A faucet turned on and off.

"Bing wants to introduce him to key employees to drive home the point that their jobs would be in jeopardy if JFW is sold."

"Smart. You've got to be happy that Deacon isn't shirking his responsibilities for a change."

Shirking his responsibilities? The man trained like a fiend seven days a week. He defined disciplined.

"He shouldn't have any responsibilities in the first place. I don't understand why his grandfather insisted Deacon have a seat on the board. He's not exactly . . ."

Not exactly what, Mama Westerman? Bright? Or easily manipulated?

"Richard said Bing has offered Deacon his position at JFW if he verbally commits now to take over when he's done fighting."

A shiver zipped down Molly's spine. Deacon's words to Maddox yesterday—*fighting for a living ain't my only option*—seemed more ominous.

"*When* being the operative word for him. Deacon. He won't give up fighting. And then there's . . . her."

Her has a name, bitch.

"So it's serious?"

"Bing says so." Julianne sniffed. "Everyone is acting like I'm supposed to be happy that he has a girlfriend after all these years."

"You're not?"

"Honestly, I thought part of the reason Deacon's always been so closed off was because he was closeted."

A gasp sounded. "No."

"Yes. Wouldn't you suspect that your son preferred men if he hadn't brought a girl home in fifteen years?"

"Julianne. You poor thing. Dealing with that worry in addition to everything else you've dealt with over the years."

Molly rolled her eyes. *What a heaping load of crap.*

"Does it make me an awful person to say I'd rather he was gay than try to understand what he sees in that woman? Sweet lord."

"Who is she?"

"Nobody. Beautiful women hang all over these fighters. They hang all over *him*. I've seen the pictures. So she wasn't at all what I expected."

And once again, you're a disappointment. You should be used to it by now.

"Well," the other woman said in a drawn-out drawl, "I hate to point out the obvious, but you *know* what she sees in him."

"Oh, I know, all right. Last night before dinner? Deacon couldn't keep his hands off her. It was such a vulgar display. So I'm betting her appeal to him is her whorish behavior." Julianne sighed. "Of course, she probably thinks that by being his whore, he'll marry her. Then she can get her chubby hands on his money."

Enough was enough.

Molly walked around the corner, straight to the sink next to Deacon's mother. She gave the woman credit; her expression didn't change a whit when she realized Molly had overheard the entire conversation.

Probably between the plastic surgery and the Botox, she can't move her facial muscles much anyway.

That thought brought on a smug smile. "I do feel the need to correct you, Julianne." Molly washed her hands and reached for a fresh hand towel. "Whores get paid to fuck. Sluts do it because they like sex. I fall into the latter category rather than the former." Then Molly sailed out of the bathroom with her head held high.

Screw you, Julianne Westerman. You are a horrible person and an awful mother. Deacon already washed his hands of you, and now so do I.

Molly nearly laughed out loud. She'd literally washed her hands in front of the woman.

Deacon walked out of the private room just as she walked in.

"Hey there."

"Hey." He pulled her into an alcove in the hallway. "Where have you been?"

"Needed a change of scenery. Why? Did you miss me?"

"Yeah." He kissed her. "You sure you're all right?"

No. I hate that your mother is a sorry excuse for a human being. "Just tired. Someone got me up early." She forced a smile. "But I'll swap sex for sleep any day."

"Me too." Deacon kissed her with infinite sweetness and then nearly blistered her lips with his sudden burst of passion.

Head spinning, she clung to him as he pressed her against the wall.

"Seriously, Deacon. This is not an alley behind some low-rent nightclub. This is a country club. Stop embarrassing yourself by acting like a horny seventeen-year-old," Julianne hissed behind them.

He'd broken the kiss the instant she'd interrupted them. But he didn't acknowledge his mother in any way. He kept those hypnotic blue eyes burning into Molly's.

Julianne harrumphed, and her footsteps faded into the distance.

Before Molly said anything, her cell phone buzzed in her skirt pocket. She pulled it out and checked the caller ID. Hardwick Designs. "Hello?"

"Molly. Thank the goddess I got you," Presley said. "I know you're with Deacon in Texas, and I wouldn't call if it wasn't an absolute emergency. But we're in major crisis mode here."

"We?"

"Me and Amery."

If Amery was at the office on a Friday night, something was majorly wrong. "What's the crisis?" Presley started talking so fast Molly couldn't understand a word. "Whoa. Slow down. Give me one second." She gave Deacon an apologetic look. "Sorry. I have to take this."

"Sounds like it. Come find me when you're done."

"Pres? Hang on until I get to a place I can talk." She cut down the hallway. "Tell me the problem."

"Something is wrong with my hard drive. So no big deal, right? I figured I'd get the files off the cloud service and we'd look at them on Amery's computer because I back up every night. But we can't access anything on the cloud service."

Presley went into a detailed explanation of everything they'd done to try to access the files. When they'd called the help line, the person told them the account didn't exist.

"What project are you looking for files on?"

"Okada. And it's the new files that Maggie sent on Tuesday. I saved them to my hard drive and then uploaded them to the cloud."

"Amery doesn't have a copy of them on her computer?"

"No. She hasn't seen the specs. Since Ronin had to go to San Francisco, she thought she'd work on them tonight. She called me in a panic when she couldn't retrieve the files, and I came down to help."

That was weird. "Is there a chance your computer got a virus?"

"There's always a chance, but I run the antivirus programs for that every Friday afternoon."

"You did that today?"

"Yes. And nothing popped."

"You didn't do a hard backup copy on thumb drives or a file sharer for those files?"

"No. Okada is strict about that."

Molly had been afraid something like this would happen. "Let's start with your computer."

For the next fifteen minutes, Molly walked her through each step, backtracking, but nothing happened except additional frustration.

If the heavy breathing on the phone was any indication, Presley had reached the freak-out zone. She said, "I hate this. Why can't I figure this shit out?"

"Because if you were a computer-tech expert, you'd be working for a company that troubleshoots technical problems."

"If we did our design work on a Mac, we wouldn't have this problem," Presley snapped.

"Bullshit," Amery said in the background.

Molly held her breath, waiting for their ongoing argument to gain traction. When it didn't, she said, "It'll be fine. Just calm down."

Amery kept yakking at Presley while Molly was trying to tell her what to do next.

"All right, all right, all right! Just stop talking at once, both of you," Presley pleaded.

"Pres, since I'll have you switch and try to access everything on my computer, I need to know that you're thinking clearly. I don't need you randomly clicking shit in a panic."

A puff of air exploded in the phone. "I am calm."

"Good. You're at my computer now?"

"Yeah. What's your main password?" Presley asked.

"OU812."

"Seriously? That is a killer password. And now you'll have to change it. Sorry. Okay, I'm on. What next?"

Molly walked her through three possible solutions and none worked. So she'd have to resort to telling them her secret. "Put me on speaker."

"Done."

"Hey, Mol. Sorry to pull you away," Amery said.

"No worries. This party sucks ass. Anyway, see the mirrored tile icon on the screen? Click on it. Same password."

"What is this?"

"A backup program in case the cloud doesn't work. Wednesday night before I left I backed up yours and Amery's hard drives and everything on the cloud to a different cloud. So you should be able to access it."

The keyboard clicked. Then Presley said, "Motherfucking hell yeah. It's all there. Every bit of it."

"Molly, you are a genius, and I have no idea what I would do without you," Amery said. "Seriously. You cannot ever leave."

Molly laughed, but it felt damn good to be needed as an integral part of Hardwick Designs. "I'm not a genius; I'm just doing my job." Which meant she never wanted to be accused of *not* doing her job, so in her paranoia, she had set up a third backup program—not that she'd admit that unless she absolutely had to.

Amery declared, "I'm giving you a raise. We'll talk as soon as you get back."

Holy crap. She hadn't seen that one coming. "Okay."

"You saved our bacon by going whole hog with a secondary backup," Presley said.

Both Molly and Amery groaned at Presley's pun.

"How are things going with Deacon's family?" Amery asked.

"They're a bunch of rich assholes, for the most part. We're at a country club right now, and I want to stab myself in the eye with the tiny olive fork so I have an excuse to leave."

"Try to remember you're in love with him, not his family."

"So noted, boss."

Guilt prodded her. If Amery had forgone a trip with Ronin to catch up on work, then Molly should be in Denver working alongside her, not stuck in Texas, where she seemed to be of little value to anyone.

She needed to talk to Deacon right away.

CHAPTER THIRTY-THREE

THE morning had started out with a bang, but this night was fizzling.

Immediately after they'd arrived, Deacon's dad started dragging him off to meet people. When it seemed like he might be able to spend more than five minutes with Molly, some crisis had occurred at Hardwick Designs, so she'd disappeared with her cell phone to do her job and troubleshoot the problem.

He wasn't sure how much time had passed since Molly had left him waiting by the door, but he was bored out of his fucking mind. It led him to imagine how Molly must have felt, left to her own devices all day and most of tonight.

He'd make it up to her.

In trying to avoid the bar—too tempting to get liquored up—and steering clear of his dad's intention to introduce him to everyone and their fucking dog, he meandered down the hallway.

It'd been years since he'd stepped foot in the Barclay Country Club. Looked like the club still put up pictures of members and their accomplishments. Even club members' grandchildren's accomplishments were lauded.

These people needed to get a damn life.

But he couldn't help smiling when he saw the newest photo on the wall. A picture of Warren after he'd won the annual junior division golf championship.

Deacon meandered, recognizing few faces in the pictures. He stopped when he reached the last grouping of photos and saw a picture of his granddad at a ribbon-cutting ceremony. The caption read:

Jefferson Westerman, at the official opening of the new golf-cart cleaning facility, generously donated by his sons, Bing and Clark, of JFW Development, in his name.

The picture was at least twenty years old. Strange to think his granddad had always looked that age to him.

There was an even older picture next to it, with the entire Westerman family. No caption indicating the occasion. But Deacon had a vague memory of the official family photo. Mostly of Clive bawling like a baby so the photographer had to retake the picture a million times. In the photo, he and Dante sat side by side, dressed identically. Even studying the picture now, he didn't know which one of the blond mop-headed twins was him.

Next in line was a picture of Tag in a cap and gown. The caption listed him as class valedictorian. He snorted. Tag had always been an overachiever.

Interesting there wasn't a picture of Clive and his accomplishments. Oh right, because he was a fucking no-talent weasel suckling at the teat of JFW.

The last image with the Westerman name caught his eye. The caption card beneath the picture read:

The Westerman twins, Deacon and Dante, enjoying a round of golf with their grandfather, Jefferson.

Deacon went utterly still. As shocking as it was to see himself with hair, it was even more shocking to realize that he'd seen that face recently. And not in the mirror.

He raced down the hallway and froze in front of the picture of his cousin Warren.

The kid looked so much like the Westerman twins at that age, it was uncanny. A warning zipped down his spine and he scrutinized the photo more closely. It went beyond a first-cousin family resemblance—Warren had been adopted and he shouldn't look anything like them.

But Warren didn't look a little like them; he looked *exactly* like them.

Head spinning, Deacon fell back onto the bench against the wall and stared at the picture, unable to tear his gaze away from it. He'd lost his virginity at age nineteen. So even if he'd knocked that first girl up . . . Warren was fifteen—not eleven—so the math didn't work.

But it worked for Dante.

He remembered his anger, guilt, and jealousy the night Dante had died, after he'd confessed he'd lost his virginity and he'd been having sex with some girl Deacon didn't know.

A girl who'd gotten pregnant?

A girl who'd given the child up for adoption?

It couldn't be coincidence that his aunt Annabelle, who'd tried for years to have a child, had adopted that baby boy.

Which meant . . . his mother had known Dante had left a child behind. But why wouldn't she raise the child herself?

Because she's a selfish, mean, nasty bitch. She didn't want you. Why would she want a sniveling kid?

His stomach twisted. Did his dad know about this?

There was only one way to find out.

By the time Deacon reached the private dining room, he'd hit the boiling point. He stalked over to where his mother sat beside his father. He looked around. Didn't look like his mother had invited her own sister and her family to the party.

Because someone like Clive or Tag, who'd known him and Dante growing up, might see the resemblance in Warren—even when Deacon himself had blocked it out.

Last night Warren had said: *I wasn't supposed to come tonight, but I just had to meet you.*

And Clive, when asked about his appearance: *Of course I wasn't invited, but when has that ever stopped me?*

Tag's surprise this morning: *No one told me about the family dinner last night.*

His mother had gone to such trouble to keep it under wraps. Too bad he was about to blow the lid off her motherfucking world. He faced her and said in a tone that hinted at his rage, "Julianne. A word. Now. Outside."

She set down her china teacup. "Deacon. Don't be rude."

"You haven't seen rude yet."

His dad looked at him strangely. "What's going on?"

"I need to talk to you both. Privately."

"Bing, dear, do you mind handling it? Gina and I were in the middle of—"

"I'm sure Dad would love to hear what I have to say about my *cousin* Warren. Since it appears he's inherited his grandfather's love of golf."

Julianne didn't miss a beat. "Gina, will you excuse us?"

"Of course."

Deacon started to walk out of the room.

"Where are we going?" Julianne demanded.

He whirled around and loomed over her. "I'd suggest a sound-proofed room so your friends don't learn the truth about what a lying, conniving bitch you are." He stormed down the hallway, so focused on not losing his shit any more than he already had that he nearly plowed Molly over when she stepped in front of him.

"Deacon?"

"Not now."

"But I need to talk to you. It's important."

Deacon stopped and glared at his parents, who'd hustled past him and ducked into a room to the left. "So is this. I have to deal with them and this situation I've been kept in the fucking dark about. I'll find you once I'm done."

"Do you need me to . . . ?"

"No."

As soon as he was in the room and had shut the door, Deacon exploded. "I don't have to ask if it's true, because I can see it with my own eyes. Warren is Dante's kid, isn't he?"

His mother looked over at his father.

"No. You look me in the fucking eye and tell me why you'd keep something like this from me."

Her eyes held the mean glint Deacon knew so well. "Shall I start with the fact you'd already run off when the girl approached me about her pregnancy? We didn't know where you were for years, Deacon. We weren't sure we'd ever see you again. So I was supposed to . . . what? Try to track down a sixteen-year-old runaway so I could ask his advice on what to do about his dead brother's unborn child?"

"Julianne," his father murmured.

Deacon slapped his hands on the table in front of his father. "How long have *you* known?"

His dad rubbed the furrow between his brows. "I found out about two weeks after you came back."

"And it didn't bother you that she kept that from you? That she willingly gave your grandson—your only physical link to your dead son—to her sister to raise?"

"Of course it bothered me. But what was I supposed to do at that point? Rip the boy away from the only parents he'd ever known? Fracture our family even more? Annabelle and Derek adore Warren. He has a happy life and everything he'd ever want or need."

Rage continued to build, and Deacon knew he hadn't hit the point of explosion yet. He didn't bother to keep his voice down, his fury absolute. "Annabelle and Derek could provide for him better than you could have? Bull. Shit." He shot his mother a disgusted look. "All because Julianne didn't want to be called *Grandma*. God forbid anyone ever thought she could be old enough to have a grandchild. That was it, wasn't it? Or maybe, since Warren's birth mother wasn't a society girl, you were afraid her lower-class traits would appear in your grandson? And how would you ever explain that at the country-club brunch?"

"Deacon," his father barked. "That is enough."

"You're trying to muzzle me because you know it's true. If Aunt Annabelle thinks her sister arranged for a private adoption out of love for her, or the child, she's got a fucking screw loose. Julianne has never done a goddamn thing if it hasn't benefitted her. She thought providing Aunt Annabelle the child she'd wanted for so long made her selfless, but it's the most selfish thing she's ever done. Julianne didn't want the boy, but she couldn't quite let him go either."

"You have no idea what I went through," his mother retorted. "Your recklessness killed two people, Deacon."

Recklessness? It was a fucking accident.

"The scandal that followed . . . You were a surly teen who didn't see it, and even if you had, you wouldn't have cared. It destroyed our lives. We had to move because the hatred for us in the community was so thick that I couldn't show my face anywhere. Everyone—and I mean everyone—assumed your father had bought off the authorities. It didn't matter that he hadn't. The mere suggestion of it made him just as guilty as you in their eyes." She took a breath. "So I lost one son, my other son vanished—and don't think for a second that your disappearance didn't cause new and ugly rumors. And then this young girl of fifteen showed up on my front doorstep claiming to be pregnant with my dead son's child. What kind of girl starts having sex at that age? She was a *child*, pregnant with a child."

"I'm surprised you believed the kid was Dante's."

"I'm not a fool," she snapped. "I'd seen this happen before in our circle; a rich man dies and a pregnant whore comes forward claiming the child is his. Before I offered her any financial compensation, I set up an in-utero DNA test. Those results validated her claim. I provided her with a safe, discreet place to live for the duration of her pregnancy, and I provided a loving future for the child she did not want."

"How much?"

"How much what?"

"How much money did her silence cost you?"

"It doesn't matter now if you know. I paid her a quarter of a million dollars. She signed every single legal stipulation without hesitation."

"Of course she did. She was fifteen fucking years old. That money probably sounded like a fortune to her." He laughed bitterly. "The joke was on her. She walked away from a real fortune by not holding on to a JFW heir."

"Her stupidity was no concern of mine—then or now."

"I'll tell you one thing, if I would've known? I wouldn't have *let* you give Dante's kid away."

"Oh, spare me your indignation." She sneered at him. "What kind of help would you have been, raising a baby? None. You were born with a silver spoon in your mouth, Deacon. You didn't have the skills to be anything to that boy except a fair-weather uncle. You would've disappointed him as much as you'd disappointed everyone else."

"Goddammit, Julianne, that's enough. You don't get to talk to him that way."

She whirled on her husband, her jaw nearly hanging on the floor. "You're taking his side?"

"There are no sides. He is our son."

"He is being an ass, as usual," she hissed. "I hate that he's standing there in judgment of me when he didn't have to deal with the consequences of his actions! We did. We had to start over. He shows up, looking like a thug, full of contempt for me, for you, for everything we ever provided him. For the future in the family business that he refused to be a part of. And now, because of a legal technicality, he can destroy it."

Her venom paralyzed him. And like the snake she was, she slithered forward, eager to sink her fangs in for the kill.

"What a slap in the face it is to your granddad that you changed the name you were born with. The name that entitles you to the inheritance that means you don't have to hold down a real job. Deacon McConnell can work out, add more tattoos, get in the ring for three or four minutes and prove he's tough. Why your grandfather didn't cut you off astounds me."

And he was done. With all of this. For good. "I'll tell you why Granddad didn't cut me loose. Because when I came back after bein' gone for years, he asked me why I left. He was the only one who did. Until Molly, he's the only one I told."

Her eyes flashed fear. She shook her head—as if asking him to keep quiet.

Fuck that. And fuck her.

Deacon opened his mouth, and his mother moved in front of her husband. "Don't listen to him, Bing. He's caused enough problems over the years. Don't let him make more for us now."

"Deacon." His father's eyes met his. "Tell me."

"Granddad knew. I don't know how, but he was the one person who understood the kind of loss I suffered after Dante died. He knew there'd be no recovering from it."

"That's because Dad had a twin who died when he was ten. He never spoke of him."

Now it made sense.

"What did you tell him, son?"

"What my mother said to me the night you left me with her." Deacon looked over at her. "She told me she wished I would've died instead of Dante. I'd known for months I repulsed her every time she looked at me. But to hear her say that she hated me?" He took a breath. "Then she told me everyone would be better off if I disappeared because losing my family was what I deserved after killing her son."

Silence.

Then his father made the most anguished noise Deacon had ever heard. He wheeled around, loomed over his wife, and yelled, "How could you?" right in her face.

"It's not what you think."

"Then explain it to me, Julianne! Explain to me why everything always comes back to you? I trusted you. I stood by you."

"But it's not—"

"No buts! Did you, or did you not, tell our only surviving son that you hated him and wished he were dead?"

Tears rolled down her face.

"Answer me, goddammit!"

"Yes, but I wasn't in my right mind! I don't remember half of what I said! God, Bing. I was in such a fog of grief—"

"Get. Out. Of. Here."

She dashed her tears away. "Bing! You don't mean that."

His father's face was pasty, and he looked to be in shock.

Deacon locked eyes with his mother. "Go. Give him some space."

She backed away slowly. Then she turned and ran from the room.

The vindication Deacon expected to feel didn't happen.

His dad lowered himself into the closest chair. Deacon followed suit.

After a bit, Deacon said, "Dad?"

"I . . . didn't know."

Not an accusatory *Why didn't you tell me?* "I know. What can I do now?"

His father reached for his hand. "Just sit with me while I try to make sense of this."

"Sure."

Deacon tried not to show his impatience after they'd been sitting there in silence for half an hour. By the time another thirty minutes passed, he was damn near ready to crawl out of his skin.

But this was his father's way—quiet contemplation. Dante had been the same way.

So does that mean you take after your mother?

No. *Fuck* no.

As much as he wanted to find Molly and tell her everything that'd happened tonight, it'd keep. She was strong enough to hold her own among this superficial crowd. And for the first time, maybe ever, Deacon didn't walk away from his dad when he needed him.

MOLLY had been pacing in the hallway since Deacon had barreled past her. His rudeness should've pissed her off, but it didn't. It scared her.

She'd never seen him like that.

So she'd heard the shouting inside the room but not the actual words exchanged. Whatever was going on . . . she knew it was bad.

Her conscience, the part that loved him, urged her to go to him.

But he had made it clear he didn't want her involved.

Isn't this the way it goes with Deacon? He keeps you in the dark. He kept from you that the reason he agreed to come to Texas was for a JFW board meeting—for a board you didn't even know he was on. You had no idea that he'd agreed to fight Watson—and you find out the same time as his family—the family he despises? Then he drops the bombshell about staying in Texas for training camp? Not to mention he ditched you today— and he abandoned you tonight. Now he's rude and uncommunicative and you just shrug it off? Offer excuses for his behavior? When he's exhibiting the same closemouthed behavior that sent you running from him the first time?

She tried not to let the doubts get a foothold, but they already had. With each minute that passed, they only grew stronger.

"I'd ask why you're hiding—but I suspect a poor farm girl like you didn't get invited to many parties like this growing up in a cornfield and you don't know how to act."

Molly faced Clive. "How astute."

"I try." Clive's gaze flicked to the door, then back to her. "But you aren't hiding because like Deacon you have zero social graces. So the question is, why are you out here and your beloved is in there?"

She said nothing.

"Sounds like a family fight and someone is unhappy. I'd ask you what's going on, but it's obvious you don't know."

"How can you be sure I wasn't tasked with watching the door so they didn't get interrupted during their family meeting?"

"Because you're pacing. If you knew what they were talking about, you wouldn't be outside the door, trying so hard to listen in, would you?"

"Are you always such a know-it-all asshole?" Molly asked in a saccharine tone.

"Pretty much." He leaned closer. "And doesn't it rankle that you're not allowed in the inner sanctum? For being the first girl-friend Deacon has brought home in years, you don't rate high enough to be involved in this family discussion?"

Stung, because he'd zeroed in on her insecurity, she retorted, "If you know so much about what's going on, why don't you tell me?"

"Because it's so much more fun to watch you twist in the wind and freak out about not knowing."

God. Clive was just like her cousins.

"I saw how you reacted last night when Deacon spoke of his

upcoming fight." His eyes gleamed with malice. "That was the first you'd heard of it. So I have to wonder if my cousin tells you anything important. How long were you together before he told you about Dante and the accident?"

Molly's face heated.

"Ah, a while, then. Even longer, I'll bet, before he gave you the rest of the story."

Don't listen to him.

"So are you one of those women who will excuse anything that 'Con Man' the big-time fighter says or does just because you're so thankful he's with you?" Clive gave her a cruel once-over. "Even without the trust fund, Deacon is out of your league."

"You know nothing about the man he is now."

"On the contrary, I know he is violent and self-centered. He's got an immense ego and a chip on his shoulder the size of Texas. He's the same privileged prick he's always been. Nothing changes with him. He does what he wants and damn the consequences."

Ooh. Sounds like Clive has his cousin pegged, doesn't it?

The voices in the room escalated.

"The smartest thing for you to do is to walk away from him. Because sooner or later, he will drive you away. That's who he is and what he does."

"Why do you care?"

"That's the thing—I don't care. But this whole situation is a train wreck, and I can't look away."

"I'd think you'd want him in a good place, Clive."

His eyes narrowed into snakelike slits. "Why?"

"So he doesn't throw his support behind Tag to sell JFW and you're out on your ass."

"Deacon telling you confidential information about a possible upcoming official vote will be seen as a breach of confidentiality, and he won't be allowed to vote. That may even get him kicked off the board." His grin defined evil, and she shivered. "You just couldn't help yourself, could you? Proving me wrong that Deacon *does* talk to you about important things."

Oh god. How had she fallen for that? "But—"

The door opened and Julianne hustled out, tears streaming down her face.

Clive intercepted her. "Aunt Julianne? What's going on?"

She shook her head. "Personal family business that he just—" Julianne glared at Molly. "Why are you still hanging around?"

"I thought Deacon might need me."

"Why don't you be a good little girlfriend and go wait for him in bed at the hotel?" she snapped.

Molly wanted to crawl into a hole. But first she wanted to puke.

Except you brought this on yourself. She thinks you're fine being Deacon's sexual plaything.

Dammit. Stuff like this always came back to bite her in the ass.

Before she could explain, Clive had his arm around Julianne's shoulders and was leading her away.

When ten more minutes passed and Deacon still hadn't appeared, Molly had enough of waiting around and supposing.

She had plans of her own to make.

CHAPTER THIRTY-FOUR

THE next morning Tag fell into step with Deacon as he started down the hallway at the JFW office building.

"You're early." He checked out Deacon's clothing—the sport coat and dress slacks he'd worn to the country club last night. "And you don't look like a bum. What's up? Did you just get out of jail or something?"

"Nope." Deacon punched the elevator button and leaned against the wall. "Fuck, I'm tired."

"Molly keep you up all night?"

Deacon scowled at him.

"Not the kiss-and-tell type. Gotta respect that." Tag leaned next to him. "How was Molly this morning?"

"I imagine she was fine. Why?"

"Imagine? Weren't you with her at the hotel?"

"No. I had to deal with the fallout after confronting Julianne and Dad. It took longer than I expected." The details weren't something he wanted to share with his cousin.

Tag stepped in front of him. "But you were with Molly last night? After the party?"

He narrowed his eyes. "Why're you bein' so fucking nosy about where I was?"

"Answer the question, Deacon."

"No. I didn't go back to the hotel last night. Like I said, some shit came to a head with my folks. Dad refused to go home. Then, when I went to find Molly to tell her what was going on, she'd already left. When I returned to Dad, he'd decided to down half a bottle of Jameson. He demanded I bring him here to his office. Then he spent an hour puking his guts out. Freaked me out, so I ended up staying with him." And after his twenty-mile run, his lack of sleep the night before, the stress with the fight, finding out about Warren, the board meeting shit, it was more like he passed out when he hit the couch in the reception area upstairs at one a.m. "Why?"

"When was the last time you talked to Molly?"

"Before the thing went down with my folks."

"How did she seem then?"

Fucking questions. "What do you mean, how did she seem?"

"Was she upset? Mad? Still crying?"

"Why was she crying?" His gut clenched. In that moment he knew he'd fucked up yet again.

Tag loomed over him. "From what I saw, you left her alone almost the whole goddamn night at the club, and then you didn't bother to tell her what was going on between you and your parents. Then Clive got his hooks into her, so why the fuck do you *think* she was crying, douche bag?"

"What did Clive say to her?"

"He said by you talking to her about a possible board vote, you violated your confidentiality agreement and he'd see you thrown off the board."

"I'd fucking welcome that," he snarled.

"But Molly doesn't know that, does she? She thinks she screwed that up for you."

Fear began to form thorns in his stomach.

"You wanna hear what she said to me when I saw her waiting for a cab? 'Now I know where I stand with him, Tag. Behind him, not beside him.'"

Deacon inhaled and unclenched his fists. "I am one man. Yesterday and last night I was pulled in three different directions."

"And none of them pulled you toward her? Then you're an even bigger idiot than I imagined."

Rage and shame filled him. In his frustration, he turned to punch the wall.

But Tag stepped forward and then crumpled inward when his belly absorbed the impact of Deacon's fist.

"Why did you do that?" Deacon demanded, taken aback.

"The wall is cement, dipshit," he wheezed. "You would've broken your fucking hand."

"So you took one for the team?"

"I've got an iron gut." Tag winced when he stood up straight. "You aren't thinking clearly. You haven't been since you stepped boots in Texas."

"You have the fucking balls to say that to me? You're the goddamn one pushing me to be here to support you on this 'sell JFW' bullshit." And now that Deacon knew his dad had Warren as an heir? No fucking way would he take Warren's future from him. "Officially, I'm no longer backing you, Tag. Selling isn't the answer, and you know it."

Tag scrubbed his hands over his face. "I know. Hearing Uncle Bing speak yesterday . . . I figured it'd be an uphill battle. Now I'm sorry I pushed you. I didn't mean to set you at odds with your dad, D. The truth is, nothing is gonna change with JFW in the immediate future, so go deal with what you *can* change. Don't fuck up your fight career because you fucked up with her. Just go fix it."

Deacon turned and ran toward the door. He didn't stop even when Tag yelled, "You're welcome."

★   ★   ★

FIFTEEN minutes later Deacon sat on the bed in their hotel room, Molly's note in his hand.

> *Deacon,*
>
> *You didn't come back to the hotel last night. While I understand you had family matters on your mind, I at least deserved the courtesy of a phone call.*

Fuck.

> *I don't know what's going on with your parents, with your board position and future at JFW, or what your plans are for after the Watson fight. I won't berate you for keeping me on the sidelines of your decisions, but I can't take this anymore either. I've gone back to Denver, where I belong. You have too many things on your mind and too much going on in your life right now to make our relationship a priority. That's not a judgment call from me, but the truth.*

What the ever-lovin' fuck? Was she breaking up with him? He read on.

> *You have an incredible chance to prove yourself in the ring and to get to the next level in your career. So go to the camp in Laredo and train with Vasquez. Win against Watson.*
>
> *You'll be angry when you read this—but please let it go. Please don't call me and leave pissed-off voice mails. Please don't hop on a plane and return to Denver to confront me in person, because we both know*

you'd eventually blame me if you're not prepared for the
fight.
     So take care of yourself. I'm sorry it came to this.
We both know it'd be best if we don't see each other for
a while.

                                        M~

     "Wrong. You'll be seeing me a lot goddamn sooner than you
think, babe."

CHAPTER THIRTY-FIVE

BOOKING a last-minute flight meant Molly had two stops and a four-hour layover. It'd take her eight hours to reach Denver.

The lack of sleep the previous night caught up with her, and she managed to sneak in a nap at the airport. But the screaming baby two rows behind her on the last leg of the trip home kept her wide-awake, giving her time to think. She didn't want to think. She wanted to block the past forty-eight hours from her memory banks entirely.

When she arrived in baggage claim at DIA, she remembered she'd ridden to the airport with Deacon. So it looked like she'd be taking a cab home.

As Molly stood in front of her apartment building with her luggage, she had a flashback of being in this exact same spot after Grams's funeral, waiting for Deacon to park her car. Hard to believe that'd been less than two months ago.

After she'd showered and unpacked, she turned on her cell phone. She hadn't wanted to deal with Deacon or anyone else while she'd been traveling.

Only one missed call—and not from Deacon. Disappointment

slugged her in the gut. She listened to the voice mail Amery had left three hours ago.

"Hey, Mol. Got your text that you were coming back a day early." Amery paused on the line. "With Ronin out of town, we need to discuss my expectations about the projects on tap this week. Come to the penthouse around nine. I'll meet you at the Black Arts main entrance. Just text me when you get this message."

Shit. Amery wasn't requesting her appearance; she was demanding it. The longer the woman was married to Ronin, the more she became like him.

Good thing she hadn't cracked open a bottle of wine since she'd be getting in her car.

To kill time, Molly jotted down a grocery list. No need to worry about Deacon's dietary needs now. That was her tipping point. She'd managed to keep from breaking down, besides a few escaped tears here and there, but this time she didn't even bother to try. She rested her forehead against the freezer door and sobbed.

Why did everything Deacon had told her about his relationship with his family seem meaningless in the face of his dismissive actions? That wasn't the Deacon she knew. That wasn't the man she'd fallen in love with. That wasn't how a man who claimed to love her should treat her.

As the rush of tears slowed to a trickle, her misery didn't cease. But she'd have put on a brave front for the next week as she figured out where she and Deacon went from here. At least she had the excuse of Deacon staying in Texas to keep people from knowing the truth.

Which is what? You left him because he hurt your feelings?

No. She left him because their relationship shouldn't be a burden to him, and that's how it'd started to feel. That's how she'd started to feel too. She'd suffered through those feelings for too many years to not have it affect her so deeply.

Since she'd be in a work situation, Molly forced herself to put on makeup and dress appropriately. After slipping on her favorite pink knit halter dress and flip-flops, she grabbed her keys and tore off her grocery list—might as well get that out of the way. Halfway to her car, she lamented the fact she'd backslid into a woman who had nothing better to do than grocery shop on a Saturday night.

Cranking the tunes in her car helped calm her so she didn't obsess over Amery's summons. Or why she hadn't heard from Deacon.

Stop it. You told him not to contact you. What did you expect?

A miracle, apparently.

By the time she reached the main door at Black Arts, Amery was waiting for her.

"Punctual, as usual."

"Not smart to keep the boss waiting."

Thankfully, Amery was too busy fussing with the excessive security system to comment on Molly's bloodshot eyes rimmed with dark circles.

They took the elevator to the fifth floor and then switched to the private elevator for the penthouse. She'd been to Ronin and Amery's place only two other times; Ronin was a fiercely private man.

Amery seemed preoccupied, which set Molly right back on edge. "Did you bring me here to fire me or something?"

"You're funny." She inserted a key into the panel and hit a button that had no floor number on it.

Holy shit. Amery was taking her to the roof. To the sanctuary she'd heard about but hadn't seen firsthand.

"You're definitely freaking me out, Mrs. Black."

Amery didn't look at her until the doors opened. "Why don't you wait by the pool? It's past the garden through the big door. Can't miss it."

"Amery—"

"Go." She practically shoved Molly out of the elevator. "And please don't be mad at me." The elevator doors closed.

Why would Molly be mad at her? Dammit. What was going on?

Standing here glaring at the elevator door won't answer your questions.

Molly breathed in deeply and exhaled before moving. As she walked down a short foyer, the rich, earthy scent of growing things filled her lungs. No lights illuminated the path through the garden. Kind of dangerous, but Ronin and Amery were the only ones who usually came up here, and they were used to navigating in the dark.

The vibrant red door separating the spaces was ajar. She pushed it open, and the sweet scent of flowers rolled over her. When she crossed the threshold, darkness was no longer an issue. Tiki torches lit up the deck around the pool. But what she saw in the pool made her jaw drop. Dozens of candles floated in the water, creating a warm glow. With each step, the floral scent became stronger.

She slowly turned around, overwhelmed by the dozens of vases of roses. When she faced forward again, he emerged from the shadows. Startled, she jumped back and closed her eyes.

He's not real. Deacon isn't here. It's just a shadow.

"Molly. Babe. Open your eyes. You're too close to the side of the pool, and it's making me nervous that you're gonna fall in."

That forced her to look at him. "What are you doing here?"

"I didn't like that you left me."

Deacon-speak for he missed her. "I'm surprised you noticed I was gone."

Not nice. But it was true.

"Well, that was a really fucking helpful note you left me as to where you'd gone. But not why."

Molly squared her shoulders. "Bullshit. You know why I left. How many times have we been in this situation?"

"Too many," he admitted.

"And you shouldn't be here in Denver. You ditching training

camp in Texas a week before a career-changing fight is only proving Maddox's point that I'm a distraction."

"Molly—"

"Save it. I explained everything in the note. And I asked you
not to do this."

"That's the thing, babe. You *don't* get to make that decision. I
do. And you sure as fuck don't get to end it with me in a fucking
note. Do you have any idea how crazy that made me?"

"Crazy enough to charter a plane, I imagine." Molly couldn't
believe he was here. And where had he gotten the idea she was
ending it? "I left you because the fight—"

"Doesn't fucking matter if I lose you over it!"

"Don't you see that's the point I was trying to make? I don't
want you or your trainers to blame me for you backing out of this
fight!" She inhaled deeply to calm herself. "We both know that's
what will happen. Dammit, Deacon. You've worked too hard for
too many years. You've only been with me for a few months."

He ran his hands over his head, then across the stubble on his
jaw. "You don't get it, do you? So I'll spell it out, literal girl. I want
you—a life with you—more than a championship belt. More than
anything in the world. Did you not hear what I told Maddox when
we were in Nebraska, woman?"

How could she forget? But she had, hadn't she?

*I could have a title fight on the line tomorrow and I still wouldn't walk
away from her. I won't ever walk away from her. She needs me, and I sure
as fuck need her.*

"I like fighting. And I'm good at it." Deacon pointed at her.
"But you? You, I love. Big difference. You should see that love
every time I look at you. You feel that love every time I touch you.
I told you that we weren't ever breaking up again. I wasn't fucking
kidding about that. So I'm here to apologize for bein' a dickhead
and to ah . . . talk."

She almost burst out laughing. He'd uttered the word *talk* like it was a communicable disease. "So talk."

"I figured you could start. Tell me exactly what I did wrong so I don't do it again. Because I swear to Christ, Molly, one small thing snowballed into a huge fucking thing. I know I ignored you, hurt you, and pissed you off. Then the next thing I knew, you were gone. It kills me that I hurt you. But none of it was intentional. And I don't want it to ever happen again. I just don't know how to stop from doin' that."

His earnestness and anguish mixed with hope—and yes, the love she saw in his eyes—was a potent combination.

Oh, man of mine, what am I going to do with you?

Show him you love him unconditionally. Teach him to be what you need.

Molly remembered Amery telling her that trying to understand a man like Ronin Black, or predict how he might react, was the hardest thing she'd ever done—but if that was the price she paid for loving him and being loved by him in return, then she'd suck it up and learn to deal with things on Ronin's level and his way.

That's what Molly needed to do now. Deacon wouldn't change overnight. But when she really thought about it . . . he'd already changed—or at least proved to her he was willing to try. The issues between them would never be as simple as him forgetting to refill the toilet paper dispenser in the bathroom. But having him here, looking at her like that, even after she'd left him in Texas . . . She would do whatever it took to make sure he looked at her that way for the rest of their lives.

But that didn't mean she wouldn't make the man grovel. Because for him, that would always be part of learning too.

"Say something," he demanded.

She gestured to the candles and the flowers. "What's all this?"

"After bein' at your place, I know you like candles and flowers and shit. So I got some. For you."

"Thought it'd help your cause, did you?"

"Figured it couldn't hurt."

"You put this together by yourself?"

He rubbed the back of his neck. "I called the orders in before I left Texas, and Knox picked up the flowers. He and I hauled it all up after Amery insisted I use the poolside as a staging area—whatever the fuck that means. Then Shi-Shi arranged the flowers, 'cause I suck at that stuff. But I lit all the candles."

"That's a lot of candles. So you've been here awhile?"

"Seems like a fucking eternity since I saw you last night." Deacon shoved his hands in the pockets of his suit pants.

She was impressed he'd dressed up. Her eyes narrowed. Wait. He was still wearing the same clothes he'd had on last night. He'd been so anxious to get to her that he hadn't taken the time to change clothes? "How did you get to Denver before me?"

"JFW jet."

"That's not fair."

"I won't play fair when it comes to you. You *know* that about me." He paused. "Look, I'm sorry I ditched you at the country club. I'm sorry I was short with you in the hallway. I'm sorry I didn't tell you what was goin' on with Dad and Julianne. There's a lot I need to tell you. And I'm really fucking sorry that I didn't call you to say I wouldn't be coming back to the hotel."

"That's a good start," she murmured.

"It is?"

"Yeah. I was worried about you."

"I know. I'm sorry."

"So what happened with your parents?"

"I'll fill you in on everything about that later. Because this right here? This is about us. Only us." He locked his gaze to hers. "Molly, do you still love me?"

His vulnerability did her in completely. He hadn't come here believing she'd fall back into his arms—but he wouldn't let her go without a fight either.

"You hurt me. And I hated that I couldn't talk to you about it. But I'm sure I hurt you too by leaving you with a *helpful fucking note.* But it wasn't a breakup note."

He remained stoic. Waiting for her to continue.

"Love isn't something that just stops. Not real love. So yes, I'm still in love with you. I don't ever want you to doubt that, Deacon."

Then he was on her. His hands cradling her face as he kissed her with hope, love, and passion.

The man definitely had the hot-makeup-kisses thing down.

When he finally released her mouth, he buried his face in her neck. "I need to hear you say it again."

"I love you."

He shuddered with relief. Then he said, "Close your eyes."

Molly obeyed him without question.

Deacon kissed the knuckles on her left hand and slipped something on her ring finger.

Her heart hammered. Blood whooshed in her ears. Did that mean what she thought it did? No. It couldn't. It was too soon, wasn't it? But what if it—

"Babe. Gotta remember to breathe."

She sucked in a huge gulp of air.

He curled his hand beneath her jaw. "Look at me."

Those amazing blue eyes were the first thing she saw.

"Marry me."

Of course the man didn't ask her; he never did anything the right way. He did it the Deacon way. And that was fine by her. "Yes."

Deacon smiled. And she wondered if she would ever get used to how gorgeous the man was when he smiled at her like that.

"Don't you wanna see the ring?"

"You have to let go of my face so I can look down."

Still smiling, he kissed her. Then he shifted back, turning her wrist so the light from the tiki torch spilled across her hand.

Stunned by the fire flashing in the diamond, she forgot to breathe again. The square-cut stone seemed awfully large in the simple platinum setting.

"Well? Do you like it?"

"It's breathtaking."

"If you look closely, there's a flaw in it. The jeweler tried to get me to pick a different stone, but I liked this one. I like the reminder that nothing is perfect. That it's better to overlook a small flaw when the rest of it is so—"

"Beautiful and perfect." Like him, her wonderful man.

"Exactly." Deacon rested his forehead to hers. "I love you more than anything—you know that, right?"

"Yes."

"But, babe, I gotta warn ya. I'm probably gonna fuck up from time to time."

She laughed. "And I'll still love you when you do."

"Thank fuck for that."

Her man—her fiancé—had such a way with words.

Then he said, "We'll figure this out."

And she believed him.

EPILOGUE

One week later . . .

"DEACON."

He stopped shadowboxing and looked over his shoulder at Ronin. "What is it?"

"Molly said to tell you they're here."

"Cool. Thanks." He grabbed a towel and mopped his face. He needed to sit down and chill out. But waiting to fight, especially for this fight, was making him antsy.

"Who's they?" Knox asked.

"My dad. My cousin Warren and his folks."

"You seem surprised they're here."

"I'm surprised *I'm* here." Last week, after he and Molly had straightened things out, he'd told her about Warren's parentage. His sweet woman had cried out of guilt for leaving him to deal with the shocking revelations alone. Then a fearful but heartfelt phone call from his aunt Annabelle had convinced him it'd be in Warren's best interest to wait until he turned eighteen to reveal his biological identity. But Deacon had asked for a chance to get to know his nephew, and Annabelle and Derek had agreed it'd be good for Warren. So the three of them and Deacon's dad had flown in for the fight.

His mother hadn't come. His father told him he believed Julianne had suffered from a psychotic episode borne of grief when she'd said such awful things to Deacon after Dante's death. And she continued to treat him the way she did out of guilt for what she'd said.

Deacon had let that go for his father's sake. If the man wanted to pretend his wife wasn't a monster, that was his business.

"You are ready, *amigo*," Vasquez said, interrupting Deacon's contemplation. "You were a beast this week."

"If we'd trained together even one more day, you'da seen my big nasty teeth, you sadistic bastard," Deacon retorted. When Deacon had tried to back out of the Watson fight, citing personal reasons, Maddox, Ronin, and even Vasquez had convinced him to stick it out. Ronin had persuaded Amery to let Molly work remotely so she could be with Deacon in Laredo while he trained. And Deacon was man enough to admit he wouldn't have made it through the week without Molly by his side. He planned to never be without her again.

Since neither of them wanted a long engagement, they were sneaking off to Corpus Christi tomorrow to get married. And maybe it made him a fucking sap, but he wanted Molly's first trip to the ocean to be unforgettable, so he'd secretly arranged for the ceremony to take place at sunset on the beach. Then the woman would have to eat her words about him not being a romantic guy. He was gonna romance the hell out of her for the next sixty years. He'd be a motherfucking *pro* at this hearts and flowers shit.

"I remember the good old days when students used to complain about that with you," Knox said, drawing Deacon's attention back to the conversation.

"They still do," Beck inserted. Then he and Knox laughed at the same time.

Maddox hustled in. "All right, everybody out. I need to prep my fighter."

Beck and Knox walked out together. Vasquez and Riggins followed.

Deacon pulled out his fight bag and tossed his hand-wrapping supplies on the bench. He already had his gauze premeasured and cut. His gauze pads were folded. He flexed his fingers, stilling the left hand when Maddox began to wrap it.

"You all right?" Maddox asked.

"I'm great."

"Cool." He paused. "They're here."

"My family? Yeah, I know."

"Not them. The Smackdown guys."

"I figured they would be, since it's a Smackdown event," Deacon said.

Maddox looked at him as he ripped off strips of tape. "I mean the Smackdown fighters are here. Specifically, the three guys in your weight class you'll be going up against after you win tonight."

"Huh. Why are you telling me this now, Mad?"

"It's my version of a pep talk."

"It sucks."

He laughed. "I've heard that before."

"Even if I lose tonight—"

"You're not gonna lose," Maddox assured him.

"But even if I do get my ass kicked, I've already signed with Smackdown, so they'll have to suck it up and come up with a new strategy for me."

Maddox lifted his head. His eyes were shrewd. "When did this signing happen?"

"Last night Molly and I had dinner with the suits. They made their pitch. My woman took the contract back to the hotel and went over it with a magnifying glass, because she's smart like that.

They agreed to strike two of the paragraphs about promotional requirements she disagreed with. So it's a done deal."

"Congrats, man. That is awesome."

Maddox's enthusiasm was completely faked—which made zero sense. "You pissed about it?"

"Nah. I'm happy for you. But since I've been helping you navigate this stuff the last year, it sorta feels like you're firing me as your business manager."

"That job never should've fallen on your shoulders, Mad, and it did by default. You're my trainer. That doesn't mean I won't talk to you about the business side of my fight career. It just means I'll be talking to Molly first."

After a moment, Maddox said, "As it should be. She's a good woman, D."

"She's the best." Deacon formed a fist with his right hand and released it. "Speaking of women . . . Presley is here."

"I thought Molly could use a friend on fight night."

No fucking way. Maddox was blushing. "Right. You brought her a thousand miles for *Molly*." Deacon couldn't resist making kissing noises.

"You're a fuckhead."

"You ain't denying that you brought Presley here for yourself, dude."

Maddox sighed. "It's complicated, all right?"

"You fucking her won't uncomplicate it."

"I'm not fucking her."

"Not yet," Deacon said. "How long has this been goin' on?"

"Since LA." Maddox finished wrapping Deacon's left hand and reached for his right. "And since when do you care about this personal crap? I thought I could count on you not to give me a rash of shit about it."

"You thought wrong. I'm a new man, bein' I'm in *lurve* and all. I'm a softer, more understanding man. A kinder, gentler—"

Deacon snorted. "Fuck. I couldn't even say that shit with a straight face."

"Yep, it's obvious you're still an asshole. So let's get back on track and go over fight strategy."

An hour later, when Deacon entered the event center, he wasn't nervous.

That's because you've got this, bro.

After the glove and body check, he scanned the seats until his gaze landed on her. Sitting in his corner.

Deacon knew that no matter what happened tonight, he'd already won what mattered most.

Continue reading for a preview of
the next book
in Lorelei James's bestselling
Blacktop Cowboys® series,

WRAPPED
AND
STRAPPED

Available in November!

HUGH nearly knocked Harlow on her ass when he entered the main reception area at the Split Rock the same time she barreled down the hallway.

He clasped her upper arms to keep them both from hitting the carpet. "Whoa, there. What's your rush?"

When Harlow's gaze snared his, he saw her baby blues were nearly indigo from anger. "I'm in desperate need to find a bigger pillow in order to smother my father."

"I thought you hated violence," Hugh drawled.

"I thought so too, but apparently even a pacifist has limits and I've reached mine. Now move it or I'll practice my first act of violence on you."

"C'mere, slugger." He towed her around the corner, crowding her against the wall, blocking her from view of the guests. His body cast hers in shadow and being this close to her reminded him of how small she was. "Take a moment and settle down."

"You just love manhandling me, don't you?"

"Yep." But he noticed she wasn't attempting to flee from him for a change. "What's Daddy doin' that's ruffled your pretty feathers?"

"Being a bigger pain in the ass than usual. It's not my fault he's stuck in his room. He's bored, but he doesn't 'feel' like reading, watching TV, or working on his laptop." She let her head fall back. "And I didn't pack my tap shoes for this trip because I didn't think I'd need to entertain him."

Hugh laughed.

Harlow looked at him strangely.

"What?"

"You laughed. You never laugh."

"Not true. I laugh around you because you crack my ass up."

That earned him a sweet smile. "At least you think I'm funny. I'm sure not tickling my dad's funny bone today."

Hugh's brain stuck on the word *bone*. *Why, yes, sweet darlin', I'd love to play a little slap and tickle with you, and then bone you to take your mind off all of your troubles.*

"I get that he hates being cooped up," she continued. "But it was his choice to come here and not return to Chicago to recuperate. Since Tierney is busy gestating baby number two, I bring his granddaughter to visit and play games with him every day. Lainie is here three times a week doing his rehab. Renner's even roped both you and Tobin into stopping by." Her gaze hooked his again. "Mandated visits from the bossman, I assume?"

"I don't mind, Harlow."

For the first time since they were in the hospital in Denver, she touched him, placing her hand on his chest. His heart skipped a beat. "I appreciate it. He's a difficult man on his best days and those have been few and far between." She wrinkled her nose. "So I don't put much stock in his claim that he's missing all his *lovely lady friends* in Chicago. That was today's complaint, by the way, the one that sent me over the edge."

"Maybe he is some kinda ladies' man on his home turf."

"You did not seriously just say that to me. Eww. That's not something I ever want to picture." Harlow broke eye contact and dropped her hand from his chest. "Anyway, thanks for keeping me from committing patricide. I'm feeling much calmer."

"Good." He tucked a flyaway section of her hair behind her ear. "How much longer are you gonna avoid me?"

"Hugh—"

"I haven't pushed because you've got a lot of family stuff on your plate. But that don't mean I'm giving up." He slid his hand around the left side of her neck, resting his thumb on the pulse point beside the hollow of her throat. "I wanna spend time with you."

"Doing what?"

Fucking you until you can't move without remembering my body on yours. "Ah. Normal date stuff."

"Such as?"

"Such as you come over and I cook you supper. Then we'll play cards. Or we'll sit in front of a fire pit. Or we'll go horseback ridin' in the moonlight."

"What if I'm not interested in any of that?"

"Then I'd go with my first choice of stripping you bare, tyin' you to my bed and reacquainting myself with every single inch of this wicked, sweet body of yours."

Harlow's pulse pounded double time at his last suggestion.

He lowered his head and placed a soft kiss on that spot. "Anything you wanna do, hippie-girl, tame or wild," he murmured against her skin, "I'll make it happen." Then he stepped back, knowing he'd probably gone too far.

The heat in her eyes morphed into a challenge. "Tell you what. If you can round up some *lovely lady friends* to keep my dad company a couple of days a week, I'll agree."

"To what?"

"Anything you wanna do, cowboy, tame or wild," she cooed in that breathy, fuck-me-now voice.

"No foolin'?"

"Not even a little bit. So what do you say?"

That's when Hugh realized Harlow was confident he couldn't deliver.

Wrong.

So wrong.

And damn was it ever hard not to grin like an idiot because he totally had this one in the fuckin' bag. "I accept your challenge."

"You do?"

"Yep. So we have a deal?"

"If you can deliver? Absolutely we have a deal."

"Done. Let's officially seal it."

She offered her hand.

He laughed. "Nice try. But you know that ain't gonna fly with me."

Harlow opened her mouth to protest and Hugh swooped right in. Taking the kiss he wanted. No sweet peck or gentle tease. He devoured her. Twisting his tongue around hers. Sucking on those full lips. Tasting the heat and need that was Harlow. Giving her back that same fire. Reminding her that the desire between them hadn't cooled one fucking bit in the past three years. If anything, it burned hotter than ever.

And don't miss *What You Need*,
which kicks off a brand-new contemporary
romance series from Lorelei James,
out in early 2016!

As the CFO of Lund Industries, Brady Lund is the poster child for responsibility. But eighty hour workweeks leave him little time for a life outside his corner office. To shake up Brady's staid existence, his brothers stage an intervention and drag him to a seedy nightclub . . . where he sees *her*, the buttoned-up blonde from the secretarial pool who's starred in his fantasies for months.

Lennox Greene is a woman with a rebellious past—which she carefully conceals beneath her conservative clothes. She knows flirting with her sexy but aloof boss during working hours is a bad idea. So when Brady shows up at her favorite dive bar, sans his usual snappy suit, and catches her cutting loose, she throws caution aside and dares him to do the same.

After sparks fly between them, Brady discovers that keeping his hands off Lennox is a much tougher challenge than he expected. She makes him feel alive for the first time in years, but the last thing he wants is to put her job in jeopardy if rumors circulate—and a small part of him wonders if he can really trust that she's not using him to get ahead.

As they grow closer, Lennox must figure out if he wants her for the accomplished woman she is—or the bad girl she was.